Andrea Bolter has always been fascinated by matters of the heart. In fact she's the one her girlfriends turn to for advice with their love-lives. A city mouse, she lives in Los Angeles with her husband and daughter. She loves travel, rock 'n roll, sitting in cafés and watching romantic comedies she's already seen a hundred times. Say hi at andreabolter.com.

Christy Jeffries graduated from the University of California, Irvine, with a degree in criminology, and received her Juris Doctor from California Western School of Law. But drafting court documents and working in law enforcement was merely an apprenticeship for her current career in the dynamic field of mummyhood and romance writing. She lives in Southern California with her patient husband, two energetic sons and one sassy grandmother. Follow her online at christyjeffries.com.

Also by Andrea Bolter

Her New York Billionaire
Her Las Vegas Wedding
The Italian's Runaway Princess

Also by Christy Jeffries

A Marine for His Mom
Waking Up Wed
From Dare to Due Date
The Matchmaking Twins
The Makeover Prescription
A Family Under the Stars
The Firefighter's Christmas Reunion
A Proposal for the Officer
The Maverick's Bridal Bargain
The Maverick's Christmas to Remember

Discover more at millsandboon.co.uk

THE PRINCE'S CINDERELLA

ANDREA BOLTER

THE SEAL'S SECRET DAUGHTER

CHRISTY JEFFRIES

MILLS & BOON

First Published in Great Britain 2019
by Mills & Boon, an imprint of HarperCollinsPublishers,
1 London Bridge Street, London, SE1 9GF

The Prince's Cinderella © 2019 Andrea Bolter
The SEAL's Secret Daughter © 2019 Christy Jeffries

ISBN: 978-0-263-27222-2

0319

MIX
Paper from
responsible sources
FSC C007454
FSC
www.fsc.org

Printed and bound in Spain
by CPI, Barcelona

THE PRINCE'S CINDERELLA

ANDREA BOLTER

CHAPTER ONE

"WELCOME TO THE headquarters of the APCF," Felice Khalif said to Marie as they proceeded down a row of work cubicles. There was a hum in the air, with the people at every desk either on the phone or focused on the computer screens in front of them. At the back of the space, Felice pointed to a small office separated from the central area by a glass wall and door. "Here's where you'll be working."

The partitioned-off room wasn't large but Marie had never had a private office before so she had to admit it gave her a buzz. Inside, a sleek glass desk was topped with boxes and stacks of paper files. A telephone bank was off to one side. Four chrome chairs sat around a glass meeting table. One large canvas with an abstract design painted in pastel colors adorned the wall.

The lone window didn't look out to the glitzy beach-front Promenade de la Croisette that Cannes on the French Riviera was known for but it did let in plenty of light. Not that it mattered, though. Marie was here to work, not to daydream out the window.

"When our events manager, Jic Gurov, suddenly quit, Alain at the Toulouse office recommended I bring you in," Felice continued. "We'll give it a try temporarily.

You'll have to jump right in. We have so much going on, and I don't really have anyone to train you."

"I'll do my best." Marie brushed her bangs away from her eyes. This was a career opportunity she could have never seen coming. A million thanks were due to Alain for recommending her for the job. Not only did he understand about the work in Toulouse that she'd had to leave unfinished, he'd also given her a glowing recommendation.

"I prepared this much for you." Felice handed Marie a single piece of paper. "Here are the upcoming events that I can confirm."

"Thanks."

Felice was right that everything was happening so fast. One minute Marie was assistant to the events coordinator for the APCF, Alliance for Parentless Children of France, at its regional office in Toulouse, and now she was at the headquarters in Cannes with a chance to become the permanent events manager if she did a good job.

France's largest nonprofit agency supporting orphaned children was a well-known organization with several field offices throughout the country. The agency was able to aid parentless children who were in the foster care system with case management, social services and transitional assistance into adulthood. An orphan herself, Marie had utilized the agency's help when she was a teenager, and the organization hired her for a job after university.

"As you know, the most important date on the calendar is our annual fund-raising gala in three weeks. The proceeds from that evening finance all of our operations for the year."

"Alain told me."

"Unfortunately, I don't think Jic has compiled all of the components for this event. Zander is coming by today to go over it with you in detail."

"Who's Zander?"

Felice heard her phone's ping and answered it. "Yes? I'll call her right back."

Marie imagined that as the agency's executive director, Felice must have many balls to juggle in the air at once. She had a matter-of-fact manner that was very professional. In her cream-colored suit, Felice lifted her eyeglasses from the chain hanging around her neck and put them on to respond to something else on her phone.

After smoothing the front of her gray trousers to try to straighten out any creases, Marie stood as tall as she could. She subtly reached behind her to tuck her blouse in tighter. At the office in Toulouse she did occasionally meet with important donors and was included in meetings, so she never dressed too informally for work. But if Felice's high-end suit was any indication, Marie might need to up her look here. After all, this was Cannes, land of the rich and famous.

At this point, she certainly didn't have money to go out and buy a new wardrobe, as much fun as that sounded. Taking a mental inventory of the clothes she did have, she figured she could put together a week of decent outfits to get started.

If she let it, Marie's mind could start swirling. There hadn't been any chance for the logistics of this unexpected job switch to be worked out. The agency was able to provide a room for her to stay in for the time being in one of its housing facilities in Cannes. But if the job became permanent, she'd have to find an apartment and give up the room she leased in Toulouse. Cannes would be a much more expensive place to live so she didn't know what she'd be able to afford. Then again, if she were to get this position permanently, there'd be a substantial salary increase.

She'd have to keep the uncertainty from getting to her during this trial period. Temporary things didn't always work out for her. One thing Marie Paquet had known all of her life was impermanence. There might be more of it to accept. Would that ever stop, would there ever be something in her life that she could count on?

Taking in the slow, measured breaths that her years spent in counseling taught her, she centered herself.

A young man came into the office and handed Felice a laptop. "Thank you, Clive."

Marie followed Felice's lead in bringing their chairs close together so that they could sit down at the table and huddle in front of the laptop. "This will be for your use. The login you had in Toulouse will work for general access. I'll give you another password to get into the files we keep confidential because they contain donor information."

"Do you know if the system logs the events chronologically, or alphabetically, or in some other order?"

"Let's hope it's chronologically so that you can prioritize." Felice opened the laptop and clicked through several folders until she found what she was looking for. "Voila."

"Great." Marie was relieved that the files were located. She was going to need all the help she could get.

"Look at your list and tell me if this corresponds. Of course, the gala in May. The Regional Managers Retreat Weekend in June?"

Marie reviewed her list. "Yes. The entry says five meals. Two dinners, two breakfasts and one lunch. Continuous snack and beverage service for both days. Transportation to and from the hotel. Multiple media setups. Breakout classrooms. Writing supplies. Goody bags. Then there's a handwritten note in red to check the hotel."

Felice opened another folder. "Donor Appreciation Luncheon in July?"

"Yes, I have that on the list although there are no specifics except winery picnic."

"Goodness, there's almost nothing in here," Felice sighed as she opened that file. "You'll have to look though this yourself and see if there's anything useful. It looks like Jic recorded his notes from meetings but didn't highlight any decisions."

Marie grabbed a pen and jotted Felice's instructions onto her printed list.

"Next, Back-to-School Support Suppers in September."

Marie's fists opened and closed repeatedly. How well she remembered those suppers that the agency hosted to aid kids in foster care who were beginning their new school years. For some, including Marie, the start of the school year was wrought with either dread or apprehension. Dread if the previous year hadn't gone well but they were returning to the same school. And apprehension if they were starting at a new school.

Kids could be cruel. But to orphans and other children in foster care, mercilessly so. The unkind ones already knew who the foster kids were, and would find ways to taunt and tease them. They'd yell out meanness to Marie that she was unwanted. That she had no family. That nobody loved her. Like many in her situ-

ation, Marie grew a thick outer shell and learned not
to cry in front of the bullies. Not that she didn't shed a
million tears in private.

The September suppers the agency held had been a
godsend for Marie. Psychologists, social workers and
education specialists were all on hand to discuss problems and develop strategies. Without them, the pressure
of the new school year might have swallowed Marie up
and left her too isolated and anxious to have succeeded
in her classes.

Now she was going to be part of creating those dinners that had meant so much to her. As an adult, she
had long accepted the fact that she would never be part
of a typical family. But by working at the agency she
was in some small way making other orphans feel that
somebody cared about them. In that, she felt great pride
and satisfaction.

"There's a note on my list to check the budget after
the gala," Marie reported to Felice.

"We'll have to see what funding the gala brings in,
in order to determine how much money we can spend
on the September suppers and how many of them we
can offer throughout the country."

"Of course."

As a teen, it had never occurred to Marie how programs the APCF provided were financed. Only that
they were able to help with the extra services people
might not be able to afford. Orphaned children sometimes had mental health issues such as depression or
post-traumatic stress disorder. Others had learning dis-
abilities or physical conditions. And, maybe most important, once they reached adulthood there was often no
place for them to turn for transitional help into higher

education or the workforce. The APCF did as much as it could for as many as it could.

Once she started working for the organization, Marie understood that any money it spent on its programs came from outside donations. She glanced up from her powwow with Felice and thanked the air surrounding her that this agency existed and that she was brought into it by one of her few schoolteachers who cared. A quick wince reminded her of some who didn't.

"I need to return a call." Felice looked up from her phone to Marie. "Why don't you continue to match up your notes and see how much information you have?"

"Okay."

"Zander has all of the data for the gala on his own computer. He's very specific about what he wants. He'll go over that with you. We're lucky to have him chairing the event this year, so let's make every effort to facilitate his plans."

"Who's Zander?" Marie realized that Felice hadn't answered when she'd asked the first time.

"Felice!" a shrill voice called out from the main office space.

"Let me go deal with that—" Felice stood up "—and let's touch base at the end of the day. After Zander comes."

As the director charged out the door, Marie asked yet again, this time to the back of her jacket, *Who* is Zander?"

What a difference a year made.

Zander de Nellay surveyed the sweeping view of the Cannes shoreline through the floor-to-ceiling sliding glass doors of his posh penthouse. The palm-tree-lined promenade of La Croisette followed the crescent-shaped curve of the sparkling Gulf of Napoule and its white-sand beaches. It was a sight to behold, indeed.

Little, if nothing, of the vista appeared any different from how it had last spring. Although then, as he had in years past, Zander had stayed in an elegant suite at one of the grand dame hotels on the promenade. And had partied every night with Hollywood film producers and the *glamorati* who flocked to Cannes from all over the world.

This season, he'd instead be ensconced in a penthouse apartment that kept the town's constant revelry at arm's length.

Gliding one of the doors open, he stepped out onto the terrace. The sun was bright but the air was crisp, a combination he'd always enjoyed. Cannes in late spring was a marvelous place to be.

Fortunately, to Zander's precise specifications, the rental agent was able to find him a suitable penthouse with a terrace that was walled-in cement rather than the typical iron balcony railing, which he wouldn't have trusted was safe enough for eighteen-month-old Abella, even though he knew she would never be outside on her own. But securely enclosed, Zander could create a little play area out here for her so that she could get plenty of the fresh sea air. He'd just need a patio umbrella or other covering to shelter her from the strength of the sun.

He shook his head to himself. A year ago Zander was an unattached bachelor, much to his mother's chagrin, with thoughts only of what suited him. He rotated his life between time spent in his native Charlegin, his apartment in Paris's tony Sixth Arrondissement and his travels throughout the world on behalf of his charitable endeavors.

Now his mind was on baby-safe balconies.

Stepping back into the penthouse's sitting room, he watched the deliveries arriving. Movers carried in the petal-pink upholstered rocking chair he'd had sent from his apartment in Paris. Rather than buying one here in Cannes, he wanted the exact chair that Abella had become comfortable with. Truth be told, he was accustomed to it, too. He loved quietly sitting in that chair with her.

Yes, one of the most eligible playboys in Europe now found himself preferring to rock baby Abella in his arms than cavorting with the high society he'd always been surrounded by. And Zander was keenly aware of the realness exchanged between them in those moments.

Heading toward the master bedroom suite, he saw Iris, a compact woman in her sixties who had been Abella's nanny since the day she was born. "Is she asleep?"

"She's just starting to rouse."

There went that funny tap in the center of Zander's chest. It was a sensation that had arrived around a year ago. The mere thought of seeing Abella pulled at his heart. Her cherubic pink cheeks and that cute way she stretched her back after a nap as if she'd been farming in the fields all day.

"The wardrobe is here," one of his assistants announced as Zander entered the master suite. "I believe you wanted to go over it."

Zander didn't really envision himself as fussy when it came to clothes. But with all the charitable organizations he endorsed and all of the fund-raising benefits and balls he attended, his wardrobe had to be appropriate. He'd come to Cannes for the spring social season and would be attending a dozen formal events and countless others that called for business attire. Even the black slacks and black shirt he wore at the moment were bespoke from the finest tailor in London.

"Create a file for me of what I'm wearing from head to toe for each event so that I don't have to think about it on that given day," he instructed the assistant. With Abella's care always on his mind, it was more important than ever that he simplify everything else. Plus, while in Cannes he planned to devote himself to chairing the APCF gala and making it the event of the season, and he needed as much time as possible to do so.

In fact, he'd be leaving the penthouse soon to go to the APCF office to meet with the event manager there. The agency's director, Felice, had informed him that the previous manager had suddenly left. Zander hoped his replacement would be up to the task of creating the kind of spectacular evening he had in mind.

If there was one thing Zander knew about, it was raising money. He made a great deal of public appearances to support good works all over the world. He gave his time and his notability freely, making it his life's work in fact. Now it was payback time. He expected many of his wealthy friends and acquaintances to donate generously to the APCF gala.

"I'll wear the white-jacketed tux for the Clean Water for Africa fund-raiser," he began. Most of the tuxedos were all black. One had traditional notch lapels, another a thin shawl collar that gave it a retro look. "This one for the cocktail reception with the film festival judges."

Another was made of velvet, a fabric that was considered very chic right now although Zander wasn't convinced it suited him. He didn't assign that one to an evening. There was the two-button he'd wear with a black shirt. Then the charcoal with the double-breasted jacket, the navy with the black lapels that he quite liked, the all-navy one and the peak-lapel gunmetal gray.

"White shirt with everything but the two-button."

Finally, he inspected the unusual tuxedo for the Mexican-themed gala that his stylist had ordered. With heavy black embroidery atop the shinier black fabric of the jacket's lapels, it was a unique piece that would fit well with the evening.

After rattling off instructions for everything from cuff links to socks, Zander turned to the second closet. There were a dozen suits with coordinating shirts, ties and shoes. Casual clothes suitable for boating or country drives. Golf and tennis wear. Beach attire. Everything was in order.

Except his mind. Thoughts of the constant socializing and the superficial women who gravitated toward him, who cared only about what they could get from him, all felt so stale. Maybe it was the baby, but a longing was starting to grow in him. For something different. Something new.

He'd RSVP'd for all the season's events as a party of two, not willing to face the firing squad alone, but really having no idea whom he'd bring along as his plus one. He'd planned to think of a platonic friend he could make easy chitchat with. Who wouldn't immediately misread his invitation to accompany him as a proposal into his world.

Misjudging a woman's intentions had only too recently stung him hard.

Frankly, he couldn't think of a woman who would fit the bill, but he'd deal with that later.

Zander left his bedroom suite. Although he told himself he'd only poke his head in to see if she was fully awake, he instead gently pushed open the door and slipped into baby Abella's bedroom.

"Well, look at you, Bell-bell." She was sitting upright in her crib, her curly blond hair tousled this way and that. "You're all the way awake already."

"Up time," she said, having only recently begun attempts at true conversation. "Up."

"Yes, Bell-bell. Up."

No further prompting was required. Zander hurried to the side of her crib to reach in, put each of his hands under the baby's arms and lift her out. He brought her against his left shoulder, as had become his routine after Iris had taught him the proper way to securely hold a baby. Zander could never figure out what the *gaga* noise Abella made was meant to signify, but she always did it when he picked her up.

She twisted herself sideways a bit to stare at Zander's face.

His eyes met hers. It was like looking in a mirror. Those dark brown, almost black, almond-shaped eyes that they had in common. The same almond eyes that his sister, Elise, had had. He could never look at Abella without thinking of his sister, his heart shattering at missing her so. Wishing he could rewrite the past so that Elise could be here right now and see how much Abella was growing and developing.

Zander and Abella continued the eye lock that they did frequently. Which he took as some kind of unspoken declaration of mutual love.

"Da," Abella said.

Da. As in Daddy.

"No, Bell-bell. Uncle Zander. Can you say Zander?"

"Da."

"Zan. How about you say Zan?"

"Da."

Each time she uttered that syllable it was with more determination and certainty than the time before, despite his protests. The word filled Zander with confusion about the decisions that were going to have to be made. Maybe not today, but soon.

He held the baby closer, inhaling the lovely smell of that fruity, organic and toxin-free shampoo Iris used on her hair.

As Zander carried Abella into the living room, a grocer arrived with food. Iris came toward him to take Abella if that was what he so desired.

Not ready to let go just yet he said, "I'll hold her for a while."

With all the comings and goings, the front door was left open. Three quick knocks against the doorjamb brought Zander's attention. It was the penthouse's rental agent, who upon spotting Zander, folded one arm rigidly across his waist and bowed forward. He sputtered in a nervous voice, "Is everything to your liking, Your Highness?"

Four hours passed before Marie looked up from her laptop. Having combed through every single file her predecessor, Jic, had left, she finally had a grasp of what information there was and what more was required for her to move forward with the APCF events calendar.

She hadn't been privy to why Jic abruptly up and left his position, only that he'd had some personal problems to attend to. The fact that some of the files were in decent shape and others were an indecipherable hodge-podge told her that Jic's departure had been hasty and unplanned. He hadn't left clear instructions for who-ever was to take over. Marie had made as many notes as she could and jotted down questions to ask Felice at the end of the day.

Out of the corner of her eye, she noticed something dark beyond the glass separating her office from the main work floor. As she lifted her face from the com-puter screen, what met her gaze was quite a surprise.

A man had his arm up, hand making a fist as if he was just about to knock on the glass to get her atten-tion. But it wasn't just any man. It was, without ques-tion, the most attractive man Marie had ever seen in her life. At least six feet three inches tall, he wore a black shirt tucked into black pants with a brown belt, topped by a brown jacket. She thought the combination of the black and brown was impossibly tasteful.

The color palette didn't stop with the clothes. His un-usually shaped eyes were the darkest of browns, practi-cally black, with his defined bone structure forming an unforgettable face. The crowning touch was a full head of thick, straight blond hair, expertly cut so that some fell forward from his forehead and the rest stayed put around his ears. Marie was sure there was never a hair out of place on the man's head.

Because he had frozen midknock, it was as if she was looking at a still photo. So she jolted when he moved to lower his arm and flash her a megawatt smile. His perfectly white teeth all but glistened in the office's harsh overhead lighting. Marie smiled back, no idea who he was or why he was in her doorway. But it wasn't often—okay, never—that an elegant and gorgeous man was grinning at her. She'd be crazy not to smile back.

While it was difficult to do anything but sit there and stare at the magnificent specimen of the human race, it occurred to Marie that she should get up and open the door to see who he was. Standing and moving toward him, she hoped her pants weren't too creased from sitting at the computer for so long. She hadn't checked her hair in hours, either, and knew that it could be an absolute mop at this point. Her lipstick had faded ages ago.

There was nothing she could do about any of that.

"Can I help you?" Marie asked after opening her door.

"Are you Marie?"

"Yes."

"Felice suggested I see you."

"Okay."

"I'm Zander de Nellay."

Oh. The gala's chairperson. Marie had been reading about him in the files.

Jic had noted three facts about Zander. Wants what he wants. Insists everything be of top-notch quality. Offering to pay the difference if anything goes over budget.

That seemed fair enough to Marie. On the private handwritten notes, Jic had doodled a little crown above Zander's name. Marie wondered if Jic was indicating that he was kind of a diva, or thought he was a king, or that he was formal and fussy.

"Marie Paquet." She thrust out her hand for a handshake. His joined hers in what she figured would be a traditional business greeting between two people who had never met.

The last thing she was expecting was for his hand to be big and strong and to convey friendliness rather than protocol. She surely wasn't prepared for the affection coming from the center of his palm to slide up her arm and down the entire right side of her body, so robust it actually made her torso bend toward it.

Once she was able to stand up straight again, she gestured for him to enter her office and closed the door behind them.

"I'm sorry. I've just started today so I haven't had a chance to set up," Marie felt compelled to explain. She didn't want him thinking she was some kind of slob with the boxes and stacks of paper everywhere cluttering up such a nice office. That was a sore spot with her because once people learned about her troubled upbringing, they assumed she was somehow unorganized or nonfunctional. It was always an uphill battle to prove them wrong.

"That's fine," Zander dismissed her concern. "This was Jic's office up until a couple of days ago and it was in the same condition then."

"Do you know why he left so suddenly?"

"I was expecting you to have the answer to that question."

"I'm sorry I don't."

Marie brushed her bangs to the side and tamped down her hair. She didn't know why she was nervous around this man, other than that he was the gala chair. It wasn't just that he was good-looking. Maybe it was that he had an undeniable air of style and class about him. Which was something Marie always admired in people. Traits that she surely knew nothing about, having grown up in whatever was the opposite of *grace* and *refinement*.

Wow, Zander de Nellay was tall. Fairly petite herself, Marie had to lean her head back to see his eyes. Although she didn't like his expression when he looked down at her. Because she imagined he was looking *down at her*.

And she'd sure as heck had enough of that in her life.

Marie reminded herself that she was projecting that onto Zander. She didn't know him well enough to be able to read his thoughts on anything, and he didn't know anything about her. A man like him, chair of a huge charity event, wearer of fine clothes, possessor of a splendid face, probably wasn't even thinking about how inexpensive Marie's trousers were or that she needed a haircut.

"Can I offer you a water or a coffee?" Felice had stressed that she was to do everything she could to assist Zander.

"I brought some." He placed his computer bag onto one of the chairs around the meeting table and pulled out his laptop and a bottle of gourmet sparkling water. "Do you have cups?"

Marie looked around the office she'd not yet had a minute to personalize. Near the telephone was a stack of disposable cups. "It seems I do," she reported and reached for them.

Zander twisted the cap off the bottle with a flourish Marie couldn't help but note. When a bit of carbonation from inside was set free, it hissed. Which was exactly how Marie was starting to feel in Zander's presence. Like she might need to let out some bubbles soon so as not to explode.

After the drinks were poured and Zander had booted up his laptop, they began.

"Why don't you bring your chair closer and we can work from my screen?" he suggested.

Even though she'd been in the exact same configuration with Felice earlier in the day, sitting next to Zander was another proposition entirely. Her awareness of him was palpable. His entire body emanated warmth. It hadn't been coming from just his palm when he'd shaken her hand.

Her fists opened and closed involuntarily.

Zander reached in his bag for something else. But when he glanced at what he retrieved, a quick smirk flashed across his face and he stuffed whatever it was back in. A second dig yielded the USB drive he'd been searching for. Naturally, curiosity racked Marie as to what the first item was.

"As I understand it," he said while reading, "the components are venue, theme, invitations, arrivals. Then there is food and beverages, rentals of tables and chairs, tableware, bar setup, buffets. Flowers, linens, tech, photography, band, auction, speeches and volunteers."

"The venue is booked and invitations have been sent, according to Jic's notes."

"Yes, months ago. Have you seen them?"

"No, I've only just started on the job today."

"There's no need to make excuses. I was merely asking if you'd seen them."

"I'm sorry. I hope they're in one of these boxes." Marie pointed to the disarray she'd inherited on her desk.

"And no need to apologize." Zander reached into

his bag again and located one of the invitations. He handed it to Marie.

Wants what he wants. Marie reread Jic's note about Zander. That was fine. Marie was detail oriented, too. That's how she'd gotten as far as she had in the APCF agency. By learning to be diligent. Not a skill she'd had any example of growing up. Except maybe toward all the wrong things.

The lavender cardstock invitation had all of the basic information. The name of the mansion that had been converted into a party location. The event date and time.

"I thought of these as more of a *save the date* kind of announcement," Zander commented. "They have no pizzazz. And they don't mention the theme."

"Had a theme been decided on? I don't see anything about it in my notes."

"No. And with three weeks to go, it's rather late in the game to be planning a big theme. But we must. I want this to be one of the most successful benefits of the social season. We have to pull out all of the stops."

Marie only theoretically understood what Zander was saying. She'd heard of lavish balls in which money-eyed guests came dressed as animals or as gangsters from the 1920s. High concepts that were designed to make the evening as impressive as it could be. With the idea that would bring in the highest donations, sponsorships and auction proceeds.

"I've only been associated with this organization for a year myself," Zander said as he scrolled through his files. "Has the annual APCF gala utilized a theme in the past? How big were the previous galas?"

"I don't know. I'll get back to you as soon as I can with that information."

"I understand that the APCF's invitation list is five hundred. And I've added my own personal five hundred. Has the agency hosted a fund-raiser of that size before?"

"I'll get the answer to that as soon as I can."

"How do you not know this? Didn't they brief you?"

"I'm sorry," Marie started again, but was getting pretty tired of apologizing. "As soon as I gather all of the information, I'll report back to you." Felice hadn't had time to fill her in on the history of the galas and Zander being so on top of everything was very intimidating.

No matter how big an event this was going to be, Marie knew she could get the job done once she had a grasp on it. It was crucial that she show Felice and the other agency bigwigs that she was capable of this position. It was time for her to take a next step up in her career, and this was an unexpected opportunity for her to show what she could do.

Proving naysayers wrong was something she'd spent a lot of her life doing. Frustration crinkled her face when she wondered if she'd ever be finished selling herself to others. Who usually doubted her from the start.

"All right." Zander made some sort of internal decision and proclamation. He transmitted full authority in every word he said, every gesture he made. Whoever he was other than chairperson for this gala, he was a force to be reckoned with. That's the kind of person Marie wanted to be. Maybe she could learn something from him. "We need to get you up to speed, and immediately."

"Yes."

Zander tapped a number into his phone. "Iris, are you able to manage until this evening?"

Whoever Iris was and whatever she was telling him

made him grin. And my, a smiling Zander de Nellay was a sight to behold. No wonder his chairing this gala was such a big deal. That smile could coax a wallet right out of its pocket.

Finishing the call, he returned his attention to Marie. "I'm starved. Let's go get some food. We'll work through the files and see where we are on every component," he commanded as if his will was always obeyed. One thing was for sure. Zander was the most compelling man Marie had ever met.

CHAPTER TWO

HALF OF ZANDER'S mind was on Marie Paquet, the young woman beside him as they left the APCF office and walked toward the center of town. The rest of his brain was on Abella, the not yet two-foot-tall girl who was the most important person in the world to him. When he'd called home, Iris let him know that everything was under control at the penthouse so that he didn't have to worry about rushing back.

That was a relief, what with the moving people and deliveries coming through, and Abella's needs to be considered. He made a mental note to give Iris some extra days off with pay once they were all settled in. A funny little trio, he, the baby niece and the widowed nanny. But a working unit nonetheless.

To the matter of the gala, he'd yet to conclude whether Marie was going to be a help or a hindrance. She seemed oddly unaware of his royal status so he'd made a point of not telling her. Because as soon as people found out, they acted differently around him. Either nervous to the point of flubbing up simple tasks, or going into over-drive to be perfect. Most people were flustered in the company of His Highness Prince Zander de Nellay of Charlegin.

It was surprising that she didn't know who he was, but it seemed there were a lot of gaps in what she'd been informed of. So at least in this first encounter, he'd let her think of him only as the event chair whom she had to satisfy, without the added distraction and onus of his title. Perhaps they'd get to know each other a bit first.

He'd come off brusque when they'd met in the office. No one could blame him, though, for being frustrated that, while he was responsible for this crucial fund-raising gala, the agency had undergone a personnel change and Marie, the replacement, was unapprised on more than just his identity.

"Do you know a place?" she asked, reshuffling the weight of a tote bag filled with paperwork on one shoulder and her laptop under the other arm.

"This way."

Reaching over to take Marie's bag off her shoulder, an unexpected sensation greeted him. As his fingertips grazed the thin fabric of her blouse in the process, Zander stiffened a little bit. His body suddenly piqued with alertness. For a good twenty paces after that, he was unable to divert his thoughts from wondering what the skin under that white shirt of Marie's might feel like if he slipped his hand underneath it. Soft as satin, he was sure of it.

It was a strange fascination. He hadn't felt curiosity about a woman in a long time.

"Do you live in Cannes?" Marie brought him back to the moment with her question, looking up to him with her big and almost completely round light blue eyes.

"I come down for the social season every spring."

"Down from where?"

"I keep an apartment in Paris. And my home is in Charlegin."

"Where is that?"

"It's a small principality near the Belgium border."

"What do you do there?"

Mashing his lips together, he suppressed a response. He wasn't used to being asked such direct inquiries. Once people knew who he was, they usually became tongue-tied or fluffed on about the weather or the rose-bushes. Marie's candor was intriguing, if unknowingly inappropriate.

"I'm involved in several charitable organizations," he answered in absolute truth. "May I?" He gestured at her laptop, taking it and slipping it into his bag along-side his own computer.

Tucking it in, his fingers again made contact with the incongruous item he had encountered when looking for the USB drive while he and Marie were still at the office. Inadvertently squeezing the malleable plastic, a quack sound echoed through the leather. How one of Abella's bath toys, the squidgy yellow duck, ended up in his bag he'd never know.

"What was that?" Marie asked in response to the sound.

"Oh, nothing." He wasn't ready to explain just yet, having learned the hard way that women tended to *ooh* and *aah* when they found out that the eligible prince was caring for a baby. And then tried to convince him that by decree of their gender they could do a better job of it than he was. When, in his experience, they were only trying to take care of themselves by worming their way into his world.

A hurtful pang reminded him that only a few months ago he'd been duped into just that.

Nothing about Marie suggested she was of that breed. But he wasn't going to be deceived, or put Abella's safety in jeopardy, ever again.

He led them to a pedestrians-only block where every other business was a café. Outdoor tables extended as far as the eye could see, each shaded from the sun with cloth awnings or umbrellas in a riot of colors. People sat chatting in groups, nursing aperitifs. Romantic couples leaned in close as they shared pastries.

Picking one of the cafés he thought he remembered from his time here last year, Zander instructed the hostess to seat them at one of the outside tables. With a pull on Marie's chair, he helped her sit and then took the wicker chair opposite her.

"Café au lait?" he suggested and after her confirmation, he ordered when the waiter arrived.

Quickly perusing the menu, he chose an herbed omelet. Marie took a bit longer to decide but once the waiter returned with the coffees, they had both made their selections.

"This is so scenic," Marie said as she surveyed the panorama from the café's patio. Palm trees dotted the horizon beyond the low buildings that lined the block. The air was clean and the sky was blue.

"Yes, Cannes is a very special place. Where are you from?"

She hesitated before answering. "North Marseilles, originally. But I was working for the APCF in Toulouse before this."

"And you've been called to service in Cannes."

"It's a great opportunity for me."

"You have no children? Parents? No husband or boy-friend to consider in a relocation?"

Marie looked downward before lifting her head only slightly and answering through her eyelashes. "No. It's just me."

Zander felt a bloom in his gut at finding out that Marie was unattached. Which was ridiculous, as if his body was betraying him. What matter was it of his whether Marie was married or spoken for?

Perhaps he was just curious. Just a year ago he was the playboy bachelor entrenched in the social scene of young royals. Where he spent his days, and nights, in the company of stunning women.

Until the world as Prince Zander knew it came crashing down. When his sister, Princess Elise, and her husband, Prince Valentin, were killed in a plane crash. And Abella, at the time six months old, was put in Zander's care.

The peculiar thing was, shifting from the jet-setter who dated the most desirable women in the most exotic places and enjoyed enviable pursuits of leisure was a much easier change than anyone would have guessed.

Truthfully, Zander had become tired of romping around. He was especially worn down by the people he met who were interested only in his title and his standing. Who never saw him for who he really was, what he cared about inside. As was personified by the one mistaken go-round with the woman who confirmed all of his suspicions.

After that, it was crystal clear. Tragedy was the cat-alyst for short-circuiting Prince Zander's lifestyle. But it was as easy as flipping a switch for him to turn his attention to one female and one female only. One who was hopefully eating her diced peaches before readying herself for a sleep.

His sister, Elise, was two years older than him, the firstborn. Which meant that Abella, her only child, was the crown princess and heir to the throne. Zander was responsible for raising not only a child, but the future ruler of their native Charlegin.

It all added up to why Zander had toy duckies in his briefcase and diced peaches on his mind. He could have hardly been bestowed a more important task than caring for Abella. Which provided a reason for him to stop surrounding himself with untrustworthy people whom he didn't even really know. He had to be very cautious with whom he brought into his orbit now, as he had the baby princess to protect.

Which was why, Zander reflected as the waiter delivered the food, the personal life of this lovely Mademoiselle Marie across the table from him should be of no interest of his.

So why was it?

Zander thought he'd seen a wash of sadness come across Marie's face when he asked if there were people in her life she was concerned about leaving behind in Toulouse.

With those big blue pools for eyes and a rose-petal mouth, she was a natural beauty. Her brown hair was a bit of a fright, with too-long fringy bangs and unruly waves tossing her locks this way and that. Yet her porcelain skin, which was so pale it was translucent, captivated his attention.

After they'd had a few bites of food for sustenance, Zander was ready to get down to business.

"In my opinion the most unforgettable galas start with a big thematic concept. It adds magic and theatricality."

"We had a hot-air balloon theme for a fund-raiser I worked on," Marie offered. "We carried it through all of the details. Table centerpieces that were small versions of the balloons with flowers coming out of the baskets. And we had party favors with miniature balloons filled with chocolates."

Zander chose his words carefully. "Marie, I'd consider that more a decorating scheme than an event theme."

Her eyes got wide. He knew she'd felt criticized, which was not his intention. But if he was going to chair a gala that was to be on par with the lavish affairs the social season was known for, Marie was going to have to expand her thinking. "I'm talking about the no-holds-barred extravaganzas like, for example, the Carnival balls that Venice is known for. They are drenched in theme from top to bottom, with venues and costumes and dinners that take your breath away."

"The APCF doesn't typically do galas on that scale."

"That's why they asked me to chair. They need to raise the kind of money the larger organizations do. So we've decided that throwing the most memorable benefit of the season will be the kickoff to a new level of fund-raising."

"I'll do my best. I've worked on dozens of events."

In reality, Zander had very clear ideas of what he wanted to do. He didn't need a sort of event manager who might not consult with him about every facet of the party. If his name was going to be linked with the APCF, everything was going to be *his* way. Perhaps someone with less experience like Marie would be a plus. He was willing to spend the next couple of days finding out if they worked well together.

With a charming smile she asked, "Do you have a personal connection to parentless children?"

That reminded him that she still didn't know who he was.

Which, actually, struck him as more than a little strange. Had she never seen his name in the news?

Sadly, Elise's and Valentin's deaths, and Zander's role in raising Abella, had garnered a lot of coverage. The story was picked up by all of the outlets when the plane crash happened a year ago. Bachelor Prince Now Daddy Day Care and plenty of other embarrassing headlines dotted every gossip website on earth at the time his family was going through such an unspeakable tragedy. How could Marie have missed learning of it? Or perhaps she just hadn't made the connection. Although she'd find out soon enough.

"Yes, the needs of orphans are something dear to my family. What about you? How did you come to work for the APCF?"

She studied him before seeming to make a decision to answer frankly, "Without the support of the agency, I wouldn't be here. I'm an orphan myself."

Think before you speak, Marie reminded herself as she sipped her coffee opposite Zander at the table. There was something so open and inviting about his face it made her want to tell him about all of the things she'd learned to keep private.

He was the kind of man girls dreamed of. Not Marie, because she'd learned the hard way long ago never to dream. But somebody else's dream come true. A man with the power and know-how to bring ideas to life. To make yesterdays disappear and tomorrows look bright.

In other words, he and those soulful almond-shaped eyes of his were dangerous. Because they could make a girl start to think about things that could never be.

"You're an orphan and now you work for the Alliance for Parentless Children of France," Zander said after putting the white porcelain coffee cup down onto its saucer. "You're exactly the reason we need the gala to be a resounding success. So that we can continue to assist parentless children all the way into adulthood."

She wasn't sure that she liked being discussed as if she was a case study students were analyzing at university. Although she was quite an example of everything that was wrong in society for orphaned children. With wounds she hoped no one would ever uncover. She'd rather die with them as memories covered in cobwebs that she kept in a tattered box in a corner of a never-visited attic. Unwrapping them only in private.

"The agency helped me get a job so I could go to university and then placed me in a position afterward."

"And event planning is where your passions lie?"

She wasn't sure why he was asking so many questions. Was he trying to determine whether she'd be able to assist him with his gala? Was he just asking out of idle inquiry? Or another motive? Fighting the urge to confide in him, she steadied herself. It wasn't often that anyone asked her about herself so she wasn't too savvy at it.

"Yes, I do like helping to bring all the pieces of an event together. Being part of a collaborative effort. Working with a team." Kind of like a family, she thought but didn't say. Because it hurt too much. "But we mainly do educational seminars and retreats. Rolls and coffee, sack lunches, that type of thing."

"Right." Zander checked his phone and with, apparently, nothing urgent there he placed it screen down on the table. "Okay, then, the first thing we need to do is announce the theme to the invitees."

Obviously, that was where his interest about her ended.

"We'll do a follow-up invitation as if we planned it that way all along," Marie offered.

"That's good. Like it was a secret we decided not to reveal right away. I want to go with some kind of costume or masquerade ball. It's classic. I think people enjoy disguising themselves with outfits and wigs so they can act with abandon. It's an innocent enough way for the guests to have a decadent evening."

"How do you have such insight into the psyche of the donors?" He surely seemed to know what he was doing.

"I've been going to charity events my entire life."

"Were your parents big donors?"

"You could say that. They made a lot of appearances."

"Oh, are they famous?"

"Something like that." He flagged the waiter. "Another café au lait, please. You?" he asked her.

"Yes, that would be nice, thank you."

Zander nodded at the waiter, who took his exit.

"A costume ball in and of itself isn't enough. We need to tell them what they're masquerading as."

Marie racked her brain. She wanted to make suggestions that Zander would like. She was in uncharted waters here. He was talking about balls the likes of which she'd never seen before. But that didn't matter—what did is that it would impress his guests.

"As I was saying earlier," he continued, "there's so

much money in Cannes, especially this time of year. All of the Hollywood glitterati are here for the film festival and half of Europe is here to ogle them. Plus, the spring galas and balls are starting so everyone is expecting to part with their money. The APCF should be getting a bigger share of the bounty."

Knowing she was just blocks away from the ultra-luxury hotels on La Croisette, where many of the rich and infamous stayed, Marie couldn't help but wonder about the lifestyles of the privileged class it seemed Zander was a part of.

What kind of care did these people take of their sons and daughters? Did they have happy homes, making sure their children felt loved and secure? Did they hug them close and protect them from harm? Or did they leave their care to others, without knowing if they were being treated right? Which type was Zander? How was he raised? Did he have children?

"Do you have children?" she couldn't help asking even though he had been cryptic when she pried into what he did for a living.

"You ask a lot of questions."

"Only the important ones."

That simply drew a chuckle from him, those dark-as-night eyes taking on a bit of glisten.

Which got her out of a tight spot. Because she wasn't one to answer the big questions, so it wasn't fair of her to ask them.

Marie's heart thumped in double time to her steps on the way back to the office. Zander was simply the most stimulating company she'd ever been in! She'd never met anyone like him. He was so sure of himself and he had an unending stream of ideas to which he encouraged discussion. She actually felt a bit slow-witted around him, though she imagined it was his innate confidence that contributed to his panache.

Not to mention how stunning he was, with those piercing eyes that caught her every hesitation, every pause, every downward glance. He read right into her. He was going to be hard to hide from. And Marie had plenty to hide.

Once she settled in at the desk in her office, she speculated on how someone became a self-assured and successful person like Zander. With her parents long dead, and in working for the good of other orphans, Marie often found herself trying to analyze what kind of upbringing led to a fully functioning adult.

She knew that two people might have grown up with exactly the same opportunities yet one could become accomplished in both vocation and personal relationships. Whereas the other might succumb to crime, substance abuse, mental illness or some other type of marginalized existence. While upbringing was not a complete predictor of someone's future, it was a start.

Did Zander have a supportive childhood with parents who sheltered him when needed and encouraged risk when that was what was called for? She couldn't help but ponder about his background. Along with what it might be like to be held in his big, long arms, though she chastised herself for that inappropriate thought as soon as she had it. Yet she simply couldn't stop imagining being enveloped by him, swept into his sureness, giving her a sense of belonging her rootless past had never allowed.

Marie shook her head. Dashing Zander was the event

chair for this very fancy benefit she found herself a part of. There wasn't to be anything personal between the two of them. Zander was a member of the upper class. Men like him didn't give a second glance to girls like her, who'd had it rough and were just scraping by. Money attracted money, confidence married confidence and so on. Wasn't that how it went? And what was she doing thinking about marrying anyway? Her love life thus far had just been links in a chain of the disappointment she had always known.

Starting with the top one, Marie moved the boxes that were on her desk and stacked them into a corner on the floor. She needed a workspace. Picking up the office phone with its many buttons, she called the front desk to find out what Felice's phone extension was. And left a message that she was available for the end-of-the-day meeting they'd agreed upon.

Before they parted Zander had asked her if she could continue working tonight and said that he'd send his driver at seven. So she'd need to finish up with Felice at the office and then go to her room to change into something more appropriate for the evening. Zander hadn't mentioned where his driver would be taking her.

After skimming through the files, Marie had a better sense of the agency's events. Some of the paperwork was from a year ago, some from five. It was a daunting prospect to have to sort through it all. She'd get to it as she could, but Felice had stressed to her that the gala was the number one priority.

Marie bit her lip, thinking again that being forced to spend lots of her time with Zander on this gala was one heck of a high-quality problem to have. Although she needed to tamp down her attraction to him, and fast!

"How did the meeting go?" Felice entered her office and closed the door. Marie looked up from the notes she was reviewing.

"Well, I think. He wants to meet with me again tonight to go into more detail."

"And you're available I hope?"

Marie bit back a snicker. Why wouldn't she be available? When she'd arrived this morning, she'd dropped off her suitcases and come straight to the office. And with no guarantees that she be promoted to the job permanently, she wouldn't even be giving up her room in Toulouse just yet. In short, Marie Paquet's life was in complete flux. Evening plans were the last thing on her mind.

"You'll need to devote yourself to Zander for the time being," Felice continued. The words *devote yourself to Zander* crawled down Marie's back, making her twitch in her seat. Devotion wasn't hard to imagine.

Perhaps there was already someone who had devoted herself to him. In fact, why on earth wouldn't there be? A smart and sophisticated man like him would surely have devotees lined up around the block. For all she knew, he was married or spoken for. Who was the Iris he had been talking to on the phone earlier today?

Regardless, Marie's task was to render this gala to everyone's satisfaction. Not to pry into Zander's relationship status.

"He talked to me about how extravagant he wants this to be. Something about being on par with the great balls of Venice. Do we have party vendors that can pull off something that ambitious?"

"This is Cannes," Felice assured. "This town knows how to throw a party better than most of the world. Of course, we have event partners up to the task."

Felice tapped into her phone. Once the ring began, she placed it on Marie's desk and hit the speaker button.

"Chef Jean Luc Malmond."

"Jean Luc, Felice here at the APCF."

"Felice, my sweet."

"We've had a bit of a staff shake-up here. And we're not entirely clear what has been settled upon for the gala's menu."

"Let me pull up my notes."

"And I have you on speakerphone with Marie Paquet, who will be our liaison for the event."

"A pleasure to meet you."

"You, too. On the phone, that is."

"As you know we have Zander de Nellay as event chair," Felice said to Jean Luc. "He wants to go lavish. I'm not sure Marie's predecessor had a grasp on the scale of the event."

"One thousand guests at the mansion," Marie added. That headcount was far larger than anything she'd ever worked on before. She was excited by the challenge. Among other things.

"I see we talked about starting with waiters passing hors d'oeuvres on trays during the cocktail hour," Jean Luc reported. "Then we seat the guests for a soup course. Followed by the entrée course with wine. Then a salad. Afterward, dessert buffets stationed at several locations in the ballroom. Continuous cocktail service in the great hall, ancillary salons and on the lawn."

"Do you have that, Marie?" Felice asked her across the desk. "You can discuss this with Zander when you meet with him tonight. See if he likes that basic outline."

"Got it."

"Jean Luc, I'm going to have Marie call you to set up a meeting this week."

"Yes, let's finalize as soon as possible. With the social season upon us, I'm like a decapitated chicken." Jean Luc let go of a laugh.

After they got off the phone, Felice helped Marie make a list of points to discuss with Zander when she saw him later.

Intrigue still nagged at Marie.

She sensed something a bit mysterious about Zander. For example, he never directly answered her innocent-enough query about what he did for work, saying only that he was affiliated with several charities.

"Felice, what does Zander do for a living?"

"Do?" Felice looked at her like she had just arrived from Mars. Marie wanted to impress the director by having all the information, but nothing in the notes said anything specifically about that. "You mean other than his royal duties?"

"Royal duties?" Marie's shoulders arched back.

"Marie, His Highness Zander de Nellay is a prince. He's the son of His Serene Highness Prince Hugh and Princess Claudine of Charlegin."

Marie's fists opened and closed. She'd just had lunch at an outdoor café with a prince? Obviously, a poor orphan from the meanest streets in North Marseilles had never met a member of royalty before.

She'd seen enough of the royals who were always on television and in magazines to know that they didn't wear regalia and crowns every time they were seen in public. Still, there was nothing about Zander, nor had he said anything, to give her any indication that he was a prince.

A prince!

"Felice, I didn't know. It wasn't anywhere in Jic's paperwork." Although she remembered in a handwritten note Jic had doodled a crown above Zander's name. Hardly a clear communiqué, but now it made sense.

"I assumed you knew, therefore it never occurred to me to mention it."

She'd be working on this gala with a prince! Why hadn't he told her who he was? It seemed like he went out of his way not to mention it.

When she saw him tonight, should she tell him that she'd only just found out? Or should she let it remain unspoken as if it was something she'd already known? Nothing in her previous reference taught her protocol for this sort of thing.

"His Highness Prince Zander de Nellay of Charlegin." Marie said it out loud to try it on for size. He'd mentioned his homeland but not that his family were the rulers there!

"It's a small principality reigned over by a prince rather than a king. Surely you heard the news a year ago when Zander's sister, Elise, who was the crown princess, and her husband were killed in a plane crash?"

Once Felice began to explain, Marie vaguely remembered hearing about that tragedy on the news. At the time she hadn't heard of Charlegin and had forgotten all about it. Royal comings and goings were of no interest to her. But she recalled the photo that had been shown on the news of Elise, a beautiful woman who, now that Marie thought about it, had those dark almond-shaped eyes the same as Zander.

"Is there a specific reason the prince is affiliated with the APCF and chairing our gala?"

"Alain really didn't fill you in, did he? Princess Elise and her husband, Prince Valentin, had a baby girl. She was left an orphan. Zander has taken her in. Princess Abella de Nellay is the next heir to the Charlegin throne."

CHAPTER THREE

MARIE WALKED DOWN the corridor to the room she was staying in. When Alain had described the facility as "nothing fancy," he hadn't been kidding. The carpet was a worn gray and the white walls were cold. He'd told her the building was a multipurpose center for the APCF, providing temporary shelter to orphans in foster care who were, perhaps, being relocated and awaiting placement. Or to those who needed to be removed from bad situations but before new arrangements could be made.

A chill swept through her at the memory, several memories in fact, of herself being in those circumstances. When frightened children were grouped together in nondescript locations to, essentially, sit around and wait to see where they were going to live next. Often fearful that as bad as their previous placement might have been, what awaited them in the future could be worse.

While there were many generous and compassionate people in the world who became foster parents, Marie hadn't had the luck to be placed with any of them. Uniformly, the six overcrowded and dirty apartments she'd been sent to over the years were habitats with adults who should not have been entrusted with the care of children.

Her parents had been no better suited. Marie had never been part of a healthy, living and breathing family. The kind she used to dream about, where people helped each other through the hard times and enjoyed each other's successes. An adult now, she'd long accepted that was never to be for her.

At twenty-five, Marie was on her own. The past might forever haunt her, but the future was hers to make or break.

The key to her room's door stuck as she pushed it into the lock and it took a couple of jimmies to fit it in. Her two suitcases were exactly where she had left them this morning after her train ride from Toulouse.

A single-sized bed with an unpainted wood nightstand beside it and a table with an armchair were the only furnishings. Sparse, institutional but clean. Time would tell whether she was in Cannes to stay, and if so, she'd look for a small place she could personalize. At least this would be a private space to think in, and her phone and the laptop Felice had given her would allow her to work and communicate as needed.

In fact, she pulled the laptop out of her bag and brought it with her as she kicked off her shoes and sat down on the bed. She propped her back against the wall and set the computer on her knees. Logging on to the internet, she had business to take care of. Research, anyway.

Into the search field she typed "Prince Zander de Nellay." Dozens of links popped up. She clicked to the first one, *Single Hot Royals*, even though the name sounded like a gossip site that may or may not contain anything true.

An hour and many websites later, she had gathered plenty of reconnaissance. Firstly, Prince Zander was incapable of taking a bad photo. Whether snapped in a tuxedo at official occasions, socializing in a tailored suit worn without a tie or on the golf course in well-fitted sportswear, the man was simply gorgeous.

Next, unsurprisingly, he had been associated romantically with several beautiful and famous women. Marie found photos of him from all over the world, either vacationing in tropical paradises or in the thick of pulsing cities, with stunning females on his arm. With an American movie star on a sailboat in the Caribbean. Riding horseback in the countryside with a London fashion model. At an Italian opera house with a Chinese ballerina.

One thing was consistent about Marie's online detective work. There were few pictures of Zander taken in the past year, other than at charitable or royal functions. After his sister and her husband died, Zander all but went into hiding. As Felice had told her that he was now the one caring for his baby niece, his absence from the party scene was understandable.

Although about six months ago, when he had been photographed he'd always had the same eight-foot-tall stick insect on his arm. A glamazon named Henriette Fontaine. Three months later, he'd made the same appearances alone. Marie's detective work added up to a conclusion that Zander was heterosexual and unmarried.

Wanting a few minutes to ready herself before she met with him again, Marie closed the laptop. She opened her suitcases and hung her limited and plain wardrobe in the room's one closet. Not sure what to wear for the evening, she flipped through her options.

He hadn't specified where they were going. So it wasn't a dinner invitation, yet it wasn't a business meeting. A suit would be wrong, but one of her few dressier dresses wouldn't be right, either.

A quick glance in the mirror on the closet door was a blaring reminder that she needed a haircut. Obviously, she wasn't planning to move to Cannes, where absolutely everyone had a "yacht chic" style that must have cost them a fortune. How would she have known that a haircut was urgent? And in her wildest dreams she couldn't have known that she'd be interacting with a prince and had to consider what to wear to spend the evening with him.

Deciding on the best middle ground she could think of, she put on a black pencil skirt with black flats. But she dressed it up with a shiny red blouse—not real silk, of course—that had a low neckline with a bow detail. Hair swept into a twist and the pearl earrings that she'd saved for a year to buy, she hoped she looked respectable. This wasn't a date, Marie kept reminding herself as she applied a bit of makeup to try to cover up the telltale signs of her very long day. She hadn't been on a date in a long time. Two years ago, in fact.

Gerard.

Marie had been on casual dates with a few men and had one boyfriend. Gerard was fifth generation of a farming family. He frequently came into Toulouse for banking and supplies, and they met at a brasserie close to the APCF's office there.

Gerard took a liking to her. Or so it seemed. Attending a sporting event or movie together, Marie thought they were at ease with each other. She didn't have a lot of friends so she appreciated Gerard's companionship. While there were warning signs from the very beginning, she shoved them aside. For a few months, she convinced herself she was happy.

But when she went with him to meet his parents, they didn't welcome her with open arms. They asked a lot of questions. She'd learned to say as little as possible about her past because people seemed to always judge her by it. Not leaving it as a mystery, they took it upon themselves to do some research. And once they found out about her, that was that. No son of theirs was going to be with a girl left orphaned by criminals. Think of the gene pool. They saw to it that the relationship didn't last long.

Gerard didn't protest. Obviously, Marie hadn't meant enough to him to defend her to his parents. No one had ever fought for her. She didn't think anyone ever would.

Yet now she was making up her face for her meeting with a prince. The juxtaposition gave her hope. People never really knew where their road would take them.

Something she did know was that she was only herself. With her checkered upbringing and her emotional scars. If she was ever to be with a man again, which she highly doubted anyway, it would have to be somebody who accepted and even loved her for who she was.

Although that was all speculation. Marie had no intention of getting into any kind of relationship with anyone again. She'd had enough hurt, neglect, betrayal and disappointment to last a lifetime. There was only one person she could count on, who had her best interests at heart.

Herself.

With a click on her purse's buckle, she left to meet the striking gala chairman who just happened to be a prince.

The buzz of the doorbell snapped Zander's attention from his paperwork. A glance down to his phone informed him it was later than he'd realized. It was time for Marie's arrival.

It had been a long day with moving into the apartment and his visit to the APCF, but there was more work ahead. While Marie was pleasant, not to mention attractive, she was not educated on the requirements for the gala. He couldn't do this alone so hoped to get her caught up quickly.

"Come in." Zander opened the door wide for her to enter.

He noticed that she had gussied herself up for the evening. The hair that had been rather adorably a mess at lunch was now pulled sleekly back. The sparkle of the round blue eyes was set off by a shade of pink lipstick that brought focus to her small and perfectly shaped mouth.

A lovely young woman had come calling. And it took Zander aback.

Until he reminded who he was, who she was, and that she had only come to work.

"Oh, my gosh!" Marie seemed to be startled as soon as she passed into the apartment. She countered with, "I mean, how nice, your…"

He waited while she took in the full panorama of the spacious living room with its solid wall of sliding glass doors leading to the terrace and the sea view beyond.

With the doors slid fully open, a twilight breeze billowed the white gauzy curtains. Inside, the blond wood combined with fabrics in shades of soothing taupes and grays gave the furniture a calm feel amid the opulence of the room. There was no denying that it was a spectacular residence.

"May I ask, is this where you live?"

"Yes, why?" That wasn't the first time Marie had blurted out a direct question that someone might consider private and not to be asked in casual conversation. He found her bluntness refreshing. People hardly ever let their thinking show when they were around His Highness Prince Zander.

"I just wasn't sure if you... I mean you can obviously affor..."

"Yes?" He folded his arms across his chest, waiting.

"You mentioned that you were only here for the season."

This exchange reinforced why he'd gotten into the habit of not introducing himself by his title to everyone he met. Marie was falling over her words just thinking of him as a wealthy philanthropist. One could only imagine how she'd act once she knew she was in the presence of a prince and a baby heir to the throne.

"Yes." He couldn't help playing along a little longer.

"I've never seen...well, what would I know? I've never been to Cannes before. It's very glamorous, isn't it?"

"For centuries now."

"I hope that if I get the job with the APCF permanently I can find an apartment in my price range. Not that you'd...well, you know what I mean."

True, Zander had never been concerned with, or even

knowledgeable of, how much a rental property cost to lease. He got the feeling Marie was well versed on the subject.

She had told him that she herself had been orphaned and that the agency had helped her. He wondered what hardships she had endured, financial or otherwise. Something unspoken about her told him that there were probably a lot.

As pretty as she was, he didn't find it hard to imagine her as a scruffy cliché of an orphan. Through the APCF he'd learned about orphaned children all over the world. Some were left parentless as a result of war or natural disasters, or freak accidents as Abella was. Others were due to the consequences of illness, poverty, suicide, addiction or crime. He had no idea how Marie had become orphaned or what her road to adulthood had been. And was more curious than he expected to be.

When they'd parted this afternoon with an agreement to reconvene tonight, he'd planned on taking her out for a working dinner. But when he arrived home, the baby was sleeping, and Iris was extremely tired and asked if he'd mind her leaving. Of course, he had his driver ferry her to the small flat he'd leased for her for their time in Cannes.

Which meant that meeting here with Marie was the only option. One he wasn't exactly comfortable with. He'd learned the hard way that he needed to shelter Abella from strangers as much as possible.

"Can I offer you a drink?" Zander asked absentmindedly, sidetracked by a peep he heard coming from the baby monitor. Perhaps Abella was waking.

"Just water, please."

Hearing no further stirring from the baby, Zander

poured two waters and gestured for Marie to join him at the sofas. They sat opposite each other.

"Let's start by talking through the gala in order of its components."

"Okay." Marie opened the folder she had brought along.

"Guests arrive via limousine or personal drivers," he began. "Do we have valets for cars that need to be parked?"

"Yes, I see here we have contracted with a company for that."

"Good. The guests exit their cars and proceed to the red carpet."

"Red carpet?" Marie tilted her head. "For the APCF fund-raiser?"

"That's how it's done. I've got prominent business-people coming, celebrities, members of royal families." He murmured the last example quickly as if it were an afterthought. "We're looking for maximum exposure. The press will be out in force to photograph the arrivals on the carpet. The gowns. The jewelry. And so on."

He meant what he said. Once his staff had put out the news that Prince Zander was hosting the gala, the royal-watching media had taken interest. Which was the plan, because all publicity would serve to raise awareness about the APCF.

While Zander wasn't among the royals whose antics made constant headlines, he found it curious that Marie didn't recognize him at all. Leveraging his position and power was how he was able to assist a number of high-profile causes. Not only was it what royals throughout history had done, it was something that made him feel good. The benevolent work was a way to pay back for the luxury and advantages that were bestowed on him as his birthright.

"So I'll need to order an actual red carpet?" she asked after a sip of her drink.

"For a costume ball, I was thinking of a black carpet. We'll light it just so, and make it mysterious and sexy."

"Sexy?" Marie clasped and unclasped her fists a few times. "Are the struggles of orphans sexy?"

"Point taken. But, yes, hidden identities and checkbooks filled with lots and lots of money are sexy."

Good heavens, Marie was not like any woman he'd ever met before! Granted, the orbit he operated in wasn't filled with ordinary people leading typical lives. The women he knew ate, slept and breathed money. They knew where it was and how to get a piece of it. And they surely knew how to spend it.

What was he going to do with this innocent Marie? As he watched that sensual mouth of hers take another sip of her drink, he thought of a few things. And then promptly reprimanded himself! Women were no longer on his agenda.

He'd get used to Marie and then she wouldn't be so fascinating. Which was reinforced when he heard another blip from the baby monitor. The sound came from the only female who mattered in his life, a position she would hold for the foreseeable future. Abella was awake and would soon want to be retrieved from her crib.

"One photo stop on the carpet should be a flower wall," Zander continued. "That's great for photos."

"What's a flower wall?" Marie leaned forward a bit, unintentionally giving Zander a nice view of the creamy skin of her neck.

On the coffee table between them sat the stack of invitations to the various balls, fund-raisers and parties that would kick off the social season. He remembered that he'd instructed an assistant to RSVP for two to all of them, that Prince Zander would be bringing a plus one. He'd still yet to figure out who that was going to be.

But to walk into one of those events without a drop-dead gorgeous woman on his arm was like to appear with a target on his back. Every female gold digger on the continent would find her way to him before the season was up, feigning interest about the baby and trying to finagle an invitation to spend time with her. Just as Henriette had a few months ago.

He needed to come up with a trustworthy female friend who could accompany him to these events so he didn't have to dodge the unwanted advances. Perhaps one of his late sister's friends, one who knew the family and wouldn't have any ulterior motives.

No, he mused, memories of Elise were the last thing he wanted. The flourishing constant reminder of her untimely death was in the very next room, haunting him every day.

Abella began to make so many cooing sounds from her room that Marie glanced over to the baby monitor.

Even though Marie was with the APCF, and didn't seem at all like the opportunist women he had known, he'd hadn't planned on inviting her to the apartment. At least not yet. But since they'd be working together closely and frequently, a proposition that filled him with a trickle of eager anticipation, he surely couldn't keep the baby a secret.

Although he took a split second to hope he wasn't making a mistake. Like his recent one, which still filled him with remorse.

When Zander stood, Marie looked unclear as to whether she was supposed to stay seated or to get up, as well. "Please, be comfortable. If you'll pardon me a moment. I'll be right back."

"Uh, okay."

"If you recall, at lunch today you asked me what connection I had to the needs of parentless children. I'm going to show you."

He wasn't able to read Marie's expression as he excused himself and made his way down the hall to Abella's room, gently opening the door that he had left ajar.

"Da." Abella recognized Zander's presence despite the room being in darkness. That she kept calling him *Da* was a problem he still hadn't figured out how to solve.

Flicking on the muted light that was contained inside a pink-and-blue unicorn lamp, he was greeted by his niece's exuberant face. "Uncle Zander is here, Bell-bell. Do you want to get up?"

"Uppie."

When he returned to the living room with Abella, Marie stood.

"This little miracle is my catalyst for concern about children left orphaned. Marie, I'd like you to meet…"

"Her Highness Crown Princess Abella de Nellay of Charlegin," Marie interrupted. "Heir to the throne."

"You *do* know who I am?" Zander's brow furrowed at the confusion. Abella nuzzled her face against his neck, filling him with that almost all-consuming need to don a suit of armor and do her bidding. While he'd convinced himself that Marie couldn't possibly be the enemy, someone's motives might not be evident at first. He was responsible for this baby, and he'd put her first in any situation. "Why didn't you say so?"

"I didn't know until Felice filled me in this afternoon. Why didn't you mention it, Your Highness? Am I supposed to call you Your Highness?"

Of course Felice had filled Marie in on his identity. The agency was planning to take full advantage of having a member of a royal family serve as the gala event chair. He'd only played along this afternoon because it seemed like Marie didn't know. And that had given him a chance to get a little bit of insight into her before the throne-and-scepter bit had her stumbling around him like she was now.

"You surely do not have to call me Your Highness or any such address unless we're in company where it's appropriate. By all means continue to call me Zander."

"Want bottie," Abella voiced her request.

While Marie watched on, he poured fresh water into Abella's cup. He and the baby still referred to it as a bottie even though she had progressed to lidded sippy cups. He was grateful for the activity as a distraction from Marie's fierce stare. She was hurt that he hadn't identified himself properly and was using that glare to fight back.

"Please, sit down again." He gestured for Marie to sit opposite him.

Abella eagerly sucked on the nozzle of her drink.

"She's...so...beautiful." The words tripped out of Marie's mouth as she looked affectionately at the baby princess.

Zander's thick fingers lightly brushed Abella's hair

backward out of her face as she drank her water. "Yes, she is."

As Abella squirreled around on his lap, Zander adjusted to accommodate her movements. Straightening one leg and bending the other, then reversing when something else caught the baby's eye. The two of them were in perpetual motion.

"May I ask again, was there a purpose in your not telling me who you were when clearly I didn't know?"

"I'm sorry, Marie," he said sincerely despite the constant shifting. "So often when I meet people in an official capacity, they don't talk to me as if I was of the same species. They feel they have to treat me with formality, and then before you know it, they're falling all over themselves."

Marie repeatedly smoothed her bangs down on her forehead, seeming uncomfortable and making Zander feel awful.

"Since, obviously, you'd discover my title soon enough," he continued, "I was trying to use the time for us to get acquainted, just person to person."

"So I was your guinea pig?"

"I apologize that must be how it seems to you. Can you forgive me?"

Marie looked around, again taking in the view beyond the terrace. She glanced down to the plush white carpeting. Studied the crystal glass that held her beverage. As if she was fully fathoming that it was a prince's water she was drinking.

All the sorts of things Zander hated. He flashed back to the last time he was with Henriette. They'd traveled to a luxurious parador in Spain for a long weekend. The way she had inspected the bed sheets and bathroom towels was just embarrassing. Zander figured when-ever he left her sight, the girl was probably looking up their monetary value online.

While he didn't suspect that anything like that was going through Marie's mind, he hated that everything, including a simple drinking glass, was how people were categorized, labeled and judged.

He had a great responsibility on his head, in Abella's well-being. Henriette had been a call to arms and he'd become quickly adept at keeping people at bay. While there were bodyguards and royal handlers in Charlegin assigned to Abella, Zander thought of her safety as his own particular job, and one he took seriously. He'd en-countered other women like Henriette who acted like they cared about the baby when really they were angling as to what *pretending* to care about the baby could gain them. Zander was making sure to have no more of that.

Marie chose her next words deliberately. "I do un-derstand a little bit about what you're talking about. People find out facts about you and then they make as-sumptions."

Which led Zander to certainty that there was more she could say but chose not to. "It sounds like you've had personal experience with that."

Marie was clearly holding something back. Even though he believed from the pit of his stomach that she meant no harm, he'd be sure not to leave her alone with the baby. Once he got to know her better, he'd reassess. After all, she did work for the APCF and Felice assured him he was in good hands.

For now, though, the metal shield was across his chest. This was his new life.

"Let's get back to the task at hand," Zander said after

succeeding in getting Abella occupied beside him with a set of plastic blocks, and more than ready to move on from the discussion of his royal status.

Abella accidently knocked her sippy cup to the floor. Marie reached down to pick it up.

"I've got it," Zander quickly blipped and snatched it from Marie's hand. Her surprised look made him aware that his action was overly defensive. What would be the harm in Marie touching something of Abella's? But was there such a thing as being *too* careful when it came to the protection of the crown princess?

In any case, should he apologize or just ignore it? Odd that he was second-guessing himself left and right around Marie.

"We were talking about the red carpet."

"Black carpet," Marie corrected, regrouping.

"The VIP guests walk the carpet, the press is out in force, etcetera."

"What about the attendees who are not, as you call them, VIP? Do they come in through the sewage system?"

Zander laughed. He couldn't help but like this woman. Her frankness and spunk were riveting. "It does sound horribly undemocratic, I know. But the reality is that the press is only interested in famous names and faces. Bringing publicity to the APCF is our goal. We have to keep our sights on that."

"No problem," she insisted with a defiantly jutted chin, then made some notes. "This is just more gala than the galas we've done before. I'm looking forward to it."

Zander glanced over again to those party invitations on the table. An idea circulated around and around his brain. Until it started to take shape and make sense.

Many birds could be killed with one stone, as the saying went. If he was going to get Marie to fathom the elaborate kind of evening he was planning for the APCF, it would be invaluable if she could see some of them unfold. He could take her along as his date for the engagements in the first few weeks of the season. Then she'd have firsthand knowledge of not one but several event styles. She'd see Cannes at its heights, when the whole city rose to the occasion of these legendary parties.

Secondly, with a woman accompanying him the pressure would be off. It wasn't hard to imagine Marie in designer gowns and with her hair and makeup styled to perfection. She'd be a fetching date and would surely ward off the hangers-on who usually planted themselves in Zander's path.

Plus it would give him and Marie an opportunity to spend plenty of time together and develop a good working relationship.

It was a genius scheme that would work on every level. Zander mentally confirmed his decision and was quite pleased with himself for thinking of it.

Almost. There was only one thing gnawing in his craw as he looked to Marie sitting opposite, with Abella still happily playing next to him. There was something about Marie that was a little too intriguing. Alluring even. Which could lead to trouble.

He could get past it, though. Between Henriette's burn that still smarted, his feelings for the baby and the massive amount of specifics to take care of for the event, he wouldn't have time for anything else.

It was a perfect plan. Wasn't it?

Marie's sweet blue eyes watched the baby play. She smiled at moments then went wide-eyed when Abella displayed her proficiency with the blocks. "Great job, Abella," she blurted at one point.

Most definitely not like the women he knew.

Her cheap shiny red blouse reminded him of her wildly windblown hair at lunch today. He'd have to buy her gowns and shoes and whatnot to attend these parties where only the finest would do.

"Marie," he said finally, after staring at her for a long while he'd thought through all the particulars. "You're going to attend some black-tie events with me in the next couple of weeks. You'll need evening wear."

CHAPTER FOUR

"I'VE NEVER WORN anything like this." The words stuttered out of Marie's mouth as she looked at herself in the shop's three-way mirror. The underslip of the midnight-blue gown fit her like a glove. It was topped by a chiffon layer to which a thousand matching crystals were affixed.

Of course, she didn't know if it was really a thousand. She only knew it was the right number of beads, not so many that the dress became flashy or over the top. No, this was subtle elegance of the kind Marie had not only never tried on but never even seen up close. She could imagine a dozen workers crafting to create this gown.

"The blue is lovely on you," Zander voted in.

Flushed by his flattery, Marie ran her hand along the scooped neckline of the dress. Its needlework and seams were expertly hidden. The inner layer felt smooth against the delicate skin of her décolleté. With a slight tug to the thin straps, she lifted the bodice of the gown a bit higher for modesty. As quietly and quickly as a stealth weapon, Pati the sales manager, a tiny woman with arthritic fingers, pinned the straps to Marie's satisfaction.

ANDREA BOLTER 65

"Thank you, Pati." Zander acknowledged her hand-iwork.

"Perhaps you'd like to wear your hair up with this gown," Pati suggested. "May I?"

Marie allowed Pati to lift her hair with a few clips to see how it would look. With the low cut of the dress's front and her hair out of the way, Marie's neck looked tall and stately. An unfamiliar description.

A couple of Marie's coworkers in Toulouse were into clothes and always encouraging her to dress more daringly or trendily. She paid them no mind. Having spent most of her life not knowing whether she'd even have clean clothes for school the next day, fashion was the furthest thing from young Marie's mind.

As an adult, she'd settled into practical and inexpensive pieces. It rarely occurred to her to replace or add to her current wardrobe unless something was so worn it would appear unprofessional. On the rare occasions she did shop, it was surely not at a store like the one they were in now.

The boutique carried formal wear from both world-renowned and local designers. Once again reminding Marie that she was in the French Riviera where sun and money informed the lifestyle. If she got the job at the APCF permanently, it would all take some getting used to.

She'd no doubt need to find her place on the *other side of the tracks*, as the saying went. Just as her ex-boyfriend, Gerard, never hesitated to remind her, she should keep her expectations low. But hopefully, there would be somewhere she could afford to live in a working-class neighborhood. Maybe she'd meet some people there. The La Croisette crowd was not her kind. Never were and never would be.

In fact, the combination of trying on the gown coupled with Prince Zander's observant eye was overwhelming. The way he looked at her was nothing like Gerard, or any other man, had. He'd picked her up earlier this morning, after deciding last night that she'd accompany him to some of the swanky fund-raisers that were on his calendar. And presto, with a snap of his fingers, she was suddenly shopping in Cannes and living in a different universe. One she could hardly fathom.

To pull off the magnitude of event Zander wanted to for the APCF, Marie was going to need an education on how events of that scale were mounted. She was grateful for the prince's invitation, although intimidated to move in a social circle she knew nothing about. Joining him for some hands-on learning was an opportunity there'd be no substitute for.

"Zander." Marie moved from the three-sided mirror over to the settee where he was sitting. She waited until Pati was well out of earshot before asking, "I appreciate your confidence in me but… I don't know how to say this…isn't it kind of obvious that I'm not the type of woman who would go to a ball on a prince's arm?"

"What kind of woman would that be?" He leaned back in his seat, legs parted as he scratched his chin.

"Don't you have well…people you live among?"

"Have you been talking to my mother?" he joked.

Although his smile was flirty, Marie pressed on.

"But aren't you supposed to be seen with women from your…planet?"

"And you're not?"

Perhaps he didn't know what a hot-button issue like belonging was to someone like Marie. Whose parents weren't capable of creating a nurturing home for a child.

And who, after they died when she was eleven, was tossed from one foster home to the next. And mercilessly teased, ridiculed for being homeless and rootless. Never being around people she trusted or felt accepted by. No one to catch her if she fell or celebrate her when she thrived. Although she was doing great by any standards in her adult life, those weren't scars that ever healed.

If Zander thought she was just as good as the selective crowd his life was built around, why did he grab Abella's sippy cup out of her hands last night as if she was infected with the bubonic plague? She could appreciate that he might not like Abella's things to be handled by strangers, but his actions surely spoke louder than his words.

Noticing that she was flustered, Zander said, "First of all, I'll bring whomever I want to a party and dare anyone to tell me otherwise." More words. "Secondly, you look fabulous, and chic, in that gown. You're not going to be wearing a sign on your back that tells everyone how much money your father makes."

"I'm an orphan. My father doesn't make anything."

"Forgive me, yes, I know that. It was just meant as a figure of speech."

"But do you think…"

He reached out and took Marie's hand. His was so solid and sturdy, tingles tracked down her body at his touch. Her neck and throat, exposed in the gown, must have turned beet red. She didn't know if she was really going to be able to hold herself together. Not only was this entire shopping expedition way out of her frame of reference, Zander himself was too much. He awakened something in her. She was hyperaware of herself in his presence and analyzing his every move.

As she had learned in counseling, when life became too much to bear Marie knew to deepen her breathing. After intaking plenty of extra oxygen, she was able to hear the words Zander spoke while he held her hand.

"This is a good idea, to give you firsthand knowledge of how these events are done. And I'll tell you something else. If you're going to stay in Cannes, I suggest you get comfortable mingling with the hoi polloi here. This is a moneyed town, full of people who have it and more who want it. An effective fund-raiser knows how to swing in the right circles."

"Yes, you're right, of course."

Pati moved toward them holding a couple of bottles of water. "Why don't we get you out of that dress and into another. Can I offer you a drink while you're changing? This, or a coffee?"

"I'd better take the dress off first!"

"Indeed." Pati turned to Zander. "Your Highness, we'll be right back."

"Zander."

Pati bowed her head. "Yes, Your Highness."

"Zander is fine, really," he said with a smirk.

Marie was completely taken aback by his warmth and humor as she followed Pati. Whatever preconceptions she might have had about the reserve of royalty was quickly being thrown out the window. But she had to caution herself not to read anything into his friendly demeanor.

A prince was never going to spend his time with the likes of her other than for the sake of his own goals, so it would be dangerous to get close to him. He had a means to an end and she was here only to serve him. That his ultimate aim was to bring as much money into the APCF as possible was certainly noble. And, she had to admit, added to his charm.

Not to mention those almond-shaped eyes that were always watching. There were those defined lips. Her eyes rolled back in her head when she allowed herself a split second of imagining what his mouth might feel like on her bare neck. Then there was that physique of his that today looked so taut under the tailored pink shirt and black jeans he was wearing. It might be heaven on earth to be in his embrace.

Pati ushered Marie back into the dressing area. Dressing *room*, singular, was the right word for it, as it was about the size of the bedroom Marie would be staying in. The walls were covered in textured wallpaper with black velvet fleurs-de-lis in a pattern. A black dais stood in the center of the room for pinning alterations.

There were mirrors everywhere. Antique armchairs upholstered in gold taffeta were arranged in a couple of groupings. Gowns on rolling racks were placed just so, as to not touch each other. A tall shoe stand with many rungs could accommodate a dozen pair. A glass case held evening bags and hair accessories. Marie had never given any thought to what a dressing room in a shop like this would look like, but it was magical.

With Pati's help, Marie stepped carefully out of the first gown. Sipping from the bottle of water, she felt uneasy seeing herself in all the mirrors with her low-cost cotton underwear amid the finery of the shop.

"The prince is very handsome, isn't he?" Pati stated rather than asked as she brought out the next dress for Marie to try.

"He is at that."

"And are you a…friend of his?"

As discreet as the manager of a designer shop in Cannes was expected to be, apparently even Pati couldn't resist prying out any data she could on Zander's relationship status. *It must be awful for him*, Marie thought to herself. People foisting themselves onto him not out of any genuine like but for self-centered reasons. In a funny way, she felt protective toward him.

"We're colleagues," she said flatly.

Marie's modeling the pewter-colored gown with the train got a "Yes!" from Zander when Pati brought her out to show him. "That will be perfect for the reception at the Carlsmon." He'd mentioned that they'd be attending a screening and party during the film festival at a hotel that was known as one of the centers of the action.

With Zander ten steps ahead of everyone else, as seemed to always be the case, he'd obviously contacted Pati ahead of time to explain what clothes Marie would need. And he was here with her making sure the selections were to his satisfaction. Marie wondered what typical days were like for His Highness, as a prince, a philanthropist and a royal baby's guardian.

Did he have an office somewhere that he reported to daily? A staff? Was it in Charlegin? Paris? With all his traversing of the world, she supposed a physical office would be impractical, not to mention unnecessary with today's technology. She considered how much about his lifestyle might have changed after the crown princess was put in his care.

Marie had to stand up very straight and force her shoulders back to wear the pewter dress properly. It was a gown for a confident woman, bold in its fit that left nothing to the imagination. It had halter-style straps with a V neckline. Under the bustline were two triangular cutouts that exposed bare skin. The geometric cutouts were echoed in the back. That little bit of skin peeking through was uncharacteristically daring for Marie. She was surprised at how much she loved it.

Having never walked in a gown with a train before, Marie got a quick course on how not to trip on the extra fabric.

"Thatta girl," Zander approved of her new posture. "You look just like one of the Hollywood stars who will be at the party."

Although Marie tried to breathe her heartbeat into not pounding, she feared it was. In a gown that probably cost more than she made in a month, Marie was going to a soiree where movie stars would be in attendance. That a girl from the *quartier nord*, as the worst streets of North Marseilles were called, with parents like hers and with the parade of incompetents who defined her adolescence after they were killed, was standing here today was unbelievable.

"Pati, what are we envisioning for the Laublie Foundation breast cancer research benefit? The theme is 'A Night in Mexico' and the dress is Mexican black tie," Zander declared and snapped Marie out of what could have had her looking back on a dark road.

"Your Highness—" Pati began.

"Zander."

"Zander," Pati finally managed with a cough, "I was thinking of black lace with some added color. May I show you what I had in mind?"

Back in the dressing room, nothing could have prepared Marie for the next dress Pati brought out, explaining that it was made from antique black lace. Marie touched the exceptional fabric, and thought it was romantic and current and timeless all at once. She couldn't believe her eyes. Her heart fluttered when Pati zipped her into it.

The fitted bodice was sleeveless with a sweetheart neckline. It skimmed her torso down to her waist. On top of the lace in a diagonal from the décolleté on the left to beyond the waistline on the right was a swath of brightly colored hand-embroidered flowers. Yellow, red, green, blue and purple against black added up to making this a dress Marie could not have imagined existed. With the help of several petticoats underneath, the skirt portion poufed out and extended to floor length.

It was a ball gown of the highest order.

Marie's jaw dropped at her visage in the mirror as Pati slipped her feet into black high-heeled sandals with a red leather bow on each. Somehow little girl dress-up had become a reality.

Prince Charming included.

As a warning, though, she shook her head at her own reflection in the mirror. There was no prince to be hers. She was only doing the job she'd been asked to, which, bizarrely, entailed wearing these exquisite clothes.

A shiver shot through her as she realized that if Zander knew any details about her, about her parents, he wouldn't want her on his arm or anywhere near him. Or near Abella. Marie hated constantly dragging her past along with her wherever she went. How she wished to not be limited by it any longer.

For now, it was all professionalism. Detached. Reveal nothing of herself. That was all she had to do. And to keep her attraction to Zander in check.

To complete this gown's look, Pati gave Marie a pair of red satin gloves that extended past her elbows.

"For that dramatic effect," Pati chirped. "And perhaps a necklace. With His Highness's approval, of course."

"Oh, my goodness." Marie couldn't help but skim one hand along the other arm to experience the shiny glide of the gloves. She surely hoped Zander liked this outfit because she knew it was the most beautiful she would ever wear as long as she lived.

After they'd finished at the dress shop, Zander led Marie toward La Croisette.

"Where are we going now?"

"Let's walk down to the beach."

He craved the sea breezes. Iris was still with Abella so he could afford a little more time out.

Zander directed them to an exclusive beach club where his family had year-round access.

"These beaches are private?" Marie exclaimed. "How is the ocean only available to certain people?"

Although he chuckled, he could grasp how strange this must all seem to her, as it would to the majority of people in the world. "Beach clubs, ball season, the film festival, Cannes can seem like another galaxy. Are you still game for taking this rocket ship with me?"

He'd noticed her habit of opening and closing her fists, which she was doing at the moment. "This is a once-in-a-lifetime chance for me to see Cannes through your eyes. I've never been on a private beach before."

"If you're going to get good at creating fund-raisers that bring in the big-money players, you should be inside their circle."

At the entrance, an attendant quickly greeted Zander. "Welcome, Your Highness. Will you be dining or in need of sporting equipment?"

"No, thank you, and you can call me Zander. We're just having a quick stroll on the beach today."

"I'll have towels and chairs for you immediately."

The afternoon had turned to dusk as they walked the length of the club's boardwalk, past the outdoor restaurant and cocktail bar, the lounge chairs and yellow-and-white-striped umbrellas set in precise rows.

Sun worshippers had begun to pull clothing over their tiny bathing suits to make their way up toward the cafés and hotels that lined the Croisette. They'd have their cocktails and change into their evening finery, emerging after dark for whatever plans were on their agenda in this fantasyland of a beach town.

"Do you want to take your shoes off and walk in the sand?" Marie asked.

"Absolutely." The way she asked thrilled him, like he was a mischievous schoolboy who was supposed to be in class but had snuck out for a short taste of freedom.

She quickly kicked her off her sandals. Zander untied his oxfords, removed his socks and cuffed his pants a couple of turns up his leg. Of course, he had fashionable beachwear back at the penthouse but they were here now, spontaneity not something Zander typically had much of. They stepped down from the boardwalk into the soft, warm sand, flashing each other a clandestine nod.

"See," she said, "even a prince can set his toes free sometimes, can't he?"

He felt his grin spread from ear to ear.

An attendant magically appeared to lay a stack of thick towels down onto a couple of loungers for their return.

"Even if he has to have his own private beach," she kidded.

As they walked toward the sparkling blue water, Zander found himself with a yearning he couldn't quite put his finger on.

There was something so genuine about Marie. It touched his heart.

Certainly the shopping excursion was a feast for the eyes, watching such a comely young woman model stunning clothing that she looked so good in. But even more fun was how innocent she was toward the whole thing, as if she herself couldn't believe she was wearing them. Hardly like the entitled girls he'd grown up around.

"What did you think of the dress shop? I take it you're unaccustomed to formal wear."

"For the events I did at the Toulouse office, I wore a black suit. With my only accessory an earpiece to keep the event running."

"At the APCF function we'll have someone else wear the earpiece. You should mingle and impress the guests. You know, you look stunning in those evening gowns."

She looked down to the sand, obviously a little embarrassed by his compliment. Which, of course, made her all the cuter.

"You've gone to a lot of trouble for me already."

He winked. "I'm sure my investment will pay off."

"Hey, are princes allowed to wink?"

"I'll check the handbook. Probably not."

Zander's phone chimed in his pocket. It was a personalized ringtone he couldn't ignore.

"Hello, Mother. How is Her Highness today?" He bugged his eyes at Marie. She bit her lip in response as their toes sunk farther into the sand. "Ah, yes, Cici. I remember. But I already have a companion for the season," he explained with a glance over to Marie. "Marie

Paquet, the event manager at the APCF. She's going to accompany me so that we can compare what's going on this spring with our gala plans… No, Mother, we're not dating…"

No, Mother, I don't know anything about her family… Yes, I know the press broadcasts every move we make.

He didn't respond aloud to that part of the conversation.

Signature Princess Claudine. A commoner who was fortunate enough to catch the eye of his father, His Serene Highness Prince Hugh, now ruler of Charlegin, Claudine was extremely concerned with the status and station of everyone she encountered. The princess was a master snoop.

"Thank you once again for the offer, Mother. I'll be sure to leave Abella at the palace if I feel the need to be the *dazzling young prince all the best girls want to get close to.*"

It was his sister Elise's expressed wish that she did not want Abella raised by her grandmother at the palace should anything happen to her and her husband. While Claudine was outwardly hurt that Elise had left instructions for Abella to be left in Zander's care if needed, it was clear that she was relieved not to have a baby to deal with. Generally, Her Highness was so busy with her art trips to Bali or on ski slopes in the States, she wasn't in one place for long.

More important, Elise and Valentin had hoped to raise a child who cared about humanity as a whole, about those less fortunate and about ways to make the planet a better place. The tutelage of Claudine was not going to bestow that onto Abella.

It was Prince Hugh who had taught those values to

his children. With all of Hugh's duties now that his own father had passed and the crown had come to sit on his head, Elise wasn't certain that he'd have time to spend with Abella and undo any superficial attitudes of Claudine's that might creep in. Elise wanted Zander to care for her child instead.

"Yes, Mother, the Hungarians, I'll be there." He eventually returned the phone to his pocket and turned to Marie. "My mother makes my love life her business."

"You're lucky to have someone who cares."

He wondered who cared about Marie.

"I am, but my mother and I seem to have different ideas about the matter."

"How so?"

Zander would publicly defend his family until the end of the earth, so he chose his words precisely. "She's been known to fix me up, and always with the wrong women. Now that I have Abella's necessities to consider, it's more important than ever to be careful who I have around."

"Did something happen?"

Henriette Fontaine, one of this mother's matches. That's what happened.

"I was seeing someone a few months ago who proved to not be as she appeared."

"In what way?"

Zander well understood that his family, and his subjects, expected him to marry an appropriate woman befitting a prince. While royalty might be permitted to marry commoners, his mother had always stressed to him that she should be one of the *best girls*, as she'd just repeated to him on the phone. Which had invariably led to superficial socialites who didn't see Zander as his own person, but only as a bank account and a palace.

Zander was putting dating aside completely for the time being.

"You can guess," he answered Marie. "She pretended to fall in love with Abella because she thought that was a route to my heart. I fell for her song and dance at first."

"Then what?"

"She started spending obscene amounts of my money, telling me it was on things for the baby. My accountants alerted me that instead she was buying jewelry for herself and treating her friends to lavish evenings out."

"She outright lied to you?"

"Then I started noticing that whenever I left the room, she'd completely ignore Abella even if she was crying or communicating a need."

"So she was just pretending to care about her?"

"The pièce de résistance was when she didn't realize I was standing behind her as she told her girlfriends she couldn't wait for Abella to be old enough to squire her away to boarding school."

"Wow."

"Yeah, wow," he minced and looked out to the sea. "I know I had been naive to let her near, but I was sincerely hurt by her deception."

"Of course you were."

He looked from the water to Marie's face, then quickly back again. He was surprised at how good it felt to talk to her. Words came easily.

"As you can imagine, I was totally unprepared to care for Abella when my sister and brother-in-law died. Even though Elise had made provisions in the case of her and Valentin's death, none of us expected it to actually happen."

"They were so young."

"Elise was a good and noble woman. The crown would have fit well on her head." He counted out five waves as they broke softly on the shore before retreating with the ebb of the tide. "It will be the great challenge of my life to properly raise her daughter."

At the shoreline, Marie was first to walk into the water and get her feet wet, encouraging Zander to follow. The setting sun provided a dramatic orange backdrop as they kicked their feet in the shallow tide.

It couldn't be more surprising but being with Marie, he found himself imagining an alternative to the Henriettes of the world. Having a connection with someone that was real, where two people could show each other who they truly were. Where what was inside them was what mattered. Who they could bare their souls with. Beyond crowns and titles, beyond class and wealth and facades.

Curiosity pecked at him. Claudine's earlier questioning motivated him to ask, "I'm learning that it's essential to be sensitive when asking questions about orphaned children. Do you mind my asking, how did your parents die?"

"They were killed," Marie answered dully.

Someday he'd be parlaying those same words to Abella, when she was old enough to understand them. He realized how difficult that was going to be. "That's terrible."

Marie pursed her lips, which made Zander question if either it was too painful for her to talk about it or if she didn't regard the death of her parents as terrible.

"I was eleven," she added.

His gut thudded for her.

"What a tragedy. You had no other family who could take you in?" He thought of his own situation. Although it was unusual and unnecessary for royalty to leave any sort of last will and testament, his sister, Elise, had gone to great lengths to document her daughter's care.

Marie kicked her feet in the water as she muttered, "My parents didn't have any contact with anyone else in our family so I didn't know them."

"No grandparents, no aunts or uncles?"

"They didn't speak to my parents."

"So if you weren't sent to live with relatives, what did happen?"

"Foster care. Six different placements."

"Six? Why?"

Marie's feet splashed in the water again, as if she was trying to bat away something.

"People fall in love with babies, not the older kids. Plus we don't fit into the clothes the foster parents keep around. We need things like books and phones. We eat more. The profit margin isn't as high."

"Isn't all of that controlled by the government? The foster parents get an allowance for your care."

"It's supposed to be. They try. But the system is overcrowded."

He had to resist the impulse to put his arm around her or hold her hand. He wanted to comfort her. "Did you feel love and affection from any of your foster parents?"

"Some of them were kinder than others. But it was a business to all of them." She bit her lip. "Hey, do you want to run?"

"Run?"

"Yes, right now. Let's just run."

He shrugged his shoulders. "Why not?"

And so they did. Two adults, one a prince, both in street clothes, ran along the shallow tide under the Cannes sunset.

They ran as if they were being chased.

Could they outrun their pasts, their destinies?

After they'd gone as far as they could, stopping with breath heavy from the exertion, Zander said, "I have to get back to the apartment. Iris has been with the baby all day and needs the evening. Let's order in some food and get work done for the gala."

He thought of the powerful film executives he'd agreed to have drinks with tonight and decided he'd tell them that something came up. He couldn't help but view his calendar through a different lens than he had in the past. Before Elise died. And he knew it was crazy, but being with Marie made him really acknowledge how much he'd changed. And had him appreciating Abella and the new life he'd created even more.

Once they returned from their exhilarating run on the beach, the club attendant handed them the personal items he'd locked up for them. "Your Highness."

Reading the young man's name tag, he replied, "Thank you, Stefan. Please, call me Zander."

Marie noticed that the prince spent a lot of time getting people to call him by his first name. He'd told her that outside of official occasions he absolutely hated being called by his title. He wanted to be regarded, and referred to, as a man like any other.

To be liked, judged or hated for himself, not his standing. While that did break with royal protocol, he didn't seem to care. This was a prince who rolled up his pants and ran on the beach. Who canceled his plans with Hollywood bigwigs because he wanted to get home to his baby niece.

A lot had become clear about Zander. Marie's internet research had identified the woman he was dating a few months ago and Zander's description of her today explained why Marie hadn't seen any recent photos of them together. It probably also explained why he was so defensive yesterday, when she had picked up Abella's sippy cup and he grabbed it out of her hand. He didn't like anyone to care for the baby. Certainly not someone who'd yet to prove herself trustworthy. Not someone who, for example, was the daughter of murdered criminals.

His Highness could buy Marie all the fancy gowns in the world. But obviously she wouldn't be a real date of the prince. She'd never belong in his world. As a matter of fact, a spark of alarm came over her at the thought that being seen in public with Zander might lead to scrutiny, to someone investigating her background. Didn't the media seem to have special powers to uncover even the most obscure buried secrets? Zander would be furious if he found out she was concealing such repugnant information about herself.

Oh, how she wished her yesteryears could be erased. That they wouldn't follow her around like a shadow that decided when and for how long she'd be allowed any sunlight. The past was that gigantic lead ball she was chained to.

She'd never be free of it.

CHAPTER FIVE

"IS THIS SIMILAR to the corporate events you've been working on?" Zander joked with Marie as they were welcomed to the Laublie Foundation for Breast Cancer Research's "A Night in Mexico." After passing through the photographers and security to get into the private party space, guests found themselves in an interior courtyard rimmed by one-story white stucco buildings with red roofs.

An enormous stone fountain dominated the center of the area. Water burst from the center of it in a high and wide spray, accentuated by colored lights alternating between milky white, bright red and sharp green denoting the colors of the Mexican flag.

"Just a little different than my typical sandwich luncheon," Marie chuckled.

The courtyard was packed with party attendees as still more made their way in.

"And you weren't kidding about guests taking the theme and dress code seriously."

"It's fun, isn't it? Don't you feel different in your gown, senorita?"

Of course she did. She'd never worn anything even close to the finery of the black lace gown with the colorful floral embroidery Zander had bought her a few days ago. But the people here probably wore luxe clothing every day, like he did.

So this was grown-up dress up, Marie thought. Surely a rich man's pleasure.

As an adolescent, moving from foster home to foster home with a tattered suitcase holding her only belongings, Marie had one itchy and pilled long black dress that she'd wear if she needed to be formal.

She remembered one time as a teenager when the school planned a dance. The girls in her class talked for weeks about shopping for new outfits and showed up in pretty party dresses. All Marie had was the ratty black dress.

The other students rolled their eyes as if that was exactly what they expected of her. As much as teenagers often complained about their parents, their troubles were nothing compared with the sloppy girl who didn't have a family at all.

Those nasty kids had no idea what it was like to be left an orphan at eleven years old. No one wanted a pre-teen like her. Babies stood a chance of being chosen for adoption. She was just a paycheck for her foster parents. Shuffled around, with no one taking an interest in her. Nowhere she ever thought of as home.

"You look incredible," Zander said, bringing her back to the courtyard, "if I neglected to mention it before."

He had sent a hair and makeup artist to style Marie for the evening. Her hair was coiffed into a dramatic sideswipe that curled into a low bun at the side of her neck. Behind her ear was a cluster of fresh red and yellow flowers, which had been delivered to her by courier earlier today.

The flower arrival had set her heart aflame. It was easy enough to fantasize that chivalrous Prince Zander was her date and that he'd sent flowers with a romantic note professing how much he was looking forward to their evening, or some such sentiment.

When she opened the box to see that it was the hairpiece she was to give the stylist employed to get her ready, Marie was a little disappointed. But, of course, this wasn't a date so there was no reason for flowers. Although the fragrant blooms arrived in a gold box tied with a ribbon, she knew it was of no more importance to Zander than if it had been a box of paper files.

Nonetheless, the whole outfit came together beautifully. And since they'd yet to speak to anyone, the fact that she wasn't a society doyenne on the arm of the prince hadn't been uncovered.

"Would you like a drink?" Zander didn't wait for an answer as he took two from the tray a waiter presented. Frosty margaritas in heavy blue glasses were prepared traditionally with salt along the rim.

Coming toward Marie and Zander were two flashy women. One a blonde with her hair up in a snug bun and wearing a pastel green dress that was so tight Marie could count the woman's ribs. She was with a redhead whose long curls were spiraled into a bun that looked of the breakfast pastry variety.

"Zander!" one called out.

"Your Highness!" the other echoed.

"Yikes," Zander whispered into Marie's ear, the warmth from his breath making her neck bend involuntarily in his direction. "I know those two. Quickly, to the tortillas." He gestured toward the other side of the courtyard where cooks in traditional Mexican garb were pressing balls of dough onto the blistering-hot *comal* grill.

Zander and Marie crept in that direction, the prince keeping watch as the two women caught sight of what they were doing. Marie could tell that he felt like game in the wild being chased by predators. One couldn't blame those girls, though, for being interested in Zander. Although he claimed that he was always surrounded by women who were only after the lifestyle and luxury that his title brought, he might have been missing one key component.

His Highness Zander de Nellay of Charlegin was one crazy-hot prince. Full stop. Indisputable. No doubt about it. And especially tonight, so dapper in his Mexican-style tuxedo with its stitching on the lapels, perfectly fitted to his tall and muscular frame. No wonder women lunged at him with hunting nets.

In fact, Marie still couldn't quite believe this remarkable man was her date, even if it was only for educational purposes.

"Oh, no, you don't," the blonde shrieked as she caught up with Zander and Marie, her redheaded cohort tagging along. "You owe me a dance back from the concert on Mykonos last summer."

"We haven't seen much of you this year, Zander. We heard you aren't dating Henriette anymore." The redhead trailed on the blonde's heels. "Have we lost you to that adorable baby daughter of yours?"

"Niece," he piped quickly.

"I'm fabulous with babies! You should let me help you take care of her," the blonde said as the heel of her white-, red- and green-sequined stiletto got caught between two of the stone tiles in the courtyard, causing her to lurch forward. A grimace twisted her face.

"I love babies, too." The redhead was not to be outdone. "They're so squishy and roly."

"I don't know that humans were intended for squishing and rolling but I appreciate your inquiry," Zander clipped in a tight baritone. "Ladies, if you'll excuse us, I see someone I've got to talk to."

Behind them, the blonde called out, "But Zander, you haven't introduced us to your date!"

Zander said to Marie as he pulled her away, "I think I told you, being a *royal bachelor* has its challenges."

"You have to always remain polite. That must be hard."

"Protocol demands that I conduct myself appropriately. I always seem to attract the prince groupies who make that a battle. Who don't want to really know me at all. They just want to be part of my advantaged life. Which is a far cry from forming genuine relationships."

"Judging books by their covers, as the saying goes." Marie knew all about that. She was constantly being evaluated against her troubled childhood. Just as she was sure Zander would judge her if he knew who her parents really were.

"I do the tuxedoes and the yachts but, day to day, I align myself with these charities so that I can help them get on with the work of improving lives."

"Your face is a double-edged sword, then."

A wistful smile came across Zander's face.

"With Abella in my care, I wish I could keep all these hangers-on away."

"Let's go inside," she offered, almost as a comfort.

Inside the ballroom, traditional dancers performed while shaking percussive maracas. Their full skirts created waves of color as they swayed through their steps and enchanted the guests.

"Marie, are you taking in all of the specifics?" Zander concerned himself with the matter at hand. "This is wonderful event design, with the margaritas and the *comal* out in the courtyard as an entry to the party."

"Yes, it was a total transition from the outside world into the private space of the party. Look at those." She pointed to the ceiling, where dozens of piñatas in the shapes of animals were hung at various lengths. "It's just gorgeous."

"Like you," he said and leaned down to give her a tiny kiss on the cheek.

Marie froze in place, stunned.

Her eyes pierced into his and her heart thumped against her chest.

After listening to it beat countless times, she snapped out of her hold. "Would you excuse me for a moment? I'm going to find the ladies' room."

Zander hadn't meant to kiss Marie. Hadn't meant to at all!

Why had he, why had he? His brain throbbed, and would until it had its answer. Maybe it was after being approached by those two aggressive party girls. Who reminded him of Henriette and the endless parade of awful women who had defined his life thus far. Marie was so definitely not like any of them. And he found himself opening up to her, perhaps actually too much.

But, in any case, a kiss on the cheek was merely a

sociable gesture, right? He hoped that was it, although he wouldn't swear to that conclusion.

Unfortunately, his mouth wouldn't stop vibrating after the feel of his lips against Marie's cheek. Surely the clouds in the sky weren't as soft as her delicate skin. His mouth had barely brushed across her face but his body reacted as if a firecracker had exploded inside him.

His behavior was dangerous. It was shocking how he hadn't had any control of himself in the moment after he'd confided in her about the royal gold diggers. His mouth was propelled to Marie's face as if an outside power had deemed it and there was nothing he could do but obey the command.

Everyone pecked everyone on the cheek at events like this, he reasoned with himself. It was no big deal. Marie had probably forgotten about a minute after it happened. He would, too.

As those reassurances ticked across his mind, he knew they were lies. The kiss dilated his eyes with desire, both physical and emotional. It was as if he hadn't known how hungry he was until someone handed him a crust of bread. He suddenly felt as if he was starving.

However, this was no time in his life to sate that craving.

He could surely have physical contact with a woman if he wanted to. After the APCF gala. And with a female other than Marie. He was free to have dalliances that meant nothing to him, and not under the same roof as Abella, of course. But there'd be no getting serious with anyone for many years to come, if ever.

Indeed, after Henriette, it had been dawning on him more and more that if he were ever to marry, his wife would effectively become Abella's mother. Not only would he have to find someone he could trust with his niece's safety and well-being, whoever he was with would have to be able and willing to accept Abella as part of the package. To be a good influence on her and to genuinely love her like her own. Zander would accept nothing less. It was a tall order.

Frankly, he doubted he'd ever meet someone like that. Which was fine with him. Abella was the one in line for the throne. As Zander was Elise's younger brother, he was not obliged to produce heirs. If he never married it might appear unconventional but wouldn't harm the royal family in any way.

So why was it that everything about Marie had thrown him into a brainstorm of new ideas and new contradictions?

Prince Zander never took his eyes off Marie as she crossed the ballroom to rejoin him after finding the ladies' room. The look on his face was off. Nostrils flared, his eyes appeared darker and darker as she approached until, at short distance, they looked almost angry. After a mental adjustment she was able to perceive, he softened but only a little.

"I was wondering why you were gone so long," he said as he presented his arm for her to slip hers through. At the feel of her hand against his muscles, sparks prickled her.

She knew she had spent a lot of time away from him after she'd excused herself, but she'd needed time to recover. In a tiny garden area that was not part of the event space, she'd practiced the deep-breathing techniques that had gotten her through many difficult situations.

Of course, she'd never had to call upon them because she'd just been kissed by an unbelievably sexy prince!

Bringing her hand to the exact spot where his lips made contact with her cheek, she'd looked up to the moon and asked it for composure. Obviously, Zander had meant the peck in a context where everyone kissed each other on the cheek as a simple pleasantry. He wasn't attracted to her or any such nonsense. He'd never know that he made her knees go as weak as if she'd drunk one of those margaritas that she actually dared not touch.

She hoped she appeared calm when, really, her legs were still wobbly.

"Take note of all of the little touches here," Zander instructed her as they recommitted to exploring the party. Of course, the kiss a few minutes ago was long gone from his mind. Proof of its irrelevance. He was professional, and she'd be the same. Outwardly, at least.

The ballroom was, indeed, decorated to the hilt in red, green and white. Massive displays of flowers sat on every table atop vividly colored tablecloths.

"These settings are outstanding," she said of the table arrangements utilizing traditional Mexican pottery rather than fancy china. "Those kinds of choices make a huge difference."

"Exactly."

"A gala of this scale must cost a fortune to produce. Doesn't that cut down the proceeds from the event?"

"There's an old expression. *It takes money to make money.* And an organization this prominent does get a lot of the components donated. The APCF isn't as high profile as the Laublie Foundation. But we can stake our place on the scene."

"That's why you want this year's gala to be spec-tacular."

"Right. So that next year I can ask for sponsors and underwriting, and point to our annual fund-raiser as one of the best events of the Cannes social season."

"Building a reputation."

"Even if I have to spend a lot of my own money on the gala this year, I'm taking the long view of how it might pay off in years to come."

"Did you support the APCF before you started tak-ing care of Abella?" Marie remained so buzzy from his kiss she hoped she wasn't babbling.

Zander still seemed skewed, too. He was such a po-lite man, he was likely worried that she'd misinterpret the little kiss he'd given her. That she'd take license to believe it had significance when, in fact, it didn't. Plus, he'd probably surprised even himself when he shared some feelings with her about the people in his life. Funny that Marie was doing a better job at keep-ing secrets than he was.

The lights began to flash red to green to white to in-dicate that it was time for the guests to take their seats. As Zander led Marie to their table, she wasn't surprised that theirs was up front and center to the stage.

The first course of the meal was served, sweet yel-low corn tamales.

As they began eating, other guests at the table kept a vigilant eye on the prince's companion. Would she choose the wrong fork or some other social faux pas that would broadcast her lack of pedigree?

Although their tablemates weren't titled, Marie guessed that none of them was the daughter or son of criminals who were murdered during a drug deal. That their parents didn't leave them in an empty apartment where they were alone and hungry for three days until a neighbor noticed something was amiss and called the police. Nor was it likely that they were tossed to and from foster homes where they were treated with a spectrum that ranged only from tolerance to neglect.

As Marie spiraled, she was about to excuse herself again to find a quiet place to do her breathing exercises. But Zander sensed that she was distraught and asked the waiter to bring her a glass of ice water. "You all right?"

Sipping slowly, she nodded and was able to regain her composure.

With colorful beams shooting in every direction, a trumpet heralded from the back of the ballroom. In came a twelve-man mariachi band, brandishing horns and guitars and violins as they began to play. In costumes of fitted pants with silver buttons down the outer leg, matching jackets and traditional wide-brimmed sombrero hats, the musicians marched into the ballroom in two lines, bringing with them a wall of sound so thrilling and effervescent it made Marie's spirit soar.

After their dramatic entrance, the band members then dispersed throughout the room while they played, stopping at different tables to perform little solos or to flirt with the older ladies and add additional good cheer. The ballroom palpitated with energy. Marie fully understood what an unforgettable event this was.

The mariachis entertained during the entrée of fish Veracruz, then speeches were made and the fundraising auction brought in lots of money. Several people came over to the table to pay their respects to, or flirt with, the prince. And Zander introduced Marie as his colleague at the APCF, encouraging them to attend their upcoming gala, as well.

Once the crowd thinned, Zander stood and pulled out Marie's chair for her to join him. "Let's go outside."

Back out at the courtyard, clusters of people stood conversing in the night air. Some watched a Mexican sandal-making demonstration. Zander brought Marie to a quieter corner where a lone musician sat on a brick ledge strumming a very large and unusual guitar. The melody was sweet and sad. Marie found herself completely mesmerized as each note wafted up into the dark sky toward the bright moon.

The moment was profoundly romantic. Zander seemed to take notice of Marie's enjoyment and put his arm around her shoulder. Together they watched the face of the guitarist as he plucked emotion out of each note, conveying more than lyrics ever could.

Zander's arm around Marie all but made her woozy. Not knowing whether she should or not, her head decided for her and fell backward onto his shoulder. He instinctively pulled her closer. In that prolonged interlude, a moment frozen in time, she allowed herself to dream about things she'd never dared before.

About what it would be like to walk through life with someone. Not a someone like her ex Gerard who thought he was too good for her. But someone who was secure, who knew that by lifting up his partner together they could reach untold highs. That was how Zander made her feel. No one in the world had ever made her feel anything even close to that before.

Indisputable facts quickly worked to pull her down from the heaven she was ascending to. Zander was never going to be with a woman like her, with a squalid past that would hang over them like a cloud for the rest of their lives. Imagine if the media found out who she was and looked into her background to see whom Prince Zander de Nellay of Charlegin was traipsing around Cannes with!

And even if that wasn't an issue, he had Abella as his priority. Uncle Prince Zander was clearly not ready to let a woman have a permanent place in his life and wouldn't be for a long time yet, something he'd articulated very clearly. Marie respected him for that. It was actually something she greatly admired about him. No one in Marie's life had ever looked out for her as he was for his niece.

It was no surprise that baby Abella had Zander's heart. Earlier this week, after they had gone shopping for the gowns and then ran on the beach, they'd gone back to his apartment to work. As soon as the nanny brought the baby into the room, Zander's eyes lit up. He held her as a father would, firmly in one arm, close and secure. Not like an inexperienced bachelor who'd had a baby foisted upon him. He was natural and authentic with Abella, as if her care came organically to him.

Zander had ordered pasta from the café next door and dutifully cut up small pieces for Abella as he and Marie ate. She'd had experience with babies as the foster homes she'd lived in housed multiple ages of children and she'd been expected to help with the younger kids. So when Zander got a phone call, it was quite logical that Marie could hold Abella.

Instead, Zander paced the opulent living room while he took his call, lifting the baby in one arm and talking through an earpiece. While part of Marie was a little offended that he wouldn't let her hold Abella, she honored his distrust, especially after that disloyal Henriette he had told her about. Marie knew he'd only even allowed her into his apartment because they had so much to do for the gala and her being an employee of the APCF lent her some credibility.

When Marie got back to her room that night, she allowed herself a few minutes of musings on Zander and Abella.

About the loving family they made together.

About almond-eyed children of her own.

Then she forced herself to shut those thoughts down because dreams never did her any good.

Just like the moment at hand, with the romantic Mexican guitar, the brilliant moon and Zander's arm around her.

In fact, as soon as Zander realized he'd had his arm around her shoulder for a while, he withdrew it. Leaving her as cold as if she was left naked in a blizzard.

They both knew nothing amorous was ever going to develop between them, and he must have reminded himself that people were watching.

Every fiber in her being screamed in protest when he withdrew his arm. Her soul cried out for him to instead take her into a full embrace. To kiss her not just again on the cheek but on her lips, her neck and even more intimate spots on her body.

That was never to be. She was going to parade around Cannes with a dynamic and gracious prince. But that would be that.

Not only would there be no romance with Zander, there couldn't even be hot reckless nights where she'd satisfy her physical attraction to him and then be done with it. The prince's casual-affair days were over. Just as well because, if she was being honest, Marie didn't think she could handle a fling with him that would come to an abrupt end.

Although she knew that she'd spend the rest of her life remembering his one and only kiss on the cheek and his one strong arm around her.

But Marie and Zander were in a business relationship. One she was fortunate to have.

Any other thoughts were just pure self-torture.

CHAPTER SIX

FUNKY MUSIC KEPT Zander company as he dressed for the film festival party at the Carlsmon Hotel. He'd fueled through a busy afternoon and now he wanted upbeat sounds to pump him up for the evening. He pulled on the pants of his tuxedo and removed the coordinating shirt from its hanger in his closet. Catching his image in the full-length mirror, he engaged in a staredown with his own face.

The unsettled feeling that beat through him was not coming from the rhythms of the song he was listening to. No, the shake-up had one basis and one basis alone. Marie Paquet. Despite everything he had been telling himself about not becoming attached to anyone, she had gotten under his skin. As a matter of fact, thoughts of her were all but driving him mad.

Buttoning up the shirt and tucking it into his pants, he asked his reflection some questions. First and foremost, how did he allow himself to plant that kiss on her cheek at the Mexico party when he'd intended nothing of the sort?

Fastening his cuff links, he commanded his eyes in the mirror to tell him why later, when the evening was winding down and they were listening to the gentle guitar in the courtyard, he put his arm around her shoulder in a way that coworkers would not have touched each other?

The Zander in the mirror had no right answers, which was an unusual predicament for him to be in. He was usually the man with all the solutions. Marie had thrown him off balance and he was losing his footing.

"You must stop this now," he reprimanded aloud to his own reflection.

But as he threaded on his tie and straightened it under the collar of his shirt, a voice inside him told him otherwise.

Marie was a breath of fresh air. Because she was so unaccustomed to the lifestyle he led, she didn't covet it. She was utterly guileless, and he never got the sense she wanted something from him, other than his help with the APCF gala. And that allowed him to tap into himself in a way that felt so pure, so emancipating.

Sitting on the bed to put on his socks and shoes, vitality coursed through him when he replayed over and over again that seemingly innocent kiss he'd given Marie. It wasn't harmless at all if he took into account the fact that he hadn't been able to stop thinking of it since. And it wasn't just one brush on the cheek that he couldn't get his brain to move past. No, it was the accompanying thoughts he was having about caressing and kissing every inch of her.

A voice low inside him demanded more. More touch, more whispers and personal conversations and knowing nods that made him believe he had some kind of special bond with her.

At his core, he knew that human connections were illogical. Attraction didn't know or care if two people

were so socially separated that they would be expected
to have nothing in common. Desire hadn't an inkling
that one person was fed with a silver spoon while the
other might not have had enough to eat. Fates weren't
the slightest bit interested in how something looked
to the masses. Destiny knew only the truth it saw before itself.

As he slid one arm and then the other through the
sleeves of his tuxedo jacket, Zander finished dressing
and begged himself to stop thinking about Marie. She'd
be accompanying him tonight and to a few more events.
They'd do the APCF benefit and then have no reason
to spend time together. If the fund-raiser was a hit,
perhaps Marie would get the permanent job in Cannes
and he'd see her once a year if he continued to chair the
gala. Other than that, there would be no cause for their
worlds to collide after this season.

The babbling he heard from Abella's baby monitor
fortified Zander's priority. This precious baby was what
mattered, and everything else took second place. Besides, he'd only just gotten acquainted with Marie. One
side of his brain questioned the wisdom of even having her in the apartment. Though he'd bet his life that
she wasn't out to deceive him in any way, some people
were masters at concealing things.

Were he ever to decide to be with a woman he'd need
to spend months, if not years, vetting her before he'd
begin to trust her around Abella, which his mistake
with Henriette reinforced.

After grabbing his phone and wallet, he slipped into
Abella's room. Iris had the crown princess in her lap
on the rocking chair.

"Are you okay for the evening?" he asked the nanny.

"Thank you, yes. Have a good time."

Zander couldn't resist tiptoeing over to give Abella a little kiss on the top of her head. As he stepped out of the room she clucked, "Bye, Da."

In front of the building where Marie was staying, Zander had his driver park so that he could greet her as she came out of the lobby. The pewter-colored gown with the geometric cutouts looked even more stunning and sexy on her than he had remembered when they bought it together.

"You are absolutely breathtaking," he couldn't help commenting as she walked toward him.

"Thank you for sending the hair and makeup squad again," she demurred with a modest smile. "I feel very glamorous." Her locks had doubled in volume and some kind of tiny shimmers were magically affixed to various strands, highlighting her expertly made-up face.

"You'd better, since the Hollywood A-list is going to be at this party."

"Just another ordinary evening for me," she joked, the sweetest blush coming to her cheeks.

Zander's chest swelled with a particular pride as he helped Marie, and the formidable train of her evening gown, into the car. He hoped he'd done enough to make sure she felt put together, knowing that meeting movie stars wasn't exactly something she was used to.

When they arrived at the Carlsmon, Zander repeated his ministrations to help Marie and the dress through the car door.

Over a hundred years old, the Carlsmon Hotel was a masterful example of French Art Nouveau architecture. It had always been one of the key meeting places for the film festival set. Countless movies and music videos had been filmed there. An enormous structure, its two distinctive domes on both the seaward corners were rumored to be inspired in design by the breasts of the architect's wife. It was, without question, the most recognizable building in Cannes.

Hundreds of cameras greeted Zander and Marie with blinding flashes. He had figured that a prince of a tiny principality was not so interesting at an event where award-winning actors and actresses would be in attendance.

Nonetheless, there was always a hungry market for photos of young royals doing anything at all. He didn't know if his appearance at this party would warrant enough attention that the press would recognize Marie as the woman he was with at the Mexico party. She wasn't used to having her name in the papers and gossip sites, so he hoped they could just pass under the radar on a night filled with brighter stars.

He gestured to take Marie's arm, which was becoming a much too familiar habit. His shoulders arched on their own volition when she gripped his bicep as they made their way down the red carpet to enter the hotel.

Behind barricades, members of the general public were allowed to congregate and take photos, calling out to the stars who waved and posed.

Marie's eyes went wide at the sight of some very recognizable faces.

Incoming party guests were ushered into the event space, a ballroom that had been converted into a screening room for the night. Ten or so movie screens were erected around the room with comfortable seating arrangements set up in clusters in front of each. With about three hundred in attendance, guests would enjoy finger foods and cocktails while they watched a documentary produced by two notable actresses on the issues of illiteracy. Proceeds from the evening were to benefit an international education organization.

"Zander!"

He recognized the voice of Asher Kraus, the Austrian race car driver he'd known for years. In years gone by, Zander and Asher had been known to rent a ski chalet where they entertained the party people of Europe for winter getaways. A time in Zander's life that seemed so shallow now.

Zander let go of Marie, noting the disquieting change to his body chemistry without her touch, in order to give his old pal a proper hug.

"This is my colleague, Marie Paquet."

"Colleague?" Asher raised an eyebrow, as if Zander had been using that word as a metaphor for something else.

As a matter of fact, he'd been making a point of introducing Marie as a colleague to as many people as possible to help her build a reputation as a relevant fundraiser. Plus, he didn't want anyone to have a cheapened image of her, to assume she was merely eye candy on the bachelor prince's arm.

Nobody would understand the turmoil that rollicked through Zander as he referred to her as a professional contact.

"Sit with us," Asher interrupted Zander's contemplations as he guided the prince and Marie over to the group he was sitting with. A stylish bunch, to be sure. Bendy women held wineglasses while the urbane men argued about which country produced the best cabernets.

The lights dimmed for the screening. Zander and

Marie sat next to each other on a small sofa. Her gown's halter top and cutouts left quite a lot of her skin uncovered and, before even meaning to, Zander made one long slide with his hand down her back as a way of ensuring she was comfortable.

The motion left him anything but, as the silken feel of her shot a maddening craving to his very center. After flashing on the number of things he'd like to explore with her while in the dark of a movie screening, he straightened up and vowed to keep his hands to himself.

One of the film's producers took to the central podium to introduce the screening.

"I love how they've done the food." Marie gestured to the cocktail tables in front of them, which adorned every grouping throughout the room. Movie theater food had been elevated to a Carlsmon Hotel level of posh. Old-timey red-and-white boxes held four different flavors of popcorn. Hot buttered, spicy, chocolate caramel and cheddar cheese all looked tempting.

"Let's try these." Zander popped one kernel into Marie's mouth and another into his own. He figured she wouldn't want to risk getting any popcorn dust on her dress. Or he wanted an excuse to feed her. He acknowledged both possibilities. Careful not to let his fingers touch her lips in the process, he fed them one of each flavor. As if they were merely conducting an inspection. Which they were.

And which shouldn't have bordered on the erotic.

Even though it did.

"That chocolate caramel is to die for," she voted in.

Bottles of old-fashioned sodas were kept cold in ice buckets. Trays with several types of sausages inside brioche rolls were the evening's equivalent of American hot dogs.

Small plastic bags lay on a tray next to bowls of assorted candies. Guests were invited to fill the bags to their liking so that they could nibble during the movie.

"Would you like me to make you a bag?" Zander asked. Asher and his friends made their selections, as well.

"I can do it," Marie insisted, helping herself to a box of the popcorn, an orange soda and a mix of every candy offered. So much for concern about her dress. Zander grinned with satisfaction. He liked a girl who chose candy over worrying about her designer gown.

Admittedly, he found himself wanting to watch her more than he did the film, but he put his attention to the screening once it began. It was quite effective in its discussion about the literacy issue and its impact on education, identity and employment.

Once the screening was over, the Carlsmon staff worked like rapid fire to remove the movie-watching groupings and turn the space back to a ballroom so that dancing and coffee service could begin.

"Let's go look at the auction items."

"Yes, I'd like to see them."

Zander took Marie's hand, oh, so supple, to navigate them over to the silent auction area.

"Yowza!" he exclaimed when they reached one of the display tables. "These are going to bring in serious money. That yellow gold and diamond watch could fetch a quarter of a million on its own."

Marie read aloud the description that accompanied a photo collage of a tropical retreat. "Weeklong stay on a private island in the South Pacific. You and eleven guests, plus a full staff, will be the only inhabitants on this hundred-acre island. Small boats and everything else you'll need to indulge in water sports and leisure pursuits will be provided. Your fun in the sun will be rewarded with meals prepared by a Michelin-starred chef. This unique property has eight bedrooms and ten bathrooms. Bidding begins at five hundred thousand."

"Nice package."

"You people live in an entirely parallel universe to the rest of us."

"You people?" he laughed.

"Let's not pretend I know what a 1963 B-Series convertible is."

Zander read the description. "Considered the best in class, this classic design has been fully updated with electronic ignition, modern sound system, wireless navigation and top-speed capability. The interior's luxury will be the envy of every motorist on the road. Bidding begins at nine hundred thousand."

Marie bugged out her eyes. "And all of these auction items were donated?"

"The gauntlet has been thrown down to us for the APCF gala, Mademoiselle Paquet. Let's see what we can do."

She filled her cheeks with air like balloons about to pop.

The band started up with a slow song, a baritone voice belting out endearments of love. People took to the dance floor.

"May I have this dance?"

As the prince led Marie to the dance floor, she was immediately swept into the music. The five-piece band was fronted by a charismatic crooner who sang about love being there all along if someone was looking for it.

When Zander circled his arm around Marie's waist for the slow dance, hearing the word *love* being sung at the same time made her light-headed. It wasn't a word she'd heard a lot in her life.

With his hand flat against her back, Zander brought her in close to him. She stiffened to his touch at first. It was simply too pleasurable, and rather than get pulled into those hands like they were a mighty wave of the ocean she tried to bolster herself at shore. While she couldn't keep a physical distance, she knew that she had to keep an emotional one.

Taking her hand in his spare one, Zander swayed them in a one-and-two, one-and-two that was something in between ballroom dancing and a more contemporary slide. They were joined so tightly that she could only press her face into the lapel of his tux. If there was a better spot on earth, Marie surely didn't know of it.

The formal fabric of his jacket smelled of a light musky cologne, nothing overbearing. The rock-hard muscles of his chest matched the solidly built arms she'd become quite familiar with. In fact, physical proximity to Zander was something she was starting to get used to, although she suspected it wasn't a very good idea.

In a few days' time, she'd been transformed from a dowdy nonprofit worker dressed in creased trousers to a woman immersed in the glitzy lifestyle of the Cannes social scene. Zander was right when he'd told her this was something she'd need to get comfortable with if she was going to be a force in the fund-raising world. With pride that she'd gotten off to an excellent start, one problem loomed large.

How could anyone be expected to spend night and day with His Highness Prince Zander de Nellay of Charlegin and not become romantically attracted to him? And wish for something beyond their professional connection? Especially when, so far, he'd kissed her on the cheek, put his arm around her, walked arm in arm and now danced with her.

Innocent enough encounters but, nonetheless, moments that awoke her from the inside and made her entire body respond. And birthed deliberations about belonging and permanence and a life shared.

On top of all of that, not only was the prince spectacularly good-looking, he was moral and caring and had a great sense of fun. Traits that would make him a fine father figure.

Even if Abella wasn't in the picture, Marie knew that royalty had an obligation to their subjects to marry the right people. After all, there were ceremonies to preside over, elders to appease and history to uphold. Royal marriages were still the serious and exclusive business that they had been for centuries.

In a million years, Marie Paquet would never be approved as a mate for Zander. A fact she kept repeating to herself as the influence of his hands directed her across the dance floor and his low vibrato murmured in her ear, "We certainly are spending a lot of time together."

"Felice had told me to report directly to you and to put any other work aside until the gala."

"Report directly to me," Zander hummed and started to say something, then decided against it. Had he been about to say that he liked the sound of that, having Marie at his beck and call? Part of her wished he did,

as confirmation that he was enjoying being thrown together as much as she was.

Which was ridiculous thinking. Yet she couldn't help
musing.

If only she could meet a man like Zander someday.
One whom she could actually have and hold and cherish, of course.

Photographers circled the dance floor. Several were
documenting the evening for the film producers who
would be able to point to a successful launch at Cannes
to bring attention to their film. But Marie suspected
some of the pictures being snapped were going to en-
tertainment magazines and gossip websites, as the public never tired of gawking at celebrities.

One woman dressed in a black T-shirt and black
pants swooped down and around the dancing couples as
she worked to get her shots. And who could blame her?

The auburn-haired actress who'd received critical ac-
claim for her performance as a Holocaust survivor was
grinding raunchily up against the award-winning actor
now making a fortune with his action hero franchise.

There was the middle-aged couple, a respected director and his television star wife, who had reportedly
split up but had eyes for only each other tonight.

A camera's flash came toward Zander and Marie,
temporarily blinding her with the power of its bright-
ness. Marie hoped the media would have no interest in
finding out whom Prince Zander was spotted with in
Cannes. Although royal gossip hounds noted his every
public move, clearly Marie wasn't famous. Even if they
were to dig, there'd probably be little or no available
information about her.

She hoped not, anyway. Prince Zander shouldn't be

mixed up with the likes of someone who had a background such as hers.

When the music changed, Zander expertly twirled Marie around the dance floor while continuing their conversation. "Tomorrow we have to finalize the costume theme."

"Okay," Marie acknowledged although now her mind had wandered far, far away. To those facts she'd rather keep private. To the eleven-year-old who had to carry in her gut the information that her parents were drug dealers who were killed during street warfare.

"We have to meet with the caterer, as well. I want to design a signature cocktail for the evening."

Marie nodded but her mind was still years back, on those same parents who were addicted to drugs themselves and made one careless mistake after the other until rival dealers were easily able to trip them up.

After some focused breathing, Marie was able to return her attention to the tall, powerful, sure prince she was dancing with. "Signature cocktail? I've never heard of that."

"When you've gone to a hundred of these parties, believe me it's the little niceties that make an impression."

He'd certainly made an impression on her. This man, with his selfless commitment to his orphaned niece, would make it his business to be sure Abella was never put in dangerous situations or in harm's way. It's what decent people did for their children.

As she continued to dance with Zander, she looked around the ballroom. Well-tended people chitchatted and sipped espressos. Marie knew that money or privilege didn't guarantee happiness. Had any of them known the embarrassment she had? The loss, the loneliness? Different circumstances, but the same pain?

Zander tightened his grip on her, an action she didn't protest. No, quite the opposite. She leaned into him, his broad chest and long arms providing the shelter that she rarely had the opportunity to seek.

Just for a minute, she told herself, as she closed her eyes and let the world slip away. She pressed into Zander to let him become her talisman, her beacon in the dark seas, her good luck charm, her hope. Just for a minute.

Marie wanted to dance for a long time, with no protest from Zander. Eventually, they stepped off the dance floor to check out the desserts. He was sure something had changed within her while they were dancing, although he couldn't put his finger on what. Now, when he looked over to see if she liked the lavish chocolate fountains, one dark, one milk and one white, Marie was not focused on the sweets. She had a distant, almost scared, look on her face.

"Yes, they're lovely," she managed in a monotone voice. "It's decadent to have three different flavors."

The words came out of her mouth as if someone else was saying them. While he intended to keep discussing the dessert, he felt an almost undeniable impulse to reach over and take her face in his hands. To kiss her over and over until whatever weighed so heavily in those blue eyes could be cast aside while their lips said everything without talking.

Lately, he'd been giving thought to what was next in his life. What the permanence and obligation of raising

Abella would bring him. How and where he wanted to spend his days.

Gazing at Marie's sweet face and replaying the internal agony he'd perceived in her triggered protective feelings. He was starting to wonder if the devotion he had for Abella couldn't also extend to a romantic love he might have room for someday.

He subtly pointed to a couple of older women at the fountains who were laughing and making a production of preparing their deserts. Skewers had been provided for guests to create spears of fruit chunks and small squares of cake that they then passed under the fountains to coat them in chocolate. The ladies were discovering that they could pass their creations under not one, not two, but all three flavors of the chocolate, creating a drippy mess that was probably delicious.

"That's a kind of specialty food that guests tell friends about the next day," Marie said.

"Exactly."

Zander's phone buzzed in his pocket, and while he generally made a rule of not taking calls while he was out with people, the vibrating sequence was specific to a text from Iris.

Abella is ill. I've given her medication and we're sitting up for the time being.

"What's wrong?" Marie snapped to attention having read the concern in Zander's face.

"The baby is sick. Have we observed enough here for tonight?"

"From what's written in the program, it looks like there will be more speeches coming."

"I'd like to bow out early and get home." Zander uttered a phrase he'd heard himself say a lot lately.

Nothing could have prepared him for the priority a child would take in his life. He knew that he'd climb mountains or swim oceans for Abella. Giving up the hobnobbing he'd spent much of his adult life doing was easy, and evenings like tonight had become the exception, not the norm.

"Are you going home now?" Marie's eyes became very round as she asked.

"Yes."

"Oh. Okay," she said, opening and closing her fists.

"*We* are going now," he clarified, grasping that she thought he was going to leave her at the party. Relief washed over her. He outstretched his hand for hers, not taking the pleasantness he felt when she did the same for granted. "Shall we?"

Exiting the party into the starry night, they watched as one of the most famous actors on earth, Ross Jarrell, made a late arrival to pandemonium from the fans who were still outside the hotel hoping for a celebrity sighting. With that much-talked-about *it* factor, confidence and sheen emanated from his every pore.

He wore his tux like it was a second skin, a shiny watch peeking out from his jacket sleeve. With a complexion no doubt polished to perfection by the world's finest estheticians, if not plastic surgeons, and a hair color chosen to erase any unwanted years, his perfection made him look almost unreal. Admirers screamed his name, and he stopped to wave for them and for the media.

"Nobody does glamour like the Hollywood crowd, do they?" It was a rhetorical question requiring no an-

swer as Zander's driver appeared at the curb and fer-
ried them away.

In his haste to get home, Zander realized he should
have had his driver drop Marie off at her room. She
was not in the fold of his life and didn't need to be
around Abella with her not feeling well. But Marie at
his side had, strangely, become the norm and it didn't
occur to him.

When they arrived at Zander's apartment, Abella
was sleeping on Iris's lap.

"She seems to be feeling better," the nanny reported.

After tossing off his tuxedo jacket, he picked up the
baby. "Thank you so much, Iris. My driver is downstairs waiting to take you home."

With Abella in the crook of his left shoulder as had
become a familiar position for both of them, he walked
around the living room knowing she was always reassured by the bit of motion. Her breathing sounded a
bit congested but she didn't feel feverish, to his relief.

He looked over to his companion in her gorgeous
gown. She was now having to move toys out of the way
so she could sit down. "Marie, if you'd like, my driver
can take you home, as well." More relaxed to see that
the baby probably had little more than a head cold, he
added, "Or I'm going to sit up with Abella for a while,
so if you're not exhausted, we could get a little work
done."

As if he'd asked a question of international importance, he eagerly awaited her answer. Given his dru-
thers, he most definitely hoped she'd stay rather than
leave right away.

"Sure, I have an idea I want to talk to you about."

Iris collected her things and headed to the door. "If there's nothing else you need…"

"Marie, would you like to get out of that dress? Iris, do you have something comfortable she can borrow?"

"Second shelf in the hallway cabinet. Help yourself."

"Thank you," Marie said to the older woman.

"Good night."

"Good night."

After Iris stepped out, Zander reached under the sleeping baby to undo his tie.

"What was the idea you were talking about?"

"It was when we were leaving the Carlsmon and we saw Ross Jarrell arrive. I was thinking how much he looked like a movie star from another era."

He heartily agreed, as Jarrell had captured Zander's attention in that moment, too. Though he'd met Ross at other events, seeing him on the red carpet with the massive fanfare and the hundreds of camera flashes he generated was otherworldly, as if he was from another planet.

"So for our gala, what if the masquerade theme was Old Hollywood? The guests could dress up like Clark Gable and Judy Garland and so on."

After he took in the idea, Zander nodded emphatically. "I love it! And with a lot of current Hollywood stars coming to the gala and here for the film festival, they'll do it up big."

"That's what I was thinking."

"We could screen some of the classic movies in areas of the party space, as decor."

"You said you wanted to do a custom cocktail. Maybe that could relate to the theme?"

"Fantastic. I think you've solved how we're going to

create the most memorable event of the season. Let's make some notes. Can I get you a brandy, or some tea?"

"Tea would be nice. You've got your hands full with the baby. I can get it for us if you'd like."

Heartened by the coziness of her offer coupled with the unfamiliarity of a woman used to fetching her own drink, he lifted a free finger to point. "Help yourself to anything in the kitchen."

Returning with a couple of mugs, she set them down on the coffee table. "I would love to get out of this dress and heels, so I'll take Iris up on her offer if you'll excuse me."

While she was gone, Zander managed to toe one shoe off and then the other without disturbing the baby.

The sight of the two mugs, with the tea bags still seeping in the hot water, touched him with their domesticity.

His jaw twitched when Marie came back into the room. In yoga pants and a plain T-shirt, she was as pretty as she'd been in the lavish gown. Barefoot, she zhooshed her hair until it looked like the slightly messy style she usually wore.

"What are you staring at?"

He hadn't realized that his gape was so blatant.

The sharp contrast to the glitz of the Carlsmon struck him like a lightning bolt. This was what life was. Yoga pants and tea bags and needy babies. It was what he was only first learning about, how to be a parent. Lessons that would take him a lifetime. Some that he would never learn.

He'd never before visualized the passage of years now running across his mind like a timeline. Abella gaining new skills as she prepares to start school. Then the schoolgirl years in the stiff uniforms. Which would be followed by the teenage years with battles for independence. She might be brought up as a royal and go to all the best schools but Zander was determined that she'd experience some of the same phases any other child would.

It occurred to him what it might be like to go through all of that with someone. A partner. To raise a child together. The right someone, of course, not some phony like Henriette or the women his mother fixed him up with.

Maybe to have children of his own someday. Effectively giving Abella a sibling or two.

With him and Elise raised by palace staff as their mother was too busy jet-setting around the world to be bothered, every day he understood more and more about why his sister was adamant that Zander be in charge of Abella were anything to happen to her and Valentin. To not let Claudine hold the reins.

Parenting was serious business. It had begun to worry Zander that although he might develop into a reasonably worthy father, Abella would need a mother figure in her life, as well. If not even more importantly than she'd need him.

He wondered about life in a typical family's home. Laughter and tears, triumphs and defeats, shared together as a team. To be loved as a man, not a prince. With a woman who brings him a cup of tea, and just as often he brings one to her. Was that what he was coming to long for?

And why, of all people, was it Marie who lit that yearning in him?

It dawned on him that for all the years he'd spent

globetrotting with his significance and position opening any door he wanted, he'd been doing his mother's
bidding. She wanted him married properly and orches-
trated a lifestyle that would put him on that journey as
soon as he reached adulthood.

Yet in all that time he'd never met anyone who touched
him inside the way Marie did. With those opaque blue
eyes of hers that seemed to go from compassionate to
wounded to intelligent and then back again. What made
her tick? Somehow, more than anything, he wanted to
know.

To her question of why he was staring he offered
only, "Sorry. Please make yourself at home."

Which she did by sitting on one of the sofas and
tucking her legs under her. Again, the informality of
her position plucked at heartstrings he never knew he
had. He sat down next to her, the baby stirring a little
bit to sprawl herself farther across his chest.

"Babies are perfect, aren't they?" Marie tilted her
head to watch Abella's face as she slept.

"They don't know enough not to be."

Was Marie aware of how perfect *she* was? Zander
sensed she didn't, that the hardships she'd known had
damaged her self-esteem.

"I'm sure what's going through Abella's little brain
is that she's safe and cared for in your arms."

"Do you think about having children?"

"I'm afraid I wouldn't know how to do it. I didn't
have the best examples of motherhood in my life."
Funny enough, neither had Zander. "It looks like you're
doing a great job with Abella so far."

Golden light shone through him at that.

"That's the greatest compliment I could ever receive."

"I respect how seriously you take your obligation toward her. Not every relative of an orphan does."

"You'd said that no relatives took you in after your parents died. What did happen?"

"Honestly, right afterward I was in kind of a daze."

"You were just eleven."

"I was put in someone's home temporarily. I think it was for about a week. They barely spoke to me. I was terrified. They didn't really have room for me and I remember sleeping on sofa cushions on the floor without a blanket. It was very cold."

Zander swallowed hard at that disturbing retelling.

Marie clenched and then released her fists.

He pointed to her hands. "I notice you often doing that."

"Nervous habit I suppose." She reached for her tea and wrapped both hands around the warm mug. Her eyes downcast.

He kissed the top of Abella's head, the baby sound asleep in his arms. "Then you were placed in longer-term foster homes? Were you treated lovingly?"

Marie shook her head no without making eye contact. "In none of them."

"And by your parents?" She signaled no again.

"Look at what you've done for yourself, Marie. After all of that, you made it through university and you have a career. You're amazing."

She smiled.

"Let me put Abella in her crib."

When Zander returned, he sat down close to Marie. Her expressive blue eyes were clouded from the late hour and perhaps the conversation. The plump lips that no longer held the red lipstick of the evening looked clean and…

Kissable. Irresistibly kissable, he thought as he leaned toward her. And unlike the peck on the cheek or the arm around her shoulder that had come before, what happened next was not spontaneous. It was not accidental.

No, as Zander brought his mouth to Marie's, the kiss he gave her had to have communicated that it was deliberate. The dominance with which he took her lips, kissing her once, then twice, then longer, bounded from inside him and wouldn't be denied.

"Marie." He suddenly pulled back. "I'm so sorry. The hour is late and…"

She looked to him with those big glassy eyes, half-shocked but clearly aroused, whispering, "Don't stop."

And he didn't. What his heart and body told him superseded any mental wisdom. He could experience her only with all his senses.

The peeking of her collarbone above the neckline of the T-shirt. The fragrance of her warm slinky skin. The taste in her mouth, like the juiciest fruit of summer. The tiny sigh that escaped from her lips. The strands of shiny hair through his fingers as he pulled her in for more electrifying kisses that he'd remember for the rest of his life.

After the last good-night kiss at the door when his driver arrived, Zander had dropped down onto the sofa, where he lay for hours, drunk on Marie.

Sometime during the wee hours, he concluded that it would now be impossible to deny that things had changed between them. Tonight's kisses were not at all like the physical contact they'd had before, which could maybe be construed as platonic affection. What was rocking through him was a truth that wouldn't be fooled.

Yes, he'd have to tuck it right back inside. He wasn't in a position to let anything develop between them. It was unfair to risk that she might feel otherwise. He really didn't know how she'd regard tonight's kisses. If she understood them as he had. An acknowledgment of their magnetism toward each other, but as an isolated incident. The last thing he'd want to do is hurt her.

The kisses had gone too far. A surge of carnal male desire combined with the camaraderie that had grown between them prompted him. The voluptuousness of her lips received many of his tender kisses. Which was then followed by a long one that was different, a penetrating kiss that lasted for five minutes and inhabited his entire body, making him lunge to her for more.

All told, Zander hadn't been able to contain himself until he'd kissed Marie probably twenty times. And was barely able to maintain the gentlemanly decorum he'd prided himself on, and the paternal concerns that now informed every move he made. In fact, he'd come quite close to letting go of all restraint entirely, which was why he'd separated from her long enough to text for his driver.

With the hungry animal in him uncaged, he envisioned leading Marie into his opulent bedroom and laying her down on the designer sheets and plush blankets afforded him. Where they'd then engage in passion taken to untold erotic heights. He wouldn't rest until he'd slowly explored all of her creamy flesh and satisfied every single longing both he and she had. And let her know that she was valued and lovable and…well, magnificent.

Unbridled lovemaking most definitely could not be on the agenda with Marie.

But a man could dream, couldn't he?

CHAPTER SEVEN

"HERE'S THE SET list from the band for the dancing portion of the evening," Zander said over bites of the salads and sips of the lemonade he'd had delivered to Marie's office.

The week had been a whirlwind. With the APCF gala quickly approaching, Marie and Zander had spent countless hours on every facet of the event. Having decided on Marie's idea of an Old Hollywood theme, they looked to apply it to every component of the party. "I told them we wanted all classic songs from movies. There are so many greats here. Do you know this one? 'Love Is a Many Splend—'?"

Marie finished her crunchy bite. Zander could have been reading from the telephone directory for the amount she was able to listen at the moment. Although she'd held herself professionally all morning, the discussion of dancing was impeding her ability to stay attentive.

All her mind could do was wander back to the night of the Carlsmon party. To Zander, resplendent in his slim-cut navy blue tuxedo. Which happened to complement her pewter-colored gown to a T.

With his big arm firmly around her waist, he'd held

her close as they danced to modern ballads. In sync, like together they could dance away all the troubles in the world. Making Marie feel that, just for a moment, her past and his present didn't matter an iota. That they looked like a couple in love, gliding and laughing as if they were totally alone rather than in a crowded ballroom filled with the wealthiest and most beautiful people on earth.

Remember, she told herself now in the confines of her spartan office, Zander was one of those people. She was not. Although she'd told him a bit about her traumatic adolescence, he didn't know even the half of how different they were, and she hoped he never would.

"'… Are a Girl's Best Friend,'" Zander finished the set list she hadn't been listening to, so fixed was she on the tones in his voice.

As much as she'd tried to forget the kiss on the cheek and his arm around her shoulder at the Mexico benefit, those were nothing compared with the kisses at his apartment after the Carlsmon party. Because, with a reasonable amount of feasibility, the peck and the arm around her shoulder might have been chaste exchanges between colleagues. Although, really, even those encounters were tinged with flirtation and romance, unless she had imagined it.

But at his apartment? No way were those kisses between coworkers, or even friends. As she watched Zander bring his lemonade to those sumptuous wide lips, her body shuddered at the recollection of his mouth on hers. Those lips that, with the smallest of movements, had taken her on a wild ride of yen rewarded with pleasure.

At the stem cell research fund-raising yacht party

last night, they'd moved together as a choreographed unit. She'd worn the blue gown with the beaded overlay, and Zander wore his tuxedo with a blue shirt that almost matched the hue. There was no division between where one of them ended and the other began. As they finished each other's sentences with a jovial banter that seemed to charm the scientist crowd on the boat that night, Marie had become more and more comfortable with the schmoozing and increasingly optimistic that their own gala would be a success.

Simply put, they worked well together. That was when she loved her job the most. Collaboration, when everybody was looking in the same direction, focused on one outcome, the success of the event. It was almost as if those involved became a family for the duration. It was a feeling that gave her immense satisfaction.

But she needed to watch herself around Zander. He already had a family, the royals on Charlegin and what he was creating with Abella.

There was no question in her mind, though, that she'd never been attracted to a man like she was to Zander. She was a moth to his candlelit flame. That night after the Carlsmon party and, if she was being honest, since the moment she met him she had been drawn to him.

To his sincerity. To the way he wielded his power with a quiet control. To his compassion. How he made her feel connected to him. And the way he was with Abella. Watching him so careful, so attentive, so decisive about what she needed was one of the most heartwarming displays Marie had ever witnessed. It wasn't just flattery when she told him how good a job she thought he was doing with her.

Nothing would ever come between him and his care

for Abella. Rather than wishing it was otherwise, Marie was grateful to know that Abella was going to receive a lifetime of loyalty and support and love even without parents. What she'd never had. A woman would be wrong to try to pull Zander from Abella's plight. Marie was happy for the baby princess.

So she'd forever treasure those life-affirming kisses from Zander, and expect nothing more. Neither one of them had instigated talking about those kisses. That Zander hadn't brought them up reinforced to Marie that they weren't important to him. Which kept her from mentioning them.

"I've got to get home," Zander finally declared after a productive afternoon. They stood. He packed his computer bag, gave Marie a very European kiss-kiss on both of her cheeks and then headed out her office door.

His departure brought a lurch forward to her shoulders as she watched the back of him stride down the corridor. Of course, she wanted him to leave and get home to the baby, who would probably be as delighted to see him as Marie was sad to have him go. Nonetheless, she'd count the minutes until she saw him again tomorrow.

Rage tasted bitter in her throat as she recalled the facts about her parents that she'd never tell Zander. Tamma and Bruno Paquet headed a ring of drug dealers that supplied illegal methamphetamines to the already downtrodden residents of the council blocks where they lived. When Tamma and Bruno discovered that their inventory had been stolen, they took to the street to confront the rival drug gang that also staked claim in the neighborhood. Whose members proceeded to shoot Marie's parents to death in the middle of the afternoon.

Unknowing and unprotected eleven-year-old Marie was in their shoddy apartment while it happened, even hearing the gunshots coming from the street, although she didn't know it was the sound of her becoming an orphan.

As Zander's broad shoulders, long legs and golden hair turned the corner and she couldn't watch him walk away any longer, unwelcome tears welled behind Marie's eyes. As she had been taught to in counseling, she concentrated on labeling her feelings.

Anger again. That was what it was. She was bona fide furious that she'd met very few men in her life whom she would consider of high quality. The kind of men who were secure in themselves. Who treated everyone with respect. Men who thought it worthwhile to see that others around them felt safe. Who communicated clearly when they were speaking and who genuinely listened.

Zander was that kind of man.

The kind she'd never have.

The only men she ever attracted were insecure types like Gerard, who found some kind of sport in pointing out their superiority. Or the few other damaged men she'd dated who weren't responsible, and she'd become their surrogate mother and caretaker.

She had never witnessed a healthy relationship in action. Her parents were two irrational people, in her memory, always dressed in ill-fitting tracksuits, yelling at and accusing each other all the time.

Even though she was too young to understand it at the time, she knew that her household hadn't been normal. That they hadn't been a happy family born from a couple's love. Through her odyssey of foster homes, Marie had never gotten close enough to any of the adults to analyze whether they were in solid relationships. There was only strife and chaos.

She'd learned to go it alone. It was the easiest and most prudent decision, and one she'd thought she was at peace with.

Until she met Zander.

In him, she'd seen how a real man treated a woman, a baby, a nanny, a party guest, a coworker. The person he was showed Marie a possibility she hadn't even considered.

And at the thought of what she'd never have, her blood ran hot.

She stood breathing slowly in her office doorway long after Zander had turned the corner out of her sight.

Felice came toward her and asked for an update. After Marie filled her in about the various aspects of the gala, she didn't want the meeting to end. Although she didn't know Felice well, as executive director for the agency Felice herself had come in contact with hundreds of orphans. And, truth be told, Marie wanted someone to talk to.

"Felice, what do you think happens to most orphaned children in foster care when they grow up?"

"I don't think we can make any generalizations. And we can only collect data on those whose whereabouts we know."

Marie nodded.

"But just like within any population," Felice continued, "there appears to be a spectrum. Many foster parents are wonderful and go to great lengths to help those in their care process the challenges a parentless child will have."

None of the foster parents Marie had fit into that category.

"As far as children in homes with not-as-attentive foster parents, we see some whose past has simply destroyed them and they never become integrated in society. There's a lot of homelessness. Then you have the people whose lack of parenting produces insecurities that they constantly stumble on. They may lead outwardly manageable lives but are never stable internally."

Marie shivered at the description of what could be her if she let it.

"Then there are those who are galvanized by what they didn't have growing up and are determined to have it as adults. Whether it's through rehabilitation or simply sheer will, many become successful adults with personal achievements and significant relationships. They partner. Have children of their own and create loving homes."

Which would Marie be?

After a meeting with Chef Jean Luc the next day, Zander informed Marie, "I'm flying home to Charlegin tomorrow. We have some Hungarian dignitaries visiting and I'm expected at the palace to make an appearance."

Disappointment flashed quickly across Marie's face at that news. He didn't think he misread it. Suddenly, he felt guilty that he hadn't mentioned the trip to her before this. But his assistant for the APCF gala hardly needed to be privy to everything Prince Zander had on his calendar.

Although Marie had become more than that and he knew it, despite his mental denials. And not just with regard to the kiss that had sent his manhood prowling, naked and primal toward her. No, there was something much larger going on with his feelings toward Marie. Which was why it bothered him that even a slight wave of unhappiness, one she quickly disguised, had flowed across her beautiful face.

"Are you taking the baby?"

"No. I'll only be gone for one night. After the reception and whoever my mother has invited for dinner, I'll fly back the next day." Mentally reviewing how much work he and Marie still had to accomplish with not much time left, he suggested, "Why don't you come with me?"

"To the palace?"

"Yes. I can't include you in the meeting with the Hungarians, of course, but the gardens are nice this time of year. You and I could work on the plane rides both ways."

It was a crazy idea but not without merit. If his mother happened to have invited any of the silly girls she always wanted him to meet, Marie would help squelch that attempt. And even though he knew he must not pursue anything further romantically with Marie, he liked having her around.

"All right," she answered without spending too much time thinking about it.

The next morning, Zander's driver shuttled him and Marie to the airport, where they boarded the small private plane hired to whisk them to Charlegin. After takeoff, an attendant served coffee and a light breakfast for the short flight.

Sitting side by side in ample tan leather seats, they watched through the windows as Cannes became smaller and farther away when they soared into the blue skies and cotton-white clouds.

"What are your parents like?" It was perhaps an inappropriate question to ask a prince whose father sat on the throne, but Zander didn't mind.

"My parents are very different from each other. My father showed me what it is to be a prince. The grace of benevolent work. He taught me to treat all people equally. To be compassionate."

"He sounds wonderful."

"He is. My mother has different concerns."

Such as flying all over the globe with her friends in the fashion industry. And measuring people by how much money they make or who their grandfather was.

Looking out the plane window, he reflected on his upbringing. His father's love for his wife sometimes clouded his ability to disagree with her. Prince Hugh had a quiet strength away from Claudine, which was when Zander and Elise got to know the best of him. Certainly they loved their mother, but it was no secret that she married their father for his title.

It was crystal clear to Zander why Elise made sure Abella would be raised by him. The weight of that responsibility tightened his jaw as he watched the plane's descent into Charlegin. Abella would rule from the palace one day, and it was his job to make sure she was fit for it. That was surely the most challenging thing he would ever do in his life. He wasn't sure if he could do it alone.

"Is everything all right?" Marie asked in the gentlest of melodies. Was something transparent in his face? And why had he begun to factor this woman beside him as part of any equation?

"I miss my sister." He felt his eyebrows furrow. "We were very close growing up."

By the time Charlegin came into clear view, Zander's mind was a jumble of memories and possibilities. He pointed to the gray stone compound and its small tower now visible through the airplane window. "There's the palace."

As soon as Zander and Marie stepped into the entrance hall of the palace, Her Highness Princess Claudine appeared from a corridor. With her hair pulled back and in an olive-colored suit with a white blouse and heels, she looked stately rather than her usual designer-label style. A nod to the visit from the Hungarians.

"Zander," she called with arms outstretched. "Where is my marvelous grandchild?"

Since his mother rarely asked about Abella, he didn't think the theatrical fanfare was necessary. Referring to the woman entering the hall beside Zander, Claudine questioned, "Where's Iris? Have you gotten a new nanny?"

"No, Mother. I left the baby in Cannes with Iris as I'm only here overnight."

"Right. No sense in all of the packing up needed to travel with her." Claudine fixed her eyes on Marie. "But you've brought someone?"

"Princess Claudine, I'd like you to meet Marie Paquet, who works with me at the APCF. She's running the gala for us."

Marie seemed unclear how to react to the introduction so bent her knees in an awkward curtsy. Zander so rarely brought anyone to the palace, he'd forgotten to brief her on protocol.

"Oh. I see. What did you say your family name is?"

"Paquet," Marie ticked out as if it was confidential. This was the same inquest Claudine had given Zander on the phone when he mentioned that Marie would be his date for some of the balls this season. His mother's obsession with social status and rank was ever-present.

"Is your family from the Riviera?"

"We're… I'm from North Marseilles."

"North Marseilles? Oh." Claudine's voice was high and clipped.

Zander could sense how uncomfortable Marie was with his mother's interrogation. Her fists opened and closed. Marie's reluctance to say much about her past gave him the indication that she might have endured pain, fear, loneliness and even mistreatment. Which tore at his heart. She had every right to keep her past private if she wanted to.

"Mother, I trust you'll be of help to Marie with the APCF gala by bringing along some of your more influential friends. Has your Monte Carlo crowd sent their RSVP yet?"

Her Highness stared at Marie as if she was looking right through her. "Zander, I don't know that any additional guests should sit in on the meeting with our Hungarian visitors today."

"Of course not," he quickly interjected. "I promised Marie she could stroll the gardens."

"Well, then. I'll join you in the green room in half an hour, Zander."

Once his mother took her leave, Zander showed Marie to the palace gardens. The late spring had brought everything into bloom and the grounds were a kaleidoscope of color and scent. With the central expanse of grass, Zander could imagine Abella running around to her heart's content. The last time he'd brought her here, she hadn't yet learned to walk. It was still hard to fathom that one day she would sit on the throne.

"This is enchanting," Marie said after surveying the vista.

"I apologize. My mother is rather…inquisitive."

"As well she should be, Zander. You're fortunate to have a mother who takes an interest in who you spend your time with."

There was Marie, taking the high road again. Even if it caused her distress.

"Yes, and she's preoccupied with my dating life."

"So she immediately assumed…"

"Exactly."

They stared down each other, both knowing that while they weren't a couple, though recent events pointed otherwise.

Perhaps it was too impulsive a decision to have brought Marie to the palace. Did he really expect any less of his mother than a full-scale examination of any woman he'd bring home? In his enthusiasm to show Marie where he grew up and where Abella would rule, he abandoned the caution that might have convinced him it was a bad idea.

Still in the shirt and slacks he'd worn for the flight, he needed to change into a suit and tie for the official introductions. The Hungarian group wanted to discuss a trade partnership with Charlegin. Any second guesses about bringing Marie along had to be put aside.

He swept his arm across the expanse of the garden. "You're welcome to explore at your leisure while I'm away. You'll find benches dotted here and there, so feel free to sit. I'll have an attendant bring out some refreshments."

"Thank you so much."

"And afterward, we'll get down to business."

"Okay."

But he lingered beside Marie rather than returning inside and getting ready for the meeting.

"O...kay," he slowly repeated. Yet his feet didn't move. Instead of getting dressed, he wanted to show Marie every little corner of the garden. To appreciate each bloom of a flower or leaf on a tree. To point out where he and Elise liked to play as children. And he most definitely wished he could take her to the secluded benches on the far end of the property. Where they could kiss in the sunlight without risk of anyone seeing them.

There was to be no more kissing Marie, he admonished himself! Yes, her hands on either side of his face was an exquisite sensation that he'd carry to his dying day. And yes, their mouths fit each other's as if it was destiny's will. Indeed, the mere memory of her kisses caused an ache in his rib cage that he still hadn't gotten rid of.

But no, he was not going to engage in any more romantic activity with her and that was that. As if that terse exchange with his mother wasn't enough, just being at the palace reinforced that Marie and he together was an impossibility. It was true that this was his world. One she would never be happy in.

"Okay," he repeated yet again, as much an affirmation to himself than anything else. "I'll see you in a bit, then."

"Knock 'em dead."

Marie's incongruous well-wishing brought a huge

smile to Zander's face as he finally turned and headed inside. He was attending the meeting as a show of family solidarity. His role was of little importance. It was simply a meet and greet. No one would be knocking anyone dead. Still, that Marie was cheering him on was so endearing he thought his heart might burst open.

The meeting went as expected. Afterward, Prince Hugh had a ceremony to attend. Claudine and Zander exited the green room and walked together in the central corridor past the portraits of Zander's ancestors on the walls.

He vaguely remembered his father's parents, whose likenesses hung above a gold-leaf table. His grandmother, Joselin, had been the crown princess whose marriage to Prince Philip—who had not been in line for the throne of his own neighboring Balfon—had been arranged shortly after they were born. After they'd married, both the royal families and their subjects had become nervous when, year after year, the couple had failed to become pregnant with an heir. Joselin had been in her forties—unheard of at that time—when Zander's father, Hugh, was finally born, to everyone's relief.

Prince Hugh was the first in the family to marry a commoner. The story went that he fell hard for Claudine when they were both at university in the Netherlands. Claudine's family was neither notable nor wealthy, so Hugh's choice of her was controversial and a disappointment to his parents. For Claudine's family, the match was a gift from heaven, as they were immediately brought into the palace fold and well cared for the rest of their lives.

"I wasn't aware you were dating," Claudine said

tightly once she and Zander were clearly out of anyone's earshot in the corridor.

"I'm not dating Marie. Remember, I told you over the phone? We're working together on the gala and she's accompanying me to some other events around town."

"You don't look at her like a colleague does."

"Must we always have this conversation? My attention is rightly on your grandchild at the moment. This is not the time in my life for women."

"Funny how the universe sometimes has plans for us that we could never see coming. I'm guessing she's not from a prominent family?"

"Mother, she's a work partner." It was maddening that his mother was so easily able to figure out that there was, in fact, a little more to the story of him and Marie than the APCF. Though he fibbed, "Nothing more."

"Then I take it you'll want her ensconced in guest quarters tonight and not in your room with you?"

"Mother!"

"Be careful, Zander. The press will have a field day with her," she cautioned and turned toward her office while Zander headed back to the garden.

There were eight at the dining table that night. Zander, Marie, Prince Hugh, Princess Claudine, an English duke and his three teenaged sons who had stopped in to pay their respects en route to Russia.

Not one, not two, but three young men with gummy smiles and frizzy hair sat opposite Zander and Marie. Claudine regaled them with travel stories. About the time an African statesman invited her to learn a weaving technique unique to his native village. Claudine asked, "Have you been to Africa, Marie?"

And about the dashing Argentine racehorse jockey who took her on a wild gallop through the Pampas. At each story, the three sons guffawed with a hiccup-like rhythm that Zander's leg under the table beside Marie's proceeded to mimic. It seemed to be about five sequences of four giggles each until they subsided and left the remaining air in the dining room to go still.

"Have you been to Argentina, Marie?"

Her Highness was making a show of pointing out that Marie wasn't in their social circle, as if it wasn't obvious. Zander had told her that the princess herself was a commoner, so Marie was surprised how much she'd gone out of her way to humiliate one of her own kind. If it weren't for Zander's reassuring hand-holding under the dinner table, Marie might not have been able to contain her embarrassment.

After the Duke and his sons had departed, Marie chatted pleasantly with Prince Hugh, an affable man who perhaps had a bit too much wine at dinner. When Zander entered the conversation, Marie explained, "I think we've decided that His Serene Highness will attend our Old Hollywood gala dressed as John Wayne."

"My son will remember that I used to be a decent horseman in my day."

Prince Zander nodded.

"We'll get you a cowboy costume with a big hat," Marie added.

Claudine joined the group and started up again, "Marie, did I see you at 'Fashion Has Passion' at the Atelier Dubois benefit last month?"

"No, Your Highness. Was that in Cannes?"

"That's right, you mentioned you weren't from the

area. But you were in Venice for the 'Circus for Change' ball, weren't you?"

"I wasn't."

"Good heavens, Claudine, no one gives a bother as to what galas Marie attended," Prince Hugh interjected.

But His Serene Highness was wrong. There were millions of people in the world who did care.

In the morning after the night spent in separate bedrooms, Zander gave Marie a tour of the palace, pointing out the works of art and gifts from foreign nations that he particularly liked. They then boarded the small plane heading back to Cannes.

As he looked out the window, he reflected on his mother's abysmal behavior. Had he known Her Highness was going to act like a dog incessantly barking to scare another one off, he wouldn't have subjected Marie to it.

Zander swiped through his tablet during the flight and scrunched his eyebrows when he came across a photo from a film festival gossip site. It was a picture of him and Marie on the dance floor at the Carlsmon party, holding each other for a slow dance.

The expression on both of their faces took Zander aback. The way they gleamed only at each other, as if they were the only ones in the room rather than two of hundreds. Anyone who saw it would surely think they were a couple in love. The caption read: *Who is the mystery brunette royal hottie Prince Zander de Nellay has been spotted with all over Cannes?*

CHAPTER EIGHT

THE CLOCK WAS ticking, Marie thought to herself as she surveyed the grand foyer of the mansion where the APCF gala would be held the next night. That the success of the evening was going to make or break her career was probably an exaggeration of the pressure, but she felt it nonetheless. With Zander's leadership, everything appeared to be in order. As if it was forbidden for anything to go wrong. Because when His Highness Prince Zander set out to do something, it got done.

She watched him across the room talking casually to one of the party supervisors. How everyone didn't melt into a puddle when they were around him, Marie had no idea. His charm was so persuasive that she couldn't set herself free from it. Between attending the parties in Cannes, spending time together with Abella, the trip to Charlegin and preparing for the gala, Marie knew her dealings with him had gone far past what was required. Let alone the kisses and the intimacies. Yet all she longed for was more. More time with him, every day, every week, every ye…

Good heavens, she tried to focus herself. She'd have no ongoing relationship with Prince Zander. How many times did she need to remind herself of that? Their lives collided here in Cannes but, after the season, he would return to his travels or the palace or his apartment in Paris. Perhaps, if she got the APCF job permanently and if he continued to support the agency, she might see him now and then.

But that was it. If there had been any question, that awful visit to the palace when Princess Claudine made her feel so unwanted sealed the fate. His Highness Zander was not going to end up with sad little Marie. Who not only hadn't traveled the world with beautiful people but was the laughingstock at the council blocks she grew up in. Where she lived in Building A on floor numbers one, three and six and Building B on floors two, five and eight as she was shuffled from one foster home to the other.

Whatever Zander might have presumed her childhood to be, he had no idea how sordid it really was. Despite the bond they shared, Marie Paquet was plainly not a candidate to spend her life with the prince.

Once again, she'd found herself in a place where she didn't belong.

"Marie, can I get your opinion?" Zander summoned her and she crossed the foyer, sucking herself up as she always did.

"How can I help?"

"Do you like these?" He pointed to a sweets tray on a side table. "Chef Jean Luc has created these individual cakes that riff on film reels, back from when movies were shot on real celluloid. To go with our theme."

Impeccable skill and artistry showed in the little round cakes. Chef Jean Luc fashioned a wrap of chocolate around the diameter of each cake so that it had the frames and spokes of a film reel. Then, with design that gave the cakes a level of flourish that would surely be noticed by every guest, the chocolate strip of film swirled up to the top of the cake in an edible curlicue.

"They're amazing. I only have one question. With the desserts served buffet style rather than table service, I wonder if guests won't be mulling about. These are rather big to eat standing up. Could Chef make them smaller? In a two-bite size?"

"Look at you, mademoiselle. A party professional! Good thinking. I'll speak with him about it." Zander flashed his megawatt smile at her, making her knees quiver so much that she subtly grabbed hold of a nearby chair to steady herself. Not giving her a moment to re-cover, he beckoned her, "Let's do a walk-through."

Past the foyer of the mansion was a grand staircase leading down to the great hall, through which six French doors opened onto a huge expanse of lawn. It was the ultimate in indoor-to-outdoor space and back again. They descended the stairs to survey the lawn, where movie screens had been set up in various locations so that through a high-tech setup, old films would be projected on each of the screens all night long to add to the fund-raiser's theme.

"Did you choose all of the movies?" she asked Zander, looking up to him in the glare of high noon, knowing the space would be magical under the moon and constellations.

"I asked an archivist from the film festival for a bit of help. One screen will show silent-era comedies, another black-and-white horror movies, another brightly colored musicals, and so on."

"It will be the talk of the town."

"Of course it will, it's Cannes!"

"I meant that as a figure of speech."

"I know. I was only teasing," Zander said with a cute elbow jab to Marie's arm that launched tingles throughout her body. His every touch, every gaze and, to be sure, every kiss held so much weight over her it was almost terrifying.

Oh, why did she finally meet a man she could foresee a *future* with who could never even have a *present* with her? After all she'd been through in her life, didn't she deserve that? Providences were cruel.

"Let's go over the table charts," Zander commanded with a guiding palm on Marie's back. Her tongue flicked the roof of her mouth as they went back inside.

Easels had been set up in the great hall with seating arrangements and party flow charts. Marie and Zander stood side by side, studying the plans. Tweaking a couple of the table assignments, Zander seemed generally satisfied.

Taking Marie by the hand, he tugged her back up the mansion's grand staircase. When they reached the top, he turned them around so they could look down on the party space. "After the black-and-gold carpet outside, the guests enter here. This will be their first sight of the great hall and the lawn beyond."

Why Zander hadn't let go of her hand after they'd reached the top of the stairs, she didn't know. But she wasn't going to be the one to break away. She'd take every second of him she could get, filling the memory bank she knew she'd cherish forever. Her fingers in his were so right. His huge hand all but surrounded hers in a joining that felt like…like home, if there was such a thing.

She allowed herself that one split second of visualizing being a guest at this ball and arriving with Prince Zander, a power couple unified in philanthropy and love. They'd party and dance the night away, peering lovingly into each other's eyes until the sun began to rise. At which point they'd go home. Wherever the location was not important as long as they were together.

Once quiet and out of their formal clothes, they'd come together in an embrace that laid them down on lush bedding to appreciate each other's bodies and the perfection of their union. They'd make love in the truest sense of the phrase, each bringing the other the rapture and delight that was the destiny of their coupling, only theirs, always.

"I think it will make a very dramatic first impression," Marie said with a dry throat as she pulled herself back. "So, guests descend the stairs…"

"And they'll be guided out to the lawn…"

"Or to the cocktail areas," Marie said as she pointed to the three social salons that extended from the great hall.

"Once most of the guests are in attendance…"

"The music starts and the tap-dancing troupe comes down the stairs doing their routine."

"That's going to be a pizzazz moment."

"The waiters will be passing out the Tinseltown Fizzes." Marie made reference to the unique cocktail Zander had commissioned for the evening.

They proceeded with their walk-through of every component, by now in such comfortable rapport with each other that they finished each other's thoughts. What had they even become? They weren't friends, they weren't lovers, but surely they were more than coworkers. Yet the closeness and the kisses hadn't changed anything. She was still not a woman he could have a future with and she needed to guard her already tattered heart before it tore apart.

Once they were done, they stood facing each other. He lifted his eyebrows. "I think that's it."

"As long as everything goes according to plans."

"I'll see you at the penthouse tonight for our costume fittings."

With that he leaned down to give her a chaste peck on the cheek, and then pivoted toward the kitchen to talk to Chef Jean Luc.

As she had done every time before, as soon as Zander was out of sight Marie brought her hand to her cheek to feel where his lips had touched it, as if she could brand each kiss into her skin to keep it safe for all of eternity.

"Come in." Zander opened the door to let in master costumer Gabin Blanc. Zander had told Marie at their first fitting that Gabin outfitted all of Cannes for these events. The big man with red hair and chapped lips entered the penthouse. He wore a smock over his white shirt and black trousers, and a tailor's measuring tape hung from around his neck.

As usual, in his left arm Zander held Abella, who was delighted when Gabin gave her pieces of fleece fabric to play with. She put one over Zander's mouth and found that hysterically funny. The sound of her innocent laughter was infectious and had the two men chuckling as they awaited Marie, who ducked into the bedroom to change.

"Whoa!" Zander exclaimed to the baby when Marie returned. "Bell-bell, do you see Marie? Doesn't she look hot?"

Indeed, Marie as Marilyn Monroe was a sight to behold in her white dress and blond wig.

"Marilyn, may I have your autograph, please?" Gabin joined in the fun.

"Va-va-voom. What a bombshell!" Zander whistled, and Abella immediately tried to imitate his sound, although it came out baby-gurgly.

"Marilyn Monroe in her heyday was the epitome of Hollywood stardom," Gabin said. "You look fab-u-*lous*. But come here while I pin and tuck a bit."

Marie dutifully reported to Gabin, who had brought a small pedestal for her to stand on while he made alterations. Zander's eyes couldn't help but follow her as she crossed the room.

The white dress was a replica of the one Monroe famously wore in *The Seven-Year Itch*, where she stood on a New York City sidewalk over a subway grate. When the train passed underground, it created a whoosh of air that escaped through the grate, blowing the dress upward and giving onlookers a peek at Monroe's shapely legs. While his Marie was far too modest to reenact anything like that, Zander couldn't keep himself from noticing that her legs did look especially fetching extended from the milky white of the dress.

As she passed by him, he also couldn't help but study the sight of her bare back, which the design of the dress left open. "She's beautiful," he sang to the baby, who seemed to know what he meant as her eyes went to Marie, as well.

"Booful," Abella echoed.

Gabin helped Marie onto the pedestal and while Zander knew he was gawking, he wasn't able to stop.

Never would he have guessed that he'd meet a woman

in Cannes who would come to captivate him in such a short period of time.

Other than the changes necessitated by the baby, he'd pictured his season on the Riviera much the same as the usual. The parties and the women who always seemed to be around if there was an introduction to him to be made. The last thing he would have expected was that he would meet someone with whom he could be ordinary and honest and not just a talking crown.

What might become of them if Zander hadn't been obliged to marry the *right* sort of woman? Marie was far more proper where it mattered than most of the frivolous girls he'd known. She cared about things with all her enthusiasm, was a force for good, and she didn't take anything for granted.

Also, *private* and *royalty* were two concepts that did not fit well together and he knew there were things in Marie's past that she was trying to keep to herself. If, and only for the sake of the mental game he was playing, Zander was ever to let public that he was dating someone she would be mercilessly stripped naked by the press. Not just once but for the rest of her life. Whatever Marie was hiding would be the top story of every royal-following newspaper, magazine and website that existed. He had the sense Marie did not want to be an open book, which was what would be required to be with him.

"She's really not my girlfriend," he confirmed to Abella in a barely audible declaration that Marie or Gabin wouldn't be able to hear.

"Girl fend," the baby yelled out, causing a pulse to Zander's jaw. Marie and Gabin turned toward them.

Abella put a piece of the fabric Gabin had given her on top of Zander's head.

Gabin returned to finishing Marie's look. In her wig of blond curls, her face didn't resemble Monroe's but the costume was undeniable. A makeup artist would add that extra touch of movie-star panache tomorrow. Although Zander surely thought the real Marie was so pretty, she didn't need any help with that face.

She stepped down from the pedestal and excused herself to take the dress and wig off. Then returned to the room in the jeans and button-down shirt she had been wearing, looking relaxed without shoes.

"Your Highness, may I do your fitting now?"

"You can call me Zander."

"Do you want me to take the baby?" Marie asked Zander.

While he'd yet to allow her to hold Abella, it occurred to him that he no longer had any reservations. He'd leave it up to Abella and read her reaction. The baby stretched her arms toward Marie, who took her from Zander and gave a tender kiss to the top of her head. Zander paused until he was sure he was confident leaving the room for a few minutes while he changed into his costume.

Turning, he heard Marie singing to Abella, *"Frère Jacques, Frère Jacques. Dormez-vous? Dormez-vous?"* Warming his heart. Certain she'd make a fine mother someday.

Playing it to the hilt, Zander soon returned to the living room. Twirling the end of his cane in his poorly fitting suit, dark wig and bowler hat, he was unmistakably dressed as early film star Charlie Chaplin's famous alter ego, The Tramp. Walking with that toddle Chaplin made famous. Marie and Gabin grinned at each other with delight at the transformation.

"I can't wait to see him with the moustache," the costumer noted.

"Look at Uncle Zander," Marie said, hoisting the baby so that she could fully see him.

"Hi, Bell-bell."

"Da!" the baby exclaimed once she made the recognition.

As Gabin made his adjustments in a final fitting, Zander liked the sight of Maria with Abella. They looked natural together. So much so that he wanted to rush to join them, to put his arms around the two females who were what mattered to him.

It took all of his will to convince himself that the optic was as phony as the too-large shoes he had on his feet. He and Abella were his life. He still wasn't planning on making any changes to that family picture.

Marie was a nervous wreck. The guests had begun to arrive for the APCF annual fund-raising gala. All of the pieces had come together and the evening was off and running with a life of its own. There was no one particular thing that Marie was worried about, only that the event would be a success. She'd opened and closed her fists so many times that her fingernails had dug scratches into her palms.

The makeup artist had come and gone, lacquering onto Marie's face every nuance of Marilyn Monroe that could be applied. The alabaster complexion, the red lips, the long false eyelashes, the heavy eyeliner and even the one signature mole on her cheek.

The wig had been set into its perfect curls that surrounded Marie's face with a sexy wave at the forehead. Shoes on. Earrings replicating the ones Monroe wore with the white dress were attached, and for that matter, pinching her ears. The look was complete.

In the small office near the mansion's kitchen that she'd commandeered as her headquarters, Marie did a final check in the mirror.

"Showtime," she said aloud to herself. As if on cue, Zander appeared as she exited the office. "Oh. Hi."

"Hello, gorgeous," he replied in a tough-guy voice that completely contradicted his head-to-toe Charlie Chaplin makeover. They both laughed. "Shall we?"

With his hand on her back, a touch that had become far too regular with all the daring clothing she'd been wearing, Zander led them toward the belly of the beast. They could hear guests reveling and the swing band that was playing on the lawn.

"Any problems?" Marie asked him.

"Only keeping this moustache on. It kept falling off with the makeup artist's usual adhesive so she used a spirit gum that's like glue."

"That will be fun trying to remove later," she joked.

"Perhaps you can help me."

Marie wasn't sure why, but her ears perked when he mentioned her helping him later. They had been together so many hours in the past weeks and perhaps she assumed that the minute the gala was over, she'd turn back into a scullery maid and never interact with the handsome prince again. Yet here he was talking about *later*.

With the baby and nanny likely to be fast asleep in the hours after the gala, Zander had booked the mansion's one hospitality suite to spend the night in so as not to disturb them. Whereas Marie was just planning to go home to her single room afterward. So she wasn't sure exactly when it was that he was talking about her help removing his moustache.

How much more time had he figured they would spend together? She surely wouldn't want to get her hopes up that he meant, for example, forever, which was what she'd come to fantasize about. Did he assume she would stay overnight here in the mansion with him?

The thought of that gave her a forbidden thrill that she worked to mask.

Zander took her hand and noticed the marks in her palm from her fingernail digs. "We've got to break you of that habit or you're going to hurt yourself." She wrinkled her nose at his timing as they rounded the corner to the great hall and he exclaimed, "Here we go."

Scarlett O'Hara and Rhett Butler were the first to say hello. The green garden party dress from *Gone with the Wind* had been re-created for Madame Fournier. The bright green leaf-patterned fabric atop the huge pouf of the white skirt was dramatic.

Monsieur Fournier, whom Zander explained owned the largest chain of pharmacies in Southern France, might have had a few years senior to Clark Gable at the time the film was made. Nonetheless, he held his own in his topcoat with a thin moustache that looked well affixed to his face.

Zander and Marie greeted the guests as if welcoming them into their own home. What would that be like, she wondered, if they were really a couple receiving guests at their Paris apartment? Regardless of the glam or wealth involved, just the mere closeness of inviting guests into their home filled Marie with a bittersweet glow.

Next, they greeted Lawrence of Arabia, who took a few minutes before recognizing the prince, his university mate. "Robin Guerin had me for supper on the tennis court every time we met," Zander told Marie as he gave his old pal a pat on the shoulder.

Waiters passed out chilled glasses of Tinseltown Fizz, the custom cocktail that contained dark grape juice to give it a gorgeous violet color.

Zander introduced Marie to the guests, emphasizing her important role at the APCF. Well versed in the programs the agency provided, Marie was able to speak articulately about how crucial the evening's proceeds would be to the organization.

As she worked the room, hobnobbing with her prince, she speculated if it was obvious to anyone that she was not of their world, but of the one they were raising funds for. In hers, there was no eco-touring in the Galapagos, like Elizabeth Taylor dressed as Cleopatra was telling her about. In Marie's life, there were no shopping excursions to New York. No hula dancing in Hawaii. No safaris in Kenya. Not even a slice of pizza in Naples.

"How's everything going?" Felice, the APCF director, came up next to her, outstanding in her costume as a crazy Bette Davis in *Whatever Happened to Baby Jane?* "This is quite an event."

"No catastrophes so far."

One thing Marie knew was that if she could, she would have Zander next to her every minute of every day. A man with both the confidence and know-how to take care of the business in front of him and to resolve any obstacle that came his way. He made everything so much better and easier.

Abella was an incredibly fortunate baby, royal or

not, to have this brilliant and conscientious man looking after her. Marie hoped she would always appreciate how lucky she was.

Applying every relaxation skill she'd ever learned, and trying not to clench her fists, she progressed through the party. When the guests sat down for dinner, she helped a too-tipsy Dorothy from *The Wizard of Oz*, who was holding her ruby slippers in her hand by that point, find a quiet corner to have a cup of coffee and straighten up. Dorothy introduced herself as a real-life real estate tycoon who was going to make a substantial donation in honor of Marie's special care.

Marie herself was too nervous to sit and eat so surveyed the room as dinner was being served. Once Zander noticed that she had no interest in sitting down, he stood to join her.

"The hearts of palm were a nice first course." The retro dinner Chef Jean Luc created was based on old menus from Hollywood restaurants where the stars used to dine.

"Now they have the filet mignon with béarnaise sauce and duchess potatoes."

"Then the endive salad."

"And the dessert buffet."

"Followed by Felice's speech."

"We're getting there, partner," Zander said as his hand went around Marie's waist, making her false eyelashes flutter. "I'm so proud of you."

Marie racked her brain, but she couldn't remember a time anyone had ever said those words to her before.

CHAPTER NINE

IN THE FINALLY empty great hall, Marie collapsed into a chair at one of the dining tables. Now in the wee hours and no more guests to impress with perfect decorum, she let her body languish, legs outstretched and her arms dangling like a rag doll. Staring up at the ceiling, which had been decorated with a moon-and-stars motif that made it seem as if the room was outdoors, she whooshed out a loud exhale.

"My sentiments exactly," Zander's voice responded. Marie craned her head to see him coming down the grand staircase, a sight for sore eyes if there ever was one. He'd half removed his Charlie Chaplin costume. Gone was the derby hat and dark wig. The moustache remained. With his natural blond hair, the contrast was comical.

Also gone were the oversize shoes and shabby top-coat he'd donned for the evening. In his remaining white shirt and black pants, along with the expensive-looking loafers he'd slipped on, he took a seat beside her and mimicked her spread-out pose on the dining chair.

"You did it," he rasped.

"We did it, Zander. There's no reason to pretend I could have done any of this without your guidance."

"My princely fairy-tale powers give me an advantage."

"No. It's because of your generosity and dedication and compassion. You don't get those traits for free just because you're a royal." He smiled. "I've learned so much through this experience, Zander."

Indeed, success at an event of this magnitude was no small feat.

"You're a good student."

"Yeah, well, let's see how well I do when I have to orchestrate one of these on my own."

"Everything worked out, didn't it?"

"I think you missed the part when Maria Von Trapp in full nun regalia tripped and fell into a pan of cherries jubilee."

They burst into laughter that echoed in the din of the cavernous hall.

"What? Where was I at the time?"

"I think I saw you out on the lawn with Humphrey Bogart. Some of the wait staff came to my rescue. But poor Sister Maria had red syrup in every fold of her habit."

"Was she intoxicated?"

"To the nines, *dahling*." Marie used a larger-than-life accent.

"That was Hyacinth Jones, an American widow who lives in Sweden. She's the unofficial cougar at all of these parties, her eyes on the younger men."

"As a matter of fact, the Good Sister squealed when a hunky waiter had to carry her away because she had cherries in her shoes. Fortunately, not a lot of guests had to witness the debacle."

"I hope she writes a fat check for the evening."

Marie sat up to take off the high-heeled white sandals that had been part of her Marilyn Monroe ensemble. She crossed one leg over the other knee so that she could rub her foot. "I danced so long with Frankenstein I thought my feet were going to fall off. Then Groucho Marx wanted a turn."

"Here." Zander turned his chair and took Marie's legs onto his lap. "Allow me."

When he wrapped his two hands around her right foot, it was as if someone had just covered her in a plush heated blanket. Her head fell backward. Even if she had wanted to object she wouldn't have been able to, his fingers were *that* therapeutic. With the skill of a masseuse, he kneaded and soothed her tired muscles, first one foot than the other.

"And you do foot massages, too?"

He batted his eyelashes in an adorable way.

How much fun this was to sit with Zander and have a recap. Actually, doing anything with Zander was fun. That was something she had never faced head-on. The inalterable fact that sharing both the good and bad times with someone made everything nicer, and might even make the intolerable tolerable. And not just with anyone but to be one of the lucky few in life who met that special person who made them feel whole, complete and part of something.

Truthfully, in the dark of lonely nights after hard days, Marie's soul did cry out for that someone she thought she'd never meet. She turned her head toward Zander and something wordless but significant passed between them.

Her legs felt the jostling when he adjusted himself in the chair.

"That feels amazing," she let slip. The words ricocheted from one side of the room to the other. "Unfortunately, I'm going to have to get those shoes back on and gather my things. It's time to go home."

"Marie, I'm sorry, I let my driver go. You know I rented the hospitality suite upstairs in the mansion for the night."

"That's okay. I'll just call a rideshare."

"At this hour? No. Why don't you stay here with me? There's plenty of room."

No, Marie. Whatever you do, say no to that offer. It had been a struggle all along to keep her attraction to Zander under wraps. She'd endured the casual touching and the not-so-innocent kissing. How much further could she go?

Oh, those kisses.

Bliss rang through her as she recounted the night of the Carlsmon party, replaying every second of what were most certainly the most exciting kisses she'd ever had. Marie's mouth yielding to Zander's. Accepting his every move. Initiating some of her own. Their lips, their tongues, fitting exactly to each other's. Both wanting more, knowing to deny themselves. Her eyelashes still flickered every time she thought of those kisses. They probably always would.

It would be too risky to share the suite with him tonight, regardless of the sleeping arrangements. That proximity would fill her head with too many what-ifs, silly unrealities about things that could never happen. Like making love. Like until eternity. The stuff dreams were made of.

"No." She eked out a sound that was sort of a half question. After a few measured breaths she tried again with, "I'd best be going."

She swung her legs off Zander's oh-so-comfortable lap and jammed her feet into her shoes. They seemed to have shrunk two sizes since she'd taken them off. Or maybe it was that her feet grew when out of the confines of the leather and in Zander's hands. When she stood up, she all but crumbled with tiredness. Having to take even one more step seemed an impossible demand.

There'd be no harm in spending the night here at the mansion with Zander, she decided.

The truth was that she wanted to make love with him. To experience the passion that they'd doled out to each other only in small amounts so far.

But she was too afraid of the hurt it would cause her afterward, when the certainty that they could never be together would be a knife to her heart.

"You must be hungry. I have a tray of cheese and fruit waiting for a bedtime snack," he coaxed as he rose from his chair.

He moved over to one of the waiter stations. From a silver ice bucket, he extracted an unopened bottle of frosty champagne. And from the glassware cart he threaded the stems of two crystal flutes in his fingers.

After a kind smile that pierced into her weary eyes, Zander lifted Marie into his arms.

A moan escaped from her throat as she wrapped her arms around his neck. Like it was the most normal thing in the world.

As they kept their gaze on each other, he carried her up the grand staircase.

Once in the suite, Zander gently placed Marie down. She immediately stepped out of her shoes, grateful to be barefoot again.

The two-room suite was as well designed and tasteful as the rest of the mansion. Built in the 1800s, it had been upgraded with every modern convenience anyone could want. The sitting room furnishings were done in dark woods and the upholstery a forest green. French doors were left open to allow in the moonlight and cool night air. To one side was a separate bedroom with a gigantic bed, carved wood posts and a dozen inviting pillows.

"May I freshen up a minute?"

"Of course," Zander replied as he uncorked the champagne bottle. He gestured toward the bathroom.

There, marble walls and surfaces were accented with gold fixtures. A glass shower had a built-in bench inside and a rain shower faucet. It looked glorious, though if Marie did use the facilities, she'd probably rather try the soaking tub. It was big enough for two people to fit in, and the whirlpool jets promised to turn sore muscles to jelly.

For now, though, she opened the taps of the sink to bring the water to a tepid temperature. Needing a bar of soap, she turned to the generous basket of toiletries that had been provided. With three options to choose from, she brought each to her nose and decided on the invigorating lemon cucumber bar. She washed her face and hands and dried them on one of the thick towels.

If she wanted to wash her hair later, she noticed that there were swanky shampoos and hair conditioners in the basket. There were lotions. Toothbrushes. Toothpaste. Deodorant. Sunscreen. How nice.

And look at that!

The basket even contained a package of condoms. She lifted the small cardboard box, tastefully white with a gold seal. If the contents were to be required, one would only have to tear the seal to open it.

How very modern and thoughtful.

Condoms.

A thousand people had populated the mansion for the gala. From the suite on the second floor, Zander could no longer hear a sound below. The staff had done as much cleaning as they'd intended to for the night. Rented tables, chairs and dinnerware would all be picked up in the morning. He knew there were security people somewhere on the premises downstairs, but they were silent.

It was just him and Marie, munching cheese in the hush of this enormous property.

"Have you ever grown a real moustache?" Marie asked Zander as they lounged on the settee in the sitting room of the suite. The Charlie Chaplin version the makeup artist had adhered to his face remained. "What does it feel like?"

"I attempted to grow one at university. It was itchy at first," Zander recalled. "It came in rather scruffy and prickly. Mother hated it. Girls I dated while I had it never said anything, so I don't know what they thought. Because, of course, one doesn't criticize a prince's choice of facial hair."

He knew he bit that out with some sarcasm. But it was absolutely true that he'd never been with a woman who had been honest with him about anything, let alone something as small a matter as his facial hair.

Except for Marie, resting beside him on the settee, never trying to be anything she wasn't.

Her pretty and sore feet were curled up between

them. It had been almost unbearably personal rubbing them in the dining room before they came upstairs. Though his thumbs so enjoyed working on all of the muscles in between the delicate bones.

Was massaging someone's feet a gift of love to them? One he was unused to bestowing or receiving? In any case, having her silky legs on his lap had been unexpectedly arousing.

Zander's mother, dressed as Holly Golightly from *Breakfast at Tiffany's*, complete with long cigarette holder, had cornered him at the gala to ask again about Marie. Apparently she still wasn't convinced by the *just coworkers* label he had been insisting on.

"You know the press will rip her to shreds," Claudine had told her son, buzzing into his ear as they watched Marie being dragged around the dance floor by a lead-footed Ben Hur.

"The press doesn't know who she is, Mother." He thought of the headline he'd caught in his news feed that questioned who the *mystery woman* was whom Prince Zander had been spotted with in Cannes. "Working for the APCF is hardly high profile."

"They'll find out, I promise you," Claudine pressed.

Zander pushed those thoughts away. They weren't together, despite his mother's assumptions. Marie's life was none of anyone's business but hers. Besides, what could be in her past that was so newsworthy?

He reached to the corner of his mouth and began to peel away the fake moustache. It wasn't as easy as it seemed. The spirit gum the makeup artist had used proved quite effective. He worked on it a smidgen at a time but without much success.

"This moustache was made to last. I can't get it off."

"Do you want help?" Marie asked.

"I think I might need some."

She unfurled her curvaceous legs and turned to face him on the settee. Leaning in, she used a fingernail to pick at the outer edge.

His entire body immediately reacted to her closeness and her finger on his face. Desire coursed through him and his mind swirled with images.

Like how when he lifted her legs to his lap in order to massage her feet, he'd allowed himself a quick caress down the length of her smooth limbs.

And that now, the pad of one small fingertip on his face was bringing a gratification grossly out of proportion to the action she was performing. It didn't matter, though. He wanted to enjoy every minute.

He shut his eyes, her face so near as she studied the task at hand. Was he imagining it or could he feel her gentle breath tickling his skin? In any case, it was delightful and made him not want the moment to end.

"You're not kidding with this glue," she sniggered.

"Do you have any suggestions?"

To his surprise, she brought her lips to his and kissed him. Not once. Not twice. And by the third time, he was intoxicated by her mouth and took her head in his hands to deepen the kiss.

"Very scratchy!" She pretended shock. He eased up, not wanting her to experience anything disagreeable. In fact, the thoughts he was having were designing ways to make her feel anything but unpleasant indeed. He could sense her smile against his face when she added, "But I didn't say I wanted to stop."

So with her encouragement he kissed her face, knowing that the coarse hairs of the moustache would create a sensation on her skin that she either loved or hated. The dulcet hum that escaped her throat gave him the answer he needed.

His mouth sought the curve of her jaw. He kissed its expanse upward to behind her earlobe. Another sigh of praise from her invigorated him further. Next, his mouth traced down the side of her neck. Once his lips found their way into the exquisite crook where neck met shoulder, he thought he might have reached heaven on earth. By then she had run her fingers through his hair, holding his head to her, wanting this as much as he did.

Breaking for a moment, he leaned back. Marie was still wearing the Marilyn Monroe wig that had been her costume. He wanted to feel her own soft hair so he easily slipped the wig off her head and tossed it to the nearby table. She reached up to remove the hairnet that had bound her own locks, and her brunette waves tumbled down around her face. "Back to me," she said quietly.

"You are always you, Marie, that's what I love about you."

Once he'd uttered those words, he couldn't take them back.

He rationalized that saying he loved something about her wasn't the same as saying that he loved her.

Although he suspected that he might. In fact. Love her.

The swell in his heart whenever she was near could have been a clue. How much he'd looked forward to each and every one of their meetings as they'd worked on the gala. How many laughs they'd shared about everyday things like couples do. How beautiful she was with Abella, respecting that Zander took his responsibility toward his niece with the utmost seriousness. How she treated him as just a sincere man, not one with whom she had to wear kid gloves or be careful what she said.

Marie made him want it all, the real romance, the real family, the real union. She had defied and destroyed every barrier to love that Zander had been able to build.

After shaking out her natural hair, she amazed him when she leaned over and, with one ferocious tug, stripped the moustache off his face.

"Ouch!" He feigned injury but was actually relieved to be rid of it.

"There you are," she sang, "the real Zander."

He encircled her in his arms and kissed the top of her head.

She leaned her neck backward to meet his face and they began another set of kisses, each one more urgent than the one before, communicating their depth of hunger for each other.

She muttered against his lips, "Yes."

Before long, Marilyn Monroe's dress and Charlie Chaplin's clothes were flung across the suite. Where they stayed until morning light replaced the pitch-dark skies.

Marie's eyelids didn't want to pop up. She had the sense she'd been drifting in and out of sleep for quite a while. It was only when her brain focused on the sound of breathing coming from beside her body did her eyes spring open wide.

It hadn't been a dream. Handsome, compassionate, spicy Prince Zander de Nellay of Charlegin was next to her in the suite's luxurious king-size bed. Their bodies were touching. They were both naked. No Charlie Chaplin moustache. No Marilyn Monroe wig. No one here to call him Your Highness.

Gingerly, she rolled over onto her side so that she could watch him sleep without waking him. With the shards of morning sunshine peeking in, Zander's skin and hair caught flecks of light in a way that made him appear almost holy, like a religious painting. Yet he wasn't a distant idol to be worshipped from afar. No, this was a vigorous man made of flesh and blood.

It wasn't hard to picture this scenario as a regular occurrence. Saying good-night to Zander as the last thing she did before going to sleep, and good-morning the first on awakening. Such ho-hum behavior between a couple, yet so meaningful.

She silently thanked him. For showing her a world she'd known nothing about. Not how to run a big gala or interact with a donor, although she'd surely be eternally grateful to him for teaching her those skills. What she was really thankful for was his kindness toward her. His belief in her abilities. His perception of her as beautiful and sexy and worthy. No one had ever made her feel that way. Inching out of the bed, still careful not to disturb his sleep, she tiptoed her way across the geometric-printed rug that covered the hardwood floors. Entering the bathroom, she fumbled for the light switch and pressed the door shut.

Evidence of what transpired last night was strewn on the countertop. That upmarket little white cardboard box of condoms that she had been so impressed with was crushed out of shape. The gold seal had been broken. The contents had been removed.

Did she look different in the bathroom mirror from

how she had the night before? Disregarding the costume, of course, but traveling behind her eyes, inside her heart, into her very center, she perceived a shift.

Yes, she and Zander had made love. Which she'd done before, with a couple of other guys she'd dated. But it occurred to her now what the phrase *make love* really meant. And she realized it was something she hadn't actually known.

Never had she been with a man who insisted that she enjoy as much pleasure as he did. Unlike those previous men, who treated her as if she were an inanimate object for their use, the lovemaking she shared with Zander was not a score sheet tracking who was doing the giving and who the taking. In fact, giving and taking had blended together to become one and the same.

Together, they'd learned each other's bodies and responses, slowly and deliberately, bringing one another other up and then higher and higher and higher still until they folded into each other's arms as one.

And now that he'd taught her what physical intimacy truly was, she'd never be able to settle for less.

Creeping back into the bedroom, she slipped on her dress and located her phone. A quick scan of messages showed there was one from Felice at the APCF. Figuring she'd better attend to that, she swiped to open it.

Didn't want you to be caught unaware, thought you should see this.

And below those words was a link to a website called *Royal Matchups*.

Dread invaded every cell in Marie's body as she tapped to the site.

The bold headline was enough to burn her stomach raw: His Hottie Highness Prince Zander's Shady Lady.

All the available air left the room and Marie's throat closed. With Zander still asleep, she gripped the wall with one hand as she read on.

We've been reporting about the mystery companion seen escorting Prince Zander de Nellay of Charlegin all over Cannes. Finally, we can confirm that the winsome mademoiselle is Marie Paquet, an employee of the Alliance for Parentless Children of France. She was assisting His Highness as he chaired the APCF's annual gala, and it seems like this pair has fun-raising in addition to fund-raising on their minds.

It's no coincidence that Marie works for the APCF as she herself was orphaned at age eleven. Readers following the news in roughneck North Marseilles might remember the double murder of a married couple there fourteen years ago. In fact, it was Marie's parents, Tamma and Bruno.

The pair were known drug suppliers to the dealers rampant in the troubled section of the city. Addicts themselves, they were shot down on the street in a hailstorm of bullets in full daylight during a turf war, while prepubescent Marie was home alone in the couple's disorderly apartment at the time.

Police found her three days later, unaware of what had happened but afraid to leave her room.

And it seems that wasn't the end of the troubles for our poor Marie…

Her palm still flat against the bedroom wall, Marie gasped. Zander rustled on the bed but didn't wake up.

So here it was. Everything she'd hoped she could keep private in her life so that she stood a chance of moving forward without being dragged down by circumstances she'd had no control over. What she'd omitted in telling Zander about herself, for fear he'd have nothing to do with her if he knew.

How naive she'd been! She'd never escape her yesterdays. They would taunt and haunt her for the rest of her life, as was their job. They would limit her options, decrease her opportunities, and could always be counted on to make her despair. Her past was an old nemesis that would shadow her until her dying day.

She read on.

The orphaned Marie, whom no other family member rushed to aid, was then set on a journey we wouldn't wish for anyone. Taken into the foster care system, she was shuffled from one from household to the next.

We shudder to think what Marie might have encountered in the six different foster homes she was sent to.

How dare the owners of this superficial website, purely for the amusement of gossip hounds with nothing better to do, investigate her background because of her association with Zander for a philanthropic project! How would they have even gathered that biography of her? She supposed that because her parents were criminals who made headlines themselves, there was no shortage of public information.

After some labored breathing to try to calm herself and identify her feelings, anger turned to humiliation. As it had so many times before.

She continued reading.

It was only after young Marie was introduced to the APCF that her fortunes improved. The agency was able to help arrange a work-study program for her to attend university. When scrappy Marie wasn't in classes, she dutifully chopped vegetables at the university's dining hall. Cheers to the APCF for also positioning her in their Toulouse office after she graduated.

Heartthrob Prince Zander has been under the radar of late, curiously not dating any of the world-class beauties he's been known to globetrot with, save for a few appearances with party girl Henriette Fontaine several months ago.

We know he's busy caring for his baby niece after his sister's tragic death, trading bubbly for baby bottles. But it looks as if he might have re-emerged, and found himself a genuine Cinderella.

Cinderella? Marie choked at the comparison.

She looked over to stunning Zander asleep on the bed, his tall muscular body fully stretched out in comfort. Marie had no idea what Zander thought about her background, if he thought about it at all. Why would he? They worked together on a project for a few weeks. That was it.

Once he read this article, he'd be furious at her and at himself for letting her get so close to Abella. Protecting the crown princess was always foremost in his mind, and knowing that they had been followed and spied on would drive him mad with guilt and regret.

Marie needed to get out of the picture. Even if Zander felt otherwise, she owed it to Abella. If Marie were part of their lives, the press and public would seek to hound and embarrass Zander and the young princess every day until the end of time. They wouldn't be able to go anywhere or do anything without reference to the daughter of slain drug dealers. Abella had already lost her parents, which would inform everything about her life. The last thing she needed was Marie to present another cross to bear.

There was no other choice.

Knowing it would be for the last time, she padded over to the bed and leaned down to Zander. She gave one final kiss to that sensual mouth that had shared so much ecstasy with her. Every molecule in her lips buzzed from the contact. Half-awake, he elongated his arms and attempted to pull her to him in an embrace. Using all her strength, she backed away. She couldn't handle lying with him again where, in his arms, she might believe the impossible was possible.

Marie hoped with all her heart that he would someday find a suitable woman. Who could be a proper princess whom Claudine and his subjects would accept, and who'd be a caring mother figure for Abella. If the press approved of her, too, that would make Zander's life much easier.

She wanted the best for him. He deserved it.

Gathering up her shoes, Marie opened the bedroom door. In stepping through the threshold, she knew that she was saying goodbye to something she would never find again. Nothing would ever replicate the connection she and Zander had come to share. Nor would she want it to. It was once in a lifetime.

Goodbye, sweet Prince.

The click of the door as she shut it behind her was surely the saddest sound she'd ever heard.

CHAPTER TEN

WHEN ZANDER WOKE up, he instinctively reached across the bed to seek the softness. The pillow he caressed was supple enough, indeed, but it was not what he was searching for. Although awakening alone had become his norm, he didn't need reminding that last night had been different. On so many levels.

Bringing the pillow to his face, he could still smell Marie's perfume. His core stirred at the memory of their union. Embracing until they'd blended into one being. Exploring one another, his hands, her hands, exciting, elevating, pleasuring. Her mouth moving from one of his shoulders to the other. His lips trailing down every vertebra of her spine. Wrapped around each other, caressing and wanting, until they joined in the most profound coupling. Their bodies fitting perfectly together as one.

"Marie?" he called out, needing her again, needing her right now.

Reality began to throb his brain like a headache. It wasn't supposed to have played out like this. He'd told himself all along not to develop romantic feelings for her. That they could never be together, therefore he would protect her feelings. And his own.

Yet once he'd lost control and kissed her that night

at the Mexico party, they were, in fact, marching toward an inevitable conclusion. And then last night, the merging of their minds, bodies and, maybe especially, their souls was even more transcendental than he could have imagined.

There was no other way to describe it. He was head over heels in love with Marie. What he was going to do about that predicament, he had no idea.

"Marie!" he called out again, hoping that she was in the sitting room or bathroom. He tossed the bedding aside and rose to scan the suite.

Her Marilyn Monroe dress and heels were gone. All he spotted was the blond wig that had been part of her costume.

Confirming that she wasn't here, he retrieved his phone to check if she'd left a message for him. He only found one from his mother, which she'd marked as urgent. As he read the *Royal Matchups* website report she'd sent, feverish blood sped through his veins like they were racetracks. His head shook back and forth as if to scream *No! No!*

Fury enveloped him. At the press. At his mother. At Marie. And especially at himself. How could he have allowed this to happen?

He picked up the blond Marilyn Monroe wig. And absentmindedly ran his fingers through it like it was Marie's own strands. As if it contained Marie's DNA, and as if that would quell the firestorm raging through him.

Marie had deceived him! He'd thought they were being open and honest but she was withholding information. He'd directly asked about her parents and who they really were. No doubt assuming that he'd have to disassociate from her if he found out the answer, she kept it from him.

He sat in his disappointment and hurt, stroking the wig.

Until anger turned to agony.

Oh, what his poor Marie had been subjected to. How absolutely terrifying it must have been to have criminals for parents, with no one to protect her. For a child to have to live in the squalor and bedlam of lawlessness and drugs was almost unthinkable. And then that they were murdered with no provisions made for Marie. The pain he felt for her was unbearable.

Zander's mother had been right, of course, that the media would find a way to trace Marie. Citing newspaper articles from fourteen years ago and a follow-up piece a few years later, those evil gossip hounds had been able to expose her. To use the information to humiliate Zander's family, and Marie herself. That he had thought for even a minute there was a chance of all this unfolding otherwise was simply the wish of a naive boy in love.

The next morning, Marie woke from fitful hours of incoherent nightmares, sinister visions filled with bursts of violent colors and distorted human screams. Yesterday was a lifetime ago, when she'd quietly left the mansion where her Zander lay sleeping after their extraordinary night. First, the success of the gala had pumped them with adrenaline and giddy pride at a job well done. Then, together and alone in the still hours, their energy fixated on each other. They engaged in celestial lovemaking, the likes of which Marie didn't know existed.

Not much more than twenty-four hours ago, she'd

lain on Egyptian cotton sheets in the arms of the strong and goodhearted prince who had entered her life and rocked it to the core.

He had treated her as an equal. Never prying about her past. And letting her fall in love with Abella, despite how carefully he guarded her. It was almost as if, along the way, Zander had come to trust Marie.

His trust. Which she had betrayed by not telling him herself about the horror stories, her horror stories. That had abruptly become public property. How silly of her to think that she could keep them private. Even people at the APCF didn't know every gruesome fact, although they'd heard similar tales hundreds of times.

But now, because of her association with Prince Zander de Nellay, the whole world was apparently entitled to slice her open and dissect inside. She could hardly fathom what it was to be him, to have every move he made be under the ever-present camera's eye that was always watching.

If only they could shut the world out and make their own rules about who was suitable for whom. Because when immersed in their own groove, she and Zander made beautiful music together. A tune she knew nothing would ever compare to. A melody she'd want to hear in her head for eternity.

Because not only was she in love with sweet Abella, she was in love with Zander.

So this was love, she mused a few days later in her solitary room. Like floating just a few inches above ground and no matter what you did, your feet wouldn't touch the floor. It could be an exquisite feeling of invincible vitality, one that inspired and motivated and gave forth endlessly renewable energy. But when all of that love was expended in vain, it was draining and exasperating and painful. A relentless reminder of what couldn't be.

As was the chrome clothing rack on wheels that Zander had sent over to hold the formalwear he'd bought her. Listlessly, she touched the black lace of the ball gown she'd worn to the Mexico party.

She noted the details of the embroidered flowers and of the threadwork. Pati at the dress shop had told her it was made from guipure lace, a specific type that had an open design and raised texture. Marie wouldn't know one lace from the other if her life depended upon it, but Pati had emphasized what a unique gown it was.

Marie had never worn satin gloves before that night and the red pair was unbelievably luxurious. Bringing one to the side of her face, she brushed it against her skin just as Zander had with his lips.

She had to avert her gaze from the Marilyn Monroe dress, with too-vivid remembrances of Zander untying the neck of the halter and skimming the fabric down her body until she was naked in his hands. She had no idea what had happened to the wig that went with it.

Individual tears dropped from Marie's eyes.

"You know, you did a great job with the gala," Felice said, leaning her head into Marie's office later that day. "Zander will be in this afternoon to close out the books."

"What?" Marie all but choked on the coffee she was sipping. She knew she'd have to see Zander again sometime. He was committed to lending his name to the APCF's pursuits and that didn't end with the gala. But she'd hoped that some time would pass before she'd have to encounter him again.

She was definitely not ready to see him strut down the corridor of work cubicles toward her office, making her prickle in anticipation as he'd done dozens of times in the past few weeks.

It would take a while before she could lock into those spectacular almond-shaped eyes that were the darkest she'd ever seen. Or to notice those muscular hands that had held her so firmly in their grip. The brawny left shoulder that competently nestled baby Abella.

No, she needed some distance before being expected to face all of that again.

"Felice," Marie sputtered before the agency director moved out of earshot. "Would it be okay if I worked from home for the rest of the day? I'm not feeling well."

That wasn't exactly the truth, but a sickness she certainly had. The most excruciating, pounding, stabbing, scorching ache anyone had ever been asked to withstand. Being near him would throw salt on those already open wounds.

Felice removed her eyeglasses and let them dangle from their chain around her neck. "I gather something personal has transpired between you and Zander," she said, reading right through Marie. "Take the rest of the day off if you want. But I don't think avoiding him is the right move."

She knew that Felice was right and she'd have to learn how to live through seeing him again.

But not today.

Please, not today.

"Here's where you've been keeping my granddaughter," Princess Claudine chided her son as she burst through his apartment door, shopping bags in tow. "I have gifts."

"Hello, Mother." Zander met her arrival, Abella in his left arm as usual.

Mother and son kissed the other on each cheek and then Claudine gave a quick pat to the baby's head. "So cute."

Claudine reached into one of the bags and extracted a pink plastic baby's rattle. She shook it for Abella, who focused her eyes on it for about five seconds before turning away. Zander's mother hadn't interacted with young children in a long time, he reasoned, so she obviously didn't compute that by eighteen months of age Abella was on to more interactive toys. Still, it was a nice gesture.

"Come out to the terrace, Mother, and we'll have a drink."

When Her Highness called Zander yesterday to tell him that she'd be in Cannes for a film festival party and would stop in to see him, he'd bridled. He was in no mood to listen to his mother's stories about the silly partygoers she kept company with and their insignificant problems.

Since the APCF gala and that obscene gossip report, Zander had been keeping to himself. He'd taken Abella in her buggy out to the seaside, which allowed him a chance to take long, contemplative walks. But he'd been returning home by nightfall, canceling engagements, staying in evening after evening. He was in a funk.

With the spongy and colorful ground covering he'd laid down on the terrace, the area had become Abella's play space as much as anything else. Which drew a curious, and probably disapproving, reaction from his mother. Nonetheless, he seated her and poured some cold drinks.

"Does she speak yet?" Claudine asked of her granddaughter.

"She has a lot of words. And is starting to string them together."

"When you were that age, we could hardly keep you quiet. We swore you had already learned to read when actually it was that you'd memorized all of the books we read aloud to you. Whereas your sister kept silent until she was almost three years old."

It was quite a surprise for Zander to hear his mother waxing nostalgic about his childhood. They both knew that his and Elise's upbringings were left mainly to nannies and palace staff, with Claudine waltzing into the nursery for overly perfumed kisses before she was off for her fabulous evenings.

Of course, any complaints on that he had were not as dire as the tragedies of Marie's childhood. But a hands-on parent his mother surely wasn't. Now, as she'd grown older, she'd apparently reinvented a history that portrayed her in a more favorable light.

At the mention of Elise, they both paused and looked out to the seashore view the terrace provided.

"Life is unpredictable," Claudine mused.

"How right you are."

Zander's thoughts moved to the anguish that had him torn up inside. Marie. When he'd gone to the APCF to finish the accounting for the gala, she wasn't at the office. His repeated calls and texts had gone unanswered. He didn't want to show up at the APCF again to look for her, as it seemed she was making it clear she didn't want any contact with him.

He should respect that.

But what about what *he* wanted?

"I can tell you're blue, Zander. Because of Marie?"

He affirmed, but his mother didn't need to be a

master detective to have figured that one out. She, too, had read the startling account of Marie's history that the media had mercilessly broadcast to the world. She added, "Frankly, that press report nauseated me."

"Me, as well."

Both mother and son knew that were he to continue to associate with Marie, it would give the media endless permission to publish demeaning and distressing personal facts about her, and grant the public and Charlegin's citizens a license to arbitrate him and his family. It would fuel an insatiable drive for stories about them, no matter where they went or what they did.

"You know I had my share of scrutiny as a commoner marrying your father."

Of course, it was many years ago when Claudine and Hugh began their courtship, before the internet and social media exploded and gave birth to constant news cycles starving for more and more content. But Zander had seen some of the unflattering newspaper clippings about the shopgirl who had caught Prince Hugh's eye. They portrayed her as an unabashed gold digger. Which she was, but it must have been hurtful to have to see her ruthlessness spelled out in print.

"You and he persevered," Zander spat with a wry twist to the corner of his mouth.

"Yes, your father loved me once."

Her words dangled in the air.

His parents had a working relationship. Fulfilling their obligations, appearing at functions and serving Charlegin's subjects. They were cordial to each other. Although Zander and his sister always knew that they weren't in love.

There were no hushed conversations or private jokes.

No stolen moments of affection. No long hours spent together.

Nothing like what he felt for Marie, for example.

"Doggie." Abella lifted the wooden piece from the animal puzzle she was playing with.

"Yes, Bell-bell, that's a dog."

"Doggie bow-wow."

"Right, a dog says bow-wow."

Abella went back to her play.

"When you brought Marie to the palace, I saw how you gazed into each other's eyes like you were the only two people on earth. And at the gala, how you interacted as a couple with a bond that was palpable."

"What are you saying, Mother?"

"That I had an ulterior motive in coming to Cannes today. I wanted to talk to you in person. To tell you that I've had a change of heart."

"How so?"

"Long ago, what the press thought of me wasn't the real issue between your father and me," Claudine confessed after a sip of her drink.

"Oh?"

"I never told you about Louis." Her mouth minced a couple of times before she spoke again. "Louis was the boy I was truly in love with. His family lived a few doors down from mine in dreadful Roubaix. Louis was a car mechanic. Blue jeans and white T-shirts, all muscle and libido. You get the idea."

Having never heard about this before, Zander was spellbound.

"My father became disabled when I was a teenager. Years hunched over factory machinery left him with constant back pain and unable to work. Mother was a laundress but didn't make enough money to support the household."

Zander vaguely remembered his maternal grandparents, who died decades earlier.

"After I met your father," Claudine continued, "I was faced with a choice."

Understanding of his mother's words washed across Zander. He laid his hand over his cheek where Marie had last kissed it. He could still feel her there. He slowly confirmed, "Stay with the boy you loved or marry the prince who would take care of your family."

"I never mentioned Louis ever again. I had no reason to hurt your father, who has shown me nothing but generosity. But I will never forget." Claudine let out a prolonged sigh before she added, "I know I wasn't an attentive mother. I think I've filled my life with silly pursuits to compensate for the love I left behind."

"And you're telling me all of this now."

"Because I don't want you to make a similar mistake." She reached across the table and put her hand over Zander's. "My greatest wish is that you follow your heart."

Were he to take his mother's advice, he knew exactly where his heart would lead him. Into the arms of the woman who had changed him forever. Learning about the terrible consequences she'd had to withstand only made him respect and admire her more. She'd grown into a brave adult who was devoted, caring and considerate. Not to mention kind and alive and passionate.

Yes, his heart belonged to Marie Paquet. He was in love with her. And wanted to spend the rest of his life with her, and didn't care a hoot what the press or anyone else had to say about it.

What's more, he suspected she loved him, too.

He wondered what his sister would think of all of this. He'd bet she'd want him to find love and to create a true family for Abella to grow up in.

"Thank you, Mother." Zander maneuvered his hand from under his mother's to on top of hers, where he gave it a squeeze.

"Now," Claudine said afterward, getting off her chair and sitting down on the ground covering next to Abella, "may I please play with my granddaughter?"

Marie glanced up from her computer when she heard a rustling just outside of her office. At eye level, she didn't see anything so went back to her work. When she heard it again, she tracked a more thorough search.

No wonder she had missed it the first time. Because walking into her office was not an adult of typical height. Bending her neck downward, Marie watched Her Highness Crown Princess Abella de Nellay of Charlegin waddle in as if she owned the place.

She sang out. *"Frère Jacques, Frère Jacques..."*

"Dormez-vous?" Marie joined her. *"Dormez-vous?"*

The interlude was followed by a massive gulp in Marie's throat as it struck her that the eighteen-month-old didn't arrive at the APCF on her own.

After acknowledging Abella's angel-like hair, Marie lifted her eyes to see the man she loved standing in her doorway.

"May I come in as well?"

Marie's eyes felt so heavy it was a struggle to keep them open. It was almost as if she didn't want to actually see Zander, so unbearable was it to know she could never have him for her own. Yet a quiet murmur told him, "Of course."

Closing the door behind him, he moved to her side of the desk, beckoning her to stand up. When she did, he hugged her right away. Her arms wrapped around him, the rigid muscles of his back pleasing to her hands. He drew her close, which sent her into a swoon she could scarcely afford. So as soon as she had the composure to, she pulled away. That was enough.

But Zander insisted she retain eye contact. "Why haven't you returned my messages?"

"You know why." She hadn't had any communication with him since creeping out of his room in the mansion the morning after the gala last week. When they had made the soul-melding, earth-shattering love that only two people who truly cared about each other could.

"No, tell me. I want to hear it in your own words."

Marie desperately needed this. In addition to the heartbreak of knowing that she and Zander couldn't be together, she was also harboring guilt about the way everything unfolded. Getting the chance to say what she hadn't would be cathartic.

"I can only sincerely apologize for not being up-front with you. I hadn't meant to keep anything a secret but I didn't think my life, my background, was of any importance as an employee for the gala. And when you asked me to attend the events around town with you, it didn't occur to me that the eyes of the world would be watching."

"That's on me. Not you," Zander said and he reached with one of his hands for hers. That warmth that always emanated from his palm flowed up her arm. "I'm the one who's responsible for my own notoriety. Frankly, I didn't think about it, either. Since I'd been shunning the limelight as much as possible, I'd forgotten how gluttonous the gossip machine can be."

"I know you have the baby to shield." She looked over at darling Abella, who was occupying herself by touching everything in Marie's office. "And you have your own reputation to guard."

He reached for her other hand so that he could hold both. "Listen to me. That's unacceptable, the idea that associating with you would somehow sully my character. To be spending my time with a smart and beautiful woman whose inner strength and fortitude has allowed her to overcome inconceivable obstacles. I'm proud, not ashamed, to be seen with you."

"We'd be chased and dismembered at every step we'd take. You don't need that. You need…"

"You," he interrupted. "I need you. Abella does, too. She'll have a kinship with you she would never find elsewhere. When she's old enough to feel the rootlessness of not having parents, you'll be there to show her the way through the darkness. We both need you."

Marie could hardly take in the words he was saying.

"I want you to come with Abella and me to live in my Paris apartment. She's getting older and needs to stay in one place. To have a routine. Other children to play with."

Zander was asking her to move to Paris with him?

"Instead of lending my name to so many causes and attending all these events, I'm starting my own charitable foundation. Run it with me. We'll do great and important work together."

Again Marie's head swam from everything he was telling her. His own foundation? Operating it with him? "Zander, we're too far apart. I don't know how to live in your world."

"I love you. And I always will. Everything else will sort itself out."

When she started to protest, he silenced her by pressing his lips to hers. His hands released hers so that his fingers could caress both sides of her face as he delivered many more kisses.

There was no defense for his kisses, despite her feeble attempt. "Zander, listen to reason. You and I can't be. The press and your subjects will…"

"What? What can they do? We'll know the truth of what matters. That I love you. And you love me." He leaned down to pick up Abella. "What does the nursery rhyme say? *Sticks and stones will break my bones but words will never hurt me?*"

With Abella in his left arm, he used his right to bring Marie into a three-person embrace. "We love Marie. Don't we, Bell-bell?"

"Ma," Abella confirmed. With her chubby pink finger, she pointed to Zander and said, "Da." And then back to Marie to repeat, "Ma."

Marie and Zander grinned into each other's eyes.

And then the little family showered each other with tickle kisses until all three of them were laughing from the pits of their happy bellies.

* * * * *

To my baby brother, Charles Duarte. Thank you for moving in and giving me this wonderful opportunity to reconnect and bond with you even more. Even though I've got more experience at life, you have grown into such a patient and wise man, I often find myself coming to you for advice. I love you, Chaddy.

It had been six months since Ethan had officially left the United States Navy and landed in the small town of Sugar Falls, Idaho, to restart his life. Yet, except for the gourmet coffee maker sitting on the counter, the tiny kitchen in the apartment he'd rented above a downtown storefront was still just as sparse as the day he'd moved in.

The place had come furnished with only the basics and every once in a while, Ethan might pick up a few things at the market to add to the fridge. But it wasn't as though he enjoyed many meals at home. For some recovering alcoholics, socializing and eating at local restaurants with full-service bars might prove to be too much of a temptation. With Ethan, though, dining out provided him with more accountability—more eyes watching to keep him in line.

Besides, when he was alone, he had too much time to think.

As the coffee brewed, he made his way back to the bathroom and cranked the shower faucet to the highest setting. He was barely under the steaming spray long enough to get wet when he heard a pounding knock.

It wasn't even 0700 yet, so the chances of someone paying him a social call this early were pretty slim. *They probably have the wrong apartment,* he thought as he washed the shampoo from his hair. Yet, the knocking continued. Ethan debated staying in the shower and just ignoring whomever was banging on his front door. But what if it was a neighbor who needed a favor? Or a friend from one of his meetings who needed some encouragement?

Stepping out on the cold tile floor, he grabbed a towel and made his way toward the hall as he dried himself.

"Hold on a sec!" he yelled, crossing to his bedroom and grabbing a pair of jeans off the top of his dresser. The knocking paused briefly, but resumed before he could get his fly buttoned. Geez, what was this person's major emergency?

He tugged one of the thermal shirts off the hanger so quickly, the plastic triangle flew off the nearly empty closet rod. Ethan barely had his arms shoved through the sleeves when he finally yanked open the front door.

A woman he didn't recognize stood outside on the narrow landing, a lit cigarette hanging from the tight, thin line that was her mouth. She flicked the cigarette over the railing, not bothering to see where it landed below, and exhaled a cloud of smoke. "Ethan Renault?"

"Can I help you?" he replied without confirming his identity.

"You the same Ethan Renault who went to Sam Houston High?"

He narrowed his gaze, studying the woman before him. There were dark circles under her eyes and a permanent crease between her brows, as though she wore a constant frown. Had he gone to school with her?

When he didn't immediately respond, she continued. "Yep, it's you all right. Your hair might be shorter, but you still do that twitching thing with your fingers that makes you look like you're about to run off at the drop of a hat."

Ethan shoved his hands in his pockets and rocked forward on the balls of his bare feet. "Do I know you?"

The woman gave a snort, as though she expected quite a different response when she showed up unannounced on a stranger's doorstep this early in the middle of February. But Ethan patiently waited her out.

It was then that he noticed someone else standing on the stairs behind her. A young girl with dark, tangled hair holding a plastic grocery store bag kept her head down, fixated at the hole on her canvas sneaker where her big toe was popping through.

"I'm Chantal DeVecchio," the woman finally said, her added eye roll conveying her annoyance at not having been recognized right away. "And this," she said, gesturing to the girl, "is your daughter, Trina."

"But I don't have a daughter," Ethan told the woman who no longer looked anything like the eighteen-year-old cheerleader he'd once taken to the prom. His chest felt as though it was caving inward and he had to straighten his back and brace a hand against the door frame.

"She's yours," Chantal said. "And it's about time you man up and take care of your responsibilities."

Ethan's spine stiffened even more at the insult to his masculinity and the implication of his negligence. His eyes darted between his former high school girlfriend and the dark-haired child who appeared to only be interested in the patterns her sneakers made on the snow-covered steps. While he didn't know much about raising kids, he at least knew better than to let them go running around without socks when it was only twenty degrees outside.

"Why didn't you call me?" What he really wanted to ask was why had Chantal waited almost twelve years to spring such a life-changing surprise on him. "Or tell me before now?"

One minute, he'd been getting ready to head out for his regular breakfast over at the Cowgirl Up Café, wondering if today would be the day he'd finally convinced the shy server who waited on him every morning to go out on a date. The next minute, someone was banging on his front door and then accusing him of being a deadbeat dad to a child he'd never even known about.

"Because I didn't find out I was pregnant until after you'd joined the Navy and shipped out. It wasn't like you left a forwarding address before you and your dad ran out of town that summer."

It was true, Ethan had enlisted right after graduation. His dad was in the oil rigging business, constantly on the move to different cities depending on the latest job. Ethan had already switched high schools five times in three years and, that summer, the only new start he'd been eager to make was the change that would finally begin his adult life.

Scanning the alley behind the row of Victorian buildings that made up the downtown business district of Sugar Falls, Ethan realized that the local merchants would soon be filling up those parking spaces. "Maybe you should come inside and we can talk about this."

"Nothing to talk about," Chantal said, snatching the plastic sack out of her—and possibly his—daughter's hand and tossing it into his entryway. A purple T-shirt spilled out and landed on his bare foot. "I can't do this anymore. I'm just not cut out for motherhood. It's your turn to step up and be a father."

She turned around and gave Trina's shoulder an awkward hug. "I'm sorry, Trina," she said, a hint of sadness creeping into her voice. "But it's for the best. You'll see."

Chantal then brushed past the girl and marched down the steps. Ethan took a few strides to chase after the woman, but only made it halfway down the staircase when he realized that the child wasn't following. Or begging her mom not to leave her. The poor thing just stood there, looking as miserable as Ethan felt.

Something was ricocheting in his chest with a thumping urgency, but his body remained perfectly still. He needed to do something, to say something, but all he could do was grip the wrought iron handrail until his brain and his body could work in sync.

What he wouldn't give for a shot of bourbon right about now. Or for a call from his AA sponsor. But no amount of booze or platitudes or even SEAL team combat training could've prepared Ethan for the blow he'd just been dealt.

Not knowing what to do, his feet grew restless and the snow squishing between his toes began to sting, causing him to take a step toward the girl. Then he froze up all over again, like that time in Kabul when he and his buddy Boscoe faced an unexpected rainstorm of firepower. One wrong move could cause everything to blow up in his face. Worse than it already had.

An engine turned over in the alley below his apartment and he looked over his shoulder in time to see Chantal speeding off in a Geo Storm that might've been yellow twenty years ago. The shredded end of a rope holding the hatchback down to the bumper dragged along the wet asphalt as she made her escape.

A shiver started between Ethan's shoulder blades and traveled its way down his back. He ran a hand through his still damp hair and faced the young girl huddled on his porch.

His gut was telling him that it couldn't be possible for him to have a daughter. However, in the right light, if the child would look up and shove some of the stringy, black hair from her eyes, Ethan might concede that she somewhat resembled his French grandmother.

To be fair to Chantal, he had to admit he hadn't exactly kept track of every person he'd ever slept with over the years, but certainly he would've remembered if he'd gotten someone pregnant. Wouldn't he?

The girl made a sniffing sound, as though her nose was running, but she still didn't raise her head or look in his direction.

Shame flooded through him at the realization that he'd never even thought to ask her if she was okay. Or to try and put the child at ease. He opened his mouth to say something but couldn't command his tongue to form any words and ended up snapping it closed again. Damn. He was already proving himself to be a crappy father.

Clearing his throat, he reminded himself that he was once a member of an elite Special Forces team and had encountered dangers far graver than an eleven-year-old landing on his doorstep. "Hi," he said. "I'm Ethan."

"I know," the girl whispered, then wrapped a scrawny arm around her waist. It was then that he noticed she wasn't even wearing a sweater, let alone a coat.

"Why don't you come inside, Trina? It's freezing out here."

The girl eventually lifted her face and his lungs seized. Her eyes weren't wide with fear, as Ethan would've expected. Nor were they filled with humiliation or hurt, which would've been understandable given the way her mother had just dumped her here. Instead, they were completely without expression. Witnessing their empty depths would've been downright spooky if he hadn't recognized that same look in his own eyes the night after his last covert ops assignment. Or recognized the identical sapphire-blue color that ran rampant in the Renault family.

Trina didn't decline his invitation, but she wasn't exactly quick to make a decision either. She had to be equally as afraid of him as he was of her. Stranger danger and all that. She must've heard her mother announce that he was her father, but that didn't mean she necessarily believed it. Well, that made two of them.

Being careful not to touch her as he stepped around her shivering form, Ethan held open the door, hoping that the heat coming from his apartment would be more inviting than the ugly used furniture inside. He was about to go into the kitchen and grab his cell phone to call for backup when finally, with an apprehensive look cast in Ethan's direction, her feet shuffled toward him.

Trina gave him a measured glance before swooping low to grab her purple T-shirt and shoving it back into her grocery bag. She held the recovered belongings close to her chest, as though they were some sort of shield that could protect her from him.

"Are you hungry?" Ethan asked. He left the front door wide-open as he walked toward the kitchen, not wanting her to feel trapped. Would she follow? Or would she run off, just as her mother had?

"Kinda," Trina replied, her voice again no louder than a whisper. She was on the thin side and he wondered when she'd had her last meal.

Ethan stared at his bare counters, knowing full well the only thing he could offer the girl right now would be a mug of triple-brewed dark roast.

"I…uh…wasn't exactly expecting company." He shoved his hands in his pockets and rocked back on his heels. "I usually eat breakfast at the café across the street."

Trina tilted her head at him, her blue eyes still empty, her arms still clutched tightly to her in apprehension. If she was truly his daughter, Ethan wanted to do the right thing by her. He just wasn't convinced that taking care of her all by himself would be the right thing.

He really could use some direction here. This town was

bursting with know-it-all busybodies who had opinions on everything from which colors to paint the historical homes to who should play point guard for the high school basketball team. Unfortunately, none of those people were currently inside his apartment.

"I've got an idea," Ethan said, but Trina's blank expression didn't waver. "I'm going to grab my coat and, uh, something for you to put on to keep warm, and we'll go across the street and grab a hot breakfast."

Surely someone over at the Cowgirl Up Café would have an idea of what he should do with the girl.

"I'll be right back," he said, walking down the hallway toward his bedroom. As he looked at the few clothes hanging in his closet, he wondered if Trina would still be standing in his living room when he came out. Or had she already made a run for it the second he turned his back? It was what he would've done in her situation.

But she was right where he'd left her when he returned with a fleece-lined hooded sweatshirt branded with the eagle and trident logo. "Here, this is the best I could come up with. But we're not going very far."

She had to drop her bag on the scuffed dining room table to take the sweatshirt from him. He sat at one of the cheap pine chairs to pull on his work boots, trying not to notice the way Trina kept having to push the sleeves up her arms to keep her hands from getting drowned by the heavy material of the borrowed sweatshirt.

Locking the front door behind him, Ethan realized that Trina was very careful not to get in front of him. She would only follow after he'd already passed. Whenever his team had infiltrated compounds and taken captives or brought in noncombatants for questioning, they'd been trained to always stay behind the enemy—to never turn their backs on a potential threat.

The thought that his own daughter might view him as a threat made his stomach go sour, however, Ethan didn't say anything as they walked down the steps to the alley and then through the narrow walkway that put them out on to Snowflake Boulevard. When they got on the main street of town, he glanced down the block toward the new public safety building that housed both the police department and the fire station. It would be so easy to lead Trina over there and drop her off. His mind calculated how long it would take him to leave her at the entrance and then hop into his secondhand truck and drive down the mountain to the Boise airport.

How long would it take to leave this whole mess behind him?

But he'd lived his life being on the move, alternating between taking on the most dangerous assignments to come through his unit and then drowning himself in a bottle to escape the unpleasantness of the world. The whole point of his leaving the Navy and relocating to Sugar Falls was so he could finally slow down, sober up and figure out what his next chapter would be.

He just hadn't expected fatherhood to be on the first page.

Monica Alvarez was balancing a tray of refilled salt and pepper shakers in one hand and a pot of decaf in the other when the tingling bell sounded above the saloon-style front doors of the Cowgirl Up Café. As a part-time waitress, early Wednesday mornings were usually her easiest shifts—most of the weekend tourists were long gone, replaced with only a handful of regulars lounging in their favorite booths, ordering their usuals, which she now had memorized. However, it wasn't the blast of frigid air coming in from outside that made the welcoming smile fade from Monica's lips.

It wasn't even the arrival of the hunky contractor who ordered the same exact breakfast—four scrambled egg whites, turkey sausage patties, sliced tomatoes and black coffee with a side of flirtatious banter—that made her pause. It was the unexpected appearance of a young girl cowering behind him that had stopped Monica in her tracks and caused the ceramic cowboy boot–shaped spice shakers on her tray to wobble.

The first time she'd waited on Ethan Renault several months ago, she'd written him off as a harmless bad boy who would eventually give up once he figured out that she wasn't interested in his type. Initially, it had been easy to brush off the sexy smirk and ignore the lazy way his thick-lashed eyes followed her as she messed up orders and proved herself to be an incompetent waitress.

But the man had been patient and stealthy and, occasionally, he'd even made her laugh. Last week, when she'd been at her real job, Ethan had come into the library and asked for a recommendation. Anyone who knew her understood that the best way to get Monica involved in a conversation was to talk about books. That's how she related best to people, by understanding them as readers firsts. Knowing a person's reading habits revealed so much, it was like a secret superpower that only librarians and booksellers possessed.

She'd given him a copy of *Rejection for Dummies* and he'd happily taken it without batting his handsome blue eyes. Then, the first thing he'd told her Monday morning was that the book was okay, but that he was waiting for the movie. While Monica hadn't had the time—or the desire—to date much since college, she'd had a feeling that his line was a lead-in and that Ethan would've asked her out to the movies if a very confused and agitated Gran hadn't called the restaurant right then and needed Monica to come home to help find the cat that they didn't own.

Today, she'd been expecting him to pick up the flirtatious banter right where he'd left off and she'd even toyed around with the idea of accepting his offer—if he asked her out, anyway—because she could barely remember the last time she'd gotten out and had a little fun for herself.

However, there was nothing jovial or flirty about the man right this second. In fact, the deep grooves along his brow and the hardened line of his jaw made him look like a completely different person—like he'd been hiding his true personality all along.

With only two other occupied booths in the restaurant this early in the morning, there were half a dozen sets of eyes trained on the new arrivals. The curious stares coupled with the silence spoke volumes and reassured Monica that she wasn't the only one who'd noticed that something was out of the ordinary.

A prickling sensation made its way down the back of her neck and she cleared her throat. "Table for two?"

"Uh…yeah," he finally said, and glanced behind him at the girl. Ethan normally walked into the restaurant with a grin and a sense of purpose, saying hello to all the locals before grabbing his favorite seat at the end of the counter. Today, though, he didn't make a move toward his usual spot despite the fact it was empty. He didn't really move at all.

"How about that table over there." Monica used her chin to nod toward an empty corner booth that was on

the opposite side of where the other diners were now blatantly staring at them.

"Great," Ethan replied, and began walking in that direction. He took a few steps, then paused and turned to
the child. "Is this okay?"

The girl's only response was to follow behind him,
her head not lifting. Something about the child tugged at
Monica's heart and reminded her of how shy and awkward she'd once been at that same age.

Monica took the tray of shakers to the prep station
and switched out the pot of decaf for regular coffee, since
Ethan normally drank at least three cups.

When she returned to their table, she passed them
both laminated menus. Not that Ethan ever needed one,
but something was definitely off about him this morning
and she no longer knew what to expect. Using the same
smile she used during the tiny tots reading circle at the
library, she faced the girl and said, "Hi. I'm Monica."

The child lifted her face and Monica gasped at the re-
semblance to Ethan. Their mouths were the same shape
and their chins shared matching dimples. If the girl's
stringy hair was washed and brushed, it would likely
be the exact inky-black shade as Ethan's, as well. Yet,
it was the bottomless sapphire-blue eyes that were the
dead giveaway.

They were definitely related.

That didn't make sense, though. Monica could've
sworn that she'd once overheard him bragging about being
single and carefree. Plus, she was positive that he'd told
Freckles, the owner of the café, that his mom died when
he was a boy and his father had passed away a few years
ago and he didn't have any other family.

So then where had this child come from?

If Freckles hadn't taken the morning off, the nosy older woman would've been asking all kinds of questions, like whether this was the girl's first time in Sugar Falls and how long was she visiting. Unfortunately, Monica wasn't quite as smooth when it came to starting conversations with the customers. Sure, she liked listening to people talk and picking up information here and there, but she didn't have that ability of asking the right kinds of questions to illicit much more than a two- or three-word response. Unless it was about their favorite books.

But a million questions were floating through her head as she stared at the child, who was having trouble keeping her hands pushed through the sleeves of the man-size sweatshirt she'd obviously borrowed from Ethan.

There was still snow outside this time of year. Where was the girl's jacket?

Monica turned over Ethan's mug and poured him a steaming cup of coffee, but he avoided eye contact so she couldn't read any clues on his normally friendly face. Turning to the girl, she said, "It's pretty cold this morning. How about some hot chocolate?"

The girl's eyes grew wide, and for an instant, an almost…craving expression flashed across her face, as though she'd never wanted anything more. Yet, her only reply was to study Ethan with a guarded look.

"Do you like hot chocolate?" Ethan asked her, and the girl nodded slowly. "Then hot chocolate it is." He turned to Monica. "This is Trina. We're still…uh…getting to know each other."

A chill spread through Monica, making her skin prickle with unease. Stumbling backward, she retreated to the prep station behind the counter. She fumbled with the bottle of chocolate sauce several times as she thought about Ethan's odd response. How did he not know the girl before now? They were clearly related.

Monica caught a movement out of the corner of her eye and turned just in time to see Trina dart into the hallway leading toward the restrooms. A hissing sound, followed by a blast of steam, drew her attention back to the complex frothing machine her boss had installed a few weeks ago and she barely got the thing shut off in time to prevent the hot milk from splattering everywhere. Monica cupped the warm mug in her trembling hands as she quickly walked to the table where Ethan was now sitting alone.

She needed to hurry if she wanted to talk to him before Trina returned from the restroom. Out of all the questions she wanted answered, the first one that came tumbling out of her mouth was, "Is she yours?"

Monica winced at her own words, her whisper-soft tone not making the personal question sound any less rude.

But Ethan either hadn't been bothered or he was too absorbed in his own thoughts to notice the impolite tone. He shrugged his shoulders, the expression on his face almost trancelike. "That's what her mother said when she left her on my front porch this morning."

"What do you mean, her mother left her on your front porch?" Monica had to brace her hand on the cowhide printed backrest of the booth. She was no longer whispering, drawing the curious stares from the other side of the restaurant.

"She knocked on my door this morning. I didn't even recognize her."

"Trina?" Disgust rose in Monica's throat. How had the man not recognized his own daughter?

"No. Her mom. I guess we dated in high school and…"

Ethan gave another shrug and it was all she could do not to grab two fistfuls of his plaid work shirt and shake the rounded muscles of his shoulders.

"You *guess*?" Monica swallowed a lump of annoyance. She wasn't only ticked off with his answer, she was angry with herself. Disappointed at how easily she'd been blinded by her building attraction to a man who didn't seem to know anything about his own daughter—including her existence. "So where is her mother now?"

"Her mother?" His brows formed a V and Monica rolled her eyes in frustration. She could handle Ethan easily enough when he was being a charming flirt, or even when he professed to be interested in her tongue-in-cheek book recommendations. However, if he was hoping this whole confused pretense would draw her sympathy, he was sorely mistaken.

"Yes. The person you dated back in high school? The mother of your child?"

"Right. Chantal drove off. She said she wasn't any good at being a mom and threw Trina's bag of clothes at me, telling me it was my turn to step up."

There was nothing more reprehensible than a man who didn't take care of his responsibilities. No amount of sex appeal or charm could make up for a lack of character. Her own father had been the same way and Monica shuddered at how close she'd come to falling under Ethan's spell.

At how close she'd come to repeating her own mother's same mistakes.

Chapter Two

Monica's growing revulsion was soon replaced with pity as Trina returned from the bathroom, her chin low and her face averted from the curious stares from the other customers as she carried a balled-up blue sweatshirt under one arm. Monica took in his daughter's lanky unwashed hair and the oversize T-shirt advertising Mesquite Muffler Mart and Automotive Repair. Not exactly a fashion staple in most preteen girls' closets.

The child's voice was low and gravelly when she whispered, "Why do they all keep looking over here?"

Monica glanced toward her Wednesday morning regulars. Scooter and Jonesy, the two older cowboys, were mostly harmless although a little gossipy at times. She couldn't say the same for the other three ladies, who apparently weren't in any hurry to leave, despite the fact they'd already paid their checks and had their own local businesses to open.

Monica had grown up in Sugar Falls and, as much as she withered under the curious stares and wagging tongues, at least she was used to the presence of the small-town busybodies. It had to be twenty times worse for a child who was also an outsider.

"You know what?" Monica stood up straighter. "The cook is out on a smoke break. Why don't you guys come on back to the kitchen and I'll fix your breakfast myself? It's much more private back there."

She was still holding the mug of hot chocolate and tried to give Trina a reassuring smile before leading the way toward the swinging door. It took a few seconds before the girl followed, and Monica pulled out the single wooden stool near a stainless steel counter for Trina, not bothering with a thought for where Ethan would sit.

He could either plop himself on the ground or go on and slither out the front door for all she cared. Instead, she had to hold back every insulting word on the tip of her tongue when Ethan finally wormed his way back into the kitchen. After all, it wouldn't be fair to say anything that might upset Trina, the poor little girl who'd just been abandoned by her own mother.

Monica added a heavy dollop of whipped cream to the mug of cocoa and handed it to the waif of a child. "Careful, it's hot."

Ethan must've left his own coffee back at the table and Monica couldn't help but shoot daggers at the man who stood by the door, his hands buried in his jean pockets and his eyes darting around nervously, as though he was also plotting his own escape. As though leaving a child behind was no different than abandoning his cup of coffee.

A knot of concern wedged between her rib cage. Monica had also grown up without a father, but at least she'd had Gran. Trina, on the other hand, didn't seem to have anyone. Maybe someone should call child protective services or even the police department and file some sort of report. She made a mental note to do some research on it. Once she got Trina fed.

"Would you like blueberries in your pancakes?" Monica asked.

Trina shot a questioning glance to her father. Or at least the man who'd sired her. "Does that cost extra?"

"I…uh…" Ethan's normally cocky voice stuttered and Monica would've laughed at how many notches his ego must've been taken down if the circumstances hadn't come at Trina's expense. He moved closer and leaned a hip against the basin of the prep sink. "You can get whatever you want. Don't worry about the cost."

The girl let out a breath and put an elbow onto the counter, resting her chin on her palm as she studied the man. Monica poured some batter onto the griddle and threw in a scoop of blueberries, constantly glancing back over her shoulder to watch the silent staring contest between father and daughter.

"Only rich people say things like 'don't worry about the cost,'" Trina said, and Monica choked back a giggle. She was glad to see that the child was finally finding her voice and speaking up. "Are you one of those guys who lives in a crappy apartment, but you're really a secret billionaire?"

"I'm not rich. And my apartment isn't *that* crappy. I mean it's not really decorated or anything because I've only lived there a few months. And I wasn't exactly expecting company."

"Ethan," Monica warned, unsure of the direction that this conversation was taking and not wanting the man to do any further damage than he'd already done by being an absent father for the past however many years. "How old are you, Trina?"

"Eleven."

"Wow." Ethan exhaled a long, slow hiss of air. "I didn't... I don't... I... Wow. I've never been in this situation before."

"It's fine if you don't want me," Trina said when Ethan apparently couldn't finish whatever it was he'd been trying to say. Whatever cheap apologies he might've offered for missing the first eleven years of her life. "I have a caseworker back in Galveston. If you call her, she'll get me a bus ticket or an emergency foster home or something."

"Have you been in foster care before?" Ethan asked, inching closer, and Monica held her breath, praying the young girl had somehow had a happy and fulfilling life up until now.

"Every year or so, my mother decides that she can't deal with me or with life and takes off somewhere. I used to live with my grandmother, but Gran died a few months ago."

"Oh," was all Ethan could say, and Monica clenched the spatula tighter, her heart clenching at the girl's casual indifference about her situation.

"I have a Gran, too," Monica offered, sliding a very uneven pancake onto a plate. Cooking wasn't exactly her forte, but neither was waitressing. "She also raised me after my father left."

Trina smiled and mumbled a "Thanks." But Monica wasn't sure if it was for the attempt at making her breakfast or for the attempt at understanding her situation. Or both.

Ethan must've heard something he didn't like, though, because he scrunched up his nose and attempted a subtle head shake at Monica. Perhaps he didn't appreciate someone pointing out the obvious comparison to another deadbeat dad, but he couldn't very well deny that he'd also left his daughter. Well, Monica supposed he *could* deny knowing about her in the first place, but he apparently knew better than to discuss all of his excuses right in front of the poor girl.

Monica set the dish in front of Trina and said, "Eat up and then we'll figure out who we need to call."

"Why would we need to call anyone?" Ethan asked. "And can I get one of those pancakes?"

"No, you may not." Monica squared her shoulders and turned toward him. Stepping behind Trina, who was drowning her plate in syrup, Monica jerked her thumb at the area in the corner where Freckles kept the stacks of flour and the cans of shortening for her famous biscuits. Walking that way, she had to wave an arm at Ethan who was slow to get the hint.

It was a tighter spot than she'd anticipated, and when he wedged his muscular six-foot frame in next to her, she was hit with the lemony scent of his shampoo. His face was only inches from hers and she lowered her gaze to the soft flannel of his work shirt and the way it stretched across his broad chest.

To get her mind off his physical nearness, Monica curled her fingers into her palms, squeezing until her nails dug into her hands. Finally, she was able to lift her head and unclench her jaw long enough to whisper, "What do you mean 'why would we need to call anyone?'"

"If she's my daughter, then she's not going back to some social worker in Galveston."

If she's his daughter? It didn't take a paternity test to prove the two looked exactly alike, including those haunted blue eyes.

"Lower your voice," she admonished, squinting past him to see if Trina had overheard. "She isn't a lost puppy. You can't just take a child home and keep her."

"Why not?" he asked, and her frustration mounted, heating her face. Or maybe it was the way his bicep brushed against her shoulder when he shoved his hands into his jean pockets.

She didn't have a legal argument, or at least she wouldn't until her shift was over and she went to the library and did some research. So Monica attempted to argue using common sense. "Because she doesn't know you, Ethan. She's got to be terrified."

"And sending her off with some stranger to a foster home wouldn't be even scarier?"

"I can hear you, you know," Trina called out, not bothering to turn around.

Monica pursed her lips and shot Ethan a pointed look of annoyance since she couldn't very well say, *Now look what you did.*

"Sorry, Trina." Ethan returned to where his daughter was seated.

Monica held her breath. She really should be back in the dining room, checking on her customers. But her heart was tearing apart at the way the girl just shrugged everything off, no longer making eye contact with the man who'd fathered her.

"I'm normally not so rude," he offered, and Monica had to give him that. In fact, Ethan was usually quite a smooth talker. Too smooth, if you asked her. "But seeing you, finding out…well, I've just been caught off guard."

Just then, Scooter Deets, one of the old-timers who ate at the café every morning, sauntered by the pass-through window and held up a hot pink coffee mug. Scooter had checked out a book on plumbing two years ago and his overdue fine was pushing triple digits. "Don't mind me, y'all. I'm just grabbing myself a refill."

Trying to fill up on gossip was more like it, Monica thought.

"I'll be right there," she said to the cowboy, who was normally hard of hearing unless there was something juicy going on. Monica turned to Trina. "Give me a couple of minutes and we'll put our heads together and figure something out."

"What's there to figure out? She's my daughter. She's coming home with me."

Monica pursed her lips and pointed to the corner of shelves so that Trina wouldn't have to listen to them talking about her. Again. This time, when he followed her, Monica steeled herself for his closeness. "What do you even know about raising a child, much less a daughter?"

"Like I said, I'm a bit out of sorts, so you'll have to forgive me for being rude," Ethan started, indicating that something rude was about to come out of his normally smirking mouth. "But it really isn't your business."

The insult hit its mark and Monica's aggravated groan sounded more like a defensive gasp. "You're right, Ethan Renault. You're not my business at all, thank God. However, someone needs to be looking out for what's best for Trina and you obviously haven't shown an interest in doing so in the past."

"I didn't even know she existed before this morning," he hissed. "So how could I have shown *anything* in the past?"

"Psfhh." Monica's hands went to her hips. "The fact that you didn't know in the first place is telling enough."

"I was in high school the last time I saw her mom. I was just a dumb kid back then. How would you like someone to judge you for what you did when you were a teenager?"

The breath caught in Monica's throat. When she'd been that age, she'd been working two jobs and studying around the clock to keep her grades high enough to win a college scholarship. She was more likely to be judged for being a boring stick-in-the-mud.

The squeaking hinge of the kitchen's back door sounded and Monica looked up, expecting to see the cook returning from his break. Instead, she saw nobody. When she glanced over to where Trina was sitting, the only thing left was an empty plate.

"Oh hell," Ethan said, running a hand through his short hair and sprinting toward the door.

The flash of panic had been evident on his face and Monica suddenly regretted every accusation she'd just thrown his way. She'd been reliving all of her old painful memories of her own father and projecting those past hurts onto an easy target.

She followed Ethan to the back door, but before she could exit, he came barreling back inside. "She's not in the alley."

"Where do you think she could've gone?" Monica gnawed on her lower lip.

"I have no idea. I really don't know anything about her. When she showed up on my doorstep an hour ago, she looked cold and hungry. I didn't have anything for her to eat so that's why we came here. I was hoping to get some answers, but now she's disappeared."

A tinkling bell sounded over the front door and Monica wanted to stomp her foot in frustration. Now wasn't the time for more customers to show up.

"Maybe she went back to your place?" Monica suggested. Every fiber in her body wanted to chase after the poor girl and keep her safe, but she couldn't until the second waitress came on duty for her shift. "You go look for her there and I'll stay here in case she comes back."

"It took me eleven years to find her," Ethan said, his eyes pleading with Monica's as though she was the only one who could help him. "I don't want to lose her again."

"I have no clue where to even look for her," Ethan said to his boss over the phone's speaker as he slowly cruised his truck up and down Snowflake Boulevard, the center of the touristy Victorian downtown. Since he was expected at his contracting job at eight, it seemed only responsible to call his employer and confide in everything that had happened.

"Maybe you should call the police department," Kane Chatterson offered.

"I'm pretty sure I heard Monica Alvarez say she was going to call when I tore out of the Cowgirl Up half an hour ago. Hold on, my call waiting is beeping." Ethan looked at his screen and saw the number. His adrenaline, which had been pumping steadily until this point, suddenly nosedived. "It's the police. I'll call you back."

Switching over to the other line, Ethan didn't bother with pleasantries. "Carmen, did you find her?"

"Monica found her in the ladies' room at the Cowgirl Up," Officer Carmen Gregson replied, and Ethan's exhale came out in a whoosh. "Apparently, she circled back and went in the front door, but Monica didn't have your cell number. I'm heading over there now, but we might want to go somewhere a little less gossipy than the local diner so we can get this worked out."

The fear clenching around his gut lessened, yet Ethan's pulse remained elevated with apprehension. And confusion. Two hours ago, he didn't even know he had a daughter, didn't know his world could be so thrown off its axis before it got shaken up and thrown again.

Ethan eased his truck off the road and scrubbed at the lower half of his face, the face he hadn't had time to shave this morning. More air released from his lungs before he asked, "What do we need to work out?"

"Just a heads-up, Renault..." The police officer, his best friend's wife, was also former military and it put Ethan more at ease to have someone use his last name. "When Monica called it in, she said the girl mentioned something about a caseworker back in Texas. That means, by law, I'm required to notify them or the local child protective services."

"Will they take her from me?" Ethan hadn't exactly been doing cartwheels at the opportunity to be a father, but there was a ball of nausea welling up in his belly at the thought of his child—someone who shared his blood—being raised by a complete stranger.

"Why don't you meet me at the café and we can walk the girl over to the station or someplace else where we can talk."

"Right," Ethan said, returning his foot to the accelerator and steering back onto the road. "I'm on my way."

Thankfully, his first instinct wasn't to stop by the bar or the liquor store before he got there—not that either would be open this early. Still, it was a relief that his steady hands now offered his mixed-up mind some focus.

Ethan again toyed with the idea of calling his sponsor to tell him about this recent development, but he didn't quite know what was going on, let alone know how to explain it. The best thing he could do was talk to Trina and the authorities and figure out his next step.

By the time he found a parking spot on the street between the Cowgirl Up Café and his apartment, Officer Gregson and Monica were already walking his way. His daughter appeared even more fragile between the two adult females, her head down and her face hidden behind a mess of stringy, limp hair.

He'd heard about dads who fell in love with their newborns right there in the delivery room. Something must be wrong with Ethan then, because he hadn't experienced an instant bond with the girl when he'd first seen her outside his door this morning. In fact, she'd been a sullen, quiet little thing who would barely look at him—not that he could blame her. But now, desperation pricked at his skin as Trina approached and he needed some sort of sign that she was okay. Or at least, that she *would* be okay.

Carmen must've taken pity on Ethan's panicked expression because she told him, "The three of us had a good talk in the ladies' room and we all agreed that everyone would feel more comfortable talking at your place so we can get a better handle on the situation."

Ethan definitely didn't have a handle on any of this and it had to be obvious. Worse, they'd most likely overwhelmed the poor girl when he and Monica stood there arguing about his inability to raise a child right in front of her, essentially driving her away. While Monica's earlier accusations still rankled at him, now wasn't the time to continue that discussion.

As the trio of females silently trudged up the stairs behind him, Ethan unlocked his front door for more visitors than his apartment had ever held at one time. At least in the few months that he'd lived there.

"I need to use the bathroom," Trina mumbled as she walked past him and toward his hallway. His first instinct was to ask the girl why she was always running to the restroom, however, it might be easier to talk with the others if he didn't have to watch his words. Plus, there wasn't a window in there so it wasn't like Trina could escape. Again.

"Is this everything she has?" Monica folded a denim pair of shorts that had fallen out of the plastic grocery bag Trina had left on the dining room table earlier. "There isn't much inside here."

"Any paperwork?" Carmen asked her, and Ethan had to bite his tongue to keep from asking why Monica was even a part of this. "It would help if we had an official name or something to go by before I call any other agencies."

For such a seemingly shy and reserved woman, Monica certainly had no problem barging into his personal life and offering up her opinions. Although, Trina had definitely opened up more when the quiet librarian and part-time waitress had spoken to her. He wondered what else she and his daughter had discussed in that ladies' room while Ethan had been tearing through town in a full panic.

"Here," Monica said, holding up a pink-and-blue document titled Birth Certificate. Despite the lenses of her glasses, he could still see the hint of accusation in the woman's brown eyes as she focused on Ethan, her forehead lifted in a questioning crease. "Your name is listed under *Father*."

What had Ethan done wrong? He'd always used protection, even back then, never relying on someone else's methods of birth control. Yet, Monica was frowning at him as though he'd gotten *her* pregnant. As if her sleeping with him would ever be a possibility now.

Her rich, dark brown hair was piled up into its usual messy ponytail of curls and he preferred her in the snug, turquoise T-shirt all the waitresses at the café sported rather than in the monotone cardigan sweaters she usually wore at the library. Ethan thought Monica had been warming up to him the past month—she'd even begun to smile at him on the mornings she'd pulled extra shifts at the Cowgirl Up. She had a cute little dimple in the side of one cheek and each time he'd caught a flash of it, Ethan felt as though someone had given him a key to Heaven.

He'd be lying if he said he hadn't already given plenty of thought to what it would be like to get her out of her clothes completely, to be able to kiss every bit of her light amber skin and hopefully be the one to make her smile, over and over. Judging by her current glare, though, he doubted that he'd ever see that dimple again, let alone find out what was underneath that T-shirt. Maybe he'd dodged a bullet by not asking her out, after all.

"Let me see that." Carmen took the certificate before studying it. "Yep, your name is definitely on it."

Ethan walked over to Carmen and scanned the paper over her shoulder. "Trina DeVecchio Renault." She even had his last name.

"Date of birth, February 8." Eleven years ago. He didn't have to do much calculating to know the timing was right. Confusion made the corners of his lips turn down. "But I never signed anything. And my birth date on it is wrong. Hell, I didn't even know about the girl until today."

"Well, someone signed off on it and that's all that matters." Carmen hooked her thumbs in her leather duty belt. "I would still need to run everything through the system to make sure the document is legitimate, but if it is, then the kinship law would apply here."

"I have no idea what that means," Ethan admitted, glancing at Monica to see if she was judging him even more for not knowing anything about family law.

"Technically," Carmen continued. "This Chantal De-Vecchio, assuming she had legal custody of the girl in the first place, gave you temporary guardianship as another family member when she left her in your care. Therefore, the state will recognize you as Trina's temporary guardian."

"Is there a note or a paper in there that says she was giving her to me?" Ethan asked, looking at the bag in Monica's hands.

"No, just two pictures." Monica held up a photograph of an older woman sitting on the front porch of a mobile home—Trina's grandmother, perhaps. The second photo was actually on shiny magazine paper and showed a basket full of calico kittens.

Even Ethan had more personal belongings and mementos when he'd shipped off to basic training.

"For whatever it's worth—" Monica gave a quick glance toward the hallway then lowered her voice to the whisper-soft tone she normally used inside the library "—when I spoke to her in the ladies' room, she admitted that she would rather stay with you than go into foster care."

"Then why did she run off?" Ethan tried to whisper back, but it sounded more like an angry hiss.

"Probably because she thought you didn't want her?"

Monica put her hands on her hips and, if Ethan had been in his right mind, he would've appreciated the way her defensive stance showed off her lush curves. He'd been trying to get this woman out of her shell for the past few months, yet now that she was finally directing some passion his way, the angry heat in her eyes caused him to take a step back.

"I'd suggest hiring an attorney and making everything legal," Carmen said, typing something into her smartphone. "But, in the meantime, depending on what the CPS records show, as long as Trina's not a ward of the court, I feel comfortable releasing her into your custody."

One advantage to living in a small town was that when people knew you, they didn't mind giving you the benefit of the doubt. Ethan finally understood the next step he would have to take.

Now, he just needed to convince a scared and abandoned little girl that he was her best option. Too bad he hadn't convinced himself yet.

Chapter Three

"But what if she changes her mind and doesn't want to stay with him?" Monica asked Carmen when the two women got downstairs and circled around to the sidewalk in front of Domino's Deli. "What if she runs away again?"

"Then I'd suggest you let Freckles know that the girl might show up at the Cowgirl Up again. Maybe she thinks of it as a safe space."

"Does that mean you think she might not feel safe with him?"

"I know you're worried about the girl." Carmen placed a reassuring hand on her shoulder. "I can't predict the future any better than you can, but I got the impression that she ran off the first time thinking she was saving face. You know, getting away before her father could reject her. Kids that age have a tendency to act tough when they're afraid. When we talked to her back in the restaurant and told her that Ethan was out searching for her and seemed

genuinely worried about her well-being, she appeared willing to give him a chance. Listen, Monica, I never would've
released her into his custody if I thought it wasn't in her
best interest."

Monica had always liked and trusted the female police
officer, who preferred mysteries while her twin sons raced
through a couple of *Magic Tree House* books a week.
They'd never really socialized much, but then again, Monica wasn't much for hanging out with her neighbors or
attending the community activities.

She was too busy working two jobs and taking care of
Gran. Being pleasant and making small talk with the customers at the restaurant took all the energy she had left.
Still, she knew how to keep her eyes and ears open and
Carmen Gregson was compassionate with the townspeople, observant on her patrols, and dedicated to her job and
family. Everyone in town valued the woman's opinion.

Looking at her watch, Monica estimated that she had
fifteen more minutes before she would have to leave for the
library. So she didn't bother keeping the hesitation from her
voice as she asked, "What do you think of Ethan Renault?"

"In what way?" Carmen was a cop and an observer.
Like Monica, she probably did her research and analyzed
things from all angles.

"As a father, I guess." Monica stated the obvious when
what she really wanted to ask—what she'd really wanted
to know for the past few months—was if she was a complete fool for having a teensy tiny crush on the man.

But her ill-advised attraction to Ethan was something
she could barely acknowledge to herself. There was no
way she would say it out loud. Besides, now certainly
wasn't the time to ask about the guy's relationship suit-

ability—which had lost all potential anyway the second Trina showed up.

Carmen turned to face her, seeming to look beyond Monica's forced casual expression and deep down into what her mind was really thinking. Wrapping an arm around her midsection, Monica toyed with the tie of her apron, trying not to feel too exposed.

"He's one of my husband's best friends, so keep in mind that my opinion might be a little biased."

Monica nodded. "Grain of salt taken."

"When I first met Ethan, I would've pegged him for a typical Navy SEAL with a cocky ego and an adrenaline complex. The type of guy who doesn't mind breaking hearts or breaking bones if it involves having a good time. Although, I'd also pegged Luke the same way and he proved me wrong. I think Ethan has been through a lot and seen a lot, yet doesn't talk about the darker stuff. Probably hides it behind that flirty smile and arrogant charm."

So Monica wasn't the only one who'd noticed the lazy, seductive grin. Or the possibility of a string of broken hearts left in his wake. Resolution made her spine stiffen and her commitment to not fall prey to his flirtatious banter intensified.

"But," Carmen continued, "I also think he takes his responsibilities seriously and he isn't afraid of a little adversity. Luke told me that of all his former teammates, Ethan was the one he trusted the most. I know the guy probably doesn't seem like the fatherly type now, but Trina is in safe hands."

Monica gave a slight nod as she exhaled, but she still held on to her doubts. Her own father had come and gone from her life many times before he'd finally left for good. She and her mom had lived with Gran until Monica was six, and when her mother passed, Gran seemed to think that her dad might come back to get her. Part of Monica had been terrified that she would have to leave her grandmother and the only home she'd ever known. But the other part of her had been excited that she could have her father back, that she might finally get to experience a dad's love. Just like Monica, Trina had to be nervous and terrified of what awaited her, but maybe she was just a little excited, too. Excited that she would now get a chance to know the man who made up part of her DNA.

Unfortunately, that excitement would soon fade once Ethan let the girl down. Even with Carmen's vote of confidence on keeping her safe, there was no way a tried-and-true bachelor like him could change his ways and provide a nurturing home to a preteen who'd just had her world turned upside down.

For Trina's sake, Monica would hope for the best. But leopards didn't change their spots. It was a good reminder for the next time she found herself attracted to a man like Ethan. Blowing a curl out of her face, she couldn't believe that she'd been secretly enjoying his flirtatious banter every Monday and Wednesday when she'd waited on him during her breakfast shift, hoping he'd ask her out.

A crackling sound shot out from the walkie-talkie on Carmen's duty belt and Monica recognized the dispatcher's voice through the static. A retiree with a tie-dye shirt and comb-over hairstyle that didn't fool anyone, Harv Jenkins preferred science fiction and the occasional graphic novel. In addition to being a part-time dispatcher, he also volunteered at the senior citizens center and had always been sweet to Gran, despite the fact that her grandmother hated his comic book drawing classes. But his words today made Monica's pulse leap. "Be advised, we just got a call about the fire alarm going off at the Alvarez house again."

The siren from the nearby fire engine rang out and a heavy ball of dread settled in Monica's stomach, a familiar feeling lately where her grandmother was concerned.

"You want me to drive you in the patrol car?" Carmen offered.

"No thanks." Monica jogged across the street toward the Cowgirl Up Café and called over her shoulder, "As long as it's not as bad as last time, I'm going to need my own car to get to work after I check on her."

She'd already left her shift at the restaurant early to help with Trina. Now she was going to be late to open the library to help with Gran. And it was Western Wednesday, which meant that she only had thirty minutes before the Louis L'Amour book club arrived for their monthly meeting in the reading room.

At this rate, Monica was going to lose both of her jobs. And then where would she and Gran be?

Trina came out of the bathroom as soon as Monica and Carmen left. Ethan thought about offering to show her around the small apartment, but honestly, there wasn't much need for a tour at this point. Besides the kitchen and combination living room–dining room, there were only two bedrooms and she'd probably already seen those on her way down the hall.

Plus, she still hadn't said much directly to him and he didn't really know what to say either.

He tried to remember what he'd been like at that age. Sullen and defiant and lonely because his dad was often out of town working for days at a time, leaving Ethan alone to fend for himself. Swallowing down his own feelings of resentment, he decided to try a different tactic.

"So, you have a caseworker back home?" he asked. She'd casually mentioned as much back in the kitchen at the Cowgirl Up as though it were no big deal. As though every eleven-year-old had one of those. If she was anything like him, she would try to put on a tough front to cover how scared she was.

Trina shrugged, but at least it was a response.

So much for the small talk. Ethan took a deep breath, steeling himself for the tougher questions he knew he needed to ask. But before he could, she turned to face him, her eyes narrowed with doubt.

"Were you really a Navy SEAL?"

Okay, so if she wasn't going to talk about herself, maybe he could lure her into a conversation by letting down his own guard. "How did you know that?"

"I'm not blind." She pointed to a class picture in a frame on his fireplace mantel. Besides the small, fake plant he'd inherited from his dad, it was the only personal item in the room. "It says 'Basic Underwater Demolition/SEALS Training.' Plus, Chantal already told me you were in the Navy."

A jolt of surprise caught him, and not just because the girl referred to her mother by first name. "What else did your mom tell you about me?"

"That you got her pregnant and then took off."

"Trina…" Ethan took a cautious step forward, dipping his chin so he could catch her eyes. "I want you to understand that I *never* would've left if I'd known about you." If she didn't believe anything else about him, he needed her to know that he'd never intentionally abandoned anyone.

Instead of giving any indication that she heard his

words, Trina pivoted as she studied everything else in the living room but him. "She once told me that you dated anyone in a skirt."

Ethan's throat tightened. Was this how eleven-year-olds talked nowadays? He didn't want to call her mother's honesty into question, but he also didn't like the idea that the deck of lies was already stacked against him. "That's not exactly a fair assessment, considering we only knew each other for a couple of months and we both were in a rush to act like grownups. I was barely eighteen at the time."

"That's how old I'll be in seven years," Trina said without looking at him.

Whoa. He did a double take as he realized she was right. He'd already missed more than half of her childhood, more than eleven birthday parties according to the birth certificate in her bag. "So, you just had a birthday, huh?"

"I guess. You know, this apartment is a total dump."

He followed her gaze down the hall to the second bedroom, which held a creaky twin bed, a cheap dresser and all the cardboard boxes he'd had shipped from his storage unit in San Diego and never got around to unpacking. "Well, it came furnished and I only moved here six months ago. Speaking of which, how did your mom know where to find me?"

That got her attention and her lips went from a pout to a half smirk. "She didn't. I did."

Her admission floored him, but before he could ask how, a knock sounded at the door. If Ethan hadn't already been studying Trina, he would've missed the apprehension flashing through her eyes before she hung her head and focused on the toe of her canvas sneaker again.

When he peeked through the peephole, he recognized Kylie Gregson, Kane's sister, and Mia McCormick. Not only was Kylie related to his boss, she was also the sister-in-law of Ethan's best friend Luke. Kylie and her best friend Mia wouldn't come to his house unless it was for a good reason. A knot formed in his stomach and he glanced back to where Trina was standing. He wanted to communicate to her that he couldn't *not* answer, but his daughter wouldn't lift her face.

Daughter. He was still getting used to that word.

The knock sounded again, this time right against his temple which was resting against the door.

Smothering a groan, Ethan twisted the knob and let the women in.

"We can't stay," Kylie explained, passing him two paper shopping bags with handles. "But we wanted to drop off some stuff for Sugar Falls' newest resident."

If it had been anyone else, Ethan might've thought they were looking for an inside scoop. But he played poker on Thursday nights with both of their husbands and knew the women were sincere.

"What is it?" he asked.

"Mostly a hodgepodge of things a girl might need," Kylie said. Trina must've shown some interest from behind him because one of their unexpected visitors looked past Ethan and spoke to his daughter. "Hi. I'm Kylie Gregson. This is Mia McCormick. She owns the dance studio in town."

Mia lifted up a pink duffel bag. "I know these probably aren't your style, but there aren't a ton of shopping options in Sugar Falls besides the sporting goods store and Designs by Doris, which tends to only carry stuff for the…uh…senior generation, shall we say? Anyway, it was the best we could do on short notice."

The women held up their offerings, but Trina didn't make a move to take anything. She just stood there in her oversize T-shirt and jeans, her blue eyes were fixated on the bags as if they contained explosives. Ethan should've probably accepted them on her behalf, but his brain was still trying to catch up and process how the women not only knew that his daughter needed new stuff, but had gotten everything together so quickly.

"Anyway, I'll be going into Boise this weekend," Kylie said, setting the bags inside the entryway, before she took a retreating step onto the landing outside his front door. "So let me know if you want to pick out some different stuff. I'd be happy to take you shopping, if your dad is okay with that."

With a wink at Ethan, she and Mia were out the door and making their way down the stairs before Ethan could even offer so much as a thanks. He'd yet to think about where he would get suitable clothes for a girl. But apparently, word had already spread about his daughter's unexpected arrival and her meager possessions. For the second time today, he was the last to figure things out and the feeling left him hollow and powerless.

"I guess my mom was right about women wanting to throw themselves at you," Trina finally said before slowly approaching the bags Kylie and Mia had left behind.

The back of his neck prickled in defense. "Those ladies are married to some of my good friends."

Trina shrugged a shoulder, then used a toe to nudge the duffel as though she was looking for a hidden booby trap before she picked it up. Ethan scooped up the bags and carried them the few feet to the ugly orange sofa.

"What about that lady Monica?" Trina asked as she looked longingly at the bags. "Was she just being nice to me because she's married to one of your friends, too?"

"Monica Alvarez isn't married," Ethan replied a bit too

quickly, then cleared his throat. And she most definitely wasn't throwing herself at him. In fact, she'd acted like she couldn't get away from Ethan fast enough this morning. Which was interesting since, normally, she shut him down with a polite shyness or an indifference that made him want to pursue her even more. Today, though, there was an edge to her that he'd never seen and her anger had been solely directed at him. People didn't get mad if they didn't care.

Did that mean that she possibly *did* care about him? A jolt of energy made its way through his bloodstream and a smile tugged at the corners of his lips as he thought of how close she'd stood when she was lecturing him in the corner of the Cowgirl Up kitchen. Of how her breasts had jutted forward when she'd—

"All this stuff is brand-new," Trina said, interrupting the inappropriate turn his thoughts had taken. "It still has tags."

She pulled out a green down jacket in a ladies' size extra-small and a pair of black pants made of a waterproof fabric that looked a few inches too long. There were also a couple of plain, long-sleeved T-shirts and a package of thick socks. Trina held the pink duffel upside down and leggings, a wraparound sweater and some sort of white, strappy tank-top thing that looked like a sports bra fell out. He couldn't be sure because Trina shoved it back into the bag too quickly for Ethan to see, which was just as well.

There was a separate sack at the bottom of one of the brown bags with the name of Lester's Pharmacy on the front. Inside, Trina found a purple toothbrush and an assortment of body lotions and hair products that smelled way more fruity than anything Ethan kept stocked in his bathroom. Every item strewn across his ugly sofa was another reminder that he had absolutely no idea what a girl her age would need.

He racked his brain trying to think of what he'd required when he was that age. Clothes, food—lots of food—a skateboard, music, video games, friends.

"I guess we should probably get you registered for school," he said, and this time he was positive that it was panic that flashed across her face. "What grade are you in?"

"I'm really tired." She shoved the new clothes—the ones he would have to eventually reimburse someone for—onto one cushion at the end of the sofa and plopped down beside them. "Can I take a nap?"

His eyes narrowed at her evasive maneuver to throw him off topic. Although, back when he was that age, he tried to avoid any discussions involving school, as well.

"Yeah. Um, I don't really have the extra room set up just yet, but you can sleep on my bed if you want. Or right here, I guess. Make yourself at home." He knew the platitude sounded forced, but he truly hoped that he could make Trina feel welcome. He just didn't quite know how to do it. "Maybe when you wake up, we can go to the grocery store or something?"

"Whatever," she replied with a yawn before curling into a ball and using the green puffy jacket as a pillow.

It was only ten in the morning and there were still a million questions Ethan wanted to ask her. But she looked depleted and a little lost and, frankly, he didn't even know where to begin. As she dozed on the sofa, Ethan opened one of his kitchen cupboards and took stock of the bare shelves. He debated whether or not he should go to Duncan's Market while his daughter was asleep, but she'd already pulled one vanishing act today. He didn't want to provide her with an opportunity to pull another.

Daughter. There was that word again, although it was coming to his mind with much more frequency considering the fact he still wasn't one hundred percent convinced Trina was his. He used the internet search engine on his smartphone and typed in the letters "DNA," but a wave of guilt crashed into him before he could add the word "test." It felt wrong to even think about blood tests and genetic proof while she was right there in the room, peacefully sleeping after what she'd been through this morning. It wasn't like he would get any answers today, anyway. Even if he did, would it change the fact that her mother had already abandoned her and she had nowhere else to go?

He shoved the phone into the back pocket of his jeans and went into the second bedroom to stare at the dozen or so cardboard boxes piled everywhere. The framed picture on his mantel had been a gift from Luke and Carmen when Ethan had moved to town. The sad-looking silk plant beside it was small enough to fit in his rucksack and served as a reminder that no matter where he went, his old man was always with him.

These boxes held the remaining contents of his life, but he couldn't exactly remember what he'd placed in them before leaving it all in storage. He rolled up his sleeves then hefted one onto his shoulder. He didn't bother opening any of them as he set to work transferring each box to his own bedroom. Whatever was in them obviously wasn't something he'd needed in the past six months. Or even longer, considering he'd likely packed them right after that last deployment that had ended in disaster and resulted in his best friend flying home in a flag-draped casket.

He honestly wasn't sure *what* he needed anymore. All he knew was what he *didn't* need—and that was to have someone else depending on him.

Because the last time he'd been responsible for another person, they'd ended up dying under his watch.

Chapter Four

"**W**hy isn't she in school?" Monica whispered when Ethan walked over to the circulation desk at the library on Thursday afternoon. Freckles sent her a text saying he hadn't come into the Cowgirl Up this morning—as if Monica cared or had all kinds of spare time to add Ethan and his daughter to her already growing list of worries.

Apparently, though, her boss felt the need to keep her apprised of things that weren't her business. And now she was mad at herself for thinking about that text all day. And even madder at the fact that she was currently taking her annoyance out on him.

"I'll get around to registering her eventually," he said, yanking off his thick jacket and revealing his normal uniform of a soft flannel shirt and jeans that fit his slim hips perfectly. "But I'm trying not to rush anything. We're still getting to know each other."

Trina was at least dressed more appropriately for the snowy weather today, so that was a point in Ethan's fatherhood column. Monica jutted her chin toward the bright green coat as it appeared between the YA aisle and the audiobooks. "I see you took her shopping for some new clothes."

"Actually, Kylie and Mia brought that stuff over."

"Then what have you guys been doing the past day and a half?" Monica hated the nosiness of her tone, but she couldn't quash her curiosity.

"Working," Ethan replied simply. She knew he and Kane Chatterson restored Victorian homes and took on general contracting jobs. In fact, she'd hired them to repair one of the walls in Gran's kitchen that had been damaged in a fire last November. The job had only taken a few days and Monica had been able to leave each morning before they'd arrived, returning home long after they were gone.

Which meant she didn't have to gaze at Ethan's muscular body, on full display as he moved around her kitchen like a member of Magic Mike's dance troupe.

"You mean you're taking her to construction sites with you?"

"I don't know what else to do with her."

That brought Monica back to her first question and she wanted to grab hold of the lapels on the man's flannel shirt and give him a good shake. "So then why isn't she in school?"

"I hate school," Trina said, setting down a stack of five books on the checkout desk. She turned to her father and asked, "Do you have a library card?"

Ethan's response was to scrunch his nose, as though his daughter had just asked him if he had four arms. "No. Why would I?"

Her groan was dramatic and typical of most kids her age. "To check out books?"

That's right. When Monica had handed Ethan the copy of *Rejection for Dummies* last week, her tummy had been too tied in knots by his knowing wink and his straight white teeth under his crooked grin. She'd been in such a hurry to get him out of the library, she hadn't even bothered to properly check out the book.

"How do we get Trina a library card?" Ethan asked.

"Fill this out." Monica handed him an application form and one of the stubby golf pencils from the plastic holder by her computer while her eyes stayed on Trina. "Why don't you like school?"

"It's boring. Do you have any of the new books by Veronica Roth?"

"Do you like that series?"

She shrugged. "It's okay."

Monica studied the girl before pointing toward the shelf with the new releases. When Trina was out of earshot, she leaned across the counter at Ethan, who was still completing the application. "Pssst. Did you even look at the books she wants?"

"No. Why?" His face was inches from her, and she could smell the mint on his breath as he whispered back. "Are they inappropriate?"

"What? No. It's just that they're at a high school reading level, which means she must be fairly smart."

"Guess the apple doesn't fall too far from the tree." He winked at her and Monica felt the heat fill her cheeks. It hadn't taken him too long to fall back into his flirtatious comfort zone.

"My point," Monica continued, her jaw tight, "is that she shouldn't be hanging out on construction sites all day."

"Are you saying that smart people can't be found at construction sites?" Something crossed his face and instead of immediately regretting her comment, Monica's blood pumped faster with frustration. She had a feeling he'd purposely chosen to twist her words into an insult.

"Not when they're supposed to be in school, Ethan."

"Maybe I should argue with you more often." His eyes turned a deeper shade, and his knowing smile returned. "I like it when you use my first name."

"Well, I like it when you don't aggravate me beyond all common sense."

"Good to know that I can make you like *something.*" Ethan gave a tiny chuckle at her gasp, and then his face grew more serious. "Listen, I'll admit that I don't know the first thing about parenthood. But Trina's been through a lot and I'm doing the best I can. I don't want to push her too much."

Some of the heat died down in Monica's veins as she studied Ethan's face for a sign of sincerity. She wanted to think he had his daughter's best interest at heart, but really, Monica didn't know the guy at all.

"What grade are you in, Trina?" she asked when the girl returned.

"Fifth, I guess."

"You guess?" Monica and Ethan repeated in unison.

Trina shrugged. "I haven't been in a while."

Ethan stood up straighter, the pint-size pencil seeming miniscule in his strong, work-roughened hands. "How long is a while?"

"It's not like I need to go, you guys. I already know most of the stuff the teacher taught, anyway."

"Actually, you *do* need to go," Ethan argued. "It's the law."

"God, now you sound like my truancy officer."

Truancy officer? That must mean the girl had a well-documented history of not attending class. She could see the muscles working in Ethan's jaw as he held himself perfectly still. Hopefully, he wasn't angry with Trina. After all, it wasn't her fault that her mother had been a...a what? Monica swallowed down the judgment.

How did she know what Trina's mother had been through? A kid herself when she'd given birth, and then never seeing the father of her child or getting any help from him whatsoever? What kind of mother would Monica have been in that situation?

"The schools here in Sugar Falls are different," Monica offered because Ethan's frozen-eyed stare suggested he could use a second voice of reason. "I know most of the teachers, and they would probably be willing to work with you if you test into a higher level than the rest of the class."

"You mean like skip a grade?" the girl asked, her eyes flickered with interest.

"I don't know about that, but they have all kinds of programs and opportunities for exceptional students."

Trina's fingers were twitching and Monica saw the girl's feet make small, retreating steps as if she didn't know whether she should take off again. "I don't even have a backpack."

"I'll tell you what," Ethan said. "Why don't we go to the school tomorrow? Monica can call her teacher friends and let them know you're coming. You can take a look around, we can maybe get you registered for those exceptional student classes, and then we'll go down to Boise this weekend and buy some school supplies?"

Exceptional student classes. Monica couldn't believe she'd used that description and she couldn't tell if Ethan knew she'd been improvising that last part. But the fact remained that the child needed to go to school.

"But how will *you* know what I need?" Trina asked Ethan, her voice laced with doubt. Then the girl turned a pair of pleading eyes to Monica. "Would you come shopping with us?"

Monica's voice stuck in her throat and she couldn't form a proper response. After all, she'd been the one to push for the girl to go to school in the first place.

Which was why, two days later, Monica found herself driving down the mountain to Boise with a former Navy SEAL and his new daughter.

Ethan wasn't sure how Trina had done it, but in less than seventy-two hours, she'd accomplished the one thing Ethan hadn't been able to do the past six months—gotten Monica Alvarez to go somewhere in public with him.

Not that it was a date. There was an eleven-year-old riding in the crew cab of his old work truck and, even though his daughter was wearing her headphones and listening to the music she'd figured out how to stream on his smartphone, Trina's presence was chaperone enough.

He'd tried to make conversation with Monica but all she'd seemed to want to discuss was how Trina was feeling—pretty healthy judging by how many groceries she'd already gone through after their initial trip to Duncan's Market; how Trina was adjusting—hard to tell since she rarely said more than a sentence or two at a time; and how the school registration went—much longer than anticipated since Trina skipped out to the girls' bathroom twice during the math assessment test. "I'm starting to wonder if she has a nervous stomach or something."

"Maybe you should take her to see a doctor?" Monica suggested in her quiet librarian voice.

"We have an appointment next week. Mrs. Dunn, the

school nurse, was able to find some vaccination records in the files her old school sent over." Ethan looked in his rearview mirror to ensure Trina was still wearing the headphones before whispering, "From what we gathered, her mother never took her so unless her grandmother got her to a doctor before she passed away, who knows when she last saw any sort of medical professional."

Monica winced. "Any word from the caseworker?"

"Not yet, which has me even more on edge because who knows what I'm going to find out from that report?" The guilt had kept Ethan up every night this week, eating away at him until all he wanted to do was drown out his crippling thoughts with a stiff drink. Flipping on his turn signal with so much force it bounced back into place, Ethan took a deep breath as he eased his foot off the accelerator. "Every time I want to get mad at Chantal for being so damn negligent with my child, I'm faced with the fact that I have no room to talk. At least she was around part of the time and did more than me."

If he'd been hoping that Monica would've said something to ease his guilt, he would have to wait longer. Trina took her earbuds out as he pulled the truck into the parking lot of the Boise Towne Square.

When was the last time he'd gone to an actual mall like this? Even before his shopping destination of choice had changed from the tactical supply store to the local hardware store, Ethan had ordered most of his stuff online. When he did come into the city for essentials, it was for new running shoes or to stock up on work jeans. Obviously, he'd never had to spend much time in the kids' department or the school supply aisle.

Looking at Monica, who was wearing a plain, gray wool coat with her jeans and an old pair of cowboy boots, he got the impression that keeping up with the latest trends wasn't her top priority either. Not that she didn't look great in her clothes, he corrected himself as the muscles in his thighs tightened. Hell, the woman would probably look good in a baggy pair of camo pants. But she was one of those no-nonsense, no-makeup-wearing types. The kind of person who dressed for function, not for fashion.

Maybe that's why his attraction to her grew every time he laid eyes on her. There was definitely something sexy about a woman who didn't have to try too hard, didn't have to flaunt it.

Monica and Trina walked across the parking lot side by side murmuring to each other and Ethan kept behind them. All he could think about was the shape of Monica's denim-clad legs while he counted down the seconds until they got inside and she removed her jacket, giving him a glimpse of her rounded backside in those jeans.

She and Trina might have been talking about which stores they needed to go to first or what they should buy, however, Ethan wanted no part of that strategy. He was just there to hand over his credit card and to carry the bags. When they entered the mall, the blast from the heater—along with Ethan's overactive imagination when it came to Monica's rear end—made him wish he would've left his own coat out in the truck.

"Some of the women in town suggested we go to that juniors store on the first floor," Monica suggested, and the entire way through the shopping center Ethan looked for a safe spot where he could hunker down and wait. Instead, he was forced to follow them into a place where the loud pop music assaulted his eardrums and the cloying, fruity perfume samples assaulted his manhood. He prayed that Monica knew what she was doing.

"I have absolutely no idea what I'm doing," Monica said twenty minutes later when she plopped down beside him on the pink velvet upholstered bench right inside the store. "This has to be the eighth time we've heard this Justin Bieber song and I haven't seen Trina since she went into the dressing room with a stack of clothes."

Ethan sprung up. "Did she take off again?"

"No, I can see her shoes under the door."

"But are they on her feet?"

"Yep. I checked." Monica tapped the side of her head, indicating she was smart enough to already think of that.

"So then why hasn't she picked anything yet?" he groaned, slouching against the glitter painted wood of the bench's backrest.

"I don't know. Some girls get really self-conscious about their bodies around this age. I know I was."

He looked her up and down, desire shooting through him. "Are you kidding? What in the world would you have to be self-conscious about?"

"I didn't always look like this, though. Just like you probably didn't always look like…" A blush stole up Monica's cheeks and he hoped it wasn't just the heat inside the mall.

"Like what?" The corner of his mouth lifted.

"Like a wall of muscle with a little head on top."

"My head's not little." Ethan rubbed at his hair that was longer than regulation. "But feel free to call me a wall of muscle anytime."

"Back to your daughter." Monica rolled her eyes. "I asked her if she needed any help or different sizes, but she insisted she was fine. At first I thought she was nervous about trying the stuff on. But now that I'm thinking about it, she *was* pretty focused on the price tags when we were looking through the racks. She could be worried about how much things cost and what you can afford."

"I can afford it," Ethan replied, his boots firmly planted apart. In fact, being a single guy without many expenses up until now meant that he could afford quite a few shopping sprees.

"That's none of my business. However, maybe you could give Trina a budget so she knows how much she can spend."

"Fine," he muttered as he clenched his fingers into fists and strode deeper into the store as though he was in full tactical gear and had just been briefed on conducting a hostage extraction. Taking note of any alternate exit routes on his way to the fitting rooms, he stealthily steered away from an entire shelf devoted to sequined pillows, averted his eyes when he passed a round clothes rack loaded down with of what could've been white training bras, and then successfully avoided knocking over a display of glitzy BFF necklaces.

"Hey, Trina," he called into the hallway leading toward the partitioned rooms. However, he had to repeat himself to be heard over the pop music blasting from the speakers, the two preteen girls squealing over their matching outfits, and a frazzled-looking mom arguing with her daughter about being too young for something called "booty shorts."

"I don't think she can hear you," Monica said from behind him.

"Well, there's no way any sane guy would willingly step foot past here." Ethan jerked his thumb toward the three-way mirror outside the entrance of the changing area.

"Hey, buddy," a guy with a shaved head whispered conspiratorially and Ethan wanted to sink in relief at the sound of another male voice in this place. "Take it from me, the fuzzy pink bench right by the doors is the closest thing they have to a demilitarized zone. Once they get you to the cash registers, it's too late."

"Can we go to the pretzel place now, Daddy?" A smiling girl about Trina's age looped her arm through the bald man's, forcing the guy to shift the two bags covered in the store's rainbow logo to his free hand.

"Only if they serve tequila there," the guy said, rolling his eyes before smirking at Ethan. "Trust me, you're gonna need a few drinks after you're done here."

"Go on," Ethan called out to the man, staring at the father and daughter as they left. "Save yourself."

Monica swatted at his bicep. But it wasn't just a longing to escape or a desire for a cold cocktail that had caused the weight of envy to settle low in Ethan's belly.

"Do you think Trina will ever look at me like that?" he asked.

"Like what?"

"Never mind." He shook his head and raised his voice as he tried calling for his daughter again. But this time, it came out way too loud and several customers turned to stare while a little boy in a stroller nearby started to cry. Probably because Ethan had just sounded like a recruit division commander shouting at a new recruit.

"Why don't I just go back and get her?" Monica finally offered and Ethan wished he would've just asked her in the first place.

But she didn't have to go very far.

Trina's eyes were wide when she hesitantly came out of the dressing room area and Ethan silently cursed himself for raising his voice earlier and probably startling her. He'd never been afraid of his own old man, probably because Louis Renault was never really home long enough to do much yelling. So it hadn't occurred to him that his own daughter might have anything to legitimately fear from him.

"Honey," Monica said to Trina, before shooting a warning glance at Ethan. Really, neither one of them knew what had happened to her in the past, but surely Monica didn't think he was capable of harming the girl. Did she? "We were just curious to see if you'd found any clothes you like yet."

Trina slowly walked toward them, wearing the same outfit she'd had on when they arrived. Her eyes were downcast and her voice soft when she replied, "I don't know."

He pressed his fingers to his temples, attempting to stimulate his brain for something to say that would take the sting out of his earlier tone. "You know, Trina, all the other girls in the store are finding clothes they like."

This brought his daughter's head up. "Do you wish I was more like the other girls?"

"No. I want you to be yourself. That's why I brought you here. So that you could pick out your *own* clothes."

Trina's face dropped. "But I don't know what I'm allowed to pick."

"Well, Ethan… I mean…your dad said that he didn't care about the prices." Monica got behind Ethan and used her shoulder to nudge the back of his bicep, making him step forward.

Technically, he *had* said that, but it wasn't like he wanted to throw his money away either. He tried not to pat the pocket containing his wallet. "If it's something you like and if you'll wear it, then let's get it."

His daughter's smile was shy and tentative at first, but when Monica nodded encouragement at the girl, Ethan realized he couldn't place a monetary value on his daughter's happiness.

Or on the feeling of Monica pressed up against his side.

* * *

A few hundred dollars later, Ethan realized that he might've gone a little overboard during a shopping spree that didn't involve a single infrared light, combat boot or armor plate. Monica had tried to warn him that he should pace himself because there were only so many hoodies an eleven-year-old needed.

"You might want to ask the cashier about signing up for their rewards program for future discounts," Monica suggested under her breath when Ethan handed over his credit card. "You'll have to do this all over again when the summer clothes come out."

Ethan gulped at the thought of making a return trip to the mall again in a couple of months. Not that he'd minded buying things for his daughter. Hell, he hadn't ever bought so much as a diaper, let alone paid child support. So a new wardrobe barely even put a dent in his guilty conscience or made up for all lost time. He just didn't want to have to be present for the process of trying on everything all over again and deciding whether to go with the denim popover dress or the flutter sleeve romper.

God, he hated the fact that he now knew what a romper was.

"No problem," he said, trying to scoop up all six large shopping bags off the counter at once. Trina was quick to grab the one he'd missed and held it close to her torso. It was the same way he'd carried his first set of Navy dress blues back to the barracks. Ethan had earned that uniform and it was the first item of clothing he'd ever had tailored especially for him. He'd grown a few sizes since then, but he still had the thing carefully packed away in one of his boxes at home.

So instead of insisting on carrying all the bags, Ethan

decided to let his child have her own moment of pride for something new. He winked at Trina before asking, "Should we go get some gedunk?"

She scrunched up her nose. "What's that?"

"Some junk food. Like a snack to reward ourselves for getting through this."

Trina nodded and all but skipped out into the mall, as though trying on all those clothes hadn't completely wiped her out. Hell, all he'd done was sit there on that stupid, safe pink bench and nod his approval, yet he was completely exhausted.

Monica hung back with Ethan as they followed the girl's lead toward the food court. He'd hoped that it was because the woman simply enjoyed his company, and he was about to switch his smile back on and say as much. However, when his daughter was out of earshot, it was clear she had something else on her mind. "You should also keep in mind that kids this age start going through their growth spurts and many of these things might not fit her next school year."

Ethan paused midstep. It was the first time he'd realized that this fatherhood deal wasn't just a one and done kind of deal. Obviously, he knew that it was a long-term responsibility, but he'd never really thought of it as more than a series of tasks. Like spec ops missions, you finish one assignment and move on to the next—a new adventure always around the corner. He hadn't quite been anticipating a repeating cycle. Like shopping. Thinking of the bald guy from earlier today made him scratch at his own head. How did other dads get through this over and over again?

Using his thumb to push against the throbbing in his temple, Ethan muttered, "I could really use something stronger than a pretzel."

Chapter Five

"What about shoes?" Trina asked around a mouthful of cinnamon-and-sugar-covered soft pretzel. Monica hadn't thought it was possible for Ethan's eyes to get any rounder today and she had to choke back a giggle at his terrified expression.

"Yeah, we should probably check out the sneaker place next." Monica pushed up her sleeves. "I'm ready to do more damage there as soon as your father is."

Yet, when Ethan remained in an apparent state of shock, Monica fluttered her lashes at him and said, "Just blink twice for yes."

"I thought we were done." He held up his plastic cup of frozen lemonade. "See, this was my reward for not going totally insane in the last store."

"That's okay," Trina murmured, tucking in her chin. "These shoes will work."

Monica followed the child's gaze to the small hole in the canvas over the big toe. She opened her mouth to chastise Ethan for his complete disregard in handling his daughter's disappointment.

But the man must've recognized the defeated expression on the girl's face because he quickly spoke up. "No, you need something more sturdy. More suited for the weather here in the mountains. And we should also get you a pair of shoes to go with that romper dress thing you picked out."

Trina's eyes lifted, flickering with hope, and Monica didn't have the heart to correct Ethan and tell him that it was really Monica who'd picked out the dress. The girl was happy with jeans and solid-colored T-shirts and sweaters. Yet, Gran always insisted that every female needed a fancier outfit for those special occasions. Not that Monica remembered the last time she'd dressed up in Sugar Falls.

The first hour of shopping had her questioning her own sanity for agreeing to run interference between Ethan and his long-lost daughter. By the time they shoved the last shoe box and bags of school supplies into the crew cab of the truck later that afternoon, though, her nerves were a little less frayed as she basked in the afterglow of a job well done.

It would've felt like a regular family outing if the three of them had any trust or confidence in the others. Unfortunately, Monica still didn't trust Ethan not to shirk his responsibilities, and Ethan didn't trust Trina not to run off, and Trina didn't quite trust anyone. Yet. But she was coming around.

As Ethan pulled onto the two-lane highway, Trina had retreated into her headphones with her music and Monica watched the sun dip lower behind the snow-covered mountains.

"So that went better than I expected," he said quietly, mirroring her own thoughts.

"Yeah, it was touch and go there for a while." Monica smiled at him, but when he returned it with a wicked grin of his own, the corner of her lip trembled. Really, the man's mouth should come with its own warning. *Caution: smirking leads to increased knee weakening.*

"I really started sweating when we walked by that booth that did the ear piercing. Thankfully, you came through and steered her toward the bookstore."

"Girls like me and Trina would rather have a new book than a pair of earrings any day."

"Yeah, you guys remind me of each other in a lot of ways."

Oh geez, did he just compare her to his eleven-year-old daughter? Or was that Monica who'd drawn the comparison? In the past few months, she'd grown accustomed to Ethan always flirting with her. Yet, ever since Trina arrived, it was like something had completely changed in his whole demeanor. Sure, he still stared at Monica when he thought she wasn't looking, but it was no longer in that playful, out-to-have-a-good-time way he used to look at her. He might throw out a bold wink here and there, but it now seemed like those were only for show, to pretend as if his whole life hadn't suddenly changed and grown more complicated.

While it made sense that he was completely out of his element with this unexpected role of fatherhood, and she should want him to be taking his responsibilities seriously, there was a teeny tiny hole right below Monica's chest that missed his more happy-go-lucky personality.

And she could hardly believe it.

"Like how?" Monica finally asked.

"Huh?" he replied, apparently lost in his own thoughts. Before Trina arrived, she never would've pinned Ethan as the quiet and contemplative type.

"How do we remind you of each other?" she clarified.

"Well, you guys are both kind of quiet and shy, but incredibly smart. Like I know there's got to be so much going on in your brain, but for the life of me, I can't figure out what you're thinking. Still, I find myself wanting to know everything about you." He lifted up his sunglasses as he cast a glance across the cab of the truck and Monica squirmed in the passenger seat. "I want to know what makes you happy, what makes you sad, what makes you tick."

"It's going to take time for you to get to know Trina like that," Monica said as she tugged on the shoulder strap of her seat belt, trying to give her neck a little relief from this sudden tightness. What she hadn't added was that Ethan had no hope of ever getting to know Monica like that. Sure, there might be times when she would lower her defenses, but she would never let her guard down with him. Or with any man ever again.

"She warmed up for a while there at the mall." Ethan glanced at his rearview mirror and then lowered his voice, forcing Monica to lean toward the center console to hear him better. "But then when we went to the office supply store, she got super withdrawn and wouldn't even make eye contact."

"I'm surprised you noticed that."

"Give me a little credit, Mon," Ethan said, his use of the shortened version of her name causing a tingling sensation in her rib cage. Great. Going on a family shopping trip with him had already created a false sense of intimacy between them. "Just because I'm uncomfortable dealing with female moods doesn't mean that I don't pay attention to them. Especially when it concerns someone I care about."

Monica tried not to look toward the backseat. It would've been a sure sign to Trina that they were talking about her. "My guess is that shopping for clothes and shoes is fun, but buying paper and pencils is a reminder that she's going to have to go to school soon. I wonder why that makes her so apprehensive."

"Probably because it's school." Ethan shrugged. "No kids I knew ever enjoyed going."

"I think it might be something more than that. Maybe she struggled with bullies at her old school or has a learning disability that makes the work tough for her."

"But you said her reading level was well above average."

"She could still struggle in other areas academically or even socially. Or maybe she had behavioral issues and used to get in trouble a lot?"

"If that's the case, the apple *really* wouldn't be falling far from the tree." His grin was finally back and Monica's heart sped up as he turned into the driveway of her grandmother's old house.

"Oh look," Trina said, pointing to the older woman standing near the snow-covered woodpile wearing a pair of patent leather tap shoes and a faded bathrobe that only came to her knobby knees. "I didn't know you guys had a kitten."

"Neither did I," Monica grumbled as she hopped out of the passenger side before Ethan could put the truck in Park.

* * *

Despite the fact that Monica had already been outside at the end of her driveway when they'd picked her up this morning, Ethan had still planned on walking her to her front door this evening. But when he saw Mrs. Alvarez standing outside in the snow with a kitten in her arms, he realized they might be here for longer than he'd anticipated.

He and Kane had done most of the repair work on the house when Mrs. Alvarez caught a frozen pizza on fire a few months ago and, after spending several days with the older woman, he knew two things. One, she didn't have a cat. Two, she only wore those fifty-year-old dance shoes when she was having one of her "episodes."

But it was Trina who got to the older woman first. "Can I hold your kitten?"

"Sure," Mrs. Alvarez replied as she handed over a ball of gray fur to his daughter. "But she's still a little sore from getting her shots today so be careful."

"Gran, did you find that cat in the woodpile?"

"What woodpile?" she asked her granddaughter. Monica pointed to the split logs stacked against the entire side of the smaller Victorian home. "Oh, that's right. The ol' furnace kept growling and hissing so much, it gave poor kitty a bad case of gas. So we came out here to get some wood for a fire."

Monica took off her glasses before pinching the bridge of her nose. Ethan cleared his throat, wanting to help ease some of her frustration. "Hey, Mrs. Alvarez, remember you promised Chief Jones that you wouldn't use the fireplace or the oven unless Monica was home."

"But she *is* home." Mrs. Alvarez gave him a dismissive wave as though her granddaughter had been there all along and hadn't just arrived with Ethan. "Wait until you try her enchiladas, Mr. Renault. It's a family recipe and she makes them just like my own *mami* did. *Mija*, is dinner ready yet?"

"Not yet, Gran," Monica said, her exhale louder than the wind whistling through the pine needles on the ancient evergreen tree near the driveway. She wrapped an arm around her grandmother's hunched shoulders. "Come on, let's go inside and get warmed up."

Trina was cooing at the kitten and, for the millionth time today, all Ethan could do was stand there frozen, unsure of what to do. If this was a hostage extraction or the detonation of an IED, he'd be much more comfortable. Being a rescuer came as easily to him as breathing. Unfortunately, he wasn't sure who needed to be rescued first—Monica or her poor, confused Gran. In his mind, he heard his BUD/S instructor's voice telling him, *Adapt and overcome.*

When his gaze fell on the wood he asked his daughter, who seemed oblivious to anything but the purring fuzz ball curled up in her hands, "Do you mind if we stay for a few minutes so I can get a fire started for them?"

"Sure. Can we have some enchiladas, too?"

Ethan grabbed a couple of logs. "I don't think there's actually any enchiladas. Mrs. Alvarez gets confused easily and must've forgotten that Monica was with us all day."

"Too bad. I'm getting kind of bored going out to eat all the time." Trina sniffed before she followed behind the two women who'd just gone into the house.

Okay, so maybe she wasn't the only one who was tired of takeout. Ethan made a mental note to learn how to make a home-cooked meal. If he could construct an improvised explosive device in the middle of an overgrown jungle or a barren desert, surely he could manage something basic. There had to be cookbooks at the library. And if not, he could always find a YouTube video to show him how.

As he knelt in front of the fireplace, he heard the two women talking in the kitchen. Their voices weren't raised, so at least nobody was yelling or seemed to be otherwise flustered. Once he finished lighting the fire, he stood up to tell them that he and Trina were going to take off.

Passing the fridge, he saw the whiteboard affixed to the front of it. Someone had used a red dry erase marker to write, "Monica is in Boise today and will be home at 6:00 p.m. Mr. Simon is next door if you need him."

"Excuse me," Monica said, brushing past him and opening the freezer to pull out a foil-covered dish. Ethan gulped, partly from her nearness and partly from his hope that she might actually be making enchiladas. Would it be horribly rude of him to swing an invite for dinner when she so clearly had her hands full dealing with her grandmother's dementia?

"So, Gran, where did you find the cat?" Monica asked as she put the frozen dish into the oven.

"I picked her up at the animal shelter this morning." Gran was sitting at the kitchen table, a blanket across her lap and the toes of her dance shoes tapping against the hardwood floor Ethan had just resanded a few months ago.

"The shelter on the way to Boise?" Monica couldn't hide the panic that flashed across her face. "Who took you there?"

From what Ethan understood, Mrs. Alvarez had lived in this house for the past forty years and had been a member of every organization and club in town. She must have friends and neighbors who were willing to take her places and help out when Monica wasn't with her.

"I drove myself." She pulled a single key out of her robe pocket and set it down on the table next to the mug of steaming water in front of her. "I found the spare in your bedroom."

"You took my car?" Monica dropped the box of chamomile tea she'd just pulled down from the cabinet. "Gran, you don't have a license anymore. You're lucky you didn't crash into someone else—oh my gosh, you didn't get in an accident did you?"

"*Mija*, I've been driving since I was thirteen years old and never had an accident."

Monica squeezed her eyes shut and took several deep breaths before she responded.

"You caused that big pileup on the highway two years ago, remember? That's why Dr. Wu took your license away." Her voice was strained, but way more reasonable than Ethan's would have been under the same circumstances.

Instead of nodding in understanding, Mrs. Alvarez rolled her eyes. "I don't even know a Dr. Wu. Your grandfather and I have always seen Dr. Jorgensen."

Ethan immediately went to retrieve the forgotten box at Monica's feet and heard her murmuring to herself. "It's probably pointless to tell her that both my grandfather and Dr. Jorgensen passed away before I was born."

He fished a tea bag out and plopped it into Mrs. Alvarez's mug of hot water. As he returned the box to the cabinet beside Monica, he lowered his own voice. "Why don't I go outside and check your car for any damage?"

"You don't have to. I can handle it." He recognized

when someone was trying to cover up and pretend they were capable of handling something themselves, despite all evidence pointing to the contrary. Hadn't he done the same thing—*said* the same thing—all those times before he'd decided to get sober?

"I know you can handle it and I wasn't implying otherwise. But we can all use an extra hand from time to time."

She tilted her head as she studied him, her left cheek sucked in as his offer hung between them. He could see the struggle behind her proud eyes and knew she was pondering whether or not she should accept his help. Whether she should rely on someone else for a change, especially a guy who had his own battles.

Ethan experienced an intense need to prove to her that he wasn't completely useless. "Mon, I can't even begin to repay you for helping me at the mall today with Trina. This is the least I can do."

Monica sighed. "Fair enough. But then we're even."

Ethan grinned at her before snatching the spare key off the table. He didn't bother pointing out that, with the way Monica and Trina had already bonded over books and shopping, he doubted that today wasn't going to be the last favor he'd have to ask of her.

Monica took Gran upstairs to change, sitting the tiny woman down on the bed so she could remove the tap shoes first. "Make sure you put them back in their special box, *mija*."

As if Monica hadn't had to put the patent leather heels away at least four times a week with these forgetful episodes coming more frequently. She studied the shoes in the worn-out shoe box with the faded Capezio logo on the top. Gran had been quite the dancer back in her day and had several VHS movies downstairs where one could catch a glimpse of Lydia Alvarez in the background as part of the ensemble cast. She even had a signed photograph of her with Elvis Presley from that time she'd been an extra in a beach party scene.

She wished Ethan could see how Gran used to be. *She wasn't always like this*, Monica often found herself explaining to random strangers in town who didn't know that her sweet and intelligent grandmother would never have tap-danced in the middle of Town Square Park wearing just her bathrobe if the woman was still in control of her faculties. Lydia Alvarez had been strong and capable and the life of the party up until a few years ago. But those glimpses of the same woman were decreasing with alarming frequency, and soon Monica herself might forget what the younger Gran was like.

Monica's loud sigh didn't alleviate any of the heaviness in her heart. By the time she returned from the closet, Gran was fast asleep on top of her blankets. Luckily, her grandmother only weighed about a hundred pounds, so while Monica couldn't lift her, she could maneuver her enough to pull the quilt out from underneath and cover her up. Standing at the doorway, she watched her grandmother sleep.

"Oh, Gran, what am I going to do with you?"

The only answer she got was a soft snore. Turning off the light, Monica squared her shoulders before heading back downstairs.

When she walked into the kitchen, she found Ethan pacing in front of the brand-new oven while Trina sat at the old Formica-covered table, holding a sleeping kitten in her arms. Apparently, it was too much to hope that the man would've done what most people do when faced with

Gran's odd behavior—pretend they hadn't noticed anything out of the ordinary and then politely find an excuse to leave as quickly as possible.

"Is everything okay?" he asked as soon as he saw her.

"Yeah. Gran fell asleep."

He shot a look toward Trina, then lowered his voice. "Is it Alzheimer's?"

Monica nodded. "She usually just wanders down the street or talks an unsuspecting passerby into a ride to town, but this is the first time she's ever taken off in my car."

"Speaking of which, there were a few little scratches and dings but it was tough for me to tell if any of it was recent." Ethan's words were a diplomatic way of saying that her Toyota Camry was nearly fifteen years old and had definitely seen better days. However, it was all she could afford when every extra dime she made went into a savings account for Gran's future medical expenses. "You might want to go out to the driveway and check to see if you recognize anything new."

The timer on the stove went off right then, making her already frazzled nerve endings pulse with each shriek of the buzzer. The last thing Monica wanted right that second was company. After all, it was much easier to pretend that nothing was wrong with her closest living relative when she didn't have an audience. But Gran took great pride in feeding any and everyone who crossed her doorstep and would be disappointed if Monica didn't offer their guests something to eat.

"Would you guys like some enchiladas? There's more than en—"

"Yes, please," Trina said rather loudly, not even letting Monica finish. She knew Ethan ate most of his meals out, so the girl's enthusiasm was probably only the result of the chance to have a home-cooked dinner.

"I don't want to impose…" Ethan's words faded as she lifted the foil off the pan and the air filled with the scent of the rich, spicy sauce.

Monica looked over her shoulder to see him staring hungrily at the cheese-covered tortillas. His front teeth scraped against his lower lip and her pulse sped up. What would it feel like to have him look at her like that? What would those teeth feel like if they lightly scraped the sensitive skin right below her…

She shivered wistfully before giving her head a quick shake. Nope. There was no point in even thinking about something so reckless. With his daughter here, Monica had been doubling her efforts to distance herself from the man. Clearly she would need to work harder at it.

Shoving the pot holders at him, she instructed, "Here, put this on the table and I'll get the plates and silverware."

"Trina, why don't you set the kitten down while we eat?" Ethan told his daughter. The girl gently put the sleeping kitty on the red vinyl chair next to her, then stood up to wash her hands at the sink.

Serving her guests gave Monica a task to focus on, even if she did so a little distractedly. She tried to pretend she was at her waitressing job and not in her own kitchen. But she never had to sit at the table with the customers while they ate, so the conversation soon stalled after a few bites.

Well, the kitten's conversation didn't stall. Apparently, as soon as it was separated from the warmth of Trina's arms, the tiny thing woke up—and didn't like being away from her holder one little bit. She meowed louder and louder until Trina lifted it off the seat and tucked the animal into the wide front pocket of her new hooded sweatshirt.

"So, what are you going to do about your grandmother?" Ethan finally asked, echoing the same question Monica had asked herself upstairs. "I mean, do you have any plans for what happens down the road?"

"I know I'll have to do something eventually…" she started, then glanced at Trina unsure of how much she should say in front of the child. The bottom line was that Gran's condition would only get worse.

"I think they have special homes," Ethan offered. "A few weeks ago we did some work on this old fisherman's cabin to get it ready to sell. His kids were moving him to a place called a memory care center."

"I know. I've looked into it. But it's not what we do in my family. I have a cousin in El Paso and when he put my aunt Bettina in a place, nobody else in the family would invite him to a backyard cookout, let alone a wedding. Besides, Gran took me and my mom in after my dad left us. When my mom passed away, Gran raised me. She gave up her golden years to care for me. The least I can do is return the favor."

"Maybe you can hire a nurse or something to be with her when you're at work?" Ethan's suggestion was probably well-intentioned, but it made the skin on the back of her neck prickle. Did he seriously think she hadn't already researched all the options? Anytime she had a down moment at the library, all she did was research.

"I've also looked into that. Even with Gran's social security and both of my jobs, I could only afford about two hours a day."

A meow sounded from Trina's midsection, drawing Monica's attention back to the current crisis at hand. She took her glasses off and set them on the table so she could relieve some of the tension building in her temples, as well as prevent her from clearly seeing the adorable kitten's face when she said, "I'm going to have to call the animal shelter tomorrow and find out what their return policy is."

Trina gasped, looking at Monica as if she'd suggested tying the kitten into a burlap bag and throwing it out into the middle of Lake Rush. Monica tried not to shrink any lower in her chair.

"Honey, it's not that I don't *want* the kitten. I'd love to have a pet. But Gran is always misplacing things and then can't remember where she left them. When I'm at work all day, I'll often come home to find her snow boots in the fridge, and the sandwich I'd made for her lunch on the floor in the mudroom. As much as she'd love to, my grandmother simply can't take care of a young, helpless kitten." Monica dragged in another deep breath. "I can't believe the people at the shelter actually let her adopt it in the first place."

"Your gran looks healthy to me." Trina tilted her head. "Is something wrong with her?"

"Physically, she's totally fine. The only medication she takes is for her high blood pressure. Other than that, she's in great shape physically. But her brain is starting to shut down and she gets confused easily and is always forgetting things, like turning off the stove before something catches fire or not watching for cars when she walks into town…in the middle of the night. I worry that she could be a danger to herself."

"My gran was the opposite," Trina said, setting down her fork after finishing the entire plate of enchiladas. "Her brain remembered everything and she was always supersmart. But she had bad knees and couldn't walk and then she got real sick and went to the hospital. I never saw her after that."

"That must have been very sad for you," Ethan said to the girl, who was using her finger to give the kitten a tiny nibble of leftover cheese. "I only met your gran two or three times when I picked up your mom for dates, but she would be sitting on her front porch working on a crossword with a plate of homemade treats beside her. She used to make the best brownies I've ever had."

When it came to his daughter, Ethan usually was at a loss for words and Monica hadn't expected him to be the one to offer comfort. Yet, sharing a happy memory of Trina's grandmother had been the perfect response. Something warm spread through Monica's chest as she studied the pair across the table.

"Chantal said Gran died because she ate too many sweets and never exercised." The fact that Trina referred to her own mother by first name chipped away at Monica's prior sympathy for the woman who'd given birth to Ethan's child. "Chantal was always worried about getting fat like Gran. That's why she took a special medicine to keep herself skinny all the time."

Monica's own father hadn't been a part of her life because he used to prefer taking a special medicine, too. The way Ethan's face had gone pale suggested that Chantal's choice of pharmaceuticals was of the same variety and was most likely illegal. While Fidel Alvarez only showed up sporadically for the occasional childhood events, at least Monica had a few good memories of her dad being loving toward her. Of him bringing her a new book and a candy ring pop before he would lift her up in his strong arms and tease that she was growing too big too quickly.

Until the last time Monica saw him, when he didn't take her in his arms at all.

Ethan cleared his throat and Monica didn't blame him for wanting to change the subject. "I bet that if you call the shelter and explain what happened, they could find a new home for the kitten."

"I can take care of Tootie."

Ethan's head whipped to the side to stare at his daughter. "Who?"

"Tootie." Trina nodded toward the kitten that was now licking red sauce off her finger. "I've been calling her that because she seems to have the toots."

Monica wrinkled her nose. "Maybe we shouldn't feed her any more enchiladas."

"Um…but you'll be at school and I'm at work," Ethan replied, not seemingly bothered by the animal's gas issues. His eyes darted back and forth between Monica and his daughter as if he was hoping someone would intervene and be the voice of reason. "Remember Monica said the kitten shouldn't be alone during the day?"

Instead of throwing him a life rope, Monica seized on the opportunity to not have to call the shelter and look like a big, evil animal hater.

"I didn't say the kitten couldn't be alone. I said I couldn't leave *Gran* alone with her." *Please don't ask me for more details than that*, Monica thought. She would hate to have Trina hear the story about how Gran found two baby skunks last spring and thought the neighbor's untrained German shepherd wouldn't bark so much if it had some new playmates. Fortunately, Mr. Simon had heard the initial growling and ran outside right away. Unfortunately, neither he nor Rambo were safe from the spray when the mama skunk swooped in to save her babies. When Gran later realized what she'd nearly done, she'd been inconsolable for days. "Cats are actually very independent and can pretty much take care of themselves."

Ethan narrowed his eyes at Monica but she quickly stood up and began occupying herself with clearing the table and taking the empty casserole pan to the sink.

"Please, can we keep Tootie?"

Even from all the way across the kitchen, Monica heard the air whoosh out of Ethan's mouth. As far as she could tell, it was the first time the child had actually asked him directly for something, rather than wait for him to offer it. Trina's request meant that she was becoming more comfortable with him.

Perhaps it was wrong to use Ethan's vulnerability with this new role of fatherhood against him, but Monica really didn't want to take the poor kitten back to the shelter. After all, it was *her* fault that she'd left her car key where Gran could find it. That made her equally responsible for finding Tootie a new home.

"Having a pet *does* teach children about responsibility." Monica looked at Ethan over the lenses of her glasses and attempted a big smile that felt completely unnatural. "It can also make them feel more secure in a new place."

"When you two tag team me like that, I don't stand a chance," Ethan groaned. "Fine, Tootie can stay at our house."

He stood up to carry his plate to the sink and Trina's whoops kept her from hearing her father when he lowered his voice, his breath caressing Monica's ear as he whispered, "But man, you're gonna owe me for this one."

Monica shivered, wondering if she'd just made a deal with the devil.

Chapter Six

"So I go to school tomorrow and then what?" Trina asked as she sat on her bed with Tootie on Sunday evening, both of them watching Ethan fix a broken drawer on her dresser so that she could finish organizing and putting away all her new clothes.

Despite being in the military for nearly ten years and accustomed to following so many rules and regulations, Ethan preferred to fly by the seat of his pants. His daughter, on the other hand, was proving to be more schedule oriented. So far today, he'd had to lay out their plans for breakfast (grabbing doughnuts at the bakery), their plans for church (he didn't attend, but apparently her grandmother had been a stickler for going every Sunday morning) and their plans for purchasing cat supplies (the pet store visit an hour ago was only slightly less overwhelming than their excursion to the mall yesterday).

But at least she was opening up and talking with him a little more.

"I'll be standing outside of the school when the bell rings at three o'clock. Maybe we can go get an ice cream at Noodie's afterward."

Seeing all the bright colored tops and leggings out of their bags really made the rest of the spare bedroom look pretty nondescript and bare. Maybe he should've let her pick out a new bedspread or something to spruce things up.

"And then what?"

"Um, you tell me about your day, I guess?" Should he already be enrolling her in sports or piano lessons or whatever it was that kids did after school?

"Okay. What happens after that?"

"Then we grab some dinner and I usually go to a meeting on Monday nights."

"What kind of meeting?" Trina asked. She was holding one of her new shoelaces up, watching Tootie bat a paw at it.

As much as he didn't want to say anything that might make him sound bad, part of his recovery was honesty. "I used to drink too much."

"You mean…" Suddenly, his daughter's animated expression grew hesitant. Perhaps even nervous.

"I'm talking about alcohol. Do you know what I mean?"

Trina bit her lip as she lowered the shoelace and looked down, refusing to meet his gaze as she slowly nodded.

Ethan dropped to his knees in front of her, needing her to see how serious he was. "Listen, I don't drink alcohol anymore. But it's important for me to go to meetings and talk with other people who have the same issue so we can support each other. Help each other stay healthy. Does that make sense?"

Trina lifted her chin just enough so she could study him out of the eye that wasn't covered behind her loose hair. "The judge told Chantal that she needed to go to meetings like that. But she had to live at rehab houses for *her* meetings and told Gran it was too hard to stay in places like that. Do you have to move into rehab, too?"

"No." Ethan flinched at being lumped in the same category as his former prom date, who he'd suspected of being strung out on something the day she'd left Trina on his doorstep. It'd been confirmed when the girl had mentioned Chantal using a "special medicine" to keep from gaining weight. "My meetings are voluntary—that means nobody forces me to go—and they only last an hour. I go once or twice a week."

Sometimes more often if he thought he needed it. Or on days when he was especially antsy or restless or in need of an outlet.

"Do I go to the meeting with you?" Trina toyed with the end of the shoelace, making Tootie think that the batting game was starting back up.

"Um, I've never seen kids there. I can ask, though. If it is something you really want to do, maybe we can get permission for you to come with me once in a while. Or we can just stay home tomorrow night. It's okay if I miss once in a while."

"No. Meetings are important," Trina said. Her voice was usually serious, but this time, it held a note of urgency, as well. "Whenever my… Chantal forgot to go to hers, we wouldn't see her for months."

The poor girl had already lost everything she'd loved. He couldn't very well allow her to worry about him falling off the wagon, too. She deserved having some stability in her life. "If it's important to you, Trina, I won't miss any meetings. We can figure everything out. You don't know this about me yet, but I'm really good at making things work."

"Maybe I can go to the library tomorrow night and hang out with Monica?"

"I think the library closes at six." Ethan stood up to pull his phone out of his pocket to check the hours online.

"Then maybe I could go to her house for dinner? She has good food there and I'll take Tootie so her grandmother can play with her and get some cuddles."

He had to admit it wasn't a bad idea. But could Ethan really impose upon the Alvarez family again?

Last night, when he'd told Monica that she would owe him, he hadn't really meant it. He just wanted to let her know that he knew what she was doing by giving the kitten to Trina, and that he might expect some appreciation from her in return. Actually, he'd prefer some cuddles of his own, but he wasn't in any sort of position to be looking for a date right now. Which was really too bad, because he'd actually enjoyed being with Monica yesterday. Don't get him wrong, he still hated the shopping. But she was so calm through it all, so understanding of what his daughter needed—of what *he* needed—that for the first time in months, Ethan didn't have to pretend he knew what he was doing. Working with Monica was the closest he'd gotten to being a member of a team since he'd left the Navy. And she was definitely the most attractive teammate he'd ever had, with her sweet dimples and her silky brown curls and her curvy...

Ugh. Ethan had been so caught up in thoughts of Monica, his phone screen had gone dark and he had to reenter his pass code, only to realize that he'd forgotten what he'd been looking up in the first place. He really needed to put that attraction on hold while he figured out what was best for Trina.

There were plenty of other people in town that he would trust to babysit Trina, but his daughter didn't know any of them. She was probably too young to stay home alone. As if reading his thoughts, she suggested, "I could just stay here by myself. After my grandma died, I lived in worse neighborhoods with Chantal and she would leave me by myself all the time."

That was it. Ethan gripped his phone tighter, determined to be the exact opposite type of parent as Chantal. They'd exchanged numbers at the mall in case anyone got lost so he already had Monica's contact info handy to type out a text. I have a really huge favor and you can say no. But I have a meeting tomorrow and can't take Trina. Is there any way she can come to your place?

He used the camera feature to snap a quick image of his daughter playing with the kitten, partly for the adorable factor (as in, *How could anyone say no to this?*) and partly to remind the woman that he'd already prepaid the favor by taking in this animal with gastrointestinal issues.

Speaking of Tootie's gas, Ethan should probably grab a can of air freshener at the market and send a picture of that to Monica, as well. Just so she could see the extent of his sacrifice for dealing with this unexpected pet.

It took another ten minutes—and several muffled curse words—for Ethan to get the dresser drawer back on the track. When he did, he was rewarded with a small grin from Trina, who was eager to finish putting away her new clothes.

Walking out of the room with his tool bag, he was also

rewarded with a text from Monica, whose straightforward "Sure" and smile emoji might have been intended as a polite response.

But that simple response also sent a tiny spark of adrenaline through him.

"Is this the sweet Trina I've been hearing all about?" Freckles boomed out when Ethan and his daughter came into the Cowgirl Up Café early Monday morning.

"Yes, ma'am," Ethan replied, and Monica witnessed his chest puff out with a bit more pride than it had the last time he'd walked through the restaurant's saloon-style doors. "Freckles, this is my daughter, Trina. Trina, allow me to introduce you to the owner of this fine establishment and the person who knows everything about what's going on in town."

"Fine establishment" might be a stretch, Monica thought, as she looked around at the bright turquoise walls covered with neon painted lassos, bedazzled horseshoes and enough cowgirl paraphernalia to host a rodeo-themed party inside every sorority house at Boise State. But her part-time boss and the popular café were definitely the center for gossip in Sugar Falls.

In fact, Freckles had been good friends with Gran for years and was the first one to point out to Monica that her grandmother might be suffering from something more than absentmindedness. A couple of years ago, it had been easy for Monica to miss the signs herself because she lived with the older woman and the changes were so gradual, it was easy to grow immune to the forgetfulness and write off the initial episodes as occasional quirkiness.

Freckles was also the one who suggested that Monica might need to start saving for Gran's health care down the road, and offered up a few extra shifts at her restaurant, despite the fact that Monica wasn't very outgoing and pretty much sucked at being a waitress at first.

"Nice to finally meet you, Trina," Freckles said around the wad of chewing gum in her mouth. "Your dad is one of my best customers, so I knew he couldn't keep you away from my famous cinnamon rolls for too long. Have a seat and I'll bring a couple out."

Trina gave a shy nod, but instead of keeping her eyes downcast she turned to look around the room, her gaze landing on Monica. "Oh! Hi."

"Hey, guys," Monica said, walking to their table with a pot of coffee. "Are you all ready for the first day of school?"

"Not really," Trina replied, her shoulders slumping under the new green jacket. "Are you sure I can't just hang out at the library and read? That's pretty much the same thing as going to school."

"Sorry, kiddo," Monica said with a sympathetic smile. "But you can come to the library after school if you want and tell me all about your day."

The girl sighed. "I can tell you about it right now. It's gonna be horrible and I'm gonna hate it."

"I hated being stuck in a classroom when I was your age, too," Freckles said, returning to the table with two fresh cinnamon rolls slathered in cream cheese frosting. "But I sure loved recess. All the boys would chase us around the playground and, sometimes, I'd even let the cute ones catch me."

Monica rolled her eyes and took her order pad out of her apron pocket. "So what can I get you for your big first day of school feast?"

"Well, we've been stocking up on cereal and Pop-Tarts

at the market lately," Ethan said, explaining why they hadn't been in for breakfast since the day Trina arrived. "So preferably something hot. Trina, do you want a few minutes to look over the menu?"

"I don't really feel like eating." The girl scooted out of the booth. "I'm gonna go to the bathroom."

"Must be a nervous stomach," Freckles said when Trina was out of earshot. "I got like that after I met my fourth husband. The man would barely look at me and my tummy would get to churning and I'd have to make a beeline for the nearest ladies' room."

Ethan's brow shot up to his hairline at Freckles's revelation of information nobody needed to hear. But he was quick to recover when he leaned forward, peering up at Monica. "Uh…the other reason I brought her in for breakfast this morning was because I was hoping you could give her some sort of pep talk?"

"Me? I'm not quite sure what I could say to make her any less nervous. I hated school, too."

"Really?" Ethan asked, his gaze traveling down the front of her and back up again. "But you're so smart. I assumed you were one of those teacher's pet types who would get straight As and be the president of the honor society and the French club and everything."

When he looked at her like that, Monica's own tummy began to flutter. "Well the straight As part is accurate, but joining any sort of society, even an academic one, would mean that I'd have to be social. And socializing isn't exactly my thing. Obviously, kids need school, but deep down I don't blame Trina for just wanting to hang out at the library and read."

Trina voluntarily returned from the restroom after only a couple of minutes—which was a vast improvement from the last time she'd been in the café and had gone there to hide—and Monica took their orders. There weren't many people in the restaurant this morning and, normally, Freckles would've been leaning against their table, chatting up a newcomer like Trina. But the owner was conspicuously busy visiting with Scooter and Jonesy, who were practically permanent fixtures in the restaurant. What was odder was the fact that Freckles kept her normally loud and joyful voice hushed and would cast occasional glances toward Ethan and Trina whenever they weren't looking.

Freckles didn't leave the old cowboys' booth until Ethan was paying his check, which was right about when Monica saw the angle of the woman's bright magenta-tinted grin and realized she was up to something.

"You know, sugar, it's such a slow morning," Freckles said to Monica as though an idea had just occurred to her and hadn't been percolating in her over-teased and heavily hair-sprayed head this whole time. Putting an orange-spandex-covered hip on the edge of the counter near the cash register, her boss continued. "Plus, you're already familiar with all the teachers and half of the kids over at that school. Why don't you take off early and go with Ethan and Trina, to ease her into her first day?"

His daughter's face lit up and it suddenly occurred to Monica that she was becoming a little too ingrained in the father-daughter-bonding experience. And Freckles was becoming a little too ingrained in the matchmaking-her-employees experience.

Monica didn't want to overshadow Ethan's role or in any way interfere with them getting to know each other better. "I doubt I'd be all that helpful. Besides, isn't the first day of school one of those big milestones that should be just the two of you?"

"Just the two of us and the other couple of hundred parents and kids at drop-off," Ethan murmured before turning to Trina and leaning down. "What would make you feel the most comfortable?"

"I'd like Monica to come with us." Trina's voice was barely over a whisper, as all the other customers around them had gotten quieter so they could overhear the sidebar conversation. "And then after school, you and me can still get ice cream at Noodie's for our milestone, whatever that is."

"Sounds like a plan to me," Ethan replied, then rose back to his full height. "As long as Monica is okay with it."

"Please?" the girl asked, the earnestness in her clear blue eyes making Monica's rib cage squeeze against her heart. She didn't know who looked more hopeful—Trina or Ethan.

"I'd really owe you." Ethan's pleading smile made her knees wobble. "Again."

That's right. She was already ahead of him in the favors department. It took every ounce of restraint not to think about Ethan's text message last night. She'd had to turn off her phone to keep from asking where he needed to go that he couldn't take a child. Since it would be after dark, she doubted it was to a work site, which only left one other explanation. Ethan had a date. With another woman.

Which was why she needed to make it clear that she would only do favors that benefitted Trina—not Ethan. A few minutes later, when he held open the truck door for her, she told him as much.

"I'm only doing this because Trina could use the moral

support." Monica shot a glance into the backseat before fixing Ethan with her most serious look. "Next time, when it comes to making your life easier, you're on your own."

Ethan offered his hand to Trina as they walked across the parking lot of the elementary school, but his daughter didn't take it. Instead, he was forced to jam his fists into his coat pockets as if he hadn't just been completely rejected by an eleven-year-old.

Yeah, she was probably too old for holding hands. She did, however, stay pretty glued to his side so he should be thankful that the girl didn't find him totally repulsive.

Monica waved to the crossing guard and several other parents who stood on the front steps of Sugar Falls Elementary School watching them approach. Trina scooted even closer to him to the point that half of her thin body was hidden behind him. Ethan's instinct was to shield her from danger, but Carmen Gregson approached wearing her full police uniform and towing two identical nine-year-old boys behind her. Ethan was eager to ask the woman if she'd been in touch with Trina's caseworker back in Texas. But with so many eyes on them, he should probably wait until after school drop-off.

"Hey, Miss Alvarez," one of the Gregson twins (he could never remember which one was Aiden and which one was Caden) ran up to Monica after twisting out of his mom's hand. "Did you get any more of those pirate detective books in yet?"

"I'm expecting a shipment today. Maybe you can come by the library later this afternoon with my friend Trina. She's new to the school."

"Are you Trina?" the other twin asked.

His daughter moved even farther behind him, her

beanie-covered head peeking out from around his bicep. So she was nervous, but at least she was curious.

Ethan loosely wrapped his arm around her shoulder, but allowed her to stay pressed close to his hip. "This is my daughter, Trina Renault. Trina, these two rascals are Aiden and Caden Gregson and they're in…uh, third grade?"

"Fourth," the pair corrected him in unison, as if Ethan should have any idea of which grades went with which age group.

"I'm in fifth," Trina's voice was faint, but at least she was talking and not running straight for the girls' room.

"That's Mr. Yasikochi's class," Caden, or possibly Aiden, replied. Ethan really should know how to tell his best friend's kids apart by now. "He's the coolest teacher here. During our last assembly, he challenged the principal and the rest of the teachers to a spelling bee and now all the students get to pick which words they gotta spell. The winner's class gets a pudding cup party."

"Do you like pudding cups?" Aiden, or possibly Caden, asked.

"I guess," Trina replied.

"Come with us," one of the twins said, pulling on her jacket sleeve. "We'll show you where the cafeteria is and where we line up after recess and where the PE teacher keeps the best dodge balls locked in her office and where…"

The boys' voices faded as they pulled a taller Trina between them and peppered her with an overload of information. When they got to the top of the steps, she looked back at Ethan, her eyes wide and uncertain.

"Go ahead, Trina," Ethan said, capturing Monica's hand to pull her along. "We'll be right behind you."

Monica made a slight squeak and her head did a double take at his fingers resting against hers. But Ethan liked having her close, he wasn't about to let go. Besides, with all the kids darting in every which direction, he didn't want to accidentally get separated from her in all this chaos. Her cheeks turned a rosy shade of pink and several of the other parents murmured to each other on the steps as she took quick tiny steps to keep up with his bigger strides.

As soon as they set foot inside the building, Ethan was hit with the scent of glue and pencil lead and industrial-strength cleaner. Apparently not much had changed in over twenty years. This place smelled exactly like every elementary school he'd ever attended. And with his father's job that required them to move every eighteen months or so, Ethan was an expert.

A shrill bell sounded, making Ethan flinch. Maybe they couldn't do anything about the aroma, yet one would think they would've developed a more pleasant ringtone by now. Man, he was glad he didn't have to stay. If hating school was a genetic trait, poor Trina must've inherited it from him.

Kids scattered in all directions—including their nine-year-old tour guides, who promised to see Trina on the playground at recess—and Monica and Ethan were left standing alone in the hallway with his daughter.

Ethan had logged at least twenty parachute maneuvers, along with countless rescue and recon missions by both land and sea into enemy territory. Yet, he'd never experienced the type of paralyzing confusion as he did right that second in the hallway of an American elementary school. Well, except for last Saturday at the mall. And the Wednesday before that when Trina arrived on his doorstep. Hell, was this constant fish-out-of-water feeling *ever* going to cease?

Thank goodness for Monica, their undesignated team leader who'd managed to wiggle away from Ethan's grasp a few minutes ago when a couple of moms cornered him about attending the next PTA meeting.

"Let's go to the front office and meet Principal Cromartie." Monica smiled at Trina while Ethan didn't get so much as a passing glance. "He usually likes to walk new students to their classrooms."

"That's right," Ethan said, recalling the principal saying as much when they'd been here last Friday to register. At the time, he'd felt as though he was signing his life away with all those forms and permission slips the admissions clerk had shoved in front of him.

Compared to all the hoops they'd had to jump through a few days ago, this morning's meeting with the principal seemed almost anticlimatic. Dr. Cromartie's skin was smooth enough to make the thin, lanky African American man appear to be in his forties, but the shock of white, wiry hair on top of his head had Ethan thinking the head of the school was much older. Either way, the gentleman had a commanding presence and spoke confidently to Trina about how well she would do in Mr. Yasikochi's class, then asked Ethan and Monica to stay outside and wait for him as he opened a door with a hand-painted sign that read *Learning is Great in Room #8.*

"Have a good day," Monica said to Trina, who was already looking at the ground.

"Remember, I'll be standing outside on the steps at three o'clock," Ethan offered what reassurance he could. They'd gone over the day's schedule several more times last night and twice this morning. "And then we'll go get ice cream."

He was hoping for at least a nod, but his daughter surprised him by lifting her face and staring right at him as she spoke. "Don't forget that I'm also going to Monica's for dinner so that you can go to your meeting."

"I won't forget," he said, lifting his hand in a wave that probably came across as way too upbeat. Trina's own hand flicked upward, but her wave wasn't even half as enthusiastic.

When the classroom door closed behind his daughter and the principal, Monica turned to him. "You have a meeting tonight?"

"Yeah." He rocked back on his heels and glanced down the hall toward the exit door. Man, it was warm in this hallway.

"What kind of meeting?"

Ethan peeled off his coat and was stuck having to loop it through his arm. He wanted to reply, *The kind that's anonymous.* But after seeing Monica's facial reaction to Trina's comment about Chantal using "medicine" to stay skinny, he didn't know if he was ready for her to judge him the same way. Before Trina, he wouldn't have had a problem answering the question. Now, however, he flashed back to the insinuation Monica had made last week in the kitchen of the Cowgirl Up Café when she'd all but accused him of being a deadbeat dad. Since then, there might've been a slight thawing in her opinion of him, but he wasn't ready to find out. Instead he shrugged as if it was no big deal. "The kind that's personal."

She lowered her eyelids skeptically. "Sounds like a date to me."

"Would you be jealous if it was a date?" He wiggled

his eyebrows while trying to tamp down the thread of hope that began to coil in his belly. If she was jealous, that meant she cared. About him.

"Not a chance." Her response would've been more believable if she hadn't added a frustrated little huff afterward.

"I think you would be." He leaned in closer, letting his eyes drop to her full mouth as she opened and closed her lips several times. However, before she could utter so much as a denial, Dr. Cromartie walked back out into the hallway to join them.

"Thanks for waiting for me," the principal said. "Would you mind coming into my office?"

The older gentleman didn't wait for a response, walking away like a man accustomed to students following him.

"Oh… I'm sure you don't need me—" Monica started, but Ethan's hand immediately found hers again and he steered them toward the front of the school.

"We came in the same car, remember?" he murmured under his breath. Plus, he wasn't about to let her off the hook so easily. If she was going to start a conversation about the subject of dating, then he would sure as hell finish it.

The smooth skin against her jaw tightened, but Monica refused to meet his gaze, stiffly allowing him to lead her into Dr. Cromartie's office.

"So we got Trina's file from her prior school," the principal said as he gestured for them to take a seat. The older man picked up a blue folder and perched on the edge of his desk. "It's not completely comprehensive because her attendance was pretty spotty the past couple of years."

"I figured as much," Ethan replied, hoping Dr.

Cromartie wasn't judging him for being the flaky parent who hadn't made her go to school. Of course, his excuse of not being in his daughter's life before now didn't exactly make him an award-winning dad either.

"According to her grades and state testing results, her grammar and language scores are off the charts. So she's a very smart girl."

Ethan sat up a little straighter, pride filling his chest at an accomplishment that didn't technically belong to him. This might actually be the first time he'd ever been in a principal's office and not gotten a stern lecture.

"However…?" Monica pressed, ruining Ethan's short-lived moment of smugness.

"However," Dr. Cromartie gave a brief nod. "When she was in third grade, one of her teachers identified Trina as having dyscalculia."

Monica made a murmuring noise and Ethan looked between the only two people in the room with college degrees. "What does dyscalcu…whatever it's called. What does that mean?"

"Dyscalculia is a developmental disorder that makes it difficult to comprehend numbers and understand math concepts. For example, someone with dyscalculia might not remember which order numbers go in, or they struggle to identify the difference between a plus sign and a minus sign. Oftentimes, people refer to it as math dyslexia."

"That explains why she was pretty adamant about not going to school," Monica offered, putting a hand on Ethan's shoulder as though she was offering him comfort. "She's been struggling in math."

As much as he enjoyed the warmth of her touch, he didn't exactly need to be consoled. In fact, his back sagged against the seat in relief. "That's great."

"I'm sorry?" Dr. Cromartie pulled his chin back. "Are you saying that you're happy about this diagnosis?"

"Well, not happy. I mean, I'm definitely *un*happy about the fact that she struggled for so long and that she never got the help she needed. I'm downright pissed that she's had to go through this and so much more without me being there to support her. But I'm relieved that we're getting some answers and that we can get her on track now. You already said she was smart, right?" Ethan asked and waited for Dr. Cromartie's slow nod of assent. "Then this math dyslexia is the only thing wrong with Trina."

"I don't know if I would characterize it as something being *wrong* with her," Monica started.

"No, of course not. I just meant that if we have an explanation for why her brain does what it does, then we can get busy and fix it."

"Well, like dyslexia, it isn't necessarily curable," Dr. Cromartie warned. "But there are specialized tutoring and strategies that can help a person overcome it."

"Great." Ethan smacked his hands together. "How do we sign her up for that class?"

"As a smaller school, we don't exactly have a budget for specialty programs like that here. There are schools in Boise that could better accommodate this sort of—"

Ethan braced his palms on his knees. "I'm not moving her. No way. She's already been through too much and I don't think it would be fair to make her start somewhere new again."

Okay, so he wasn't just looking out for Trina's best interests in that regard. He also preferred not to uproot himself when he was just getting settled and had developed a dependable support system. Just like on the airplanes when they tell people to put on their own oxygen masks before helping others, Ethan's personal self-care would be essential if he truly wanted to be a better parent for his daughter. Really, it'd be better for *both* of them if they could avoid having any more disruptions in their lives.

"We have after-school tutors who come into the library a few days a week," Monica offered, placing a calming hand on top of his twitching fingers. "I can ask around to see if there's someone who specializes in dyscalculia. But you'd probably have to pay them out of pocket."

He studied the woman who sat beside him, the woman who was consistently a source of quiet strength and seemed to always know the answers before he could even think of the questions. He flipped his palm over, lacing his fingers through hers and giving them an instinctive squeeze in appreciation. God, it felt good not to be sitting here alone.

"I might not be rich, but I'll spend every damn dime on Trina's education if that's what it takes to get her where she needs to be. Maybe it didn't matter to Chantal, but it does to me. I want to help her the best way I can." He smiled gratefully at Monica, and looked back at Dr. Cromartie. "We'll start working on this as soon as we find the right tutor."

It also meant that Ethan would be spending a lot more time at the library.

Chapter Seven

"Hey, Monica," Nurse Dunn called, poking her head out of the health office. The woman wore medical scrubs covered with teddy bears and carried a coffee mug stamped with two different shades of lipstick. "Were you talking to Dr. Cromartie about the open school librarian position?"

"Um…" Monica tried not to look at Ethan behind her or in any way signal that they'd just been in the principal's office together. "No. We were just going over some tutoring programs at the city library."

"Oh." Nurse Dunn's eyes landed on Ethan's hand which had somehow nestled its way into Monica's again. The first time they'd held hands had been so they could stay together as they fought traffic in the crowded hallway. Then, in the office, the gesture had been more of a show of emotional support between friends. Now, though, his firm, wide grip was a little more difficult to write off as platonic. In fact, she didn't know what burned more—the area just below her wrist where his thumb was tracing slow, steady circles, or her cheeks that were flaming with mortification. "Well, if you know anyone who is interested, send them our way."

"I will," Monica replied, but it came out in a muffle and she had to clear her throat to repeat herself.

She stepped into the hallway, hoping that the quicker she walked, the easier it would be to dislodge Ethan's hand. But the man wasn't letting go. Obviously, she could yank hers away, however, that would only serve as an admission that his touch had any sort of effect on her. So she kept her spine stiff and her head facing forward and tried to pretend that she hadn't even noticed how overwhelming, yet natural, it felt to have his long, work-roughened fingers settled against hers.

There'd been such a suffocating warmth in the school hallway that Monica sucked in deep gulps of the cold February air when they got outside. She should've steeled herself better for the sudden drop in temperature, though, because her shoulders let out an uncontrollable shiver, causing Ethan to release her hand so that he could wrap that arm around her waist and pull her toward him.

His body shielded the wind from her and it was tough not to notice how perfectly she fit against him.

Okay. She'd only allow herself to enjoy the strength and warmth of his protective arm for a few more steps. But before they could make it past the sidewalk, Carmen caught up with them in the parking lot.

"My boys forgot these in the back of my squad car. I swear if their heads weren't attached, they'd forget those, too." She held up two lunch boxes—one Batman and one Spider-Man. "Anyway, I'm glad I caught you guys alone."

Monica opened her mouth to argue that despite the way she was pressed up to his side, she and Ethan weren't really alone. At least not like *that*. And not on purpose. However, Carmen didn't bat an eye as she continued, "I got a call from Trina's caseworker this morning."

"What did they say?" Ethan stiffened beside her, but didn't let go. Monica could only imagine the type of information he would need to brace himself for. Her own muscles were probably equally as tense at that moment.

"She reiterated pretty much what Trina already told you. Chantal DeVecchio has had numerous arrests for drug-related charges. Irene DeVecchio, Trina's grandmother, primarily raised her seeing as how Chantal was in and out of jail and rehab so often. The Texas Department of Family and Protective Services didn't open the case until Irene's health began to decline and Trina's school attendance suffered. The caseworker was assigned primarily to help with social services and to watch over the situation and make reports. She'd even referred them to family court to get Trina's guardianship legally established and to look into the possibility of other relatives raising the girl if and when Irene could no longer do so. She said your name came up when Trina asked her to do a search for her father."

"Trina mentioned that she'd been the one to find me, not her mom." Ethan lifted his face toward the cloudless sky, but his eyes were squeezed shut and his hand slipped from her waist to find hers once again—as if he was dizzy and Monica was the only thing grounding him. "I wanted to ask her more about that, but she shuts down if I try to get too much information from her at once."

"The caseworker said that when Irene passed away, Chantal took off with Trina and they stayed off the radar for a while. She was relieved when I told her that the girl was here with you."

"Does that mean they'll let her stay with me?" Ethan's normally unexpressive eyes were flooded with determination and resolve. She'd seen him friendly, she'd seen him charming, she'd even seen him confused. But this was the second time this morning she'd witnessed his intensity when it came to Trina's well-being. Maybe he was truly serious about wanting his daughter, after all.

Carmen's expression was a bit more guarded. "Texas is referring the case to the authorities here in Idaho. They'll be in contact with you soon to set up a home visit."

"A home visit for what?"

"To make sure that you're providing Trina with suitable living conditions and to probably interview you both to determine if being in your custody is in her best interest."

Ethan let out a whooshing breath, his shoulders relaxing. "What do you think, Carmen? You think I can pass the home visit so that they'll let me keep her?"

"My personal opinion? Of course they will. My professional opinion, however, is that you never know what can happen in these kinds of situations. Like I told you last week, it might be beneficial to retain an attorney, just to make sure all the legalities are in order."

Ethan nodded, then looked at Monica. "What about you, Mon? If you were the caseworker, would you let me keep her?"

Her tummy quivered at his use of the intimate nickname again and her body grew warm at the realization that he craved her reassurance. If he'd asked her to direct him to the family law treatises or the top-rated parenting books, it'd be no problem. Yet, here in the real world—away from the reference desk—she would only be offering him false hope.

Before she could say as much, the phone in the back pocket of her jeans vibrated.

"Excuse me for a sec," she said, stepping away to answer the call from an unknown number. "Hello?"

"Hey, Monica, this is Marcia over at Duncan's Market." Marcia only stopped in the library once a year or so to browse the self-help books, yet always left empty-handed. She'd also been a few years ahead of Monica in high school and even back then was well established as one of the most notorious gossips in town.

"Hi, Marcia. What can I do for you?" Scrunching her nose, Monica thought, *Please let this phone call be about the Motivational Mondays book club and not about why Monica has been spending so much time lately with Ethan Renault.*

"The reason I'm calling is because your grandmother came in this morning to do some shopping, but when she got to the checkout line, she didn't seem to have her purse."

A knot of dread formed in the pit of Monica's stomach. "Is she still there?"

"She is. She got pretty agitated so Mauricio, our deli manager, took her into the back office to talk about rotisserie chicken recipes. I think it's calming her down, but you should probably swing by and pick her up."

Ethan approached, his dark brow lifted in a silent question. Monica covered the mouthpiece of the phone and whispered, "Gran's over at the market. I have to go get her."

He nodded, so Monica removed her hand to speak

into the phone just as Ethan added, "Tell them we're on our way."

Marcia gasped on the other end. "Oh my. Is that a man I just heard in the background?"

Monica's cheeks flooded with heat and she squeaked out, "I'll be right there."

Ethan drove Monica straight to Duncan's Market and, despite the fact that she insisted he leave her there, he followed her into the store. "Your car is still at the café and I don't have to be on the job site until ten o'clock. So unless you want your gran walking to your car in her bathrobe and tap shoes, you should probably let me give you guys a ride."

"But then Marcia Duncan is going to know that we were together this morning," Monica said through clenched teeth as she forced a smile and a wave at one of the cashiers.

"It's Sugar Falls and all the parents and teachers just saw us at the elementary school together." He glanced down at the titanium chronograph watch the guys in his platoon gave him for setting a record on the combat diver qualifications course. "I'm sure Marcia, as well as the rest of the five thousand people who live within the city limits, already know you were with me. In fact, they've probably been speculating on it for at least a good hour by now."

"Oh hey there, Ethan," Marcia greeted them in the same syrupy tone she'd used when she'd followed him and Trina around the store last week, pointing out all the specials while not-so-subtly throwing in a leading question. *We have strawberry Pop-Tarts on sale. Do* you *have strawberry Pop-Tarts back in…where are you from again, dear?* As they'd stocked up on groceries, Marcia had tried to stock up on gossip about the person everyone else in town was referring to as his secret daughter. "I thought I recognized your voice when I was on the phone with Monica, but I knew she'd already left the café to go to… where were you guys so early this morning?"

See, Ethan shot Monica a knowing look, but her head was on a swivel—probably scanning the store for her wayward grandmother—and didn't seem to register anything else. Not wanting to give in to Marcia's blatant attempts to fish for information, he asked, "Is Mrs. Alvarez still here?"

"She's back here. Mauricio is trying to keep her calm by letting her chop up cabbage for coleslaw, but she refuses to wear the disposable gloves or put her hair up in the hairnet. So we won't be able to sell any of it."

"There you are, *mija*," Gran said to Monica when they entered the deli prep kitchen. "And you brought your handsome friend with you again."

"Hi, Gran." Monica's tone was laced with caution. He recognized it as the same one he used when he wanted to ask Trina a question and didn't want to scare her off. "We stopped by to give you a ride home. You remember *Mr. Renault*, don't you?"

Ethan would've laughed at the way Monica emphasized his formal name, as if that would lead Marcia—or anyone else—to think there wasn't anything casual going on between them. But now wasn't the time to be teasing her about the status of their relationship. Not only because her grandmother was possibly in a delicate mental state, but also because he wasn't exactly sure of the definition of their relationship at that point.

"Of course I remember you, Ethan," Gran replied, then

winked at the store owner. "He spends quite a bit of time at our house, you know."

Monica's cheeks turned a charming shade of crimson. "That was back in November when he was working on our kitchen, Gran."

"And he stayed over very late after he brought you home the other night, *mija*."

"Oh my." Marcia's eyes couldn't get any rounder and her mouth hung open like one of those bottom-feeding catfish hanging out at the Lake Rush docks waiting for someone to drop a tasty morsel their way.

Ethan's fingers twitched. "Mrs. Alvarez, if you're all done here, why don't we head on back to your place and maybe you can make me something for lunch?"

Really, he wasn't very hungry after adding that cinnamon roll to his normal breakfast earlier. Plus, it wasn't exactly lunchtime, but when they'd worked on her house, the older woman had seemed to enjoy plying him and Kane with homemade food no matter what time of day it was.

"For you, *mijo*, I'll make some fresh *conchas* and that Mexican hot chocolate you like," Gran said, using the masculine version of the endearment she usually reserved for her granddaughter. "But I'll have to stop at the market on the way home and pick up some things."

Monica's breath came out in a sigh. "Gran, we're at the market right now."

"Oh, well then that's convenient." The woman took off the service deli apron someone had given her, revealing the shabby bathrobe she'd been wearing underneath. Her feet gave off a musical ping with each step as she walked across the tile floor. She looped her frail arm through Monica's, stifling a yawn. "*Mija*, go grab us a cart so we can do our shopping."

"Um, Mrs. Alvarez—" Marcia lifted her plump fingers in a small wave "—you still have your cart of groceries over by the register. Remember, you told us not to put anything back until Monica got here with your purse."

Monica patted her jacket pockets. "That might be an issue. I left my own purse at the café when I took off with Ethan this morning."

"So then you want me to put the groceries in the cart away?" Marcia scratched the frizzy blond hair on top of her head. "All of them?"

"*Donde estan, mija?*" Mrs. Alvarez's face grew pinched. "*Donde esta la comida que acabo de compare? Y por que me esta viendo asi la gorda?*"

Ethan had to rely on some of the Spanish phrases he'd learned back when he'd been stationed in San Diego near the border. But he understood enough to know that the older woman had just taken a turn and didn't know where they were or what had happened to the food she'd just bought. She'd also made an unflattering remark about Marcia Duncan's size, judging by the tight grin Mauricio Norte was trying to hide and the shushing sounds Monica was making at her.

Ethan fished the keys out of his pocket and handed them to Monica. "Why don't you take Gran to the truck and I'll pay for the groceries?"

"Come on," Marcia said, casting a narrowed look at Mrs. Alvarez who was now speaking in rapid-fire Spanish. "We already scanned everything and have it bagged up front."

Ethan followed the owner of the market to the cash register and didn't even ask what was in the two shopping carts. He just wanted to get out of there and get Monica and her grandmother home.

When he got to the parking lot, Gran was already in the backseat. Her lips were moving, but no sound came out as she slouched against the armrest and stared vacantly out the window.

"Oh my gosh," Monica said when she saw all the bags in the two carts he towed behind him. "Why in the world was she buying so much food? I don't even want to know how much money I owe you for all that."

Ethan was glad he'd crumpled up the receipt and shoved it deep into his coat pocket on the way outside. He doubted Monica had an extra two hundred dollars lying around to pay him back. Not that he'd let her.

"We can figure all that out later." Ethan jerked his head toward the cab of his truck. "How's she doing?"

"Exhausted." Monica reached into one of the carts to haul out a paper bag. "Every time she has an episode it takes a lot out of her, physically."

Ethan lowered his tailgate and, when he took the bag of groceries from her, the backs of his fingers inadvertently grazed the underside of her breast. A current of electricity shot through his body and he dropped the bag, making a loud *thunk* against the metal shopping cart.

He'd touched women before. Hell, he'd even touched Monica before and they'd pretty much been holding hands at the school all morning. But that was more out of necessity. Sort of. It was also before Marcia Duncan made it a point to suggest that their relationship was more than just friendship.

Now, though, it was different since they were both aware of their attraction and this time the accidental contact through her wool coat sent waves up one of his arms and down the other. The blush rising over her neck told him that she'd felt the same sensation. In fact, Monica refused to look at him as they finished loading the rest of the bags into the truck, which was a sure sign that his touch had equally affected her.

And that made him feel pretty damn good.

Their house was only a mile away from the store, yet Gran was lightly snoring by the time Ethan pulled into the driveway. Monica turned around in her seat to wake her grandmother, but Ethan put his finger to his mouth. "Let her sleep. I can carry her upstairs."

Seeing her tiny and frail grandmother cradled in Ethan's arms would have been touching if it hadn't reminded Monica of the way someone would carry a child. It broke Monica's heart to sit back and watch such a strong woman grow increasingly dependent with each passing day.

Leading the way to Gran's bedroom, Monica pulled the quilted cover back so that he could get her sleeping grandmother settled on the bed. She reached down to unbuckle the strap of Gran's tap shoe and gasped at the maroon-colored bruise on the papery thin skin underneath.

"Looks like a blood blister," Ethan whispered. "How do you think it happened?"

"Hard to say. She usually gets them just by bumping into something. But the rest of her feet are all purplish and raw—like she maybe walked all the way to the store."

Monica's car was still at the café and most of the nearby neighbors knew better than to give her grandmother a ride when she was dressed like this. Thankfully, some of her neighbors tended to stop by and check in on Gran because they knew Monica couldn't afford a full-time caregiver when she was at work. She never would've been able to manage it without all the added help. Although, she had to wonder if she was managing anything anymore.

"Do you need me to help up here or should I bring the groceries in?" Ethan's fingers quivered slightly before he shoved them in his pockets.

The guy was definitely itching to get out of here. Not that she could blame him. To an outsider, Gran's behavior must seem totally crazy. "If you could just set the bags on the front porch, I'll get them from there."

Just like two days ago, Monica carefully repacked the dance shoes in their box and pulled the quilt up over her grandmother. Also, just like two days ago, when she returned downstairs, she found Ethan in her kitchen—his coat tossed over a chair as he put three cartons of eggs in the refrigerator.

He glanced at her when she entered, but didn't stop what he was doing. "I wasn't sure where everything went, so I guessed. The good news is that you won't be running out of pickles anytime soon."

He nodded toward the open pantry cabinet with an entire shelf dedicated to duplicate jars of the same dill variety and Monica sighed. "Gran is always afraid of running out of certain things. The crazy thing is that she doesn't even like pickles, so they just sit there until I can go through and sneak a few containers out at a time. Same thing with the diet root beer and the grape jelly. I'm worried that the people who run the canned food drives are going to ask me to stop donating so often."

"That explains the stash of Oreos I found hidden on the top shelf."

"Actually, those are mine. Gran thinks store-bought cookies are a sin, but I lived on them during finals week at college and now, anytime I'm stressed, it's like my body craves them."

"I'm guessing you're stressed pretty often?" Ethan lifted two five-pound bags of rice and she tried not to stare at the way it made the muscles under his snug thermal T-shirt stretch.

"Some days—like today—are a little rougher than others."

He paused. "Maybe I shouldn't bring Trina over tonight, after all?"

"No, Gran'll be up and at 'em in a couple of hours. Usually, when she wakes up after having an episode, it's like a reboot. You know how if you get too many windows running on your computer, you can shut it off and then restart it to get it working faster?" Monica waited for Ethan's slow nod. "That's what her brain does. So she'll most likely remember that Trina is coming tonight and will want to make something special for dinner. It's probably why she went to the store in the first place."

"Well, I wouldn't want to disappoint Gran." Ethan's smile was back and Monica's knees went as soft as the fresh loaf of white bread in her hands. "But I don't want it to be any extra work for you."

"Actually, Trina will be a positive distraction for Gran. Really, it'd be helping me to have her over. Besides, who else is going to eat all this food?"

They worked in silence emptying the rest of the bags. When they finished, Ethan lifted both of his arms over his head to stretch, causing the hem of his shirt to rise and reveal a strip of smooth, chiseled skin just above his belt line.

Monica's mouth went dry and her head went a little

fuzzy as she imagined what it would be like to undo the first button on his fly.

Oh boy. She really needed to get him out of her house before her imagination led her down a dangerous path. Forcing herself to swallow, she asked, "Shouldn't you be heading back to work now?"

He looked at the heavy-duty watch on his wrist. "Probably. Are you going to stay here to watch your grandmother or do you need a lift back to your car?"

Monica groaned as she sank into one of the dining room chairs. "I can't afford to miss any more work. Let me call one of our neighbors and see if they can come over and check on her a few times."

Mr. Simon had recently retired and Monica pulled out her cell phone to call him while Ethan sent his own boss a text.

After hanging up, she ran upstairs to change out of her boots and Cowgirl Up T-shirt and into something more appropriate for the library. She checked on Gran one more time, planting a soft kiss on the older woman's spotted cheek before switching on the long-range baby monitor they'd purchased a few months ago.

Monica asked Ethan to lock up as she navigated across the snowy grass as quickly as her narrow pencil skirt would allow. Mr. Simon was already on his own porch to take the monitor's walkie-talkie unit so he could listen to Gran while he was working in his garage.

"That Ethan Renault?" Mr. Simon asked, nodding toward Ethan's truck.

"Oh. Um, yes. He's giving me a ride back to the café to get my car."

"Your gran tells us you're spending a lot of time with him lately." Mr. Simon was nice enough, but he tended to read a few too many true crime stories and was suspicious of anyone he hadn't known for at least twenty years.

"I wouldn't say *a lot*…"

"Heard you went down to Boise with him to go shopping."

"News travels fast." *As usual*, Monica wanted to add. "But did you also hear we went with his eleven-year-old daughter?"

"Might've heard something about that. My wife thinks he's in the market for a new mom for his little girl. But I told Deb that everyone in town knows he was interested in you long before the child showed up—"

"Okay, well I better get going, Mr. Simon. Call me when Gran wakes up."

When Monica climbed into Ethan's truck, her fingers fumbled with the seat belt buckle as she kept replaying Mr. Simon's words about everyone thinking Ethan was interested in her. Her neighbor, though, was also a known conspiracy theorist who'd once questioned whether the government could listen in on the baby monitor, so she shouldn't give his illogical opinion another thought.

"Here," Ethan said, putting his hand over hers. Her skin hummed to life, just like it had when he'd accidentally brushed against her breast in the parking lot at the market. And when he'd spontaneously grabbed her hand for reassurance in the elementary school hallway before that. He snapped the metal mechanism into place, allowing his thumb to trace over hers afterward. "It can be tricky sometimes."

She stared at his tanned, callused fingers, mesmerized by the slow and gentle strokes he made against the ridge of her knuckle and all the way to her crescent-shaped nail.

Pull away, her brain told her.

Touch him back, her lower parts dared her.

Fortunately, her brain won out, but not until he'd made his way all the way to the tender flesh of her wrist. Her elbow hit the hard part of the glove box because she'd jerked her arm back so quickly.

He gave her a knowing smile, but instead of talking about what had just happened, Ethan thankfully put the truck in gear. When they turned onto Snowflake Boulevard, he asked, "How long do you think your gran will sleep?"

Monica shrugged, relieved they were talking about anything other than the way her body always responded to him. "It just depends on how bad the episode was. It's like her brain is working so hard to make sense of the world around her, that her body stops working in order to send all of the energy up there. Spanish is her first language, so when she reverts to it like she did earlier at the store, I know it's just a matter of time before she shuts down. I really appreciate the fact that you were there to drive us home."

"Pretty soon we're gonna need a scorecard to keep track of how many favors we owe each other."

"Maybe we shouldn't be keeping count of who owes who what." Or of how much time they were spending together. It was a slippery slope to be indebted to someone she was finding it harder and harder to resist. She squared her shoulders against the seat. "We're friends. That's what friends do. Help each other out."

"So that's all we are, huh?" he asked as he parked in front of the Cowgirl Up Café. "Friends?"

"Yep." She opened the door and jumped down from the cab before her eyes proved her mouth wrong. "I'm just your friend, Ethan."

"Well, that's more than we were a few weeks ago, so I guess we're making a little progress." His upper teeth did that thing where they scraped against his lower lip and she commanded her feet to move. But they ignored her and chose to obey him when he called out, "Hold on!"

Ethan opened his own door and, as he made his way around the truck, Monica gulped in enough cold air to fight the rising temperature inside her.

"You forgot this," he said, holding up the half apron she'd taken off on the way to Trina's school earlier. Before she could snatch it from him, he had already looped the strings around her back and was tying it just above her belly button. This time, though, when his fingers grazed against her torso she was positive that it was no accident. "And just for the record, my meeting tonight is not a date."

"And just for the record, it wouldn't be any of my business if it *was* a date." There, that sounded strong enough and almost believable. In fact, as she walked away, her knees grew steadier with each step until she almost believed it herself.

Chapter Eight

Ethan didn't realize how badly he'd needed to attend an AA meeting until he sat in that room at the community rec center on Monday night. Alcoholism could be a disease of loneliness and isolation—no matter how busy or social he was. Being with others who battled the same disease made Ethan feel a little less alone.

He and Commodore Russell were standing by the coffee machine in back when the older man removed the toothpick from his mouth and said, "You know what the Big Book says about shouldering the burdens and troubles of others?"

Ethan inhaled deeply and replied, "We find that we're soon overcome by them. But aren't Trina's burdens also my burdens?"

"Yep. But you don't want your burdens to become hers."

The old guy had a point. Ethan's sobriety was more important to him now than ever before. If that meant fortifying himself with more meetings, then that's what he'd do. Trina deserved to have him be the best father he could be.

However, he didn't want to overuse his goodwill with Monica—such as it might be—to ask her to keep babysitting Trina in the evenings. So before he left, he made a mental note to look into the AA sessions held during the day at Shadowview, the military hospital thirty minutes away.

Both Trina and Gran were yawning when he arrived at the Alvarez house to pick up his daughter and the gassy kitten. But neither one looked as exhausted as Monica. The circles under her eyes were faint, and her usually proud shoulders seemed to sag.

"How'd it go?" he asked her when she came out of the kitchen and met him in the entryway.

"Great. Gran taught Trina how to make flour tortillas and how to do Elvis's signature hip shake. Trina read some of her book to Gran and kept her from feeding Tootie too many black beans while I made a few phone calls. That reminds me, I lined up a math tutor to come to the library tomorrow. He's a graduate student down at Boise State, so he can only come on Tuesday and Thursday afternoons."

"You are incredible," he said, reaching out both of his arms in praise. Actually, his instinct had been to lift her up in a celebratory hug, but Ethan had stopped himself just in time. A pink flush crept up Monica's cheeks, perhaps from his compliment or perhaps because she knew that he'd been about to touch her again before he caught himself.

He hoped it was because she was also thinking about the last time he'd touched her and how *both* of their faces had filled with heat. Testing the waters, he softly placed a hand on her shoulder. "Seriously, Monica. I can't even begin to tell you how much I appreciate everything you've done for me these past few days."

Her indrawn gasp was as abrupt as her glance at his fingers. Yep. She was thinking about their physical attraction, too.

"Well, technically, I was doing it to help Trina," she said before dramatically lifting her own arms in a stretch as she yawned loudly. The move was probably intended to dislodge his hand, and it worked. Although, she probably didn't realize that it also caused a few of the buttons on her white blouse to gap, giving him a glimpse of a light pink lacy bra underneath. After a second yawn, she added, "But I'm also extremely grateful to you for helping me out at the market this morning."

Ethan lifted the corner of his mouth in a sly smile before repeating her own words. "Well, technically, I was doing it to help Gran. Although, I wouldn't be opposed to us helping each other—"

Monica's third and suspiciously fake yawn cut him off. "Whew. Sorry about that. It sure has been a long and interesting day."

"Then I don't want to keep you away from your bed." What Ethan really meant was that he wouldn't mind carrying her to bed himself. After briefly going upstairs earlier this morning, he'd found himself wondering about Monica's bedroom all afternoon. But with her grandmother and his daughter putting away Elvis records in the living room a few feet away, it wasn't as though he could just sweep the sleepy, sexy woman up into his arms. Instead, he cleared his throat and looked over his shoulder. "Come on, Tri, let's head home."

His daughter patted Mrs. Alvarez's hand, which was the biggest display of affection he'd witnessed from the child—at least to another human. She had plenty of affection for the bean-eating kitten.

"Come back again, soon," Mrs. Alvarez offered, and Monica didn't correct the older woman or otherwise appear to be put out.

Well, if Ethan had a clear shot, he was certainly going to take it. "Perhaps next Monday?" he suggested.

"Perfect," Mrs. Alvarez said while Monica just yawned. Probably too exhausted to protest.

The following morning, since Trina seemed to do best with a routine, Ethan took her to the Cowgirl Up Café again for breakfast, despite the fact that Monica was usually off on Tuesdays. On the way to school, they discussed the tutor and then confirmed their afternoon schedule at least three more times.

The same discussion took place every day that week and by Friday, he decided to drive down to Boise again to get Trina her own cell phone so she wouldn't have to stress about being forgotten at school.

"Text me or call me whenever you need to," he'd told her. And she did. Every day during her lunch break. At first, it was a passive reminder, such as "See u at 3." Then he began responding with memes of inspirational cat posters, such as the kitten with its paws attached to a window curtain and the slogan "Hang in there."

After a few days, she would write back "lol" or use a smiley face emoji, which was an improvement considering she still didn't smile that often in person.

By the second week of March, he honestly couldn't say that he'd gotten any more comfortable with his new role as Trina's primary caregiver, but they definitely had bonded over cat memes and had an established daily pattern that he could anticipate.

The mornings were still the easiest part of his day, even

though they were a bit rushed and consisted of cereal more often than made-to-order eggs at the Cowgirl Up Café. Swinging a hammer and climbing ladders on his various job sites gave him something physical he could focus on, although he was in serious need of anything a little more athletic.

He was always outside of the school at exactly three o'clock to pick up Trina, which would've been the highlight of his day if she didn't always look so miserable and defeated every time she came out the doors. Or if he could've avoided the other parents who were constantly trying to get him to bring two dozen treats for the bake sale or help organize the popcorn fund-raiser or chaperone the band field trip.

His daughter wasn't even in band.

Even the evenings weren't as difficult as he'd expected them to be, since he was usually busy not-burning (or sometimes phoning in) dinner while looking over Trina's homework or scratching his head at some of the characters on the YouTube videos she liked to watch. By the time he dropped in his rack at night to get some shut-eye, he was so mentally exhausted, sleep came easier than it ever had.

No, the biggest struggle for Ethan came in the late afternoons. "Happy hour time," he used to call it, back before any time of the day had become happy hour to him. He grew restless and antsy and even bored during that two-hour window when he transitioned from being a full-time working adult to being a full-time responsible parent. The worst was when Trina was at the library for tutoring on Tuesdays and Thursdays.

Ethan was left with absolutely nothing to do but sit in his truck and try not to think about drinking, or sit at a distant table in the library and try not to think about what

Monica would look like underneath her boxy cardigan sweaters and her stiff, button-up blouses.

That second Thursday afternoon in March, he'd finally decided to change into some workout clothes and go for a long-distance run while he waited for Trina. But he'd only made it a couple of miles when the rain began to pour down and—even though he'd run in much worse conditions than these—he turned back. He was soaking wet by the time he got to the library and thought about going home to change, but then he would've been late to pick up his daughter.

Walking in the library, Ethan's shoes squished and leaked water onto the old parquet floors. A mom whipped her head around, giving him the stink eye and putting her finger to her lips in the universal sign to be quiet. The old building was built in the late nineteenth century and, while it was both historical and unique, the architect apparently hadn't taken into account that the hexagon shape and open second-story floor plan only added to the acoustics and amplified every little peep.

His daughter was usually in one of the study rooms upstairs and there was no way to get there in these shoes without announcing his every step. Maybe he'd just find Monica instead and tell her to let Trina know he'd be a few minutes late.

"Hey," he said when he finally spotted the librarian in the hidden recesses of the nonfiction section, kneeling down near the lower shelf and passing a kid an oversize volume on frogs.

She dropped the book before the kid could take it, but the young boy didn't even notice because both pairs of eyes were on him.

"You're all wet, man," the boy stated the obvious, picking up his frog book and giving Ethan a gap-toothed grin before walking away.

Monica remained on her knees, though her lips parted and her glasses slipped down her nose as she aimed her gaze directly at his torso.

Extending his hand, he asked, "Do you need help getting up?"

"You're all wet," she said, not making any move to accept his offer or to otherwise rise to her feet. In fact, she continued to study him, making his skin heat under the cold, clinging fabric of his soaked shirt.

"So I've been told," he replied, his chest jutting out as though he was silently inviting her to look her fill.

"Your clothes are practically plastered to every muscle on your—"

The water trailing down his outstretched hand dripped onto her gray skirt, unfortunately drawing her attention from whatever it was she'd been about to say. But judging by the way her cheeks had gone crimson and her pupils had dilated, she didn't have to say anything. Monica was more than attracted to him, he realized with a satisfied smile. She was aroused.

She gave her head a little shake before putting her own palm in his. When he yanked her to her feet, he didn't release her. Rather, he used the momentum to pull her toward him. Monica put a hand on his chest, probably just to brace herself from getting any closer, and his heart hammered underneath her slender, delicate fingers.

"You're all wet." Monica knew she was repeating herself, but her dazed mind couldn't form any other thought as her pulse pounded in her ears.

"And *you're* all flushed," Ethan said with a smirk before leaning his wet face closer to hers. He stopped just short of kissing her, though, and her eyes darted down just in time to see his lips part ever so slightly in invitation.

Monica knew it was a mistake before she'd even risen up on her tiptoes. One minute she was looking for a book about the habitats of tree frogs and the next she had her lips planted all over a dripping wet Ethan Renault. She could taste the rain on his lips as her mouth slanted over his.

Her tongue was as eager as her hands that were gripping the damp fabric on his shoulders for leverage, pressing him up against the life science and zoology shelves. Or were those the foreign language shelves behind him? She didn't know and she no longer cared. All that mattered was that she'd finally let go of this attraction she'd been struggling to hold back for so long, and now she was making up for lost time.

His hands splayed around her lower back, just below her waist, as his tongue lazily stroked against hers. She was rushed and frenzied while he was slow and methodical, easing their kiss into a rhythm.

Reminding herself to breathe through her nose, she inhaled the salty, tangy scent of his skin and the familiar, musty smell of lignin from the books surrounding them. Kissing Ethan was like reading a fast-paced thriller set in a faraway land while being in the comfort of her own home. His mouth was a wild adventure, as exciting and thrilling as being on a roller coaster, while his steady arms were solid and reassuring, the safety bar keeping her in place as she enjoyed the ride.

Monica let her hands travel down his chest, exploring the hard peaks and ridged valleys of his muscles. His mouth trailed kisses across her jaw and she threw back her head, drawing in another ragged breath.

She was just slipping her fingers under the hem of his wet T-shirt when Ethan jumped away so quickly, his head thunked against the oak shelf behind him. Monica's initial instinct was to moan in disappointment. Yet, when she caught the panicked look in his eye, she nearly groaned in embarrassment for shocking him with her forwardness.

But the groan didn't come from Monica. It came from the eleven-year-old girl at the end of the aisle who'd just seen them.

Ethan didn't bother to say so much as a goodbye, let alone give Monica a proper thank-you. After all, what was there to say following a kiss like that?

He'd had to chase after Trina, who'd shot him a withering look before stomping toward the exit, her yellow backpack bouncing with each purposeful step as she broke out into a run in the parking lot. Luckily, the onslaught of rain must have discouraged her from taking off down the street, and she headed directly for his truck instead.

She was struggling with the door handle when he pulled up beside her to unlock the truck with his remote. He opened it for her, but couldn't even find the words to ask her what had her so upset. Not that his daughter was really one for coming out and discussing any uncomfortable feelings—a trait she'd probably inherited from him. Besides, Ethan had a feeling he already knew what was wrong. The problem was he didn't know how to fix the situation without making things worse.

While he'd never let uncertainty or poor planning prevent him from completing a mission before, fatherhood was proving to be the one assignment that left him in a constant state of doubt. At least when he'd been on deployments, he'd had the backing of his team and his squad leaders. Had his own dad ever felt this alone and confused? Feelings of ineptness filled Ethan as he climbed into the driver's seat.

He sighed as he put the key in the ignition, but before he could turn over the engine, Trina surprised him by saying, "Things were just starting to get normal. Why did you have to mess it all up by kissing *her*?"

In Ethan's defense, Monica had kissed *him* first. But since his daughter was showing some anger instead of the casual indifference she usually exhibited toward him, he wasn't about to miss an opportunity to find out what she was really thinking. Unfortunately, Trina's blue eyes had gone dark and stormy and glared at him with such accusation, he nearly winced.

Perhaps their standard operating procedure of mostly ignoring each other would've been preferable—just like remaining strapped into a perfectly good airplane would've been preferable to someone who was afraid of heights. But he was already at the free fall altitude and his parachute was packed with the rip cord in his hand. He had to make the jump.

Wiping the raindrops from his confused brow, he replied, "I thought you liked Monica."

Okay. Even he knew that sounded lame.

"I do." Trina crossed her arms and looked out the window.

"Well, I like Monica, too." He put his arm along the top of the bench seat as he turned to face her. It was also his way of letting her know that he wasn't going anywhere until they talked about why she was so upset.

"Sure you do. *For now.*"

He ran a hand through his wet hair as he exhaled. He'd heard that teenagers came equipped with plenty of sarcasm and attitude, but he'd hoped for a few more years of getting to know his daughter before he'd have to experience the full effects of adolescent hormones. "Trina, I'm trying to understand why you're upset. I really am. But I'm gonna need you to walk me through this."

"Chantal said that all men leave. But I was hoping that you would be different. Then again, you left us, too, so I don't see how."

Okay, so apparently this had something to do with her mother and him. That was just one more sin that Ethan was never going to live down. He could follow his twelve steps and try and make amends all he wanted, but some things were out of his hands. Circumstances were already too far gone and it wasn't fair for him to pretend that he could undo the past. He sighed and attempted a different approach.

"Tri, when I was younger, my mom told my dad she wanted a divorce."

"So your mom left you, too?" She lifted her lips into a quasi snarl. "That makes it okay for you to leave?"

"Not exactly. My parents shared custody of me. I was with my mom during the week and with my dad on the weekends. I hated it. So that Christmas, all I wanted from Santa was to have all of us back together in the same house."

"Only babies believe in Santa." She snorted, adding condescension to the current display of charming pre-teen attitude.

"Well, I was five," he replied a bit too defensively. Yep, ignoring each other would have definitely been preferable. Or perhaps he could've found a suitable cat meme for this situation.

His daughter waited a few beats then asked, "So I'm guessing they didn't get back together?"

"Nope. My mom died in a car crash with her new boyfriend on Christmas Eve."

Trina's face softened, but it wasn't his intent to garner

any sympathy points or to make this conversation about him. "What I'm trying to say is that I know what you're going through. It's normal for kids to hold out hope that their parents will eventually get back together."

"Wait. You think that I want you to get back together with Chantal?"

"Isn't that why you're mad at me for kissing Monica?"

"As if!" Trina rolled her eyes.

"Then why else wouldn't you want me to date her?"

Her brows shot up. "Are you guys dating?"

"Not formally."

"Exactly." Trina nodded as if everything was perfectly clear. However Ethan was more puzzled than before.

"Help me out here, Tri. Please."

"Chantal said that you left as soon as you got what you wanted from her."

"And what did she say I wanted from her?"

Trina shrugged. "I don't know. I guess the same thing as all those other men who came over but never took her out on dates. Kissing and gross stuff like that."

A chill went down Ethan's spine and a cold rage spread through his body. If Chantal knew what was best for her, she better stay long gone. Trina must've sensed the shift from his confusion to his disgust because she scooted closer toward the door, as if she needed to be ready to get away from him, too.

"I'm not mad," he lied to his daughter as he fought to unclench his hands. At least, he wasn't mad at *her*. "You can always tell me anything—say whatever is on your mind."

She studied him for several moments before taking a deep breath. "If you and Monica aren't dating and you're just kissing her, then that means you're gonna leave her, too."

Ethan closed his eyes and let his head fall back against the headrest. "So you *don't* want me to leave Monica?"

"No. I like her. And I like Gran."

"I like them, too, Tri. But just because we like somebody, doesn't mean that they'll like us back."

"You don't think Monica likes us?"

"Well, I know she likes *you*," he replied honestly. "She smiles a lot when you're around and she always has books set aside for you and she asks me how you're doing in school all the time."

"Hmm," Trina said, tilting her chin. "Maybe she likes you, too, then."

"Why do you think that?"

"Because last Monday night when we were eating, she asked about you."

Ethan's chest expanded. Now they were getting somewhere. "Oh yeah? What did she want to know about me?"

"She wanted to know if you were getting any better at making dinner. Then today, she told me she had a cookbook for you at the checkout desk. It's called *Crock Pot for Dummies*." Trina giggled at the last part.

"So that's two out of three," Ethan shrugged as though he didn't really care one way or the other. He knew better than to rely on a kid for matchmaking experience, but since he rarely got to engage in real conversations with his daughter, he convinced himself that he should ask more questions. "What about Monica smiling when I'm around?"

"Hmmm. It's more like a frown whenever you're talking to her. But when you're *not* talking to her, she does kinda stare at you. A lot."

"Wait. How does she stare at me?"

Trina grinned. "The same way she was looking at you after you kissed her."

Chapter Nine

The following Monday night, as he drove to the Alvarez house to pick up Trina after his meeting, Ethan thought about how he could get Monica alone, running through several scenarios in his mind. He needed to talk to her about that kiss between the library shelves last Thursday, mostly to explain why he'd left in such a hurry. While he hadn't been expecting it, he also hadn't been quite ready for it to end. In fact, who knew how far out of control things would've gotten if Trina hadn't interrupted them?

Thoughts of Monica's mouth against his had filled up his weekend to the point that he'd gone so stir-crazy being cooped up in his apartment, he'd needed a physical release. The weekends were usually his time to get outdoors and do something that fueled his adrenaline and reminded him that he was alive. Unfortunately, his choices in extreme sports were now somewhat limited with an eleven-year-old in tow.

It was still a bit too early in the season to get out on the rapids, so he couldn't take Trina white-water rafting. He'd tried to teach her how to snowboard on Saturday, but all the recent rain had made what little snow remained on the runs pretty icy and she'd given up after only two falls.

She'd been a good sport, though, asking to hang out in the lodge with the book she'd brought along so that he could spend an hour or so out on the slopes. They'd driven down to Boise on Sunday to try out an indoor rock climbing gym, but it wasn't the same as scaling up a granite cliff or, better yet, boulder jumping.

So by the time he pulled the truck in front of Monica's house, his nerves were humming with energy. Monica was already on the porch and he smiled at her apparent eagerness for his arrival.

Until he got closer and saw her face.

"What happened?" he asked as he crossed the front yard.

She was twisting a cloth towel in her hands. "I was in the kitchen doing dishes and didn't even hear them leave."

"Hear who leave?"

"Gran and Trina. They were in the living room listening to one of her Elvis records and then the needle started skipping. When I went in there to check on them, they were gone."

Gone. The word was a punch to Ethan's gut. "Maybe they went for a walk?"

Monica shook her head. "They took my car. I tried to call you, but it went straight to voice mail."

Ethan checked his phone. He'd turned off the ringer when he was at the meeting and forgot to switch it back on.

"Let's go find them," he said as he jogged to his truck.

"No, they're already on their way back. I called the police right away and Carmen found them at Noodie's getting ice cream. Here they are now."

A squad car turned onto the street and Ethan's stomach sank as if he'd swallowed a rock. He never wanted to see his child in the backseat of a police car again.

When he opened the door, Trina flew into his arms. "Shh, honey, it's okay," he told her as she clung to him.

Mrs. Alvarez's eyes were huge and her face was pale as Monica helped her out of the front seat.

"I don't know why I did that, *mija*." Gran handed Monica's purse to her, which was probably how the older woman had gotten the car keys.

"Oh, Gran," Monica said, pulling her into an embrace. "Are you okay?"

"Just a little shook up. We left your car at the ice cream shop. Officer Gregson wouldn't let me drive it back."

"I can get it in the morning," Monica offered. "Come on, let's get you into bed now."

When the two women went inside, Ethan gently set Trina down and kept a protective arm around her.

"It was a pretty bad episode this time," Carmen started, but her walkie-talkie crackled to life. "Tell Monica that I'll swing by in the morning and give her a lift to get her car."

Ethan waved her off and would've bundled his daughter into the safety of his truck and taken her straight home, but when he opened his passenger door for her, she shook her head. "Tootie's still in the house. I have to go get her."

Monica was just coming down the stairs when they got into the entryway. "Ethan, I am so sorry that this happened on my watch."

"Don't worry about it. Everyone is safe and sound. Besides, how could you have stopped it?"

"That's what's eating me up. I couldn't stop it, short of locking Gran up and turning our home into a prison."

"It's my fault," Trina said, her lips curled downward as

134   *THE SEAL'S SECRET DAUGHTER*

the toe of her sneaker tapped at a dark spot on the hardwood floor. "I just didn't want her to go alone. I called out to Monica, but I don't think she heard me over the record player. Gran kept calling me Bettina and saying, 'Don't tell Mom.'"

"Bettina is Gran's sister." Monica took off her glasses to rub the bridge of her nose. "Sometimes she has flashbacks to when she was a kid and gets the past confused with the present."

"Then I guess that would make you her mom?" Ethan suggested, not knowing what else to say. He didn't want Monica beating herself up over something she couldn't really control.

"Sometimes I feel like that." Her dark, silky hair was loose and curly and Ethan realized it was the first time he'd seen it out of a ponytail or messy bun. When was the last time she'd ever been able to actually let her hair down and relax?

"Well, I still shoulda ran and got you," Trina said, her face filled with remorse. "But she seemed so happy and I thought I could just…you know…take care of her myself. When we got to the ice cream place, though, she was all confused and didn't know who I was or who she was and I started to get real scared. The teenager behind the counter started yelling at her and Gran started yelling back and then the teenager called us nutjobs and threatened to call the cops if we didn't leave and that's when Officer Gregson showed up."

"*Mija*—" the older woman was holding her tap shoes in one hand as she came down the stairs "—I have a craving for some ice cream. Let's run into town and oh… Hi there, Ethan. What are you and Trina doing here?"

His daughter's eyes were wide and she took a step closer to him, but her courage surprised him when she spoke calmly to the older woman. "We already went to get ice cream, Gran. Remember?"

"Oh. That's right." Mrs. Alvarez turned to Ethan and it was as though he could see the entire events of the evening pass across her face as her memory returned. In fact, suddenly, the woman looked much older than her eighty-something years. "I hope you're not mad at me for getting arrested with your little girl."

"Nobody got arrested, Gran," Monica said, gently removing the dance shoes from the frail woman's bony hand. "Officer Gregson gave you a ride home because you seemed pretty confused."

"That's been happening a lot, huh, *mija*? Me getting confused."

Monica's eyes filled with tears, but she swiped them away quickly. Her voice broke when she replied, "Yes, Gran. You have Alzheimer's. It makes you forget things sometimes."

Mrs. Alvarez's face fell and Ethan could only imagine the complex emotions she was going through as the significance of the diagnosis settled over her. How many times had she and Monica probably had this same exact conversation, both of them reliving the painful revelation each time?

Nobody spoke for several seconds, until Gran reached out and stroked her granddaughter's upper arm. "I suppose it must be terribly difficult for you, taking care of me."

"You took care of me, Gran. It's only fair that I take care of you."

The older woman studied Ethan for several seconds before her eyes returned to Monica. "But when I took care of you, I'd already experienced the best years of my life. You're too young for such a burden, *mija*. You need to be out on dates and having fun and thinking about starting a family of your own."

"I already have a family, Gran." She lowered her voice before switching to Spanish. "*Tu es mi familia.*"

But the older woman shook her head as she patted Monica's hand. "Tell her, Ethan. Tell my girl that she should be going out on dates."

"I've been trying to get her out on a date for six months, Mrs. Alvarez." He shrugged, resorting to what came natural to him in tense, uncomfortable moments like these. Teasing. "But your granddaughter won't listen to me."

"If I was in a home, she'd go out with you."

"This *is* your home, Gran."

"Oh, *mija*, you know what I mean. I saw the brochure in the trash can last week. That one you brought home with the pictures of all those gray-haired people gardening and swimming in a big fancy pool and playing bingo. What was it called?"

"Legacy Village," Monica sighed, but her shoulders were ramrod straight and Ethan could tell that the fight hadn't left her. "It's a memory care center."

"Meh," her grandmother tsked. "They probably won't help me get my memory back, but maybe we should check it out all the same?"

"Gran, I'm not going to take you there."

"Then I'll have Ethan take me there. You'll take me right, *mijo*?"

"I'd rather take you out dancing, Mrs. Alvarez," he said, attempting another wisecrack to cover the fact that he wished he could be anywhere but there, thrust into the middle of an extremely personal family conversation.

"Oh, *mijo*, I'd spin circles around you. But Monica would love to go dancing with you."

"Gran," she warned her grandmother, and Ethan would've laughed at how tight Monica's jaw had locked down if his own wasn't still sore from clenching it a few minutes ago when he'd thought his daughter was missing again.

"There's a dance at the VFW for St. Patrick's Day," Mrs. Alvarez continued. "Why don't you two go to that?"

Monica said something about Gran's memory only working when it was convenient. Or inconvenient. He couldn't be sure because she'd mumbled the sarcastic remark under her breath.

"I'll tell you what, Mrs. Alvarez," Ethan replied. "Why don't we go over to Legacy Village on Saturday and check it out, then we can all go to the St. Patrick's Day dance afterward together?"

"Oh, what a brilliant plan. You're such a smart one." She patted his hand before looking at Monica. "Isn't he smart, *mija*?"

Monica narrowed her eyes as she sized up both of them. "I think the word you're looking for is sneaky."

On Saturday morning, Ethan and Trina arrived on Monica's front porch to take her and Gran to Legacy Village, just as he'd promised. Or threatened, depending on who was asked.

Monica had seen him on Tuesday and Thursday at the library, but they'd only talked about two things: how Trina's math tutoring was going—she was already learning tools for telling numbers and symbols apart. And how Gran was feeling—more episodes and forgetfulness this week, but so far no sneaking out of the house.

What Monica and Ethan still hadn't discussed was that heat-filled, mind-boggling and totally unexpected kiss a little over a week ago.

Maybe it hadn't made much of an impression on him, Monica decided after he still hadn't mentioned it when she'd ran into him and Trina getting sub sandwiches at Domino's Deli on Wednesday night. The man had probably kissed more women than she could count and her pathetic and awkward attempt at a make out session in the very public library was just another check mark for his man credentials.

So if Ethan could pretend that nothing physical had happened between them, then so could she. In fact, she was surprised that he'd shown up at all today.

"You guys made it," she said when she answered the door Saturday morning.

His wide shoulders went back and his chin went up. "Did you think we wouldn't?"

"I just know that most people wouldn't want to go tour a retirement home on their day off. I wouldn't have blamed you if you'd found something more fun to do. Like jumping a motorcycle across the Sugar River Gorge?"

Everyone in town knew that Ethan was quite the daredevil and adrenaline junkie. The other day in the library, Trina had mentioned the recent snowboarding and rock climbing excursions and how she needed to start downloading books onto her smartphone so she could read when he dragged her along on his adventures.

"Nope. Motorcycle jumping is always on Sundays." He wiggled his eyebrows before lowering his voice. "Besides, I would've blamed *myself* if I didn't make it today. Contrary to the way you always look down your nose at me, I don't take my promises or my commitments lightly."

Monica's throat grew tight. She wasn't ready to be one of Ethan's commitments. "I doubt Gran even remembers that you said you would come with us. Or, you know, about that other thing tonight."

Monica tried to give him a dismissive wave of her hand, hoping he'd forgotten about the second half of the bargain he'd made with her grandmother. But Ethan folded his arms across his chest. "It doesn't matter what Mrs. Alvarez remembers. If *I* say I'm going to do something, then I'm going to do it. Unless, of course, you found another date for the St. Patrick's Day Dance tonight?"

Oh great. He loudly mentioned the very thing she'd been trying to avoid right as Gran walked out of the kitchen with the handles of a wicker basket looped over her arm.

"That's right, the St. Patrick's Day Dance is tonight. I hope we're back from the picnic in time for you kids to go."

"Gran, we're not going on a picnic today." She shot Ethan a knowing look. *See, she wouldn't have remembered if you hadn't brought it up.* "We're going to Legacy Village to take a tour."

"Is that the old folks home?" her grandmother asked.

"It's a memory care center," Trina offered.

"Oh, and you brought Bettina with you."

"Actually, Gran that's not—"

"It's okay if she calls me that," Trina said softly, and Monica could've hugged the girl for being so understanding.

"Well, then what are we waiting for?" Gran asked as she walked out to Ethan's truck carrying the picnic basket. Her tap shoes pinged against the sidewalk, but at least she'd been willing to put on a pair of stretchy pants and a cardigan sweater over her favorite leotard instead of her old bathrobe.

"Thank you for always being so sweet with her," Monica whispered to Trina as they followed Ethan and Gran outside. "Sometimes, she mistakes me for her sister, too."

"Well, I've never been anyone's sister, so I don't mind."

"Me neither." Monica smiled and gave Trina's shoulder a little squeeze. The girl didn't flinch or back away, so they were definitely making progress.

Legacy Village was located near the military hospital, thirty minutes down the mountain. Monica sat quietly beside Trina in the back of the crew cab and tried not to look at the digital clock on Ethan's dash or think about how much time it would take to visit Gran every day. Or worse, to get to Gran if she had a major episode and needed Monica.

Her grandmother kept up a steady stream of conversation, regaling Ethan with tales of her glory days as a backup dancer in Hollywood during the sixties. "Have you seen my picture with Elvis?"

"The one on your fireplace mantel? I did see that," Ethan said for the fifth time in only ten minutes. "Did the King ask you for your autograph?"

Gran giggled and playfully swatted at Ethan's shoulder. "No, but he did ask me to teach him how to do the frug."

"What's the frug?" Trina asked.

"It's a dance where you…um…you move your… I can't exactly remember." Gran turned to look at Monica and her expression was slack, her eyes blinking several times. "How far away is this picnic, anyway?"

"We're almost there," Ethan said, and Gran's head snapped back to him. Alarm spread through Monica because her grandmother was now frowning.

"No. This isn't it. The Fourth of July picnic is always in Town Square Park and this is definitely not the way to Town Square Park." Gran's face had gone pale and she pivoted in her seat again, her eyes darting frantically between Trina and Monica as she clutched her purse against her chest. "Aren't you two going to stop him? The driver is taking us to the wrong place."

"Gran." Monica put a calming hand on the older woman's shoulder, but Gran jumped away from her, knocking her bony elbow into the dashboard. Monica's heart crumpled at the realization that her own grandmother was suddenly terrified of her.

"Stop calling me that. Where are you people taking me? I want to go back. Turn around. I'll call the police." Gran reached for the door handle, as if she planned to leap out of a vehicle doing fifty miles an hour down a two-lane highway. Thankfully, Ethan had locked the doors when they'd first gotten inside. He looked in the rearview mirror at Monica, his brows raised as though to ask her what she wanted him to do.

"Gran, it's me, Monica. Your granddaughter..." she started again, but her grandmother had managed to get her window halfway down and was yelling for help in Spanish. Luckily, the bike lane was empty, but what if someone thought they were abducting her? What if someone reported them to adult protective services? Fear paralyzed Monica as her brain ran through every worst-case scenario.

"Siri, play Elvis," Trina said into her smartphone and the beginning strains of "Viva Las Vegas" came out of the speaker. It took Gran a few seconds to recognize the intro of the congo drums, but by the time the King began crooning the chorus, Monica's grandmother was already breathing more steadily.

Monica's own breathing, though, didn't settle until the next song began and Gran started tapping her fingers along to the beat of "Suspicious Minds."

Exhaling through her nose, Monica slouched against the backseat, trying to get her heart rate under control. Suspicious minds, indeed. The appropriateness of the lyrics wasn't lost on her. Or on Ethan, apparently, who kept glancing at her in the rearview mirror.

"Hey, did I ever tell you guys that I have a photo of me with Elvis?" Gran asked, as though she hadn't been in full paranoia mode a few minutes ago, about to fling her frail body out of a moving vehicle in order to get away from the one person in the world who loved her the most.

"No kidding?" Ethan said casually, despite the fact that his fingers were still clenched around the steering wheel at the ten-and-two position. "I'd really love to see that picture sometime."

"It's on the fireplace mantel at home. Right next to Monica's college graduation picture. I always knew my *mija* would go to college."

"Did you ever go to college, Mrs. Alvarez?" Trina asked.

"I didn't even finish high school, dear. I had my first professional audition when I was fifteen. I had to lie about my age, of course…" Gran continued talking about her short-lived dance career and Monica closed her eyes as she massaged her temples, crisis temporarily averted. For now.

She'd read all the books, done all the research. She knew that people with Alzheimer's responded well to familiar music and stories about their youth. More important, she'd experienced Gran being confused and forgetting who she was at least several times a day. But her grandmother had never looked at her with those terrified eyes, as if Monica was out to hurt her or cause damage.

Instead of responding properly to the situation, though, Monica herself panicked and had just sat there frozen. Guilt washed over her as she replayed her own incompetence in bringing Gran down from such a chilling episode. Rather, it had been a quick thinking eleven-year-old who'd saved the day.

Chapter Ten

Monica knew within the first ten minutes of the tour that there was no way she could leave her grandmother at Legacy Village. It was too big, too full of people who also needed help—some appearing more incapacitated or dependent than her own grandmother. Gran could get lost in a place like this. Or worse, forgotten. But Monica smiled and nodded and followed the intake nurse, a middle-aged woman with purple hair and a name tag that said NICOLE in large print, as she showed them the independent living apartments and the water aerobics pool, and the full-service dining options.

"They sure have a lot of old people here," Gran said to no one in particular as they passed several residents parked in wheelchairs near the "Drive-In Theater," which was really just a big movie room with a huge screen on one wall and murals painted with old-fashioned cars on the other walls.

Monica didn't point out the fact that her grandmother was of a similar age as the majority of residents, and Trina kept her phone in her hand, probably prepared to play more Elvis songs in case another one of Gran's episodes began.

Nicole was talking to Gran about the activities calendar when Ethan put his hand on Monica's waist and leaned toward her. "So what do you think?"

"It's clean. And the people seem nice. But I don't think it's for Gran."

"She seems to like it so far." He nodded to Gran who was waving at a silver-haired woman hunched over a walker as though they were long-lost friends.

"Well, I'm sure they're only showing us the best parts."

"Now you sound like your neighbor Mr. Simon." Ethan didn't remove his hand and his lips lowered toward her temple. "He wrote down my license plate number the other day."

"He writes down everyone's license plate numbers. He also regularly posts to the neighborhood watch app every time Mrs. Fitzroy gets a package delivery because he thinks the UPS driver has the same style mustache as someone on the Crime Stoppers website."

"Exactly. Why do you guys always think the worst of people?" Ethan's warm breath against her hairline was currently preventing her from doing any thinking at all. Besides, Monica was only being cautious. She certainly wasn't as bad as Mr. Simon.

"Listen, I'm not saying there's anything wrong with the place. It's fine for other people's grandparents. But it's not what I want for Gran."

"It might not be what you want, but it's what she needs that matters."

"She *needs* to be home with me." Monica crossed her arms in front of herself, her determined stance causing Ethan to return to his full height. "Nobody here will love her the way I love her."

"Of course you love her. But are we just going to pretend that that incident in the car didn't just happen? She was terrified, Monica. Hell, *you* were terrified."

"Only because I was afraid of how it might affect Trina," she mumbled.

Ethan's sigh was heavy as he ran a hand through his hair. "Man, Trina was the only one of us who kept her cool. Even *I* reverted to my hostage extraction training and was about to jump across the bench seat and haul Gran against me to keep her from hurting herself."

"*Mija*, look, they have dance classes here." Gran pointed to something on the five-by-five-foot activity calendar on the wall. Geez, everything was written in such big letters around here. "It's called Music and Motion and it starts after dinner."

"Actually—" Nicole pushed a purple strand of hair behind her ear "—our usual dance teacher who leads that class just had hip surgery and we don't know when she'll be back."

"I could teach the class," Gran offered. Then she did a hop shuffle followed by a double brush-back in her tap shoes to prove it.

"You certainly could teach it," Nicole replied with a bright smile, as though she was perfectly accustomed to indulging irrational people in their false delusions. Monica immediately pegged the woman for a science fiction reader. "I bet the residents would adore having a sub for the usual teacher. But I should warn you, Mrs. Alvarez.

Many of your students aren't quite as mobile as you. Some might even need to stay in the chairs and just clap along."

Wait. What? They were actually going to let her grandmother teach a dance class? This could go wrong on so many levels.

"Um, I don't want to be a party pooper here or anything, but I'm supposed to go to a sleepover at Kayla Patrelli's house tonight," Trina said in a low voice meant just for her father. However, Monica was so on edge from the car ride there and the tour that was now taking way longer than she'd anticipated, that her senses were incredibly heightened, especially her hearing. "I've never been to one before and we're supposed to be at her family's restaurant at four o'clock 'cause her mom is gonna let us make our own pizzas."

"I can drive you back to Sugar Falls, Trina, and then return for Monica and Gran later." Ethan was being more than accommodating and Monica had to wonder if he was just trying to escape the crazy again. Was he worried that Gran would have a meltdown if they told her she couldn't go to the dance class?

"That'll never work, *mijo*," Gran told Ethan. "The St. Patrick's Day Dance starts at seven tonight and you promised you'd take my granddaughter. I can just stay here at the hotel after I teach my class. That way you two can go on your date and have the night to yourselves."

"Oh, Gran, no." Monica gulped and her cheeks burned in mortification. "I'm not going on a *date* with—" She stopped when she saw the confusion filling her grandmother's eyes. She didn't need a repeat of what happened an hour ago on the ride there. "I mean, it's not a hotel. It's a...." She looked at Nicole for some help.

"You know, oftentimes, we have potential residents

stay overnight. Sort of like a trial run. Mrs. Alvarez would be welcome to stay here tonight to try us out."

"Did you know that when I was living in Hollywood, a group of us girls auditioned to be dancers on a cruise ship?" Gran's eyes went bright and her smile was wide, making Monica hope this story would prove to be a happy distraction. "First-class meals included and we could travel the world while entertaining the guests and putting on shows. I was the only one who got a callback and my friend Darla was so jealous that I got hired and she didn't."

"I don't remember you ever mentioning working on a cruise ship, Gran," Monica said, used to these little detours and scrambling to navigate them back to the current issue at hand. Or in this case, avoid the current issue at hand, which was Monica going out with Ethan. Alone.

"Well, right before we set sail, I found out I was pregnant with your dad. I married your grandpa, and that was the end of that." Gran made a tsking sound and shook her head. "Aw, but you should have seen that ship, *mija*. It was so big and fancy. Kind of like this hotel."

Oh boy. The pleading look on the older woman's face clued Monica into the fact that this story wasn't just a diversion. Gran actually thought she would be reliving her youth. How could Monica deny her grandmother the opportunity?

Ethan must've sensed her train of thought because he leaned in again and said, "It's only one night."

After Ethan dropped Trina off at Patrelli's Italian Restaurant, he walked to his apartment to get ready for his first date with Monica.

Well, it wasn't exactly a date. At least, not the kind

Ethan had in mind when he'd first decided he'd wanted to ask Monica out all those months ago. On the way home from Legacy Village, she'd tried to tell him that they didn't need to go to the St. Patrick's Day Dance, but Trina had insisted that Gran would find out if they didn't go and would be very disappointed. Just like they'd all been disappointed to find out that the picnic basket Gran had packed contained only pickles.

What did one even wear to a St. Patrick's Day party, anyway? Besides green? The only thing he really knew about the holiday was that it involved corned beef and co-pious amounts of green beer. In fact, he'd always thought the celebrations were just an excuse to get drunk. And he definitely couldn't do that tonight. When Monica had suggested she meet him at the VFW hall, he'd made a joke about being the designated driver then told her he'd pick her up at seven.

Standing on her front step, Ethan's chest grew heavy with each knock. He refused to believe he was nervous be-cause of her. He never used to get nervous around women. But the sight of Monica opening the door made him catch his breath. She was wearing a green, silky dress that hit just below her thighs. Her tan cowboy boots drew even more attention to her long, sexy legs.

She must've caught him staring, because she tugged at the ruffled hem of her dress. "Is it too short? Maybe I should go back inside and change."

"No, it's perfect. Sorry for staring, but I'm used to see-ing you in jeans at the café and those long, skinny skirts you always have on at the library." He was also staring be-cause he'd never seen a more incredible set of legs, but say-ing so out loud would certainly scare her off. "Is it new?"

Monica grabbed her purse and a denim jacket off the

table in the entryway. "No, I've had it since I was in high school. Apparently, I've grown a bit since then, but it was the only green item of clothing in my closet. You ready to get this over with?"

"Is going out dancing really going to be a chore for you?" he asked, trying not to sound insulted. It was definitely easier to come across as lighthearted and the life of the party when he had a few drinks in him.

"Sorry. It's not you. I'm just not into big crowds and parties and making small talk with everyone who'll be asking me about Gran."

Some people might ask her about Gran, but a few of the bolder ones would likely ask her about where she'd been hiding those legs. He held the truck door open for her. "So we'll make an appearance. Maybe dance to a song or two so we can honestly tell your grandmother that we participated. Then we'll take off and you can call and check on things at Legacy Village."

Monica ducked her head, but not before he caught the sheepish expression. "I've already called twice."

"Good. Now I don't feel so overprotective for already stopping by Patrelli's to make sure Trina had her phone charger in case she needs to get a hold of me."

"Oh my gosh, I can't even begin to thank Trina for all her help with Gran today, for being so patient and springing into action like that with the music. I owe that girl another trip to the mall."

"She'd probably rather have a trip to the bookstore. Or a new e-reader so she doesn't have to download everything onto her phone."

"Hmm." Monica gave a dreamy smile as she looked out the window. "I can't even believe she's the same girl that you brought into the café a few weeks ago. She's really bloomed since she's been with you, Ethan."

"You sound surprised."

She held up her palm. "I wasn't trying to offend you."

"No, I know. I'm surprised, too."

They parked and went inside the VFW. It was already crowded and he was holding Monica's hand again, but she was stiffer than usual. Man, he'd never had to work this hard to get a woman to relax around him. Was she embarrassed to be seen with him?

"It looks like an army of leprechauns threw up in here," Ethan said over the band doing their rendition of the Dropkick Murphys on stage. Big Rhonda and the Roadsters played most of the local gigs and always tailored their playlist for the occasion.

Monica wrapped her free arm across her waist, but at least she kept her head raised. "I heard the kids at the elementary school did the shamrocks and pots of gold decorations."

"That explains why there's so many rainbows made out of construction paper. I was beginning to question the crafting skills of my fellow veterans."

Her smile was tight, as though she appreciated his joke, but was too uncomfortable to actually laugh out loud. "The VFW is donating 25 percent of the proceeds back to the school tonight. So I guess we better do our part and grab something to drink."

This was it. Ethan steeled his courage and gave a nod as he followed her over to the crowded bar.

Seeing the rows of liquor bottles lined up against the mirrored shelves behind the bartender no longer made him sweat with the inner battle of denying himself something he desperately wanted. Nor was he threatened by the fact that the bartender was married to one of the guys in his Monday night meetings and would surely tell her husband that Ethan had relapsed if he ordered anything stronger than a soda. No, the thing that had him gritting his teeth and pushing up the long sleeves of his black shirt was the conversation that would be sure to follow after he ordered.

"I'll take a pint of Guinness," Monica said to the bartender over the deafening sound of the bagpipes the lead singer was attempting to play.

"I'll have a Diet Coke," Ethan finally said, and the woman behind the bar gave him a slight nod of approval. Not that they both weren't well aware that an alcoholic could easily get their hands on a drink at a party like this.

Monica tilted her head and, before she even opened her lips, Ethan knew what her question would be. "You're not having a beer? It's St. Patrick's Day."

Unless it was an old Navy buddy who didn't know he'd gotten sober, Ethan could usually respond with a simple explanation of *I don't drink* and those who were polite didn't push. But Monica deserved to know the full truth instead of a puzzling nonresponse.

"You know those meetings I go to on Monday nights?" he asked and watched her face as the pieces fell into place. "They're AA meetings. I'm an alcoholic, Monica."

She didn't flinch or back away in disgust and she didn't narrow her eyes at him. However, she did study him for an uncomfortable amount of time without saying anything.

The weight of her stare settled over him despite the fact that his head was pivoting around to everyone else in the hall so that he wouldn't have to make eye contact with her. Ethan's fingers began twitching and he scratched the back of his neck.

"I changed my mind," Monica told the bartender when

the woman set a frothy pint on the polished oak in front of them. "I'll have a Diet Coke, too."

"No," Ethan replied immediately, his skin prickling with unease. He gave the bartender a pointed look and said, "No, she'll keep the Guinness."

Monica put a hand on his bicep, but his muscles were far too tight for her touch to penetrate his senses. "Ethan, if you're not going to drink, then—"

"Don't do that, Mon. Don't treat me differently now that you know."

"I'm not trying to treat you differently. It's just that I don't want to…" She trailed off, the same way most people did when they didn't know how they should act in front of an alcoholic.

"Tempt me?" he asked, then tried to ease the awkwardness by giving her a wink. "Listen, that dress you have on is way more tempting than some bitter, dark draft beer."

His words had the desired effect and a warm blush spread across her cheeks. He watched the muscles in her neck constrict as she swallowed before replying. "Honestly, it's okay. I don't even drink that often. The only reason I ordered it was because everyone else had them and I thought it would help me relax."

"Well, I'm all for you relaxing—" he passed the beer to her "—and cutting loose a little bit."

It was then that her eyes narrowed. The last thing he wanted was for her to think he was going to try to take advantage of her. Or couldn't be trusted.

"Fine." He took the beer back and handed it to the bartender, who was now ignoring her other customers and actively watching their conversation. "She'll have a Diet Coke. But keep the Guinness on my tab and give it to one of those ol' boys at the end of the bar over there."

Monica followed his nod toward several older men who'd probably never been to Ireland but were wearing matching green sashes and tweed caps and singing along to "Whiskey in the Jar."

Ethan took their diet sodas and they made their way to an abandoned table in the corner, but not before several local townspeople said hello or tried to wave them over toward the dance floor. Ethan gave most people a nod, but Monica kept her eyes faced forward as though she didn't see anyone or anything except for the safety of the perimeter of the room.

Yep, the gossips' tongues would be wagging tonight. He pulled out a metal folding chair for Monica and then moved another one closer beside her so they could talk without having to yell over the music.

His date might be shy, but she was also intelligent and curious, so it didn't take her long to ask, "So how long have you been…uh…"

"Sober?"

She nodded as she took a sip from her straw.

"Almost eighteen months."

"Do you still struggle with it?"

"I'd be lying if I said I didn't. Every day can be a struggle, but some days are easier than others. And I've gotten much better at knowing my red flags and staying in tune with what my body needs."

"What do you mean 'what your body needs'?" she asked, and he couldn't stop himself from looking down at her bare legs, her thighs more exposed by the way her dress had shifted higher when she sat down. She followed his gaze and cleared her throat.

He didn't bother to hide his guilt behind his smirk. "When I'm excited or angry or full of energy, my body craves an outlet, a way to release some of the adrenaline I tend to build up. When I'm bored or lonely or thinking about things that I've messed up in the past, my body craves a distraction to keep me from dwelling on all the crap. I used to use alcohol to regulate both, but that's no longer an option. Part of the appeal when I made my decision to move to Sugar Falls was the fact that there's no shortage of extreme sports here to keep me engaged."

"I heard you were an adrenaline junkie."

"You could say that."

"Sounds like being a Navy SEAL was the perfect job for you."

"It was. Until it wasn't."

The lines above her nose creased into a V. "Why do I feel like there's a story behind that?"

He gave a light chuckle, but his chest felt hollow inside. "Let's save that story for our second date."

"Ethan." She turned her shoulders toward him and took a deep breath. "It's one thing to joke about this being a date, but I think we both know that nothing serious can happen between us."

"Do we *both* know that? Because I have a feeling *you* only came to that conclusion after you found out about me being in recovery."

"No, that has nothing to do with it." She leaned forward. "I'll admit that I toyed with the idea of going out with you, but that was before."

"Before you found out I was an alcoholic?" he asked and took a gulp of his soda, wishing it had just a splash of something stronger to sting his throat. To burn away the shame filling his chest.

"No. Before Trina showed up and Gran got worse and we both had to deal with all these other complications of having family members depending on us." She pushed her glasses up farther on her nose, the serious librarian about to call him to task. "My whole life is centered around my grandmother right now and it wouldn't be fair to get involved in a relationship when I can't fully commit to it. You can't honestly tell me that your life hasn't been thrown out of whack by finding out you have a daughter."

"It one hundred percent has been thrown off." He rolled his shoulders back as though he was preparing to do some heavy lifting. "But hell, I was never really relationship material to start with. Nobody is saying we need to commit to anything, Mon. But if you're attracted to me and I'm attracted to you, I don't see why we can't spend time together and help each other out with mutual needs."

One eyebrow shot above the rim of her glasses. "Mutual needs?"

Crap. He used to be much smoother at this sort of thing.

"Okay, that didn't come out the way I meant. I just know that I like being with you. I also like helping you out. Listen, we can both agree that we have too much going on to get serious about anything else, but we also both needed someone to step in and ease the tension. Come on, don't you ever need a break?" He hesitated. "A physical release?"

"Physical release?" she hissed, looking at the nearby tables, probably to make sure nobody overheard them. Her cheeks were now stained pink, her full lower lip twisted between her teeth as she watched him. "I hope this is your way of asking me to be your partner for one of your extreme sports."

"Right now, I just want you to be my dance partner," he said when the strains of "Danny Boy" started. He stood up and pulled her to her feet. "We can discuss how extreme and how physical we want to get after that."

Chapter Eleven

Monica let Ethan pull her close on the dance floor, her body fitting perfectly against his.

She'd known that there were AA meetings at the community rec center on Monday nights, but she hadn't even put two and two together and figured out that was where he went when he'd leave Trina at her house.

That's how blind she'd allowed herself to become when it came to the man.

Not that it should matter that he was a recovering alcoholic, but having experienced her own father's preferences for addiction over family and everything else, Monica couldn't help but think of Ethan differently now.

The problem was that her body didn't think of him differently. Her arms still had a will of their own as they wrapped around his neck and her hips took charge of everything else below as they swayed against him.

When the song ended, he didn't release his grip from her waist, but he did lean back and wait for her to lift her head from his shoulder. "So we've officially fulfilled our promise to your gran. Now what?"

Now we go home and never see each other again, was what she should've said. However, it wasn't like she could simply avoid him or go back to pretending that he was just some flirtatious customer she could forget about at the end of her shift. They would obviously have to interact in the future, their lives in this small town were already too intertwined.

His gaze was heated, his grin was smug and his earlier words were still ricocheting inside her head.

Don't you ever need a break? A physical release?

From the very center of her core nestled against him, to her fingertips resting along his open collar, Monica ached with a need for some sort of release. As he waited for her answer, the challenge hung in the air between them. If he'd just put the proverbial ball in her court, the least she could do was control what happened from here on out.

There were plenty of things in her life right now that she couldn't control, including her body's reaction to him. If they got the physical stuff out of the way once and for all, though, her mind would be able to focus on the bigger picture around her. And Ethan Renault was definitely not a part of Monica's bigger picture.

She'd already made it clear that neither one of them were in any position to enter into a serious relationship, and really, a carefree bachelor like him would be grateful that she didn't want anything more.

This was the type of relationship her mom had warned her about. The kind where she didn't use her head, and put her own physical needs first. Yet, if she was careful—and

Monica was always careful—she should be able to keep things strictly physical with Ethan. That way, her heart would stay safe and her mind would stay sane.

Monica might've wrestled with the decision all night, but a shimmying, eighty-something-year-old in a green leather bustier and shamrock-shaped sunglasses wiggled up beside them and tossed a plastic strand of beads over Ethan's head.

"Hey, Lieutenant Renault, you gonna stand here all night making schmoopie eyes at my favorite waitress or are you two gonna dance?" Freckles asked.

"That depends." Ethan lifted his dark brow at Monica.

"You only live once, darlin'." Freckles winked at her before stage-whispering, "I don't think I need to tell you what *I'd* do if I had a man like *him* looking at me like *that*."

Monica nearly shrieked out loud as her boss gave her a playful swat on the rear before boogying off. Swallowing down her embarrassment and not wanting to cause any more of a scene, Monica finally answered Ethan's original question about what to do next. "Now we go back to my place."

She didn't have to repeat herself. He was already holding her hand, pulling her through the crowd of people who'd arrived late. If they hadn't left their jackets and her purse at the table, she was sure Ethan would've hauled her straight to the car right then. As it was, it took them another five minutes to collect their things because people kept stopping them to ask about Gran.

By the time they got to the parking lot, Monica's cheeks were sore from the fake smile she'd pasted on every time she'd told a neighbor or an old friend that her grandmother was doing as well as could be expected.

Her nerves were shot and her pulse was humming from Ethan's steady grip and the way he'd stayed by her side, continuously steering her away from any uncomfortable conversations as he guided her toward the exit.

"Normally, I try to duck out of a party with nobody seeing me," she admitted when they got to his truck. "But that was the smoothest, quickest escape I've ever had to suffer through. How did you learn to work a room like that?"

"Hostage negotiation training."

Of course. He'd been a part of one of the most elite special forces in the military. Not that she planned to go up against him in battle, but it was a reminder that he was likely more skilled when it came to outmaneuvering and outstrategizing.

Ethan shifted into reverse and then put his arm across the seat. But instead of looking out the rear window, he lifted his fingers and toyed with one of her loose curls. "So, we're going back to your place?"

"Yes," she said, then gulped, hoping he didn't hear the quiver in her voice. "But we should establish a few guidelines."

"What kind of guidelines?"

"The usual, I guess. You probably have more experience in this department than me."

"Are we talking about sex?"

"*Casual* sex," she clarified.

"Right. And you think *I'm* more experienced?"

"Than me? Definitely."

"Sounds like you don't know me very well."

"Okay, then let's start there." She hadn't gone through the same training as him, but she'd once read a book about negotiations. Hopefully, that was close enough to at least give off the appearance that she knew what she was talking about. "Rule one. No need to get to know each other that well. This is just physical. It's not a job interview."

"We're going to have rules?" Ethan's fingers tapped against the seat back. "Sounds pretty job-like if you ask me."

"Rule two," she continued. "Our families and our work come first. So we can only…you know…be together when we're not otherwise occupied."

"Rule three," he countered. "Let's not have so many rules."

"No, we need them to keep us from taking this attraction to the next level. It would be good for both of us if we set out the boundaries ahead of time."

His heat-filled gaze across the dim lights of the dashboard was just as intense as a caress, causing a shiver to race down her spine. "I will never do anything that would make you uncomfortable, Mon. At least, not on purpose. Contrary to what you might think about me, I'm not totally undisciplined. I do have some self-control."

"I don't think you're undisciplined," she protested.

He chuckled. "Are you trying to convince me? Or convince yourself?"

"I'm convinced that you're the only regular customer in the café who always orders the same healthy breakfast every morning. A boring diet like that takes a lot of discipline."

"Hmm," he replied, not sounding completely persuaded by her weak example as he finally backed out of the parking lot.

Okay, so maybe Monica *had* doubted his self-control, especially when it came to him being around so many alcoholic drinks at the VFW earlier. She'd read that addicts often lied to cover up their vices. In fact, Ethan's unsuitability worked in her favor because it would allow her to get close to him physically, while requiring her to maintain her distance emotionally.

He remained quiet throughout the short drive to her house and didn't say anything as he followed behind her up to the front porch, waiting patiently while she unlocked the door and then switched on the light in the entryway. It was odd enough going inside and not having Gran there waiting for her, but Ethan's silent and controlled movements were even more unsettling. Either he was holding himself back, waiting for her to change her mind. Or he was conserving his energy, a predator preparing to pounce upon his prey.

Sliding the dead bolt home gave her a boost of courage, a feeling of being the one in command. The decision had been made and Ethan was still here, watching her as she stood there shifting her weight from one leg to the other. "So how does this work? Do I offer you some coffee or something, or do we just head straight upstairs?"

"You mean you haven't already put a rule in place for one-night stands?"

The phrase made her wince, even though Monica had been the one to originally introduce the option of casual sex. "Is that what this is? A one-and-done kind of thing?"

"Rule four," he said, closing the distance between them. "Let's not put any time limits on anything."

Cupping her cheek, his face was only inches away from hers. He lifted his other hand and gently removed her glasses and set them on the small entry table. She could feel the ruffle along the V-neckline of her dress flutter against her chest as it rose and fell. One deep breath. Two deep breaths. Three… When his lips melded against hers, she didn't think about any more breaths or any more rules. She didn't think about anything but being closer to him and the barrier of his shirt that was now the only thing standing in her way.

Her fingers worked frantically over the buttons while her tongue dove in deeper in an attempt to stake her claim inside his mouth. When she finally got underneath, the heat from his bare chest set her palms on fire as she stroked every muscle, every ridge as though she needed to memorize the feel of him.

Something tugged against her arms and she moaned as her hands were pulled away from exploring his torso. But then she realized he was only relieving her of her jacket and her fingers returned to him as soon as she was free of the faded denim. His own hands slid to her hips and then behind to her rear end as he pulled her to him, pressing her against the hard length of desire under his zipper.

The house had grown chilly from the March evening and cool air kissed at the backs of her thighs as he slowly moved the silky fabric of her dress higher until it was bunched around her waist. Monica reached behind her to unzip the back, but his hands followed and one palm cupped the nape of her neck as he worked the zipper down.

His fingers trailed against her shoulders and she felt the dress delicately glide against her, bringing a heightened awareness to her skin as it dropped to the ground at her feet. Her bra followed the same route and the next thing she knew, she was standing in front of the man in nothing but her panties and her cowboy boots.

"Wow," he said, his voice low and throaty and warming every inch of her exposed flesh. When Ethan stared at her like that, Monica no longer felt shy or awkward.

She felt bold and powerful and capable of bringing a man to his knees. "I've spent the last six months imagining what you would look like when I finally got you naked, but nothing in my fantasies could've prepared me for how perfect the reality is. You are so much more than I expected."

"Finally got me naked?" she asked, reaching for his belt buckle. "You were pretty sure of yourself, huh?"

He lifted only one finger and traced it so lightly against her hardened nipple, her head tilted back as she whimpered.

"The only thing I was sure of was that I wasn't going to stop wanting you until I had you, Mon. And even now, I doubt that one time will be enough."

"Good, because I don't want to wait anymore." She brought her mouth back to his and kissed him deeply as she pressed her flat palms against the warm skin under his waistband, working his pants over the well-rounded curve of his butt until they joined her dress on the floor.

Ethan's hands were stroking and massaging and driving her mad as he hauled her against him. Breaking his lips away, he kissed a trail across her jaw, down her neck and to the same breast he'd been teasing earlier. He dropped to his knees in front of her, his hands continuing their descent over her hips, her thighs, her knees and her calves.

His lips had moved to the sensitive spot right below her belly button and after that, she didn't know where his hands went. Or what he'd done with her panties. Monica's breathing was already labored, but when Ethan's tongue dove into the center of her heat, she began to suck in quick gasps of air through her moans.

The first time she'd kissed him had been in the middle

of the book stacks at the library where anyone could've seen them. Now she was standing in the entryway of her house—still wearing her boots—as Ethan's tongue flicked and stroked and brought her to the highest peaks of desire. Apparently, her shameless response to him knew no bounds, and she no longer cared.

"I need you." Spreading her fingers through the short hair on his scalp, she eased his head up, watched him rise to his feet as his lips made their way back up to her face. "Now."

"You have me," he smirked. He walked her backward and when they got to the staircase, Monica thought he was going to lift her up and carry her upstairs.

But she didn't want to wait another second. She lowered herself to the second step, pulling him down with her. His lean hips slid between her thighs and she felt the rigid length of his manhood against the area he'd just so thoroughly kissed.

His chest pressed into her breasts and his face hovered over hers, his breath just as quick and frantic as hers when he asked, "Right here? On the stairs?"

She answered by pulling his lower lip into her mouth and suckling it.

His groan was low and a thrill shot through her at the knowledge that she could drive him just as wild as he was driving her.

"I need to grab something," he mumbled, but didn't take his eyes off her as he stretched an arm behind him and fumbled with his discarded pants. When he returned, he was already tearing open the package. As he rolled the condom on, the latex scent of the prophylactic mingled with the scent of her desire and Monica's thighs instinctively drew him closer, knowing her release was only moments away.

Pausing as his tip entered her, he closed his eyes and held himself perfectly still, as though he wanted to savor the moment. Monica drew in a ragged breath. "Ethan, please..."

With another groan, Ethan thrust forward, filling her as he lifted her hips. He wrapped his forearms against her waist, shielding her lower back from the wood planks of the stairs as he withdrew and plunged into her again and again. As the tempo built, Monica brought her knees around him, clinging tightly to every inch of him as her body shuddered and then shattered against him.

Ethan had never yelled out during sex before, but his ears were still echoing and his throat was hoarse from the way Monica's name had been torn from his mouth when he'd completely lost himself inside of her.

He eased his arms from behind her back and rested on his knees, which had never left the ground floor. Ethan couldn't believe he'd taken her right there on the stairs, but he certainly didn't mind the sight of her wearing nothing but a sheen of sweat and her cowboy boots.

His lips curved into a self-congratulatory grin as he stood and reached to pull her to her feet. She gave a contented sigh and his chest puffed out at the knowledge that he'd done a thorough job of satisfying her. So much for her one-and-done concern.

"Should we head to your room for round two?" he asked as he nuzzled his mouth against the warmth of her neck.

"I don't know if my legs are strong enough to climb the stairs yet."

"I've carried rucksacks heavier than you," he said before lifting her up vertically.

She let out a shriek before wrapping her calves around him again. He'd already made it up the first two steps when a muted ringtone sounded from his pants pocket on the floor below.

Monica stiffened before looking around frantically, probably to make sure they hadn't been caught again. Setting her back on her feet, he said, "Let me just make sure it's nothing important."

It took him a moment to dig the phone out of the pocket of his tangled pants. When he saw Trina's name on the screen, his heart jumped into his throat. "Hello?"

"Uh, hi. It's me. Trina." Her voice was hesitant and came out as a whisper, sending his pulse into overdrive. Something was wrong.

"What's wrong?"

"Oh, um, nothing?" There was a slight echo to her words and he told himself that she wasn't in any immediate danger.

"Are you in the bathroom?"

"Yeah? Um... I just wanted to see what you were doing?" Everything she said came out as a question.

Monica had already found her glasses and was pulling on her dress, concern etched all over her face. Obviously, he wasn't about to tell his daughter *exactly* what he was doing, but Trina knew he was supposed to be at a dance with Monica and she was smart enough to pick up on the fact there was no music playing in the background. "I was just dropping Mon off at her house. How are things going at the Patrellis'?"

Please say everything's okay, he thought. Not just because he wanted his daughter to be making friends and having a good time, but also because he wanted to continue having his own good time, as well. Man, that made him sound like a selfish ass.

"Um, it's okay, I guess? They have a lot of kids."

Ethan remembered spending the night at his best friend's house when he'd been the same age. The Phillips family also had a lot of kids and their house was full of noise and fun and arguments and life. He'd loved going over there and pretending he was just one more sibling. However, Trina wasn't the same way. She liked reading and listening to music by herself and anything else that involved being quiet. Which meant she was probably miserable over there.

Looking at Monica, her lips swollen and her cheeks raw from the whisker burn of his five o'clock shadow, Ethan swallowed a lump of disappointment and asked his daughter, "Want me to come pick you up?"

"No. Maybe. I don't want Kayla to think I'm a baby."

The fact that she was even admitting that much made Ethan want to run to her rescue.

"Why don't you tell her that Tootie won't settle down and go to sleep because she's missing you?" he offered. It was a valid enough excuse since that kitten had meowed like crazy at him after he'd returned to the apartment earlier this afternoon without Trina. "I'm leaving the Alvarez house now and should be there in about five."

He heard a sigh of relief coming from the other end. "Thank you, Dad."

The air left his lungs as he stared at the disconnected phone in his hands. It was the first time his daughter had actually called him Dad and not just in reference. A warmth spread through him and it felt as though the leader of the free world had just placed a medal of honor around his neck.

"Is everything okay?" Monica asked.

"Trina called me Dad," he said as he grinned stupidly at Monica. "She's never called me that before."

Monica's own mouth formed a surprise O before returning his smile. "That's incredible." Then her face dropped as she lifted her brows. "But did something happen at the Patrellis'?"

Ethan had done the casual thing with women before, but in his experience, a woman didn't appreciate being ditched before the night ended—no matter which call of duty summoned him. Monica had said she wanted to keep things physical and he was now about to put her wishes to the test.

"She didn't want to admit it, but she was a little nervous and would be more comfortable if I pick her up." He waited for a pout or an attempt to convince him otherwise.

"Poor Trina," Monica tsked before handing him his shirt. "I used to hate sleepovers when I was a girl. All that forced talking and staying up late and pretending to like another parents' cooking? It would always throw me off my routine and make me feel unsettled."

The way she shoved his shoes at him while he was still yanking a leg through his pants was beginning to make Ethan feel a bit unsettled himself. Apparently, she was pretty eager to see him leave. He tried not to be bothered by it. "So you don't mind if I take a rain check on coming upstairs with you?"

"Ethan, no promises or commitments, remember?" Her eyes darted around to everything else in the room but him as she reached behind her back to work up the zipper of her dress.

Unsure of whether her words were meant as a reminder that he didn't owe her anything, or a reminder that she wasn't guaranteeing anything in the future, he brought his finger to her chin and tilted up her face until she was forced to look directly at him. "You don't have to commit to anything, Mon. But I have no problem promising that I'm going to want you again. And soon."

Chapter Twelve

Monica pressed her fingers to her swollen lips after Ethan gave her a parting kiss.

Turning to climb the stairs, she avoided looking at the lower steps where they'd just made love. No, not made love, she corrected herself. They'd just had uncomplicated sex. Uncomplicated, mind-blowing, soul-reaching, earth-shattering sex.

And he'd promised to make her feel that way all over again. Perhaps they might even make it to an actual bed next time.

Nope, she wasn't going to go there, Monica told herself as she stepped into the hot shower and scrubbed the scent of his musky cologne off her skin. She shouldn't be looking forward to there even being a next time. Monica would never depend on a man for anything, not even uncomplicated, mind-blowing, soul-reaching, earth-shattering sex.

Especially from a man that had a history of leaving

town when a better offer came along. While Ethan might currently be proving himself to be a decent father, Monica knew that it couldn't last forever. Even a supposedly reformed bad boy might eventually get restless and take off. Although, he hadn't hesitated to go get Trina when she'd called and wanted to come home. In fact, he'd been downright giddy at the fact that his daughter had finally called him Dad. So at least the man's priorities were in order. For now.

When she climbed into her bed, her head barely hit the pillow before she was fast asleep. She slept hard and deep and didn't so much as dream until something startled her awake and she shot up in her bed. The house was way too dark and way too quiet.

Gran.

She'd forgotten to check on her. Monica's bare feet padded quickly down the dark hall toward her grandmother's room and when she saw the quilt perfectly made up on the bed, a kernel of panic rose in her chest. The digital clock with the jumbo numbers beside Gran's bed blinked 3:06 a.m. And then her sleepy brain finally clicked into place and she remembered her grandmother was staying at Legacy Village tonight.

See. Getting involved with Ethan was already making Monica forget about her responsibilities. Bringing him home last night had been a huge mistake.

Monica raced downstairs and held her breath as she fumbled in her purse, looking for her cell phone and praying she wouldn't find any missed calls from her grandmother. She let out a deep exhale when the screen came up blank. Nicole, the intake nurse, had told her that she could call the nursing desk anytime to check on Gran. But surely they would've notified her by now if there had been any problems. Carrying her phone back to her bed, Monica vowed to put all thoughts of Ethan out of her mind and to try to go back to sleep.

Unfortunately, she tossed and turned the rest of the night, reliving every touch, every kiss and every stroke.

Monica drove straight to Legacy Village on Sunday morning, finding a happy Gran holding court at the breakfast buffet and showing a woman wearing zebra-print slippers and a plastic tiara how to use the waffle iron.

"Look, Hector—" Gran reached across the toppings station and passed the can of whipped cream to an elderly man with the biggest earlobes Monica had ever seen "—my granddaughter's plane finally landed. How was the flight, *mija*?"

"My name is Gary, lady," the man grumbled before putting the whipped cream and three bananas into the hidden compartment under the seat of his walker and shuffling off.

"Are you ready to go home, Gran?" Monica asked, casting another look at Gary, who grabbed a few spoons out of the silverware caddy and slipped them into his pocket.

"Already?" her grandmother asked. "Can't we stay another night at the hotel? Please?"

Monica observed all of the residents sitting at their little tables in groups of four and six. The dining room was decorated more like an upscale country club than the Cowgirl Up Café, but it was just as crowded and lively as the Sugar Falls restaurant on a Sunday morning.

"But we always make *sopa* together on Sunday nights." Really, just like the enchiladas, Gran made everything herself while Monica just supervised.

"*Mija*, you know how to make *sopa* just fine by your-self. Besides, they're having church services at ten. They have a lady minister who comes in and we don't even have to go anywhere. Then they're having a piano player this afternoon and obviously they're going to need someone to lead the dancing." Gran lowered her voice to a whisper, "Some of these people are so stiff and bored, they don't even get up to dance unless someone encourages them."

Probably because more than half of the residents ap-peared to have limited mobility, Monica thought as the wire basket on an electric scooter clipped her elbow, its occupant speeding by toward the omelet station.

"Good morning, Mrs. Alvarez." Nicole appeared, her hair in a sleek purple bob today. "I heard you had quite the active night last evening."

Monica's stomach sank as she braced herself for the worst. No telling what kind of mischief her grandmother had gotten into. Please don't let it involve fire damage or monetary compensation, Monica prayed silently. There was no way they could afford any more setbacks.

"So does that mean I'm gonna get the job?" Gran clapped her hands together.

"I think we can work out a suitable offer," Nicole re-plied. "Do you mind if I speak with your agent about it?"

Oh boy. Were they really going to keep up the cruise ship dancer pretense?

"Be straight with me," Monica told Nicole when Gran went to assist a resident who was falling asleep in his chair and losing his grip on his cream cheese-slathered bagel. "How did she do?"

"She was quite the spitfire," Nicole chuckled.

"I'm so sorry. I can take her home right now—"

"Monica, no." The nurse waved her palm back and

forth. "I didn't mean that in a bad way. I meant she was actually very energetic and helped liven things up around here. She even got a conga line going at one point. Then last night's movie was *Blue Hawaii*, so she was practically a celebrity. The night nurse said she slept soundly until six this morning and then found her way to the kitchen and helped Reynaldo get the bacon and sausage going for breakfast."

"Oh no, you can't let Gran near a stove without proper supervision."

"Monica." Nicole folded her hands together in front of her chest. "I understand that you know your grandmother better than we do. But we want our residents to engage in the normal activities they're used to doing at home. Everyone on our staff—from our electrician to our chef to our night janitors—is trained to supervise and engage with residents just like Mrs. Alvarez. We have locks and security measures in place where we need them, but we also have a wealth of compassion and understanding for what our residents are missing from their old lives."

Monica sighed. "I just don't want her to get hurt. Or endanger others."

"I'm not going to promise that she won't ever have mishaps. Her condition is going to get worse and she's going to start having more bad days than good. We understand that she can't help it and we certainly don't expect perfect behavior from any of our residents. But we're well equipped to deal with any situation that comes up."

It was more than Monica could say for herself.

"Why don't you bring down some of her things and let her stay for the entire week and see how she does before you make a decision?" Nicole suggested. "No promises or commitments."

No promises or commitments. Monica's heart sank at the phrase that was now becoming all too familiar in her life.

On Sunday evening, Ethan went back and forth with whether he should call Monica. Mostly, he just wanted to hear her voice and know that she wasn't mad at him for leaving so abruptly on Saturday night. But he also was curious to find out how her grandmother had done with the sleepover at Legacy Village.

He paced along the boxes stacked against his bedroom wall until Tootie began attacking his foot every time he did an about-face, swatting at the shoelace on his hiking boot. In the past couple of weeks, her tiny kitten teeth had chewed through the laces of one of his favorite pairs of running shoes and both of his work boots. She'd also shredded through several toilet paper rolls; regularly used the ugly orange sofa as a scratching post; and tore up the school cafeteria menu he'd taped to the refrigerator, as well as the math worksheet Trina had "accidentally" forgotten on the kitchen table.

They'd learned to close the bathroom door before leaving the house, as well as put all their shoes away in the closets. But the poor sofa was out of luck until Ethan had time to build a mini cat condo. Trina said that Tootie was punishing them for abandoning her during the day to go to school and work. But the thing was a cat. Wasn't she supposed to want to be left alone?

Alone. Tomorrow was his Monday night meeting and he still needed someone to watch Trina for him. Ethan's mind sprang into action. That would be a perfect excuse to call Monica.

Unfortunately, his daughter was reading a book in the living room and, with the thin walls of his apartment, he didn't want her overhearing anything in the event Monica said she couldn't watch her. Trina didn't need any added rejection in her life.

Ethan pulled his phone out of his pocket as the first pricks of Tootie's claws began their assent up the leg of his jeans. He scooped her up and put her on his shoulder, which, other than Trina's lap, was the kitten's favorite place to be. Unfortunately, he got rewarded for his efforts with a puff of gas from under her tail.

"Geez, cat, what did you eat?" He scrunched up his nose as he started a text to Monica. How did your gran do with her trial stay at the place?

The little bubble popped up on his screen, indicating that she was responding and Ethan shuddered. Although, the sensation probably came from Tootie's whiskers as she used her nose to explore the area behind his ear.

Gran did really well. In fact she wanted to stay longer, surprisingly. Nicole said she could extend the trial to a week so I drove home and packed some of Gran's things and her blood pressure meds, then went back to have dinner with her and sign some papers. I just got home and I'm drained.

Did you get any sleep? he began to type then quickly deleted the words. It would've been a good opening to bring up what they'd done last night, however, he didn't want to scare her off too quickly. Are you working tomorrow?

Yes. Both jobs. Then I was thinking that Trina and I could go down and visit Gran while you're at your meeting.

Thank God she'd brought it up so he didn't have to sound like a jerk for wanting to add more responsibility to her already full plate. Are you sure you don't mind having Trina tomorrow? I know things have changed with your gran and I don't want to inconvenience you.

Trina's not an inconvenience. And Gran will want to see her. The response bubble popped up again and then disappeared, as though she too had just deleted something.

Were you going to add that YOU wanted to see ME, as well?

Actually, I was going to add that I didn't want you to miss your meeting.

"She thinks I lack self-control," he explained to Tootie, who'd curled herself into a ball on his shoulder.

And maybe he did, because he couldn't stop himself from typing, Well, I'm looking forward to seeing you. Maybe after my meeting we can pick up where we left off?

Bubbles appeared then disappeared at least three times and Ethan chuckled at how flustered she must be if she kept deleting her responses. Finally she replied, Not in front of your daughter.

His mouth lifted at the corners. She hadn't completely shot him down. She was merely forcing him to make some adjustments to his launch coordinates.

Luckily, Ethan didn't try anything in front of his daughter when he'd dropped her off earlier Monday evening. Probably because Monica planned ahead and already had her purse and keys in her hand when they'd pulled up to her house.

Tootie was a hit with the residents at Legacy Village— especially with Hector/Gary, who'd tried to sneak the kitten into the hidden compartment of his walker and take her back to his room with the rest of the items he'd pocketed along the way.

Her grandmother had been happy to see her and Trina at first, but then Gran had switched into her cruise director mode during bingo, ditching them to stand in front of the room and calling out the numbers. When they'd left, Gran had acted as though she didn't even know them and said, "Have a safe flight home."

Monica was exhausted and slightly depressed when she and Trina got into the car to return to Sugar Falls. On the return trip, they talked about her upcoming book report for school and Tootie's new diet and maybe trying to stay over at Kayla Patrelli's house again. But Monica knew something else was still on the girl's mind as they drove home, because she didn't even bother with her headphones.

The one subject Trina hadn't brought up so far tonight was her father. As much as Monica didn't want to discuss the man either, she had a feeling that Ethan was the looming elephant in the room—or the car, so to speak. If she didn't steer the conversation in that direction, how would she know if Trina was truly doing okay?

"So, how do you like living in Sugar Falls?" Monica asked, chickening out at the last moment.

"I like it." Her reply was simple and followed by silence. So apparently, that subject was a dead end.

"How about your apartment? Are you and Tootie pretty comfortable living there?"

"It's okay. It kinda smells like pastrami all the time because we live on top of a deli. My dad said the case-worker is going to come Wednesday afternoon and check us out. I kinda…" Trina's voice trailed off.

"You kinda what?" Monica pushed.

"I kinda wish it had more decorations in it, like your house does. I don't want the caseworker to think it's too plain, like it could belong to anyone."

"You mean you want it to look lived-in?"

The girl kept her head down as she stroked Tootie's gray fur. "Yeah. I want her to think it's a good place for me to stay."

Monica's heart stretched and her throat tightened. Trina *wanted* to stay with her father. Ethan would be so happy to know this. "If you want, I can bring some stuff over tomorrow to help spruce the place up."

Trina's face lifted, revealing a bright smile. "Maybe some stuff from your house? I don't want to get anything brand-new because then it will look obvious, like we're trying too hard. And pictures. We'll need some pictures in frames."

The kid was smart, Monica had to give it to her. "I definitely have some old frames. But we'll have our work cut out for us if we need to decorate *and* get some photos made up in less than forty-eight hours."

"I've been taking a few on my phone, but maybe we should get a shot of all of us together."

"All of *who* together?" Monica asked, her knuckles stiffening as she gripped the steering wheel.

"You, me, Dad and Gran."

Oh no. The poor child was under the impression that they were some sort of family unit, or at least she was hoping to portray them as such. A nugget of shame lodged in Monica's belly and she knew the thing would only get bigger if she didn't level with Trina.

"I don't know if…" Monica started, but didn't know how to finish without insulting the girl or making her feel rejected.

"I don't mean like a family photo or anything. But just something showing that me and Dad have what they call 'a support system.'" Trina was smart *and* she'd done her research.

Monica slowly exhaled. "If it's okay with your dad, then it's okay with me."

"Are you kidding? My dad will do anything if you tell him to. I know he asks your advice for stuff all the time. And he's always staring at you with those googly eyes."

"Your dad does not have googly eyes," Monica replied, already regretting the curiosity lacing her voice. Really, Ethan's eyes always were sort of empty and hard to read, even when he'd been flirting with her at the café. At least they used to be. Before Trina had arrived. Now they were mostly full of confusion and concern and occasionally lust.

"I know you guys kissed." Trina was now staring directly at her. Monica kept her eyes on the road, but the girl's scrutiny continued to drill into her.

Shifting in her seat, she asked, "How do you know he kissed me on Saturday night?"

"I was talking about when I saw you in the library, remember? Why? Did you kiss *again* after your date?"

Monica's brain spun as excuses pinged through her mind. She wanted to deny everything, but Trina was too old and too smart not to see through it. Pulling up to the first stoplight in town, Monica decided she'd have to change tactics. "Honey, I want you to know that *you* are your father's main priority. No matter what happens between him and me, we will always think about you first. Both of us only want to do what's best for you."

"So then you *are* dating?" Trina's lids lowered the same way they did when she was calculating math problems with her tutor in the library, but she didn't so much as blink. "Like officially?"

"No, not officially. We're just friends," Monica said as she turned onto her street. Ethan's truck was already waiting at the curb in front of her house. "I think."

Chapter Thirteen

"Hi, Dad," Trina said when she opened the door. The kitten, startled awake by the dome light, suddenly jumped out and made a beeline for the bushes. "Tootie! Come back!"

Just when Monica didn't think her nerves could handle any more stimulation tonight, Ethan took off after the animal.

"I'll get her," Ethan said, getting flat on his belly under the thick hedge of junipers along the property line. He made several mewing sounds before pleading with the kitten, "Come here, Tootie, that's a good girl. You want a little piece of cheese? Daddy will get you a little piece of cheese if you come out…"

"What in the heck are you doing?" Mr. Simon muttered from the other side of the hedge, making Tootie scamper deeper into the dense branches.

"I'm trying to get my daughter's kitten out of the

bushes." Ethan stood up and brushed the dirt off his chest and flat abdomen before looking over the five-foot-tall hedge at her neighbor. "Why are you wearing night vision goggles?"

"I heard some kids were gonna be out toilet papering tonight and I plan to catch them in the act." Mr. Simon was dressed in all black and his camouflage face paint only made the grooves of his wrinkles stand out. "But if they see you all out here having a party, they'll likely get scared and take off."

"You know you can call the police to handle that sort of thing," Ethan offered.

"Already did. But Officer Gregson says they don't have the resources to conduct an all-night stakeout, so here I am."

A rustling sounded in the branches and Ethan dropped back down to the ground. "Come on, Tootie," he pleaded again. But the cat didn't seem to care.

"I thought you were supposed to be a Navy SEAL." Mr. Simon shifted his night vision goggles to rest on top of his receding hairline. "What kind of Navy SEAL can't get a little cat out of some bushes?"

"Monica." Ethan twisted his neck to glance up at her. Even from that angle and in the dim glow of the streetlight, she could tell that he was having a tough time keeping his grin in check. "Could you please get me a slice of cheese so I can bribe the cat out without having to resort to my elite spec ops skills to navigate through this maze of juniper branches? Preferably before Mr. Simon asks to see my DD214 forms as proof of my service."

"Aye, aye, Lieutenant." Monica gave a mock salute before heading inside to the kitchen. When she returned,

Trina was on her knees beside her dad making clicking sounds and calling for her kitten.

The girl turned to Monica. "Mr. Simon was just telling us that he read a book about a cat burglar who literally stole people's cats."

"Yep. The Feline Felon. You know, they never did catch him." Monica's retired neighbor really needed to find a new hobby. Considering the size of this overgrown hedge separating their yards, maybe Monica should refer him to the gardening section the next time he came to the library.

"Hurry, Dad," Trina said, using her phone's flashlight app as Ethan took the wrapped slice Monica had just handed him.

Monica glared at Mr. Simon before kneeling on the ground to get a better look. "Nobody's going to steal Tootie."

Ethan didn't even need to hold the cheese out. The kitten was already sashaying out of the branches at the sound of the cellophane wrapper.

Trina scooped Tootie up quickly and chastised her while simultaneously nuzzling the gray fur on the animal's neck.

"We better get this little escape artist home." Ethan handed his daughter the yellow cheese before standing up. After he'd brushed himself off again a second time, he scratched the cat behind her ears as Trina fed her. The trembling sensation in Monica's lower regions was no doubt coming from her ovaries.

Walking toward his truck, Ethan asked Monica, "How was Gran?"

"She was okay. Didn't know who we were after the first thirty minutes, but she seemed really happy to be at that place. Don't you think, Trina?" Monica apparently now needed the confirmation of an eleven-year-old girl to justify that it was okay to put her grandmother in a home.

"She sure was smiling and laughing a whole lot," Trina replied, as she climbed into the front seat with Tootie cradled under one arm. "Hey, Dad, Monica said she's going to bring some stuff over to our house tomorrow so we can decorate for the home visit."

If Ethan didn't want Monica's involvement in his personal family business, now would've been the perfect time for him to speak up. Instead, he just smiled and dropped a kiss to Monica's temple. "Cool. We'll see you tomorrow, then. I'll make dinner for us."

Monica's face burned all the way to the roots of her hair.

"Can I tell the caseworker you guys are dating?" Trina asked her dad through the open window before looking at Monica. "I mean, you said you wanted to do the best thing for me and I think the best thing would be for the caseworker to know that my dad has a girlfriend and that she's part of our support system."

"What caseworker?" The question came from behind the bushes. "Like an investigator? What are they investigating?"

"Good luck with your stakeout, Mr. Simon." Ethan waved at the neighbor. "Let me know if you ever need to borrow my night vision goggles. They're modified with four tubes for a field of view of 97 degrees. They're also military grade and come complete with a government restriction."

A thumbs-up popped above the hedge and Monica squeezed her eyes shut behind her glasses to keep from rolling them.

When she opened her lids, Ethan was less than a foot away and her legs gave a wobble as she waited for him to kiss her, right there in front of his daughter. Again.

Instead of using his lips, though, the challenge in his eyes had a deeper impact on her nerves. "Bye, Mon. See you tomorrow at six."

Tuesday night, Monica arrived at the apartment carrying two boxes filled with quilts, throw pillows and some knickknacks that put Ethan's crooked, fake plant to shame. He wasn't sure that anything could spruce the place up, but he was willing to give it a shot if it meant he wouldn't lose Trina.

Monica even came bearing already framed photographs. She put a picture of Trina and Tootie playing tug-of-war with a shoelace in Ethan's room and a picture of Ethan wearing his tool belt and a flannel shirt in Trina's room. On the fireplace mantel, she put a picture of him and Trina riding the ski lift—looking like happy father and daughter adventurers, despite the fact that Trina had taken the lift right back down. There was also a picture of Trina and Gran doing a dance move in the Alvarezes' living room.

"Who took these?" he asked, absently scratching at the back of his neck. He certainly didn't remember posing for any of them.

"I found the first two on Gran's phone and got them developed. I took the one of Trina and Gran dancing, and Freckles didn't tell me how she came by the one of you guys on the slopes. It's a small town and I guess she has her connections."

He'd assumed that most people in town knew that Monica was helping him with Trina, but hope threaded through him at the realization that she wasn't keeping their relationship a secret. In fact, she was obviously enlisting the help of the locals in an effort to be a part of this support system Trina kept mentioning.

As Monica stood in his living room surveying her handiwork of throw pillows and knitted afghans and half-burned pillar candles, Ethan came up behind her. When he put his hands around her waist, she startled but she didn't pull away. She peeked behind them, probably to make sure Trina wasn't in the room, and then she leaned back against him. *Man, this felt right.* Lowering his lips to her neck, he asked, "What about a photo with you in it?"

She stiffened, but he didn't let her go far. Moving to the other side of her neck, he murmured, "Maybe I'll ask around over at the VFW and see if anyone got a shot of you in that short green dress. Wearing those sexy cowboy boots…"

She sighed as his fingers crept underneath her soft, blue sweater and danced along her warm skin as his palms made their way over her rib cage.

"When can I see you again?" he asked, his lips now just behind her ear. He felt her shudder, but the oven timer squawked and she practically jumped out of his arms.

As they utilized the polka-dot tablecloth she'd brought over, he sat across the dining table from her, eating a pre-made chicken potpie he'd picked up from the café and watching her try and pretend that she wasn't thinking about their next time together.

On Wednesday afternoon, despite Trina needing several reassurances from him in the morning that everything would be fine—as well as two bathroom passes while she was at school—the home visit went off without a hitch. The first thing Ethan did was offer up a prayer of thanks that nobody, especially his daughter, had seen through his false bravado. The second thing he did was send Monica a text message to celebrate the caseworker's recommendation that Trina stay with him.

She was at Legacy Village and replied with a picture of Gran painting a very unfortunate likeness of Elvis during the watercolor class. My grandmother thinks you look like him.

Ethan chuckled to himself before typing a response. I'll take it. You can give it to me tomorrow night when we meet at Patrelli's to celebrate.

She met them for dinner on Thursday night and, when Trina went into the back room of the restaurant to play arcade games, Ethan reached across the table and took Monica's hand. "When are we going to see each other again?"

"I'm seeing you right now," she said, but her eyes dropped to his lips and all of his blood dropped to his lower parts.

"You know what I mean."

"Maybe this weekend?" Monica's voice came out in a shy whisper and Ethan doubted he could wait that long.

Friday morning, he dropped off Trina at school and when Monica arrived to the library nearly an hour before it opened, he was waiting in the parking lot with a stack of books Trina had checked out and already read.

"I hope you're not here to pick up that new Navy SEAL book that came out on Tuesday," Monica said as she exited her car. "Mr. Simon beat you to it and checked it out yesterday."

"Mr. Simon can keep it," he replied, trying to keep his lips from sneering in disgust. An embedded journalist had written a fictionalized account of Ethan's unit and, from what he'd heard from Luke, the story contained a rather heroic retelling of the night Boscoe had died. "I already lived the nonfiction version and it's something I'd like to forget."

He felt the weight of her gaze as she studied him. "So that was you in the book? The one who single-handedly fought off all those insurgents in the middle of a crowded marketplace? And then carried your partner's body up to the roof and jumped across several buildings to make it to the medic's helicopter?"

"Well, I remember there being a lot more to the story than that." Specifically, the part about how he'd been the one to inadvertently lead his partner into the ambush in the first place. Monica tilted her head, her eyes full of comfort and a willingness to listen. However, Ethan didn't get many moments alone with the woman and he didn't want to waste the current one by talking about his past mistakes. He held up the stack of Trina's books. "Anyway, I'm actually just bringing these back."

"You know you can use the book return." Monica pointed to the metal box with a drop slot. "You didn't need to wait for me to get here."

"Maybe I just wanted to get you alone."

She looked at her watch, then looked at him, then looked at the empty parking lot. "I have to open the library in forty-five minutes."

"All I need is thirty," he replied with a hopeful lift of his forehead.

Inside the closet-sized storage room behind the circulation desk, Ethan hoisted Monica onto a metal book trolley and then proceeded to prove that he only needed half that amount of time.

She sighed contentedly when he withdrew from her and he couldn't help but watch her flushed chest rise and fall with each breath afterward.

He was already looking forward to the next time he could see her. "Someday, we'll have to actually make it to a bedroom."

"Well, we certainly shouldn't make a habit of doing it here." She felt around the shelf beside her until her hand landed on her discarded glasses. When she got them on, he helped her down to her feet before she tugged her skirt back over her hips.

"I'd suggest going to my job site next time, but starting Monday, Kane and I are building a new fish cleaning station near the Lake Rush boat launch."

"Is the city paying for that? Because the council postponed their vote on my request to expand our audiobook collection."

"Don't worry. Nobody is paying for it." He held up his palms. She lifted an eyebrow and he continued, "I've been known to give back to the community on occasion."

"You're racking up quite the list of good deeds, Ethan Renault." Monica folded her arms in front of her. "In fact, I've seen your name on the visitor log over at Legacy Village every day this week."

"Well, the day shift nurse said I'm the only one who can get your gran to slow down long enough between activities to drink a meal replacement shake."

Monica rubbed at the crease between her brows.

"What's wrong? Are you worried about your grandmother?"

"Well, that. And the fact that I'm not so sure we should be crossing all these boundaries and becoming so involved in each other's lives."

Ethan buttoned up the front of his jeans. "Don't you think it's a little too late for that, Mon?"

* * *

Nicole was heading quickly in her direction when Monica finally arrived at the check-in desk at Legacy Village later that afternoon. On the phone, the nurse had explained that they had things under control, but wanted to keep Monica informed about this latest episode.

The whole drive down there, though, she'd been beating herself up over the fact that she couldn't rush to Gran's aid sooner. But at least her grandmother was being taken care of by professionals and wasn't home alone or wreaking havoc on the local businesses on Snowflake Boulevard. By the time she'd pulled into the parking lot, Monica wasn't any closer to deciding if a memory care center was the right choice or not.

"Sorry I couldn't get here sooner," Monica said, already dreading the worst. "We had our teen reading challenge meeting and I couldn't close the library until four. Is she okay?"

"She's doing better now. Our doctor was making rounds and gave her a little sedative. She isn't asleep yet, but she's not crying anymore. Ethan is in her room with her."

"Ethan's here?" Monica asked, slapping the visitor sticker on her chest as she strode down the hall with Nicole on her heels.

"I called him when you said you couldn't be here right away. Mrs. Alvarez kept asking for *mijo* and I've heard her call him that before."

Trina was sitting in one of the overstuffed chairs in the hallway alcove near Gran's room, her headphones in her ears and her backpack at her feet. It must've been a really bad episode if Ethan had come straight from the school and was making his daughter wait outside.

When Monica slipped inside the room, she saw Ethan in a chair near Gran's bed. The older woman was fully dressed, but under the covers and holding Ethan's hand.

"Gran?" Monica whispered, brushing the silver hair off her grandmother's forehead. Her paper-thin eyelids fluttered open.

"There you are, Bettina. Look who came to stay at the hotel. My *mijo*." Gran's bony fingers squeezed against Ethan's hand and she mumbled something in Spanish that sounded like a recited prayer.

"That was nice of you to come keep her company, Ethan," Monica said.

"It's not Ethan," Gran replied, her words forceful yet somewhat slurred. "It's Fidel. My Fidel. He's finally home."

Ethan smiled when Gran patted his cheek but, when the older woman closed her eyes again, he got Monica's attention and mouthed the words, "Who's Fidel?"

"My dad." Monica hadn't replied out loud either, but just feeling the answer against her lips pierced her heart. She sat on the edge of the bed and her grandmother looked up. "How are you feeling, Gran?"

"Never been better." Gran's smile was faint, but genuine. "I have my son home and we're finally going to be a family. Look at all those muscles he built up while he was at the academy."

What academy? A prickling of unease spread through Monica as her grandmother kept talking.

"Don't I have the best son in the world, Bettina? He's always taken such good care of me."

Monica's jaw locked into place to keep her from responding the way she wanted to. She knew that she wasn't supposed to correct someone who was confused by Alzheimer's as long as their confusion wasn't harming them. But Gran's current bout with mistaken identity was bringing back some pretty painful memories for Monica. Especially since her deceased, deadbeat father was now getting unfair credit and glowing accolades when it was *she* who'd put her life on hold to take care of her grandmother.

"My *mijo* is going to take such good care of his baby girl, too," Gran continued to no one in particular, now. "As soon as he puts all those bad guys away, he will come home and take care of us. I know it."

Gran mumbled something else before her eyes drifted closed and remained that way for a few minutes, suggesting the sedative had finally taken full effect.

"Nicole said that a lot of people with dementia or Alzheimer's can get pretty anxious around this time of day." Ethan's voice was soft and low, probably because he didn't want to wake Gran again and have her confuse him for her low-life son. "The nurses called it 'sundowners' because it comes on when the sun goes down. It's not exactly my best time of the day either."

She knew he was trying to help, trying to make Monica feel better, but his compassion and understanding were only driving that wedge of unease in deeper. Between her guilt for leaving her grandmother at a nursing home and her sudden resentment that Gran wasn't even aware of how hard Monica was trying to do her best, she was dealing with too many emotions to add an ill-advised attraction to a single father to the mix.

Her grandmother let out a snore and Ethan gently extracted his hand and stood up. "The doctor said once the sedative took effect, she'd probably be out for the night. I've got to go get Trina some dinner. You wanna come with?"

"No, I'm not very hungry. What do you think she meant when she said you got back from the academy?"

Ethan lifted his shoulders. "Did your dad go to some sort of prep school?"

"Nope. He was a local kid, as far as I know," she replied, thinking of the boxes in the attic where Gran had stored her father's old things. Obviously, her grandmother had been beyond confused and clearly hadn't known what she'd been talking about. Although. This was different. Most of her episodes were usually centered around something she wanted or something that had actually happened in her past. Gran had never completely made something up out of the blue before.

"Okay, so maybe we can still get together this weekend?" Ethan asked.

"Sure," she said absently, as she focused on Gran's slurred words. Dealing with her grandmother's episodes had become such a part of Monica's routine, it was hard not to worry that the disease had become contagious. If her own mind was now slipping, as well.

Ethan studied Monica for a few more moments before placing a light kiss on her lips and walking out the door. She moved to the chair he'd vacated, but after about five minutes, when it became clear that Gran wasn't going to wake up and answer her questions anytime soon, Monica headed out to the parking lot and drove straight home.

Determination fueling her.

Chapter Fourteen

The return trip up the mountain was a complete blur, as though Monica's hands and feet were operating on autopilot, while her mind spun out of control. Letting herself in the house, she dropped her purse at the door and grabbed a package of Oreos from the kitchen before heading up to the attic.

Two hours later, Monica was sore from sitting cross-legged on the uneven wooden slats. Her eyes hurt from the lack of decent lighting and her brain was even more confused than when she'd started this pointless task.

The boxes contained all the same pictures and trophies and high school yearbooks she'd seen before. Her dad had been an all-star in both track and baseball at Sugar Falls High School, and had graduated as salutatorian. He'd gotten a scholarship to the University of Idaho, which was where he'd met her mom. There were a couple of wedding photos, but that was where all the clues ended. So how did her father fall into such a bad crowd?

The memories she had of him were few and far between, but most of them involved him leaving for long periods of time and then returning later with a book and a tight squeeze, teasing her about how big she was getting. She remembered looking forward to those visits, but she also recalled Fidel Alvarez's sudden presence having the opposite effect on his wife. And how could Monica enjoy seeing her dad when her mom was so clearly miserable?

One time, he'd showed up on a motorcycle, stayed a night or two and then fought with her mother before leaving in the middle of the night. When Monica was six, she'd gone on a long road trip with just her and her mom. She couldn't think of the name of the prison, but she remembered being fascinated by all the tattoos covering his arms when they sat across from him in the visiting area. She also recalled him being upset with her mother for bringing Monica.

Her mom had said that her dad would rather live with a bunch of druggies and crooks than be with his own family. That's when she'd made Monica promise never to fall in love with the same type of guy—a guy who didn't put his family first.

After her mother died, Monica made a promise to herself to not even give the man who'd fathered her a second thought. There'd been a couple of times in high school when she'd see his name on one of the plaques in the trophy case and she'd thought about doing some online research to find out more about him. After all, he obviously had a criminal record and she might be genetically predisposed and at risk for heading down the same unfortunate path.

Then she'd come to her senses and convinced herself that any answers she might uncover would only depress her. Instead, she'd buckled down on her studies and wouldn't attend so much as a school dance, let alone a party, just to prove that she was nothing like him.

The sound of a lawn mower rumbled to life and Monica looked at the time on her cell phone. It was almost seven o'clock on a Friday evening, which meant that Mr. Simon must be getting a late start on his yard maintenance. Either that or he needed a ploy to spy on poor Mrs. Fitzroy's delivery driver.

Wait. Mr. Simon had lived next door to Gran since before Monica was born. Maybe he could give her some insight about the man who'd abandoned her. Her legs revolted when she rose to her feet, but her circulation was back to normal by the time she got outside and waved down her neighbor.

"What can I do for you, Monica?" Mr. Simon had shut off his lawn mower, but he was blatantly staring at the big brown truck now driving away. His eyes narrowed behind his wire-rimmed glasses. "Awful late in the day to deliver a package."

"Mr. Simon, do you remember my father?"

"Fidel? Of course. Who wouldn't remember him?"

His daughter, Monica thought. "Gran's been asking about him a lot. Can you tell me anything?"

"Boy, that guy could run. Won the eight hundred meter at state two years in a row. He was a couple of years behind me at high school, but he was smarter than anyone I ever hung around. And he loved pickles."

"No, I know all about when he was young." Except the pickles part, which finally explained Gran's surplus in the pantry. She was hoping her son would be coming home to eat them. "But what can you tell me about him after he got married?"

Mr. Simon let out a low whistle.

Monica twisted her lower lip between her teeth. "Tell me."

"Well, I hate to say it, but he really never should've married your mom. Not with his lifestyle."

Monica seized on the opening she needed. "What about his lifestyle?"

"Come to think of it, that boyfriend of yours reminds me of Fidel in a lot of ways." Mr. Simon tapped his chin and Monica felt every muscle inside of her coil at the comparison. Ethan most definitely was not her boyfriend, but she wasn't going to argue the small details when she needed to understand the bigger picture.

"Why? Is it because of his…" She had almost said *addiction*, but at the last second caught herself. Talking about Ethan's alcoholism would've been a violation of his trust. "Lifestyle?"

"Fidel was one of those macho hero types. Always good at sports and always wanting to save the world. He was this happy-go-lucky guy who was the life of the party and could fit in with anyone. Nobody was surprised when he joined the DEA after college. But when he started taking on those undercover assignments, your mom was not having it. And who could blame her?"

"DEA? You mean Drug Enforcement Administration?" Maybe Mr. Simon had read a few too many true crime books. "Are you sure?"

"You mean your grandma didn't tell you?"

Monica shook her head. Nobody had told her. "I thought he was on the other side of the law, so to speak. My mom took me to visit him in prison before she died.

He got so mad at her and wouldn't even look at me, let alone hug me."

"Yep, your gran told me about that. That was back before we had a local police force. I had to organize the neighborhood watch so we could take turns keeping an eye out to make sure none of his associates came looking for you."

"What do you mean his *associates*?"

"The kind he was infiltrating. Fidel had gone so deep undercover, even the prison guards didn't know he was a special agent. Your mom drove you down to Florence, Colorado, to show him that his work was causing him to miss out on your childhood."

"They fought in the visiting area," Monica said softly. "He yelled at her."

"It was actually a pretty reckless thing for your mom to do. Fidel was investigating a major drug ring that ended up taking down a dozen or so guards, four supervisors and the assistant warden. By bringing you to that prison, she was painting a target on both of your backs and providing his enemies with the perfect means to exact their revenge. Even when the case was over and he was done testifying, he still stayed away just to make sure you were safe. He died shortly after that in a routine drug bust that went bad. At least, that's what they told your grandmother."

"Is that why I wasn't allowed to go to his funeral?"

"That would be my guess. He was Lydia's only son and she was already devastated. You were all she had left after that." Mr. Simon jabbed a finger in the air. "Actually, I have some pictures of him and you when you were a baby. The neighborhood threw a big party when he came home from the academy. Things were a little tense around here after he died so your gran asked me to hold onto some of his awards and the newspaper articles just in case any of those bad dudes he put away came looking for you. There's a *Law and Order* marathon on tonight, but I can look for them tomorrow and bring them over."

Monica thanked her neighbor and returned to the house in a daze. Gran hadn't avoided talking about her dad because she was too sad. She'd done it to keep Monica safe. Now that she thought about it, even her mother had never come out and called Fidel a drug addict. But they'd never filled in any of the blanks either, and Monica had been left to think the worst.

The pieces of a puzzle she hadn't known existed began clicking into place. Her father showing up late for her birthday party and her mom yelling at him for missing it. Her father disappearing for stretches of time and then reappearing out of the blue with disheveled hair and an overgrown beard that made her mom complain there was no way she was going to take family pictures with him until he "cleaned up his act."

Her entire childhood, she'd thought her father was some lowlife, some criminal. That his addiction had come before anything else. Apparently, his addiction hadn't been to drugs, but to his career.

She saw a missed text from Ethan, but Monica's head was still swimming and she didn't want to think about anything but how wrong she'd been about everything in her life up until now.

The entire weekend went by and Ethan didn't hear from Monica. He knew she'd been stressed out about that incident at Legacy Village the previous Friday, so he hadn't wanted to push her.

On Monday afternoon, he was going to send her a

text asking her whether he should make alternate arrangements for Trina, but when his daughter came home
from school, she said Kayla Patrelli invited her to Bring a
Friend night at the Snowflake Dance Academy. He'd been
hoping she would express some sort of interest in an ex-
tracurricular activity that involved actually being active.

Plus, maybe Monica was right. They'd been getting
too involved in each other's lives lately.

On Tuesday afternoon, when he brought Trina to tutoring, Monica kept her distance. However, several times
he caught her watching him, her expression leery as if he
had suddenly grown two heads.

"Why are you looking at me like that?" he asked her
when he passed by the checkout desk.

"Like what?" Monica kept her eyes averted, as though
she was now suddenly too busy to notice him standing
right in front of her. She was opening book covers and
scanning barcodes and stacking them on the same metal
trolley where he'd made love to her a few mornings ago.

"You haven't returned any of my texts. Did something
happen on Friday after I left Legacy Village?"

Her hands stilled over a cellophane-covered copy of *The
Great Gatsby*. When her eyes finally rose to his, they were
somewhat vacant behind the lenses of her glasses. "I found
out that my father wasn't who I thought he was. My grandmother never told me the truth. And now she's at the point
where she can hardly remember what the truth is anymore."

"Mon, she's still your family even if you're not related
by blood." Ethan leaned his elbows on the polished wood
counter separating them. "When Trina first showed up, I
thought about getting DNA tests. But even if I didn't already believe deep down that she was mine, I would've

wanted her anyway. I'm sure your grandmother feels the same about you."

The creased V appeared above her nose before she shoved her glasses back into place. "No, I'm not talking about biologically. I mean my dad wasn't some drug dealing criminal. He was actually an undercover DEA agent."

"Oh yeah. I read that he took down one of the biggest drug operations in the federal prison system."

Monica's head drew back. "How did you know that?"

"I did an internet search. I wanted to know more about the guy your gran was mistaking me for in case I needed to get her settled down again."

"Why have you been so good to her?" Monica asked. "You have all of your own issues with your meetings and your job and becoming a full-time single dad overnight. You've already got me to sleep with you. So why are you still hanging around and being nice to Gran?"

"Because I want to do more than just sleep with you, Monica."

"Why?" she asked, her neck stretching back as she looked up at him. He realized the mistrust he'd thought she'd overcome was back in full force. "What does an adrenaline junkie like you see in a bookworm like me?"

"Because you're smart and you're serious and you're stable."

"Stable? Wow. You really know how to get a girl's pulse racing." She turned to look at the same boy who had been asking her for the frog book a couple of weeks ago, and was now on his tippy-toes, using the second shelf of the medical section as a stepladder. "Do you need me to help you find something, Choogie?"

With a final stretch, the boy toppled over a hefty volume on human anatomy. "Nope, Miz Monica. I got it."

Choogie kept the cover turned toward his chest as he

ran-walked to a back table where the Gregson twins were eagerly awaiting them. Monica groaned under her breath. "Last week, they found a stash of *National Geographic* magazines in the Friends of the Library donation pile. I'm going to have to go check on them before they get to the chapter on reproductive parts."

"Then I'll make this quick." Ethan remembered what it was like to be curious at that age and wanted to tell the boys that no book was going to make the opposite sex any less mysterious. Taking a fortifying breath, he continued. "I moved around a lot when I was a kid. Then, when I was in the Navy, I never slept in the same bed longer than six months at a time. Usually way less than that. So when I say stable, I mean I like the fact that you were born and raised here and that you're established in the community and not going anywhere. I want to settle down, Mon. I want to belong somewhere and I want my daughter to have what I never experienced."

"Most of the single women who live in Sugar Falls are just as stable," Monica challenged.

"But it's calm when I'm with you. More importantly, *I'm* calm when I'm with you. Like I don't need to jump out of a plane or dive off a cliff or race down a mountain when you're around. I'm not saying I won't do those things in the future. But when we're together, I'm not looking for anything else to stir my blood. I liked you before Trina ever showed up, but then I saw you with her and I was an absolute goner. You know what to do for her before I can even figure out the right question to ask. She needs you almost as much as I do."

"Ethan, I don't think I can be needed by anyone else right now. Between my jobs and Gran, I'm barely keeping my head above water."

"So then why don't you depend on someone else for a change?" he asked.

"Like you?" She rolled her eyes and his chest filled with disappointment. "You're renting a furnished apartment by the month and you haven't even unpacked those boxes in your bedroom yet. You said that you wanted stability. Well, so do I."

Monica hadn't even tried to ease the blow before walking away to retrieve the book Choogie and the Gregson twins were now hovering over. She'd left Ethan standing there to contemplate the absolute reality of her harsh words.

He needed her, but he had absolutely nothing that she needed.

On Wednesday morning, Ethan was supposed to run electrical wiring to Freckles's backyard gazebo for her new hot tub. Kane was Freckles's nephew by marriage and, when the café owner told him and Ethan about some of the best hot tub parties she'd attended in the seventies, Kane had picked up his tool bag and told Ethan, "You're on your own."

So when the dark clouds finally opened up to deliver the spring showers the weather channel had predicted, Ethan rolled up the conduit and wires and decided not to get electrocuted that day. There was an AA meeting he could attend at Shadowview at ten, but when Ethan went home to change into some dry clothes, he saw Tootie sitting on top of the cardboard boxes, gnawing at one of the corners.

Well, he thought, pushing up his sleeves, if he wanted Monica to think he was stable, maybe he should take her advice and finally unpack these boxes once and for all.

The first one was easy. Mostly papers and files. He scanned over his performance ratings from the Navy and his father's last banking statement that the attorney had sent him after his old man had passed away. Between his small inheritance from his dad and all the extra deployment pay he'd stashed away, there was no reason why he couldn't buy one of the older Victorian homes over on Pinecone Court and fix it up for him and Trina. That would definitely demonstrate to him and everyone else that he was just as stable as the next person.

The second box had some photos and several plaques and awards from his days on the team. Maybe if he found a place with a den or an office conversion, he could hang some of these on the wall.

When he got to the third box, though, Ethan wanted to close it back up as soon as he opened it. Standing up, he went to the kitchen to make another cup of coffee. Tootie meowed, as she always did anytime someone got close to the refrigerator. "The vet said no more snacks. If I have to become stable, then your digestive tract needs to become stable, as well."

He downed half the cup before carrying it back into his bedroom and facing the box that contained some of Damon Boscoe's personal effects. The ones he was supposed to send to his buddy's family more than two years ago. The faded T-shirt advertising the Recovery Tour he'd gotten when he and Ethan snuck off base to go to an Eminem concert. The sweat-stained bandana printed with the Texas flag that Boscoe always wore under his helmet. The tied stack of letters from his mom that smelled like vanilla cookies. He shifted through more pictures and then his eyes landed on it. Boscoe's lucky shell he'd found in the sand after barely passing their combat dive phase. It still had his friend's blood on it from the night Ethan had held him in his arms as the desert sky lit up with gunfire rounds and missiles while they'd waited for backup to arrive.

Losing a team member in battle was something Ethan had been through before. But with Boscoe it had been different. Both of them were from Texas, they'd ridden together on the same bus to recruit training and they'd been stationed to the same destroyer after graduation. They'd even received their letters welcoming them to BUD/S training on the same day. Boscoe had been the only brother he'd ever known.

And Ethan had killed him.

Or at least, he hadn't saved him.

After a full investigation, the inquiry board determined that Ethan hadn't been at fault for the attack that had taken Boscoe's life. But Ethan hadn't been at his best either. He'd polished off a bottle of vodka the night before, after celebrating the capture of one of the top ranking terrorists in the area. His head was still fuzzy and his entire body was hungover when the base commander had ordered them to follow up on a tip about a possible retaliation attack. If Ethan had been thinking clearly, he never would've walked into that marketplace without suspecting a trap.

Ethan's responses had been slower and his best friend had paid the price. He'd like to say that he got sober the very next day. But it wasn't until Luke Gregson was standing on the tarmac beside him back in the States as they lowered Boscoe's casket from the plane. Luke told Ethan about his first wife dying in a DUI and how he'd always blamed himself for not speaking up sooner and getting a loved one the help they needed. Luke had then handed him a flyer listing all the local AA meetings near the Coronado base.

Ethan now dug in the cardboard box again and picked up the piece of paper that Luke had given him that day. It was crumpled and stained with pizza sauce and had been covering half a bottle of Jim Beam.

That's right, the memory slammed into Ethan. He'd

been drinking when he'd originally packed this box. He'd gone to refill his cup with ice, and saw the list of AA meetings he'd thrown in the trash. He'd been completely sloshed when he'd called the number on the flyer and didn't remember taping the box closed that night.

Now, as he held the glass neck of the bottle in his hand, he realized that day eighteen months ago was the first time Ethan hadn't finished a bottle. So much had changed since that night and he would like to think he was strong enough in his recovery to keep the half-empty bottle as some sort of trophy. Some sort of reminder that he'd stopped mid-drink and never needed a drop of booze again.

But then he looked outside his bedroom door, at the floral quilt covering his daughter's bed, and he knew that nothing would be worth losing her. He wasn't even going to risk the possibility of temptation. Standing up, he didn't bother taking the time to walk all the way to the kitchen sink. Instead, he went straight to the bathroom and began pouring the contents down the toilet.

Unfortunately, he'd left the door open too long and Tootie decided it was the perfect time to attack the unattended toilet paper roll. The kitten missed her target, though, and knocked into Ethan, causing him to splash a fair amount of bourbon all over the front of his clean T-shirt.

He was about to change into another, but his cell phone vibrated in his pocket.

"Hi, Dad." Trina's voice echoed off the acoustics of what must've been the girls' bathroom.

"Trina, what's wrong? Why aren't you in class?"

"Can you come to the school? I really need you."

"I'll be there in five minutes," Ethan said, already halfway down the steps outside before he disconnected.

Chapter Fifteen

When Monica arrived in the girls' bathroom at Sugar Falls Elementary, Ethan was already there and sitting on the counter between two sinks, apparently not caring that a gaggle of schoolgirls could walk in at any second.

And he smelled like a distillery. Had he been drinking? Disappointment made her legs turn to lead as she walked closer to the sinks, but she'd deal with him later.

"Where's Trina?" Monica asked. "What happened?"

Ethan used his thumb to gesture toward one of the closed stall doors and that was when she noticed his daughter's shoes underneath.

Had Ethan shown up drunk at the school and made some sort of scene?

The lock slid open and Trina emerged with her phone in her hands. The girl wasn't looking down or hiding her face, though. In fact, she didn't appear to be upset at all.

"I got your text that you were here, honey," Monica told the girl. "Why are you hiding in the bathroom?"

"It's Wednesday," Trina said, as though that explained everything.

"Are you worried about your math test?" Ethan asked his daughter, and Monica realized he was just as clueless as to why Trina had resorted to hiding out in the bathroom. Again. "I thought that was tomorrow."

Monica glared at Ethan and mouthed, *Are you drunk?*

He frowned at her and gave a quick shake of his head before hopping off the counter. Hmm, he appeared steady enough on his feet.

She would've assessed his sobriety more, however, Trina began speaking again. "No. I'm not worried about my math test. I mean, I will be tomorrow, but I figured the sooner I got you guys together the better."

"Okay, so it's Wednesday and you've got us both here, Trina. She wouldn't tell me what was going on until you arrived," Ethan told Monica then turned back to his daughter. "Is everything okay?"

"No, it's not." Trina planted her hands on her hips. "Both of you guys have told me that you want to do what's best for me, right?"

"Definitely," Monica replied at the same time Ethan said, "Of course."

She and Ethan were now standing side by side and Trina's brows were lifted in challenge as she faced them. "Well, it's best for me if you guys are dating and making each other happy."

Ethan lifted his eyes to the ceiling and made a choking noise that suspiciously sounded like a smothered chuckle. Monica opened her mouth to protest, but Trina held up her palms. "I know you two haven't been talking. Dad, you were looking at your cell phone every five minutes last weekend waiting to hear from her. And, Monica, when we visited Gran on Sunday, she told me that you were crazy about my dad and it would be up to me to get you back together."

"Honey, you can't listen to what Gran says half the time—" Monica started, but Trina cut her off by pointing her little eleven-year-old finger right at them.

"Gran told me that was exactly what you'd say. When I saw you staring at my dad in the library yesterday I knew she was right."

Ethan's nose made a hissing sound as he drew in a deep breath. "So you decided the best way to get us together was to call both of us and tell us that it was an emergency and we needed to meet you in the girls' room in the middle of the school day?"

"I never said it was an emergency. But it's Wednesday and my tutoring session tomorrow got canceled so I knew that I needed to do something quick or else you guys wouldn't see each other until next Monday again. It worked when Gran had you both show up together, so I figured it would work for me."

"It's more complicated than just getting us alone to talk." Monica looked at Ethan. "Back me up here anytime."

Ethan merely shrugged, the fabric of his shirt releasing its boozy odor in the air. "No harm ever came from talking."

"Okay, so you guys have about twenty minutes until the lunch bell rings and everyone heads this way." Trina put her cell phone in the back pocket of her jeans. "I have to go back to class right now, but I'll be in the cafeteria later if you need my advice."

Advice for what? Monica thought. But as the door closed behind the girl, Monica wanted to call out and ask her to come back so she wouldn't have to face Ethan alone.

"So what do you want to discuss first?" he asked, leaning a hip against the bathroom counter as though he was ready to settle in for the long haul.

A little girl wearing pigtails and a laminated hall pass around her neck shoved through the door and paused. She looked back and forth between Ethan and Monica before glancing up at the sign on the door that clearly read Girls.

"We were just leaving," Ethan told the child as he cupped Monica's elbow and steered her into the hall. She thought she'd gotten another reprieve, but then he added, "We can finish our discussion outside."

When they got out to the parking lot, it was still drizzling and Ethan watched Monica clean the splatters off her glasses. "It's really coming down, huh?"

"It's barely a mist," he pointed out. "Or are you so desperate to avoid me, you're going to pretend we're in a category four hurricane?"

"I haven't been avoiding you." She wrapped her arms around her waist and stared at the empty flagpole behind him.

"Okay, well I see we're not going to get anywhere by actually talking about what's going on." Ethan's lower lip curved into a frown as he nodded. "Let me know when you're ready to have a conversation."

He pulled the keys out of his pocket and Monica made a sputtering sound. "Are you sure you should be driving in your condition?"

"In what condition?" Ethan had seen the way she'd

looked at him in disgust earlier when she'd walked inside the bathroom and took her first whiff of him. But he wanted to hear her say it out loud. She didn't trust him.

"Oh come on, Ethan. You smell like you've been doing shots all morning."

"No, I smell like I was dumping a bottle of bourbon down the toilet and a kitten tried to attack the toilet paper roll and knocked the contents all over me."

"Why did you have a bottle of bourbon in the bathroom?"

"I found it when I was finally going through those boxes in an effort to get 'stable' for you." Oh great. He'd just used air quotes. There was no pretending that he wasn't completely off his rocker now. "But then I got a call from Trina and I practically flew over here."

"Oh."

"Oh?" Ethan moved both of his hands on his hips. "That's all I get is an 'oh'?"

"I'm sorry for thinking you had a relapse." Her curls were getting tighter in the rain and she shoved a hand through them.

"I'm not going to pretend that it doesn't hurt to know that you doubt me, Monica. And I'm not going to pretend that there's no chance I'll ever have a relapse. I'm a work in progress, okay? But at least I'm trying to put myself out there."

"I'm having uncomplicated, mind-blowing, soul-reaching, earth-shattering sex with the most attractive man I've ever laid my eyes on," she said, and Ethan felt the edges of his mouth reverse course and turn up into a grin. So she thought their sex was mind-blowing, too? He would've followed up on that last part, but she wasn't done talking. "At least I thought it would be uncomplicated until all of my emotions got involved. Do you have any idea how outside of my comfort zone that is? You don't think I'm putting myself out there, too?"

Ethan had to tamp down the pride rising in his chest so he could keep her talking. "I think you're upset about your grandmother and you're dealing with all this new stuff about your dad. But I also think it's easier for you to hold me off at a distance."

"Don't you see that I *have* to keep you at a distance, Ethan? That I have to protect myself?"

"Protect yourself from what?"

"From falling in love with you!" she yelled in a very nonlibrarian way.

Ethan's lungs seized at her admission, and then his pulse sprang back to life so quickly, his heart felt as if it was blasting against his rib cage. "Why would you want to stop doing that?"

"What if you left?" she asked, her voice no longer as confident as when she'd been yelling.

"What if *you* did?" he countered.

"Why would I leave?"

"I don't know. Maybe for the same reasons you think I might. The past four weeks, you've been refusing to make any promises and commitments, yet that didn't stop me from falling absolutely completely crazy in love with you."

"But you're a risk-taker, Ethan. I'm not like you."

"Not when it comes to my emotions, I'm not. But I also know that I can't stay safe and let life pass me by."

"Are you saying that I'm letting life pass me by?"

"I believe it was your gran who said that."

"But you clearly agree with her," Monica accused.

"Listen. The other day, you asked me why I was attracted to you and I put it all out there, yet you *still* blew me off. My feelings weren't enough for you. *I* wasn't enough for you."

"Of course you're enough for me. You're more than I have ever wanted. But happily-ever-afters are only in books. We need more than just a connection. Than just a physical attraction."

"So you admit that you're attracted to me?" Ethan exhaled. "At least that's a start."

"I think we established that on my staircase and then again in the closet behind the circulation desk at the library." The dampness in the air coupled with the heat radiating from Monica's blushing cheeks made her glasses steam up.

"That's why you had sex with me." He carefully took her glasses off and used his dry T-shirt under his flannel to wipe them clean before setting them back on her nose. "But why did you help me so much with Trina? Why did you share so much of yourself with me?"

Monica took a deep breath, then shuddered. "Because you're strong and you're resilient and you don't give up. I love that when you're completely out of your element, you still do your best to get things right. I love the fact that you try to understand Trina and where she's coming from, rather than defend yourself or push her to see things your way. I love the fact that you go to visit a little old lady every day, even though she doesn't know who you are most of the time, and that you patiently wait for your daughter at shopping malls and public restrooms despite the fact that you'd rather be skydiving off a cliff somewhere. I love the fact that when I'm in your arms, your eyes don't look so empty anymore. And I love the fact that you completely proved me wrong about the kind of man you are."

He stepped to her and brushed her hair away from her cheek. "You're using the L-word an awful lot. Does that mean that you're rethinking that whole no-promises, no-commitments thing?"

"I was rethinking it before I ever said it." She put her hands on his shoulders and sighed. "I love you, Ethan Renault."

The words floated around him, a sense of peace settling over him. He wanted to kiss her but he also wanted to stare at her and memorize the exact way she was looking at him right that second.

"I love you, too, Monica Alvarez," he said, feeling the words all the way down to his bones. "I know that things in our lives are crazy and chaotic and between Trina and your gran, we don't know what the next day will bring. All I can do is love you through it."

Monica's hands linked behind his neck and she pulled his head toward hers. "And all I can do is love you back."

Epilogue

The morning of April 8 was sunny and bright. It was also exactly two months since Trina's actual birth date, but Ethan insisted he wasn't going to wait until the following year to celebrate his daughter. Monica and Trina hung decorations in the backyard while Ethan drove to Legacy Village to check Gran out for the day so she could attend the belated birthday party.

Trina had invited several kids from her class, but when word got out that Ethan was renting an inflatable obstacle course and a bungee jumping trampoline, everyone from the neighborhood wanted to come celebrate the eleven-year-old.

"*Mija*, this is exactly what this house needed," her grandmother said, transferring a sleeping Tootie to the crook of her arm as she took the cup of frozen lemonade Monica brought her. "Children and friends and music and laughter. But why didn't you ask me to cook the food?"

"Well, Ethan lives above Domino's Deli and Mr. Domino offered to do the catering. Plus, I wanted you to sit back and enjoy the party." Gran had been pretty with it since she'd arrived a couple of hours ago, but that didn't mean that Monica was going to let her guard down when it came to sudden episodes. "How're you feeling, Gran?"

"I'm about as good as you'd expect. Some days are better than others."

"Do you hate it at Legacy Village? You don't have to go back."

"Actually, I rather enjoy it. Even when I feel like my old self, I enjoy it. You were always a quiet thing and, after your dad died, I had to keep to myself more. But I like people. I like being social and helping the other residents at the home. No offense, *mija*, but living at the house was so boring. You were always gone at work and I couldn't drive or have any fun. It's better that I'm there."

"I miss you, though, Gran." Tears filled Monica's eyes and she hated that she sounded like a spoiled child. Especially since they were surrounded by so many people who'd come there for a party.

"You miss who I *was*," her grandmother replied. "So do I. Unfortunately, I can't be that person anymore."

"Okay. But the house is pretty quiet without you."

"Then do what you did today. Bring some life into it."

"You *are* my life, Gran."

"No, you need a *real* life. Invite Ethan and Trina to move in with you. They can even bring their little cat with them."

Monica felt the heat climb her neck. It'd only been a few weeks since she and Ethan had admitted that they loved each other. She didn't want to scare the guy off as soon as she got him. "I think Ethan and Trina are happy living at their apartment."

"Actually—" Ethan sat down on one of the rented folding chairs next to them on the deck "—Trina hates the apartment and thinks it's too plain. Even with the borrowed decorations. I've always loved the houses on this street, though. Especially this one. When I was doing work on the kitchen a few months ago, I kept envisioning a sunroom right over there off the nook."

"You know, I always wanted one of those." Gran's eyes brightened. "I would've used it for a dance studio, but you could probably also make it a reading room for Monica and Trina."

Ethan's eyes locked on Monica as he took a chug of his own cup of frozen lemonade. When he set the drink down, he revealed that sexy smirk above that even sexier chin dimple. "I'm willing to make anything that Monica and Trina want."

Trina ran up to the deck right at that second, and passed Gran a piece of chocolate birthday cake. "Did you convince them yet?"

"I'm working on it, *mija*." Gran stage-whispered to the girl.

"Convince us of what?" Monica narrowed her eyes.

"You know, since you're building things, I also always wanted my own gazebo. Right over there." Gran pointed to the spruce tree in the corner. "It doesn't have to be as big as the one in Town Square Park, but something big enough for…oh…let's say a wedding ceremony? Think you can build one of those wedding gazebos, Ethan?"

Monica felt the heat rushing up her face and scooted to the edge of her seat, facing her grandmother so she could tell her to stop making such crazy suggestions. But Ethan's voice interrupted her.

"One wedding gazebo coming up." When Monica turned back around, Ethan was down on his knee, holding out a small box.

Everyone in the backyard went completely silent. Except for a lycra-clad Freckles, who'd just been launched on the bungee jump and was shrieking with laughter. Monica's stomach boinged just as hard.

She looked down at the ring box and then back at his sapphire-blue eyes, no longer hollow, but full of laughter and love and hope. "Is that...? Are you...?"

"I love you, Monica Alvarez. And if you marry me and promise me a life of stability, I'll promise you a life of adventure."

All she could do was nod and Ethan didn't bother putting the ring on her finger because he was too busy lifting her into his arms, her cowboy boots coming off the ground.

A cheer rose from everyone in the backyard and Trina jumped up and down before extending her hand to Gran's and giving the older woman a high five.

Theirs wouldn't be the typical family, and Monica knew they'd have their share of ups and downs down the road. But there was nobody else she'd rather have by her side.

* * * * *